THE
TRAINWRECKERS

Also by Sean Lynch

HOLD BACK THE NIGHT

The Guns of Samuel Pritchard

COTTONMOUTH
DEATH RATTLE
THE BLOOD OF INNOCENTS

THE TRAINWRECKERS

THE GUNS OF SAMUEL PRITCHARD

SEAN LYNCH

PINNACLE BOOKS
Kensington Publishing Corp.
www.kensingtonbooks.com

PINNACLE BOOKS are published by

Kensington Publishing Corp.
119 West 40th Street
New York, NY 10018

All Kensington titles, imprints, and distributed lines are available at special quantity discounts for bulk purchases for sales promotion, premiums, fund-raising, educational, or institutional use.

Special book excerpts or customized printings can also be created to fit specific needs. For details, write or phone the office of the Kensington Sales Manager: Attn.: Sales Department. Kensington Publishing Corp., 119 West 40th Street, New York, NY 10018. Phone: 1-800-221-2647.

PINNACLE BOOKS and the Pinnacle logo are Reg. U.S. Pat. & TM Off.

First Printing: November 2021
ISBN-13: 978-0-7860-4856-4
ISBN-13: 978-0-7860-4857-1 (eBook)

10 9 8 7 6 5 4 3 2 1

Printed in the United States of America

*This book is dedicated
to everyone who roots and toots.*

Chapter 1

"Atherton!" a voice shouted from outside the café. "Smokin' Joe Atherton! I know you're in there! Come out and face me you yellow, backshootin', son-of-a-bitch!"

"Good lord," Idelle exclaimed. She instinctively pulled her infant son closer and looked anxiously across the table at the faces of her husband, David "Ditch" Clemson, and her brother, Samuel Pritchard. "Who's that shouting in the street? And what on earth does he want with you, Samuel?"

"Don't rightly know," Pritchard drawled around a forkful of eggs.

It was early morning, and the trio were seated in Perkins's Diner, across the town square from the marshal's office. Ditch Clemson, Atherton's mayor, was leaving on the morning train to Kansas City to attend a meeting between a pair of railroad executives and a number of other mayors in the region. Ditch's wife Idelle and six-month-old son Samuel, named after her brother and Ditch's lifelong friend, town Marshal and Jackson

County Sheriff Samuel Pritchard, had risen to share breakfast and see her husband off at the train station.

"Whoever he is," Ditch said, "he sounds riled."

"I know you can hear me!" the voice outside continued. "Come out of that café, you gutless trash! You hearin' me, Atherton?"

"I reckon he does," Pritchard observed.

Samuel Pritchard, formerly known under the alias Joe Atherton, sighed, wiped his mouth, and withdrew the napkin tucked into the collar of his button-front shirt as he pushed himself from the table and rose to his full, six-and-one-half-foot, height. He scooped up his Stetson from where it rested on the back of his chair and placed it on top of his head, covering the bullet scar on his forehead over the right eye.

Only twenty-nine years old, Pritchard had left Atherton as a teenager. He'd fled his hometown after his father, Thomas Pritchard, was lynched by Atherton's corrupt mayor Burnell Shipley, their home was burned, the family's lumber business was stolen, and his mother was forced to wed Shipley to prevent the murders of her only son and nine-year-old daughter, Idelle.

But instead of keeping his word to Samuel's mother and sparing her son's life, Shipley's hired lawmen took him to the banks of the Missouri River, bound him, placed him on his knees, and executed the big youth with a .36 caliber ball to the forehead. Ditch Clemson watched the horrific scene play out from nearby woods, and wept as the murderers buried his friend in a shallow grave and rode off.

When Ditch dug the body up, intending to re-bury the corpse next to his father's grave, he was dumbfounded to discover his friend was still alive. The lead ball skirted Pritchard's skull beneath the skin and exited on the opposite side, creating what appeared to be a through-and-through head shot. In reality, the injury was only a flesh wound that merely knocked the big teenager out.

Ditch nursed his friend back to health, and the pair fled Missouri for Arkansas to join the Confederate Army. Pritchard, fearing for his mother's and sister's lives if word got back to Atherton that he was still alive, enlisted under the alias Joe Atherton, the name of his hometown. He also began a lifelong habit of daily pistol practice and was never again without at least a pair of revolvers. He swore an oath that nevermore would a gun be aimed at him without the ability to shoot back.

After a series of harrowing adventures as Confederate guerilla raiders, Ditch and Pritchard went south to Texas after the war and parted ways. Ditch found success as a cattle rancher, while Pritchard was recruited into the Texas Rangers on the basis of his reputation as a mankiller and his uncanny ability with all manner of firearms, particularly those of the one-handed variety.

Before long, Joe Atherton became known far and wide as Ranger "Smokin'" Joe Atherton because it was said anyone who went up against him would soon find themselves, "smokin' in hell." The actual number of men Pritchard, under the moniker Joe Atherton, put down as a Confederate guerilla and Texas Ranger wasn't known, but nonetheless a subject of heated debate in saloons, gambling halls, and bordellos ranging from Chicago to San Francisco and all the way from the Dakota Territories to the Pecos River.

After a decade of rangering for the Republic of Texas,

Pritchard's reputation only grew. And after the murder of his beloved fiancée, Caroline, he re-joined Ditch and avenged her. Only then, more than ten years after fleeing their home as boys, did the duo, now battle-hardened men, return to Missouri. There they faced-down the ruthless Burnell Shipley, the man who'd ruled Atherton like a feudal warlord since the day they'd fled, and his mob of badge-wearing, hired gunmen.

When the dust settled after the Battle of Atherton, as it had since become known, Shipley and all of his hired guns were dead. But so was Pritchard and Idelle's mother, Dovie, and Ditch's brother, Paul. All that Shipley had stolen was returned to its rightful owners, and peace and prosperity reigned once more in the sleepy river town of Atherton, Missouri.

Samuel Pritchard was finally able to abandon the alias Joe Atherton and resume his God-given name. After Ditch was elected Atherton's mayor, he persuaded his huge friend to assume the duties of Atherton's town marshal. Pritchard reluctantly agreed, and pinned on the star primarily out of a desire to remain close to his sister and Ditch, the only family he had left. And since the birth of his nephew Samuel in December, Pritchard's protective instincts only increased. He was also, again reluctantly, elected sheriff of Jackson County, since Atherton was the county seat.

But there were many who refused to forget the name Smokin' Joe Atherton, despite the fact that Pritchard no longer used it. To such men, motivated by a desire for notoriety, revenge, spite, or a craving to earn a man-killing reputation of their own, the fact that Smokin' Joe

Atherton was now a small-town lawman named Samuel Pritchard, and no longer a gunfighter, mattered not a whit.

Serving alongside Pritchard in his duties as town marshal and county sheriff were two deputies; Toby "Tater" Jessup, a portly, middle-aged, good-natured, former livery-man who mostly tended to the caretaking of the office and jail and who rarely carried a gun, and Count Florian Strobl, an expatriate Austrian nobleman and professional duelist who had come to Atherton to kill Pritchard to collect a bounty. After Pritchard spared Strobl's life, "The Count," as Tater teasingly called him, became fiercely loyal to the towering young lawman.

"You'd better get your sorry ass out here and face me," the voice outside hollered, "or I'll start a-shootin' up your hogwallow of a town! You listenin', Atherton?"

As if to punctuate his words, a pistol shot rang out. The sound startled little Samuel, nestled in his mother's arms, who began to cry.

Pritchard took a second to adjust the hang of his dual holsters, each containing a Single Action Army revolver chambered in a .45 Colt and suspended from separate, cartridge-laden, belts. The revolvers sported custom, five-and-one-half-inch barrels, which he couldn't know wouldn't be offered by the Colt factory as regular production items called the "Artillery Model" for another few months. He'd won the guns in a shooting contest in Abilene, Kansas, against a martinet Yankee pistoleer.

"I'll go along with you," Ditch said, standing up.

"You will not," Pritchard said, putting his massive hand on his medium-sized friend's shoulder. "You'll stay right here and look after my sister and nephew, who also happen to be your wife and son."

"But Samuel—"

"But nothin'," Pritchard cut him off. "You ain't even heeled. You're stayin' here, and that's final. We don't know if that fool outside is alone? Might be, he's got a confederate hidin' out of sight with a rifle? You fetch Dady Perkins's scattergun from the kitchen and be prepared to use it if anybody gets past me and comes into this diner with hostile intent."

"Okay," Ditch said, recognizing the wisdom in his friend's words. He'd fought too many battles alongside Pritchard to remember, and trusted his friend's judgment over all others in such matters.

Dady Perkins overheard Pritchard's admonition from behind the café's counter and wordlessly handed her double-barreled shotgun over to Ditch. He automatically broke open the action and checked the loads.

"What are you going to do, Samuel?" Idelle asked, as she soothed her crying son.

"Why, go outside and have a word with that irate feller," he answered, heading for the diner's door. "What else?"

Chapter 2

"Put your backs into it, you lazy curs," the man on horseback said around his wad of tobacco. He withdrew a watch from his vest pocket and glanced at its face. "Train'll be here any minute."

"Mighty easy for you to say," one of the men working on the tracks retorted, "a-sittin up on that big ole horse, pretty-as-you-please."

"That's how it goes when you're in charge," the mounted man said. He was tall and obese, and sat upon a huge draft horse beneath a fancy felt top hat sporting a rattlesnake band and turkey feather. "You get to sit up on a horse in the cool mornin' air and watch others scratch in the dirt like Chinamen. Get paid a lot more, too."

The others grumbled and cursed but continued working.

A dozen men, all armed, were uprooting a section of railroad track a couple of miles west of the town of Sugar Creek, which was twelve miles southwest of Atherton. It was hard work, as a portion of the track they were dislodging lay partially across the bridge spanning Rock Creek. The bridge had been replaced and upgraded by the

Missouri Pacific Railroad, formerly the Pacific Railroad, less than a year before. The men's horses were tied to trees concealed in the woodline, fifty yards away.

"How much more of this iron rail do you want us to dig up?" another man said, pausing to lean on his prybar and mop his face with his handkerchief. "We've already dug up durn-near twenty feet worth of track?"

"Keep on diggin' until I say otherwise," the Big Man in the top hat answered. "I'll let you boys know when you've pulled up enough rail. And hurry the hell up."

Pritchard stepped out of the diner into the bright morning sunlight. It was early May, and still cool in the mornings. Twenty-five feet from the doorway, standing in the middle of the street, was the owner of the voice he'd heard from inside the diner.

"You the feller who interrupted my breakfast?" Pritchard asked him.

"You're damn right I am," said the man.

Calling the voice's owner a man was a stretch. He was no more than eighteen or nineteen years of age, but looked much younger, and stood perhaps five-feet-six-inches in height. He had a scrawny build, a narrow face, and close-set, dark, eyes. His hat was pushed forward on his head, and his weak chin jutted out defiantly. He wore a pair of low-slung, holstered, pistols, tied down to his thighs with leather cords. Both bony hands were poised above the butts of his revolvers.

Pritchard slowly stepped off the plank boardwalk and into the street. "I presume you're also the feller who fired that pistol shot I just heard?"

"You're damn right I did," the man sneered.

"The discharge of firearms within Atherton's town limits is strictly prohibited," Pritchard said, "unless done so in the course of self-defense or to put down a sufferin' animal. It would appear you've done neither."

"I don't give a damn about your bog-trot of a town's stupid laws," the man spat.

Citizens began peering out of doors and windows. The scrawny young man noticed the onlookers and a smile began to spread across his face.

"What's your name?" Pritchard asked.

"Name's Delbert Greaves," he answered, elevating his voice for all to hear. "Folks'll be rememberin' it after today."

"Do you have a problem with me?" Pritchard said.

"Damn right," Greaves said. "I hear tell Joe Atherton is the fastest, deadliest, gun hand around. Folks say he's quicker than buttered lightnin' and can shoot out the eye of a bouncin' jackrabbit. Ended scores of pistoleros, they say. Been hearin' that kinda talk since I was in short britches."

"You don't look long out of short britches today," Pritchard said, "and I don't go by the name Atherton anymore."

Greaves's smile vanished, and his face reddened. "I heard tell about that, too. Heard you'd gone yeller and took up another name. Samuel Pritchard, you calls yourself now. Sheriff of Jackson County, and marshal of this here town of Atherton, I'm told."

"Pritchard happens to be my real name," Pritchard said.

"Maybe it is," Greaves said, "and maybe it ain't. I

didn't come lookin' for Marshal Samuel Pritchard. I come south from Iowa lookin' for Smokin' Joe Atherton."

"And your business with him?"

"I'm gonna put him into the boneyard."

"Any particular reason?" Pritchard asked.

"Even if I had one," Greaves smirked, "it ain't gonna matter none to you. Not when you're lyin' down in the dirt, spittin' out your last breath."

"I know your reason," Pritchard said, "even if you don't."

"Oh yeah? Whyen't you tell me, Atherton?"

"I already told you once," Pritchard said, "that ain't my name. Your reason for bracin' me is the same as many others who've braced me before. Loud-mouthed little nobodies from nowhere, full of blusteration, who think that because they can shoot a tin can off a rail fence, or plug a defenseless drunk in the back, they're pistoleers and mankillers to be feared and respected. Fools who believe if they end me, they'll become somethin' besides a loud-mouthed little nobody."

"You callin' me a nobody?"

"Don't have to," Pritchard said. "That's what you are, and you know it. Otherwise, you wouldn't be here in Atherton's streets actin' the fool and callin' me out."

Greaves's face tightened and his fingers twitched over the walnut stocks of his revolvers. "I'm done talkin'," he said. "It's time to slap leather."

"Fair enough," Pritchard said. "How about we draw on the count of three?"

"Suits me," Greaves said. "Get ready to die, Smokin' Joe Atherton."

"One," Pritchard said, looking past Greaves and winking.

"I'm ready for you," Greaves said. His entire body was tensed like a compressed spring.

"Two," Pritchard said.

Deputy Florian Strobl brought the butt of one of his nickel-plated, Chamelot Delvigne revolvers squarely down on Delbert Greaves's skull. While Pritchard engaged him in conversation, Strobl silently crept up from behind. At Pritchard's signal, the agile deputy brained the would-be gunfighter, who collapsed instantly to the street.

"Zat should take ze piss and vinegar out of him," Strobl said in his aristocratic Austrian accent.

Pritchard walked over to the unconscious Greaves and removed both of his revolvers. He handed them to Tater Jessup, who'd emerged from the marshal's office.

"Lock this lunkhead up," he directed his deputies. "We'll bring him before Judge Pearson this afternoon."

"What're you gonna be doin'," Tater grunted as he and Strobl lifted Greaves, "while we're a-luggin' this here prisoner off to jail?"

"I'm walkin' Ditch and Idelle to the station," Pritchard said, as citizens receded through their doors and windows and resumed their tasks. "He's got a train to catch."

Chapter 3

Pritchard held his nephew while his sister Idelle hugged her husband. They were at the railroad station, situated at the outskirts of Atherton. Little Samuel chortled and tugged on Pritchard's star.

"You be careful on the road, Ditch Clemson," Idelle cautioned her husband. "You come back to me just as soon as you can."

"I'm only going to Kansas City," Ditch reminded her. "Ain't like I'm going off to California. I'll be back day after tomorrow on the afternoon train."

"I know," Idelle grumbled. "I still wish you didn't have to go."

"Got no choice," Ditch said. "I'm the mayor of this town, remember?"

"What's this trip all about?" Pritchard asked.

"A meetin' has been called by a big railroad boss, John Brody, and some of the mayors in western Missouri," Ditch explained. "It's to be held in Kansas City, where Brody's railroad company is headquartered. A representative from the governor's office is supposed to be there, too."

"What's it all about?" Pritchard asked.

"It's no secret there's going to be a new railway line cutting across the state. A lot of federal money is on the table. The two biggest railroad companies in these parts, the Missouri Pacific and the Brody Line, are competing amongst themselves to see which one of 'em gets the lion's share of that big government contract. Depending on how the contest shakes out, a lot of towns with rail lines running through them now could potentially see their lines pulled or diverted. Other towns, currently without rail lines, might get themselves one or find their existing tracks, if they have 'em already, expanded."

"Sounds to me like the two railroad companies are playin' a winner-take-all poker game?"

"That's exactly right, Samuel," Ditch agreed. "The owner of each railroad company is hoping to force the other to sell out or fold before the contract is formally awarded. It's a well-known fact that neither Brody nor Jason Gould, the owner of the Missouri Pacific, has a reputation for a willingness to compromise or share. It's also a well-known fact that neither one of them is above dealin' from the bottom of the deck to win."

"That explains why you're goin' to Kansas City, all right," Pritchard said.

"Got no choice. This is a case of either being at the dinner or on the menu. The new governor, Hardin, claims he'll take into consideration the recommendations of the local town mayors when it comes to deciding which of the two railroad companies should be awarded the government contract. I guess we'll find out if that's true."

"If it is," Pritchard said, "it explains why Brody is

a-courtin' all you mayors in Kansas City. He wants your endorsement."

"It ain't just Brody who's extendin' invitations to all the mayors," Ditch said. "Jason Gould invited all of us to Saint Louis next week, presumably for the same reason. Both of those railroad bosses are a-tryin' to curry our favor."

"It's a courtship, all right," Pritchard said. "But I get the feelin' if you mayors choose the wrong suitor they'll be hell to pay from the one who lost out. And the other railroad who gets the contract," he finished. "I reckon the victorious railroad boss won't go easy on the towns that didn't endorse his line."

"That pretty much sums it up," Ditch said. "Brody and Gould are both powerful and vengeful men. You don't get to be a railroad baron by forgivin' those who trespass against you. Neither one will balk at crushin' those mayors and towns who stand against 'em, if that's how the chips fall."

"You'll do right by Atherton," Pritchard said, patting his friend on the shoulder. "You've always had a noggin for business, Ditch."

Pritchard wasn't idly complimenting his friend. After the war the two young men, along with Ditch's brother Paul, pooled their stakes and headed south to Texas. Together they bought twenty-thousand acres of dirt in Taylor County, just south of what would one day become Abilene. They also bought four-hundred head of cattle.

Not long after that, circumstances occurred that led Pritchard to the Texas Rangers. Ditch and his brother prospered in the cattle business. A few years later, joined once again by Pritchard, the Clemson brothers drove over three-thousand head of Texas longhorns north to Abilene, Kansas, where they sold the herd and made their fortunes.

"I'm gonna need every bit of that business sense in Kansas City," Ditch conceded, "and then some. This ain't just my decision; it's a decision the rest of the mayors and I will have to agree on. United we stand, divided we fall."

"I'm sure you'll convince the other mayors to do the right thing," Pritchard said.

"I'm gonna try," Ditch said. "It ain't but a few hours by rail to Kansas City, and all the other mayors from these parts will be joining me on the same train. I hope to spend the trip conferring with them. I'd surely like to convince everybody to hold off on choosing between one of the two railroads until we've had an opportunity to meet with both Brody and Gould, and hear their separate offers."

"Mind your cards when dealing with John Brody," Pritchard said, dodging one of Samuel's pudgy hands that was tugging on his nose.

"You've had dealings with Brody before?"

"Met him once," Pritchard said. "He was one of Cottonmouth Quincy's clients. He paid Cottonmouth's hired guns to buffalo landowners off their properties and to thump or shoot any of his rail workers, mostly Chinese folk, who got outta line. That oughta tell you all you need to know about John Brody."

"I'll keep that in mind," Ditch said.

"I tried to have a warrant sworn out for his arrest after the Cottonmouth affair," Pritchard went on, "but that fell apart when Governor Woodson left office. Now I can't even try. Brody has too much money and clout with the new four-eyed governor, Charles Henry Hardin."

"Good morning, Mayor Clemson," Doctor Mauldin

greeted them. He nodded to Pritchard and tipped his hat to Idelle.

"You taking the train today, too?" Ditch asked Atherton's only physician.

"I am," Mauldin acknowledged. "I go into Kansas City a couple of times a month to pick up medical supplies, but this is a special trip. I'm going to interview a young physician. See if I can't entice him to consider moving his practice from the big city here to Atherton?"

"Good luck," Ditch said. "Lord knows Atherton could use another sawbones."

Doc Mauldin was in his late sixties and the only doctor in Atherton. He'd made no secret of his desire to bring another to town to better serve Atherton's growing population and ease the burden of his busy practice.

Ditch kissed Idelle, who took his son Samuel from her brother, and shook Pritchard's hand. "I'll see you in a couple of days, Samuel."

"We'll be here," Pritchard said. He and his sister waved as Ditch followed Doctor Mauldin across the platform. There they boarded separate cars before the westbound train steamed off.

Chapter 4

The train sped westward at the blistering speed of thirteen miles per hour. At that rate, taking into consideration the numerous stops in small towns and villages along the way to drop off or pick up passengers, freight, mail, or livestock, it would take at least three hours to traverse the approximately twenty-five miles to Kansas City.

Ditch was in the train's second passenger car, which had been reserved exclusively for the use of the dozen or so mayors en route to the meeting in Kansas City. All other regular passengers had been relegated to the other cars. A thick cloud of pipe, cigar, and cigarette smoke filled the cabin, and despite the early hour, more than a few bottles were being passed around. The train had been underway from Atherton for less than an hour.

"It stinks, I tell you," the mayor of Keytesville declared around his cigar. "I don't trust them two crooked railroad barons any farther than I can sling 'em. They've got something up their sleeves. Why else would the owners of the two biggest railroads, The Brody Line and Missouri Pacific, be willing to pay for railway tickets, and a night's stay at the fanciest hotels in Kansas City and Saint

Louis, just to get us all together for a meetin'? The whole thing smells like a swindle, if you ask me."

"It doesn't cost the railroads anything to ferry us to Kansas City or Saint Louis to meet with their owners," the Springfield mayor said loftily. "And since Brody and Gould also own the hotels they'll be putting us up in, it doesn't cost them much to host us." He held up a bottle and cigar. "Brody was kind enough to pay for this private car, even if it is on Gould's train, and stock it with smoked fish, cigars, and good whiskey. That was right hospitable of him, I say. I'll bet when Gould finds out what Brody did for us, he'll ferry us to Saint Louis in a train car twice as big and fancy as this one, with dancing girls and a brass band." The other mayors laughed and emptied their glasses.

"What can it hurt to enjoy their hospitality?" the Springfield mayor continued. "Why not benefit from the two trips and listen to what each of them has to say? I suggest we bask in the bounty of our hosts while we can."

"Easy for you to say," the mayor of Westphalia challenged. "You've already got a passel of railroad lines runnin' smack-dab through your city. Not to mention, your town's big and important, like Jefferson City. You don't have to worry about one of the railroads takin' away or movin' your only line. Osage County's got but one rail runnin' through it. If either of the railroad companies were to divert that line, Westphalia is gonna dry up like a parched well." He pointed his finger around the car at his fellow mayors. "How about your towns?"

The jovial tone vanished.

"Can't you see them two railroad bosses are a-tryin' to fatten us up like calves to the slaughter?" the Keytesville mayor added. "A little whiskey, a train ride, and a night's stay on a feather bed in a fancy hotel ain't gonna make me forget who I'm dealin' with!"

"Why don't you relax," the Springfield mayor said, "and have a drink?"

A chorus of voices erupted, drowning each other out in argument. Ditch stood and motioned for everyone to quiet down.

"There's no point scrappin' amongst ourselves," Ditch said, once the politicians had silenced. "We don't yet know what the two railroad bosses want to discuss, nor what our new governor's stake in all this is? Or hadn't any of you considered what ole Charlie Hardin's relationship to John Brody or Jason Gould might be?"

Ditch could tell by the faces of the mayors that most had not considered the governor's role.

"I think it's safe to say," Ditch went on, "that neither railroad would be ferryin' us all the way to Kansas City or Saint Louis unless they wanted somethin'. I agree with the mayors of Keytesville and Springfield; I do believe the railroads are trying to butter us up. Brody just got the first crack at us, that's all. But I also agree with the mayor of Springfield; I'm keeping an open mind. I propose we all agree to stick together, and act as one, regardless of what the railroad companies have to say during these two meetings. No matter what their intentions, the railroads will be bettin' on our respective towns and cities having separate interests, and us mayors squabbling amongst one another. But if we act in solidarity, they'll have a much harder time buffaloing any single one of us into something that none of us want. What say you?"

"For such a young feller," the Columbia mayor said,

"Mayor Clemson is speaking mighty savvy words. I second his wise proposal. None of us should agree to nothin', as far as the railroads go, until after both meetings are done and unless the majority consents."

A murmur of agreement broke out as glasses were again filled and raised. The Missouri politicos were still drinking when the train's whistle abruptly sounded. An instant later, the ear-splitting screech of metal-grinding-against-metal erupted as the brakes were fully applied. The mayors lurched and stumbled as the train's engineer desperately tried to halt the locomotive.

"It's comin' 'round the bend," one of the men called out.

"I can see that for myself, you idjit," the Big Man in the top hat said. "Ditch them tools," he ordered. "Get mounted, and be sure to cover up your faces."

A dozen men obeyed. They raced to the woodline, tossed their tools in a pile, and climbed into their saddles. Some pulled neckerchiefs past their noses while others put on burlap sacks over their heads, replete with cut-out eyeholes reminiscent of the masks worn by partisan raiders during the war. The man in the feathered top hat covered his mouth and most of his thick beard with his kerchief and drew one of his pistols.

"You all know your jobs," the man in the top hat said. "When it's over, we'll meet back here at this spot. Any questions?"

None of the men said anything. All drew their pistols.

"Here she comes," the man in the top hat said.

* * *

By the time the engineer saw the gap in the tracks, it was too late. Whoever had removed almost forty feet of rail had done so strategically, knowing the westbound train would be encountering the gap in the tracks while navigating a blind curve. The train was just west of Sugar Creek, where it had stopped to off-load a pallet of grain and pick up a family of five heading to Topeka to attend a religious jamboree.

The location of the gap in the tracks had also been selected due to the lay of the land. Not only was that portion of the track along a curve, but it was also approaching the short bridge over Rock Creek. When the engine hit the gap, having barely slowed despite the application of brakes, the sound of splintering wood could be heard for only an instant before the train derailed. The locomotive careened onto its left side and toppled over the bridge, twenty feet down into the creek. First the engine flipped, then the coal car, baggage car, the passenger cars, freight car, mail car, livestock car, and finally the caboose.

The shriek of the engine was lost in the thundering concussion as the train crashed into the creek and collapsed like a giant iron accordion. The screams of the terrified passengers and crew mingled with the braying of animals in the livestock car as it came to rest amidst a geyser of dirt and water.

It took a moment for Ditch to recover his senses and realize where he was. He found himself waking up, and he wondered how long he'd been out? The last thing he remembered was standing on a bench, the sound of the train's whistle, and then a tremendous crashing noise. His head throbbed.

The air was thick with dust, and the sounds of shouts, moans, and screams could be heard all around him. He was lying on his back, and when he tried to sit up, he discovered he couldn't. His left leg was pinned under something large and heavy.

That's when the pain hit him. His left leg was on fire. Ditch wiped the grit and blood out of his eyes and looked around. The scene he beheld was a horrifying one.

He was lying on the passenger car's ceiling. The car had collapsed as it overturned, and had caved in on the remainder of the compartment. Mangled bodies, and parts of bodies, were strewn about. Ditch recognized them as belonging to what were once his fellow Missouri mayors. He hadn't witnessed such carnage since the war.

Ditch also found blood on his face, his right arm immobile and aching, and his left leg below the knee inescapably trapped beneath a crushing wall of debris.

Many of the men in the car were clearly dead. Others moaned or cried out in agony. Ditch could only wonder if the people in the other passenger cars, which were carrying the train's regular travelers, had fared any better?

Ditch saw water seeping into the car, felt cool liquid trickle over him, and welcomed its awakening effect. That's when he came fully to his senses and grasped that the train had derailed over the Rock Creek Bridge, plummeted into the shallow water below, and came to rest in the creek.

Ditch saw a trio of men climbing through the wreckage. He started to wave to them for help but stopped himself when he noticed, with alarm, that they were all wearing masks or neckerchiefs over their faces and wielding pistols. One of them was very large and wore a fancy top hat with an ornate snakeskin band and prominent feather. It became clear to him, in that instant, that the train's derailment was no accident.

"This here's the right car," one of the men said to the others, as they clambered their way through the wreckage. "Ain't no women or kids in this one. Only menfolk, and all of 'em wearin' fancy suits like they was a-goin' to a Sunday church meetin'."

"This is the car we want, all right," the man in the top hat agreed.

"Looks like the bulk of our work's been done for us," the third man said, scanning what was left of the car. He pointed at the mangled bodies with his revolver. "Most of these boys have already been put to rest."

"Check 'em anyways," the man in the top hat ordered. "Strip 'em of what money and trinkets they have and finish 'em off."

The pair of gunmen went from body-to-body while the man in the top hat supervised. They rifled pockets for wallets, watches, and jewelry, stuffing the items they seized into a burlap sack, and then moved on to the next dead or dying politician. Most of the mayors in the demolished car were dead, some severely injured, and a couple were wounded to lesser degrees. One of the casualties, groggy and believing the newcomers were rescuing him, reached out his hands as Ditch had almost done.

For his efforts he received a bullet.

The two masked men made their way through the demolished train car and shot the surviving politicians as they encountered them. The only ones they didn't shoot were those who were already dead.

Ditch lay immobile with his eyes closed, playing possum, trying to ignore the slaughter and hoping they would believe him deceased. He could hear them moving closer, rifling bodies, and tried not to wince at each shot or at the desperate pleas of those begging for their lives.

Ditch was unarmed, and cursed himself for disregarding Pritchard's advice about carrying a pistol while traveling. A veteran of the war and no stranger to gunplay, Ditch typically didn't wear a gun, unlike his tall friend, who was never without at least two.

The systematic killing continued. The acrid smell of gunsmoke filled the car. Finally, Ditch sensed the gunmen standing over him. He tried not to flinch when he felt a boot kick him in the ribs. Despite his attempt to play dead, he released an involuntary grunt due to the excruciating pain in his left leg.

"That's all of 'em put to rest," Ditch heard one of the gunmen announce, "except this one. He's still among the livin'."

"Don't look like he'll be with us for long," the other masked gunmen said.

Ditch felt the barrel of a revolver press against his forehead. He opened his eyes and looked up to find a masked man squatting next to him.

"Don't finish him yet," the man in the top hat said.

Ditch felt the barrel move away. The gun's owner relieved him of his wallet, watch, and wedding ring.

"How bad is he hurt?" the man in the top hat asked.

"Head's busted up," came the answer, "and it looks like

he's got a broken arm, but one of his legs is pinned and mashed all to hell. He's bleedin' out fast. Iffen I had to guess, he ain't long for this world." The man in the top hat peered at Ditch's trapped leg and nodded to himself, as if confirming the assessment.

"What's your name?" he asked Ditch.

"None of your business," Ditch replied through clenched teeth. The pain and fury of his predicament notwithstanding, he wasn't going to give his killers any satisfaction.

"Brave feller, ain't he?" one of the gunmen chuckled.

The man in the top hat accepted Ditch's watch and ring from one of the other men. He opened the watch and found a photograph of Idelle inside.

"Mighty fine lookin' young woman," the man in the top hat said. "After today, she'll be a widow and in need of comfortin.' Whyn't you tell me which Missouri town you're the mayor of, so's me and my boys can pay her a visit? We'd be more'n happy to console the bereaved."

"Sure," one of the others chimed in from beneath his mask. "We could take turns consolin' her." His partner laughed.

"Who says I'm a mayor?" Ditch said, straining to conceal the agony from his voice.

"I happen to know everybody in this here car is a mayor," the man in the top hat said. "At least they were before this particular train ride."

Ditch chose silence as his retort.

The man in the top hat pocketed Ditch's watch and ring and took a step closer. "Do you know who I am, boy?"

"How could I?" Ditch said. "You're hidin' behind a mask, ain't you?"

"My name's Jem Rupe," the man in the top hat said, without removing his mask. "Heard of me?"

"I've heard the name," Ditch said, shaking his head to fight the pain and remain conscious. "If that's who you are, this ain't the first train you've wrecked."

"It surely ain't."

Their conversation was interrupted by the sound of an explosion somewhere outside. The blast echoed for several long seconds. The noise was followed by whoops, cheers, and a chorus of gunshots.

"That'd be the boys blowin' the safe from inside the mail car," one of the men said.

"See to it," Rupe told one of his two companions. "Make sure none of what's in that safe finds its way into the boys' pockets." The gunmen scrambled from the wrecked car to comply.

"We gotta be on our way," Rupe said to Ditch, nodding to the other gunman. "I'd put a bullet to you, but that'd be doin' you a mercy and a waste of a good bullet. By the looks of that leg of yours, and how much blood you're a-leakin', you're goin' goslin shortly. Adios, Mayor. Iffen I run into your wife, I'll be sure and give her your howdy-do's."

"I'll be a-given' her somethin' else," the other gunman chuckled.

The two gunmen departed the car leaving Ditch trapped with his tortured thoughts.

Chapter 5

It was mid-morning by the time Pritchard got back to town. He'd driven his sister and nephew back to their stately home, a mile outside Atherton's city limits, after seeing Ditch off on the train. The house sat on land once owned by their family, stolen by Burnell Shipley's gang, and recovered a decade later in the aftermath of the Battle of Atherton. The building was an impressive, two-story, brick affair, re-built by Ditch in the wake of the original structure being burned to the ground during the war.

Pritchard made sure his sister and little Samuel were settled, declined her offer of coffee by reminding her of his law enforcement duties in town, and rode back to Atherton aboard Rusty, his thirteen-year-old Morgan. Rusty, who stood over eighteen hands tall and had been his faithful companion since the war, made the trek to Ditch and Idelle's house tied to the back of the buckboard.

When Pritchard entered the marshal's office, which also served as his home by virtue of the private sleeping quarters he kept in a small room in the back, he found Deputies Florian Strobl and Tater Jessup seated at his desk. They were playing cards using matchsticks as poker chips. Neither wore their hats or coats. Strobl examined his hand through his monocle, a cigarette dangling from his lips, while Tater scratched his sizable belly and squinted down at his cards. Tater wore no gun, as usual, but Strobl's matching pair of Chamelot Delvigne revolvers rested in dual shoulder holsters underneath his arms.

Behind them, sitting on a bunk in one of the locked cells, sat Delbert Greaves. When Pritchard strolled in, he jumped to his feet with an expression of fury on his face.

"'Bout time you showed your yeller hide," Greaves snarled. "I knew you was afraid to face me. Havin' your deputy sneak up on me unawares and crack me on the noggin from behind was a cowardly act and unbefitten' of a self-respectin' lawman. All because you was afraid to face me fair and square. When I get outta here, I'm a-gonna—"

"Does that little rooster ever stop crowin'?" Pritchard asked nonchalantly, as he hung his hat and coat and removed his gun belts.

"He's been squawkin' somethin' awful," Tater affirmed, "ever since he woke up. Goin' on and on about how he's a-gonna gun me and Florian here, and then you, Samuel. Fancies himself a real curly wolf. He's powerful desperate to have his name bandied about in the same breath as Wild Bill and Dallas Stoudenmire. I've never before, in all my days, heard a solitary fool spew so much blusteration."

"It won't be blusteration when I'm a-standin' over your punctuated corpse," Greaves barked at Tater. "You ask anyone, back in Wapello County, how fast I am? They'll tell you, all right. When Del Greaves passes by, folks step aside 'cause they know I can draw and shoot quicker'n spit. I'm faster than anybody, you'll see. Sure as hell faster than you, Yellow Joe Atherton. I'll shoot that piss-colored stripe right off'n your back. I'll have to, 'cause you already done proved you ain't got the sand to show me your front and face me proper."

"Faster with a gun," Strobl said around his smoke without looking up from his cards, "isn't necessarily better with a gun. You should be thanking me for bonking you, Mr. Greaves. A bonking you may awaken from. Had you pulled on Marshal Pritchard, you would not now be in jail annoying us with your childish boasting. You would be in Simon Tilley's funeral parlor, across town, slumbering silently in a pine box."

"So you say," Greaves spat. "We'll find out soon enough. You can't keep me locked up in this hoosegow forever, Marshal. When I get out, I'll be a-gunnin' for you. All of you."

Pritchard sighed. "Get in line," he said. "In the meantime, would you mind hobblin' your lip? You prattle on like you've got a case of the backdoor trots, 'cept it's your mouth doin' the leakin' instead of your backside."

While Greaves cursed at Pritchard's comment, Tater guffawed and Strobl chuckled. Greaves's face got even redder. "Laugh all you want," he hissed, "but you won't be laughin' long. Not after I get outta this hoosegow and get my hands on my pistols. None of you will be a-laughin'. You'll be runnin' for your ever-lovin' lives."

"Lord," Tater said, "what a peacock."

"Would you please be silent?" Pritchard asked Greaves. "We've got the gist of your bobbery, and are full-aware of how you'll be sendin' us all to the bone orchard with your smokin'-fast shootin' irons. But meantime, while you're in our company in this jail, we'd sorely appreciate a little peace and quiet."

"I speak my mind," Greaves argued. "I say what I want, when I want, and you can't do nothin' to stop me. I may be locked up, Marshal, but you can't harness my mouth."

"Fetch the bucket," Pritchard told Tater.

"Right away." Tater grinned, setting down his cards and rising from the table. "I was gonna fold anyway. Florian's been bestin' me every hand. I know he ain't cheatin', 'cause that would go against his Eur-O-Peen code of honor, but I can't for the life of me figure out how he's a-doin' it?"

"Maybe it's your poker face?" Strobl suggested, peering up at Tater through his monocle. "Normally, when bluffing at cards, one doesn't cross their eyes, belch, or break wind."

"Haw, haw, haw," Tater retorted, as Pritchard hid his grin. Tater, whose nickname was earned for his physique and affinity for spuds, ambled to the closet, retrieved a tin bucket, and went outside to the pump.

"I'll shoot that lookin' glass right outta your eye," Greaves goaded Strobl. "You just watch me, Frenchy. Your wife will be a-cryin' in her soup."

"I am not married," Strobl said, "and I am not French."

"I don't care where you're from," Greaves said. "It's where you're a-goin' that matters. You're goin' to hell on a shutter, and I'm a-gonna send you."

Strobl stood, removed his monocle, and stretched. "When does our noisy prisoner get his day in court?" he asked Pritchard. "I grow weary of the bumpkin's company."

"Who're you callin' a bumpkin? You'd best know I'll

be gettin' payback for that knot on my head." Strobl ignored him.

"I visited Judge Pearson on the way over here," Pritchard answered his deputy. "He'll see us after lunch."

"Eat hearty, boys," Greaves jeered. "It'll likely be your last meal. Your next victuals is gonna be blue whistlers outta my pistols."

"I might shoot myself," Strobl said, "and save the bragging whelp the trouble. Such a course of action is infinitely preferable to the sound of his voice."

"I might join you," Pritchard said.

Tater returned to the office carrying the bucket. It was now full of water.

"You're all yellow," Greaves continued, "not just your cowardly marshal. All together you three so-called lawmen ain't worth the manure on the underside of my boots. Killin' you three peckerwoods will be like stompin' a trio of bugs."

"Shall I?" Tater said.

"Fire away," Pritchard nodded.

Tater emptied the bucket on Greaves through the bars of his cell. He shut up long enough to gasp as the frigid liquid drenched him.

"You filthy dogs!" he sputtered. With his hair matted and his clothes soaked, he looked even smaller and skinnier than before. "I'm gonna kill you all for this!"

"Didn't he already say that?" Tater asked. "Your turn," he said, handing the bucket to Strobl.

"With pleasure," Strobl accepted the bucket. He briskly strode from the office.

"Where's he goin'?" Greaves demanded.

"Out to the pump," Tater answered. "It's only about twenty feet yonder. Don't worry none. He'll be back in a minute."

"I'll ask you again," Pritchard said to the prisoner. "Will you be silent?"

"My words givin' you the shivers, Marshal?" Greaves challenged.

"Nope," Pritchard answered. "Just an earache. Kinda like a preacher who won't stop sermonizing at a wake, not realizin' that one of his flock is dead and the other parishioners are a-wishin' they were." Strobl re-entered the jail carrying the re-filled bucket.

"I ain't gonna be silenced merely because you're too scared to hear what I have to say."

Pritchard signaled to Strobl, who drenched Greaves again. This time, the prisoner tried to turn and flinch. It was to no avail. He shuddered, shivered, and then rushed the bars in a rage.

Strobl handed the bucket to Pritchard. He took it and made for the door.

"You bastards!" Greaves howled.

"We can do this all day and all night," Pritchard said, as he reached the door. "It's but a few steps to the pump, that well ain't gonna dry up anytime soon, and whoever's fetchin' the water earns a momentary rest from your mouth."

"All right," Greaves conceded. "I'll button up. But only because the next time I speak it'll be my guns doin' the talkin'."

"So we heard," Pritchard said. He handed the bucket

to Tater to return to the closet, and was closing the office door, when John Babbit rushed in.

Babbit owned and operated the town's only newspaper, the *Athertonian,* and did double-duty as Atherton's telegraph operator. He'd sprinted from his office and was out-of-breath.

"Marshal Pritchard," he got out between gasps, "something terrible has happened."

"Take it easy, John," Pritchard soothed. "What's got you so riled?"

"The train," he panted, "the one that left this morning. It's crashed. Went off the bridge over Rock Creek. Just got a telegram from the nearby town of Sugar Creek."

"That's only a dozen miles from here," Tater spoke up.

"The telegram said a lot of the passengers were killed," Babbit went on, "and a lot more are hurt bad. The Clay County sheriff is asking for volunteers to help. He's already notified the army and the governor's office. The railroads, too."

Pritchard's mind instantly went to Ditch.

"What should I do?" Babbit asked.

"You send off a telegram to Sheriff Gusman in Clay County and tell him every man I can raise in Atherton will be on the way directly."

Babbit scurried off. Pritchard turned to Tater. "Get to the church," he said to his deputy, "and have Pastor Donaldson ring the bell. I want every able-bodied hand in the county mustered. We'll need wagons, medicine, blankets, bandages, and plenty of tools. Your job, Tater, is to take charge of organizing the efforts from here in town and gettin' folks off to that wreck as fast as you can."

"You can count on me, Samuel," Tater said, grabbing his hat and coat and rushing from the office.

"Florian," Pritchard said to Strobl, as he belted on his guns, "the town is yours. Deputize anybody you need to help keep the peace."

"And you?" Strobl asked, already knowing the answer.

"I'll be makin' for Rock Creek," he answered, putting on his hat. "Ditch was on that train."

"What should I tell your sister?"

"Tell her to stay calm," he said, "and that I'll get word back to her about Ditch as soon as I can. She'll want to go herself but don't let her leave, no matter how much she squawks. Whether Ditch is alive or not, it won't do her any good to eyeball what's left of that train."

"As you say, Samuel."

Pritchard grabbed his .44-40 Winchester carbine, a box of cartridges, and his coat, and started again for the door.

"I surely hope Mayor Clemson is all right," Strobl said solemnly. "Why the rifle?"

"Been my experience," Pritchard said, "during the war, that in places where lots of folks are dead the cats, coyotes, wolves, and buzzards ain't far behind."

"An unpleasant prospect," Strobl said, remembering his own wartime service in Europe, "but nonetheless true."

"Don't be too frightened, Yellow Joe Atherton," Greaves couldn't help himself from taunting. "Buzzards and bobcats can't shoot you in your skunk-yellow back."

Pritchard dropped his coat, rifle, and the box of cartridges on the desk, snatched the jail keys from a desk drawer, and had the cell door opened in a flash. He grabbed the snickering Greaves by the collar and lifted the skinny, wet, would-be gunman's face up to his own.

"My name is not Atherton," he said, his voice barely a whisper. "Not anymore. The next time you call me anything but Marshal Pritchard, and with a smile on your face when you say it, I will break you in half like November cornstalk. Comprende?"

Greaves's feet were well off the ground. All he could do was nod.

Pritchard slowly lowered the quaking Greaves. He exited the cell, which Strobl locked behind him.

"Forget the water," Pritchard said to Strobl as he retrieved his rifle, coat, and cartridges and headed again for the door. "If the pipsqueak pistol fighter opens his yap again, bust him over the head once more with your revolver. If that don't quell his mouth, shoot him."

"With pleasure," Strobl repeated.

Chapter 6

By keeping Rusty at a steady trot, Pritchard made the dozen or so miles to the derailed train at Rock Creek Bridge in under two hours. He stopped in the town of Sugar Creek long enough to water the big Morgan and observe that most of the townsfolk there had already gathered supplies and headed off to the wreck to lend a hand.

As he steered Rusty around the same curve that the train had navigated before meeting its fate, Pritchard took in the landscape before him.

The bridge over the creek was mostly intact, despite its missing track, but the engine, coal car, passenger cars, and the baggage car were on their tops or sides twenty feet below. Trailing behind them up the bank were the freight car, livestock car, mail car, and caboose. The mail car and caboose, though off the tracks and on the embankment, were still upright. Pritchard knew at a glance, when he saw the discarded rails and the gap in the tracks, that the derailment was no accident.

Hundreds of people scurried about in two separate, hastily erected camps, one on each side of the creek. Pritchard observed that the camp set up on the east side of the damaged bridge was composed mostly of railroad workers from the Missouri Pacific Railroad, and the camp on the west bank composed of personnel from the Brody Railroad. Dazed and injured passengers sat on the eastern embankment, attended by the caring hands of dozens of volunteers.

Pritchard noticed plenty of men in army uniform. Several large fires were burning under heavy cauldrons, a mess tent had been set up, and a hospital had been established in the largest tent.

Men scampered over the demolished train. Pritchard surmised that not all of the survivors had been rescued yet, and that crews were also engaged in the unenviable task of removing bodies from the twisted ruins. More than two-dozen, tarpaulin-covered corpses lay side-by-side at the crest of the creek, with another body being added every few minutes.

Pritchard tied Rusty to a wagon and headed for the row of bodies. One by one he lifted the tarps and examined the deceased. As he viewed the cadavers, he noticed all but a few were adult males. One was a small boy he recognized as belonging to a family from Atherton. Some of the dead men he recognized as mayors of towns and villages in western Missouri. Many, to his surprise, bore gunshot wounds to the head.

"You there," a soldier yelled at him, "get away from those bodies!"

Pritchard stood and faced him. "I'm Marshal Samuel Pritchard, from Atherton," he announced, "and the Jackson County Sheriff. One of this train's last stops was in my town. I have a right to know if any of my citizens have met their end."

"I ain't gonna tell you again," the soldier said, unslinging his rifle. "Step away."

"At ease, Private," a voice behind Pritchard said. He turned to find a uniformed officer approaching.

"I'm Major Duncan, commander of the barracks at Independence," the officer said. "You don't know me, Marshal, but I know you. Your reputation precedes you."

"Beggin' your pardon, sir," the soldier said, "but just 'cause this feller says he's Samuel Pritchard, don't make it so."

"Would you mind removing your hat, Marshal?" Duncan asked.

Pritchard took off his hat and swept back his white-blond hair to reveal the bullet scar decorating his forehead. The private's eyes widened.

"How many six-and-a-half-foot-tall men do you know, Private," Major Duncan said, "wear a lawman's star, a pair of revolvers, and a bullet hole in their skull?"

"Sorry, sir."

"As you were," Duncan said to the sentry.

"I'm lookin' for my friend," Pritchard told the major. "He's the mayor of Atherton. His name is Clemson."

"You didn't find him here?" Duncan asked, pointing to the line of bodies.

"Nope, nor among the survivors bein' attended to over yonder."

"I'm sorry to be the one to say it," Duncan said, "but there are still a number of bodies yet to be recovered from the train. All three passenger cars are filled with dead travelers. It's possible his body hasn't yet been brought out."

Pritchard's heart sank. He knew if Ditch were alive,

he'd have already spotted his energetic friend. Ditch was a natural leader, and would have been among the rescuers organizing the relief effort and rendering aid to others, if he was able.

"There is another possibility," Major Duncan said. "The hospital tent. Quite a few of the passengers were gravely wounded. My unit's surgeon, along with several other volunteer physicians from neighboring towns, are doing what they can. Let's check there, shall we?"

Major Duncan escorted Pritchard to the surgery tent. It was packed with blood-covered doctors, nurses, and orderlies. One of the surgeons working inside was Dr. Mauldin.

"Doc," Pritchard greeted, as he approached Atherton's only physician. He noticed Mauldin's forehead was bandaged and one of the lenses in his glasses was cracked. He was busy stitching up a nasty gash on a young man's torso.

"Samuel," Mauldin acknowledged Pritchard without looking up from his task. "Good to see you, Marshal. It's been one helluva morning."

"So I noticed," Pritchard said. "Are you all right?"

"Been better," Mauldin said, "but after seeing so many who didn't come out of this train wreck alive, I'm not complaining."

"Have you seen Ditch?"

"I have," Mauldin said. "he's in the convalescent tent, next door." Mauldin looked up from his work and his eyes met Pritchard's. "I did what I could, Samuel."

Pritchard mumbled "Thanks," and rushed out of the surgical tent. He had to remove his hat and stoop to enter the smaller convalescent tent adjacent to the surgery.

Dozens of people lay on cots within the dim lighting inside the tent. All looked in various stages of severe injury, had already been treated by the surgeons, and were being attended by nurses. Most were moaning or crying out. Some were on the brink of imminent death.

"Samuel!"

Pritchard found Ditch lying on a cot covered with a blanket. His head was wrapped in gauze and his right arm was in a sling. He looked feverish and was soaked in sweat.

"It sure is good to see you," Pritchard said, putting on a smile. "I thought for a minute—"

"Almost was," Ditch interrupted. "If it wasn't for Doc Mauldin being on the same train, I'd have gone to my glory for sure." He lifted the blanket. His left leg was missing below the knee.

"Hell," Pritchard said, deliberately exhibiting no astonishment and widening his smile, "you always were a slowpoke, anyhow. One less limb won't slow you down none."

Ditch grimaced and coughed. "Damned leg got pinned and crushed. I was bleedin' out. Ole Doc Mauldin showed up with that black bag of his and sawed it off right there in that smashed-up train car. For the record, I don't recommend the experience unless you've got some laudanum in you, or at least a quantity of good whiskey."

"I'm right sorry, Ditch," Pritchard said.

"Nothin' to be sorry about," Ditch said. "Had to be done. If Doc hadn't taken my leg and stopped the bleedin', your sister would be a widow. As it is, she's married to a cripple."

"None of that talk," Pritchard said. "You're a better

man on one leg than any man I know on two. Idelle and your boy are gonna be right grateful to know you're still among us."

"How about you?" Ditch asked with a wink. "Are you grateful I'm still alive?"

"Not me," Pritchard joshed. "You've always been a righteous pain in my backside."

It took effort for Pritchard to feign jocularity. Inside, he was furious. Ditch Clemson had been his neighbor and friend since they were small boys. It was Ditch who helped him bury his father, exact vengeance on the men who lynched him, and dug him up from his shallow grave, headshot and just shy of perdition.

Together they'd escaped a prisoner-of-war camp, enlisted as Confederate guerilla fighters, fought a war, hunted down and avenged Pritchard's murdered fiancée, and stood shoulder-to-shoulder to rain down retribution on the man who'd forced them to flee their home as innocent boys in the first place, only to return a decade later as hardened men to set things right. He and Ditch had fought countless battles together, during and after the war, and in his mind no more reliable partner, brother, or friend could be found. That Ditch had married his little sister Idelle, and was the father of his nephew Samuel, only compounded the internal rage Pritchard felt at what had befallen his comrade.

"This train wreck weren't no accident," Ditch said. "It was derailed deliberate, Samuel."

"I know," Pritchard said. "Gonna find out who done it."

"It was Jem Rupe," Ditch said, "and some of his boys."

"Arkansas Jeremiah Rupe?" Pritchard said incredulously. "You sure about that?"

"That's what the man said," Ditch answered with a cough. "Never met Rupe myself, but it looked like him from what I've heard tell of his appearance. He was a big feller, wearin' a mask with a soup catcher hanging below it, under a top hat sportin' a snake band and a turkey feather."

"Ain't heard that name in a while," Pritchard remarked. "Not since the war. Gotta admit, this sure looks like Rupe's work. Lord knows, Jem's got a history of wreckin' trains."

"Son-of-a-bitch stole my wedding ring," Ditch said. "Took my watch, too. When he saw the picture of Idelle inside it, he told me he was gonna find her and have his way with her."

"That so?" Pritchard said, as his fists clenched. "Ain't a-gonna happen. On my oath, Ditch; Jem Rupe and any-body ridin' with him is gonna rue this day. I'll see him barkin' blood or swingin' from a branch, so help me God."

"Wish I was ridin' with you," Ditch said, his voice straining. "Got a score to settle."

"Don't you worry none about that," Pritchard said. "I'll settle the score for the both of us. All you've got to do is get well, and get back on your . . ."

Pritchard stopped himself before he finished the sentence. "Sorry, Ditch."

"Forget it, Samuel. I know what you meant."

"You're going to have to leave," a nurse scolded Pritchard. "This man needs to rest, not converse. You must go."

"There's something else you should know," Ditch said, grabbing Pritchard's arm with his good hand.

"Whatever it is," the nurse said, "it'll have to wait."

"Can't wait," Ditch shot back at her.

"Go on, Ditch," Pritchard said, holding up one massive hand to silence the nurse before she could upbraid them again. "Speak your mind."

"Jem knew beforehand it was only mayors in our passenger car," Ditch said. "The way him and his men spoke, they were set on us, particular."

"The hell you say?" Pritchard repeated, his voice barely a whisper.

"No doubt about it, partner," Ditch said.

"That'll be quite enough, Marshal," the nurse said. "If you don't leave now, I'll alert the major."

"My apologies," Pritchard said to her. "I'll be on my way." He stood as upright as the tent would allow. "I'll find a wagon to get you back to Atherton," he told his friend. "Meantime, you rest easy."

"I'll be all right," Ditch said. "You've got a man's work to do, Samuel. Get to it. But do me a favor, will you? Tell Idelle—"

Pritchard cut him off. "I'll tell Idelle exactly what she needs to hear. Don't you fret none." He left the tent with his fists still clenched and his jaw set.

Chapter 7

Thirteen riders galloped toward the stopped train, which was halted on the tracks only a few miles east of Kansas City. The locomotive wasn't a regular, but instead a special dispatched by the Brody Railroad Company out of their Kansas City depot to assist in the response to the wrecked train at Rock Creek. The engine was hauling boxcars loaded with tools and supplies, and the passenger cars were filled with able-bodied workmen.

Even though the wrecked train belonged to the rival Missouri Pacific Railroad, it was in both companies' interests to get the bridge repaired, the tracks cleared, the missing rail replaced, and the line operating again as soon as possible.

The rival railroad company's relief trains were coming from opposite directions. The Brody train had approached the disaster from the west, in Kansas City, and the Missouri Pacific relief train had come from the east, in Saint Louis.

Two of the boxcars on the halted Brody train had their sliding doors already open and ramps extended. The thirteen horsemen rode up, dismounted, and led their animals into one of the cars where attendants were waiting to unsaddle the animals. The riders then scurried into the other boxcar. A moment later the ramps were pulled up, the boxcar doors closed, and the train got under way.

Inside the boxcar housing the riders were several men already waiting. Two of them were attendants, like those who'd received the horses in the other car. They'd lit lanterns, and had tables set up with food and beer. The riders began doffing their masks and clothes. They put all of their personal items, including their hats, coats, and boots, into one large wooden box, and their pistols and cartridge belts into another. They then began donning overalls, work boots, gloves, and caps.

The other two men wore fancy suits. One was a freakishly tall, skinny, man with dull eyes, a sallow face, a drooping mustache, and wide-brimmed hat. The other was of medium height but stocky, and wore a bowler and a handlebar mustache. Both men wore pistols belted around their waists.

"Where's the money?" the man in the bowler asked the big, bearded, man in the top hat. He had just tossed his feathered headgear into the box, and was busy soaping up his face for a shave with a mirror, a bowl of water, and a razor provided by the attendants.

"In the bags," he answered, pointing to a bulging set of saddlebags next to a cloth bag on the floor. "The money and trinkets belonging to the passengers are in the burlap sack." He began to hastily scrape off his beard.

The tall man bent to examine the saddlebags and burlap sack. He held aloft a fistful of currency for his partner to acknowledge.

"Any trouble with the safe?"

"Nah," the Big Man replied as he cleared his chin.

"Popped open like a whore's knees. Only trouble we encountered was the guard in the mail car. Stubborn feller, he was. His bull-headed ways earned him a bullet."

"What about the other task?"

"Done just like you wanted. Nobody in that particular train car walked away. Every man not bedded down by the derailment was put to rest by our pistols." He paused his shaving. "All but one, that is."

"You left a mayor alive?"

"You told me to leave somebody alive to tell the tale, didn't you?"

"Not one of the mayors, you fool," the man in the bowler protested. "I expected you to have the sense to reveal yourself to one of the passengers in the other train car, not one of the mayors. They were all supposed to be eliminated. Why couldn't one of the other passengers tell the story?"

"Those in the other passenger car were mostly women and children." The Big Man shook his head. "Them who might've born witness were hysterified, and couldn't be counted on to remember their own names, much less the one I gave 'em. Don't worry none; the politician we left kickin' won't be kickin' for long. Just long enough to tell his tale, I reckon. He was all busted up in the crash. His leg was smashed flat and he was bleedin' out. Likely he's already expired."

"Likely ain't certain." The man in the bowler scowled. "Your instructions were clear. You were supposed to end all of the mayors. Those were your orders."

"Like I told you," the Big Man said, "he's probably already done expired."

The man in the bowler shook his head at the Big Man in disgust. "Probably isn't certainly," he said.

"What about our payment?" the Big Man asked, ignoring the disdain.

"You'll be compensated," the man in the bowler said. "Just like we agreed."

"When? My boys want their money now. So do I."

"When it's convenient," the man in the bowler said. "Remember our agreement. After we get to the wreck, you and your men are to mix in with the other workers and assist with repairing the bridge and tracks. You'll be paid after the work is done, when the entire outfit pulls out."

"My men are gun hands, not railroad laborers."

"Don't be a fool. There are going to be posses scouring the territory in all directions looking for Jem Rupe and a dozen riders. The safest place for you and your boys to be is the last place any lawmen will look, which is right under their noses at the train wreck."

"Iffen you say so," the Big Man said, finishing his shave and toweling off his face. "But there'd best be no tricks. We'll do as you say, and toil amongst the rest of your rail workers, but if you or your boss try to crawfish they'll be hell to pay."

"Are you threatening me?" the man in the bowler said. He parted his coat and placed his hand on his revolver. The tall man with him suddenly stood up from where he knelt counting money, faster than a man of his size would typically be expected to move. He also parted his coat.

The Big, now clean-shaven, Man glared back at the shorter man in the bowler and his tall associate. He was painfully conscious that neither he, nor any of his men, were still armed, having placed their guns into the trunk.

"I ain't makin' no threats," he said evenly. "I'm sayin' we're owed money, that's all."

"You'll get what's coming to you," the man in the bowler said.

Chapter 8

"Time to go," Strobl said, as he unlocked the cell door. "Judge Pearson is waiting."

Delbert Greaves, still damp from his earlier soaking, muttered under his breath. He walked from his cell past Deputy Tater Jessup with his shoulders slumped.

Tater spent the remainder of the morning and the early afternoon rounding up and organizing volunteers to make the journey to the site of the train wreck. A number of Atherton's residents had relatives who were aboard.

"We are going to walk across town to the courthouse," Strobl said in his Austrian-accented English. "We'll have no trouble, Mr. Greaves, will we?"

"When I decide to give you trouble," Greaves said, "you'll know it."

"Always gotta be the hard case," Tater said, shaking his head. "Tell me, son, why're you so hell-bent on gettin' yourself shot dead?"

"Who says I'll get shot dead?"

"That's how all you would-be gunslingers and pistol fighters end up," Tater said. "Seen it a dozen times if I've seen it once. Oh, you might put a few notches on your pistol before you feed the buzzards, but sooner or later hombres like you always end up perforated before your time. That's 'cause there's always another fame-hungry whelp just like you nippin' at your heels to become the next 'fastest gun in the territory.' Iffen you don't change your ways that'll be your end."

"Since when did you become my pa?"

"I ain't your pa," Tater said. "But iffen I were, you can bet you'd be spendin' time in the woodshed on the business end of my razor strop."

"Just you try it," Greaves said. "I'll—"

"I know, I know," Tater cut off Greaves's tirade. "You'll shoot me dead with your blazin' fast pistols. I hate to break it to you, kid, but you've already told me that a time or two before."

"It's all he's said," Strobl commented.

The two deputies, with Greaves walking ahead of them, escorted their prisoner across the square to the new courthouse. The two-story building was completed only last year, and sat in the center of town.

Atherton had become a prosperous place since Samuel's return. With its stewardship wrested from Burnell Shipley, the booming lumber, ranching, river transport, and agricultural interests worked full time to keep the railroad boxcars and barges stocked with goods for buyers at all points on the compass.

The streets were largely deserted in the middle of the afternoon, a result of so many townsfolk heading off to help with the train tragedy.

Judge Pearson, a sober man whose reliable temperament and good judgment were well-known to all in Atherton, was putting on his black robe when the trio arrived. There was no one else in the courtroom.

"Court's now in session," Pearson announced, taking his seat behind the bench. "What have we here?"

"Delbert Greaves, Your Honor," Tater said, as he and Strobl removed their hats, "hailing from Wapello County, Iowa. He's charged with callin' out the marshal this mornin', threatenin' his life, firin' his pistol within town limits, and disturbin' the peace."

"I believe I heard that shot," Pearson remarked. "Durn near made me spill my morning coffee." He looked sternly down at Greaves. "Those are serious charges, son. How do you plead?"

"I ain't your son," Greaves said. "And I ain't got nothin' to say to you, your yellow-bellied marshal, or anyone else in this stinkhole of a town."

Pearson's eyebrows lifted. "Tell me, Deputy Jessup, where is the marshal?"

"He lit out this mornin' for Rock Creek and the train wreck, as soon as he heard of it. Ditch was on board."

"I see," Judge Pearson said, rubbing his chin. He was a good friend of Mayor Ditch Clemson.

"He lit out, all right," Greaves said. "But it weren't on account of no train wreck. He was afraid, pure and simple. A-scared to face me in a fair fight."

"Young man," Pearson said, "you are not only ill-mannered, but you are also an imbecile. I know Marshal Pritchard. That you stand before me in this court, alive and breathing, is a testament to Marshal Pritchard's restraint. He chose to let you see another sunrise."

"I'm callin' you a liar," Greaves said.

"I've heard enough," Pearson said, pounding his gavel

once. "Guilty on all charges. That's fifty dollars, each count, for a fine of two-hundred dollars."

"That's pure robbery!" Greaves protested. "I ain't got that kind of money!"

"Two-hundred dollars or six months in jail," Pearson added. "Take your choice."

"Six months? Are you crazy?"

"Evidently it is you, Mr. Greaves, who is the crazy one," Pearson said, "if you think Atherton is a place where strangers are permitted to openly challenge our law enforcement officers to duels, threaten their lives, discharge firearms promiscuously, and disturb our peace and quiet. What'll it be? The fine or the jail?"

"I've only got four dollars," Greaves said. "I don't even have a horse to sell. I came into town on the train."

"Then it looks like you'll be stayin' awhile," Tater said, "as a guest of our jail." He let out a long sigh. "Though I ain't sure which of us is the one bein' punished?"

"Might I make a suggestion?" Strobl said to the judge.

"Go on ahead, Deputy."

"May I suggest, in the interests of justice, that the prisoner's fine be reduced to thirty-nine dollars on the condition he immediately leave town and never return?"

"Why that amount?" Pearson asked.

"The prisoner owns two Colt's Army revolvers," Strobl explained. "Both are in virtually new condition. He also owns a pair of fancy, hand-tooled, belt holsters. These items are currently locked in the safe in our jail. I have it on good authority that Wynn Samples, at the Atherton Mercantile, will pay fifteen dollars each for the guns and five for the belt and holsters. That, along with the four dollars in Greaves's possession, should cover the court's costs and pay for a rail ticket out of town."

"An excellent suggestion, Deputy Strobl," Pearson said.

"You can't sell my guns!" Greaves roared. "Not for fifteen dollars apiece, anyhow! I paid twenty dollars each for them guns! This town's not only full of cowards, it's full of thieves!"

"Then enjoy your stay in Atherton," Judge Pearson said. "If you behave, you might be out by Thanksgiving. Court's adjourned."

"Wait a minute," Greaves said, lowering his voice. "I'll take your damned offer, Judge. I ain't gonna spend no six months locked up."

"Very well," Pearson said. "The sentence is hereby amended to your release, providing you forfeit your guns, leave town, and never return. I authorize your arrest, on sight, should you enter the town of Atherton again."

"I'll take Mr. Greaves to the train station directly," Strobl said.

Strobl, Tater, and Greaves left the courtroom. "If it's okay with you, Florian," Tater said, "I'll leave you to escort our prisoner to the station by your lonesome. I've got to ride out to the Clemsons' and tell Idelle what happened to Ditch's train. I don't want her hearin' it from anyone else."

"Good luck," Strobl said.

The Austrian deputy walked the sullen Greaves through Atherton to the train station. He purchased a ticket north, billing it to the town, and pointed to the passenger car.

"Let's not meet again," Strobl said.

"You'd best hope our trails don't cross," Greaves said,

as he boarded the train. "I ain't forgettin' what you and this town of yours done to me."

"Remember what you will," Strobl said, "as long as you don't return to Atherton. Auf wiedersehen." The deputy turned and walked away.

"I'll be back, Frenchy," Greaves said under his breath, once Strobl was out of earshot. "You can count on it."

Chapter 9

By sundown, the makeshift camps on both sides of the creek had expanded to more than a dozen large tents, countless small ones, and an endless stream of freight wagons. Hundreds of workers from both railroads, and an equal number of volunteers, had arrived, as well as another platoon of soldiers from the army barracks at Independence.

Two more trains had arrived, in addition to the two already at the site. A small private train belonging to the Brody Railroad Company, headquartered in Kansas City, had rolled in from the west. Another private train from the Missouri Pacific Railroad, in Saint Louis, had entered from the east. Each of the new trains sat halted on opposite sides of the Rock Creek Bridge, and served as headquarters for their respective railroad companies.

Work on the damaged tracks had ceased for the day, not only due to the encroaching darkness but because even darker clouds were rolling in. May was the unofficial start of twister season in Missouri, and heavy storms at this time of year were not uncommon.

Pritchard walked across what was left of the Rock

Creek railroad bridge. He ignored the stares of the retiring workers, who gazed up at the towering lawman in his Texas-style hat, boots, and garb, as he passed by them on their trudge to the mess tent.

Once he crossed the bridge, Pritchard strode along the tracks until he reached the Brody headquarters train, one-hundred yards west of the creek. A few workmen were still milling about, but there were also several private railroad detectives, dressed in town suits and armed with rifles, standing guard. Near the first passenger car, which was a highly ornate affair, were a pair of soldiers being halted by a quartet of the detectives. Pritchard approached the fancy car.

"Where do you think you're going?" one of the railroad detectives demanded.

"Into that-there train car," Pritchard said, pointing.

"No, you ain't, cowboy," the detective said. "That's Mr. Brody's private car. He's conducting an important meeting. He left orders he wasn't to be disturbed."

"How do you know I wasn't invited?" Pritchard asked.

"The army's been invited," the detective said. "So has the boss of the Missouri Pacific Railroad and the Lieutenant Governor. But you, cowpuncher, ain't invited."

"He wouldn't let us in, either," one of the soldiers explained. "Only our commanding officer, Major Duncan, was allowed to enter."

"My name's Samuel Pritchard," Pritchard explained, "and I ain't no cowboy. I'm the town marshal of Atherton and the Jackson County sheriff. For your information, this here train is wrecked in Jackson County. I reckon if the State of Missouri, the army, and the two big railroads are bein' represented in that meetin', there oughta be somebody representin' the county, too. Quite a few Jackson County folks lost their lives today travelin' this rail line."

"So?" the detective said.

"So," Pritchard said, "I'll be attendin' that meetin'. Step aside."

"Or what?" the detective said.

"I already done told you," Pritchard said, "I'm a-goin' into that-there train car. You'd best give ground."

The detective grinned, looked back at his three companions, levered a cartridge into his rifle, and brought the weapon up horizontally across his chest in an obvious gesture to deny Pritchard further progress toward the train car. "What are you going to do if I don't, Marshal?"

With astonishing speed, Pritchard snatched the rifle from the sneering detective's grasp. He immediately slammed it back into the man's face, which rendered him instantly unconscious. Then he pivoted and brought up the rifle before the other dumbfounded detectives could lever cartridges into their own carbines. All three found themselves staring into the barrel of the lever gun in Pritchard's hands.

"Lose them rifles," Pritchard ordered. The detectives complied. "Now git!" The trio scrambled hastily away. He snatched the rifle from the detective and tossed it off into the darkness.

The two wide-eyed soldiers watched Pritchard step over the railroad detective lying unconscious at his feet and climb the steps to the private car. He stopped before he reached the door and looked over his shoulder.

"You boys a-comin' or ain't ya?"

The two soldiers grinned at each other and scampered aboard behind him. Without knocking, Pritchard went into the car with the two soldiers on his heels. Everyone inside looked up as they entered.

The car was even more expensively furnished inside. Polished bookshelves filled with leather-bound volumes decorated one wall and a beautiful, well-stocked, bar adorned the opposite. There was a large mahogany desk and an elaborate map table in the center.

Four men sat in thickly padded leather chairs, each holding a snifter of brandy. An older man in a white jacket and gloves stood solemnly in one corner awaiting an order.

Pritchard recognized three of the men; John Brody, the owner of the Brody Railroad, Major Duncan, whom he'd met earlier that afternoon, and Missouri's lieutenant governor, Norman J. Coleman. The other man was a stranger whom he presumed represented the Missouri Pacific Railroad, the Brody Railroad's main rival.

"What is the meaning of this interruption?" Brody demanded, standing up. "This is a private meeting."

"Evenin', Mr. Brody," Pritchard said pleasantly. He removed his hat, revealing his bullet scar. "You remember me, don't you?"

"I most certainly do," Brody said, making no attempt to hide his outrage. He was a short, balding, florid man in his sixties wearing a costly suit that was carefully tailored to conceal his girth. "The last time we met was in Dominic Quincy's office, in Saint Louis. You struck him in the face, if I recall. Broke his nose. You also shot off one of his arms."

"That's generally how I treat folks who put up cash money to have me killed," Pritchard said.

"If I'm not mistaken," Brody said contemptuously, "you eventually killed him, did you not?"

"Actually," Pritchard said, "it was one of my deputies who killed ole Cottonmouth. Put a load of buckshot into his belly while he was in the act of tryin' to murder my pregnant sister. Far as I'm concerned, killin' ole Cottonmouth was akin to steppin' on a bug."

"I also remember, during our first meeting," Brody continued, "you called me a 'crooked tycoon' and threatened to have a warrant sworn out for my arrest."

"Governor Woodson was all for it," Pritchard said. "But Silas Woodson ain't in office anymore, is he? Which explains why you're a-courtin' Governor Hardin."

"That's preposterous," Brody declared. "Who says I'm doing any such thing?"

"Playing hostess to his sidekick says so," Pritchard said, pointing his hat at Lieutenant Governor Coleman. Coleman, a thin, stiff-looking, man with a full head of white hair, looked uneasily around the car. He avoided Pritchard's gaze.

"What do you want?" Brody asked.

"Only to join the meetin'," Pritchard said. "Seems you forgot to send the Jackson County Sheriff an invitation. By the way, I'm the county sheriff."

"I didn't forget," Brody scoffed. "You weren't invited."

"That's what the feller outside told me," Pritchard said. "Right before he spit out all his teeth and fell asleep." The two soldiers snickered but stopped when Major Duncan directed a sharp glare at them.

"Ain't you going to introduce me?" Pritchard said, pointing his hat this time at the stranger in the room.

He was a raven-haired man in his fifties with a heavy beard and dark eyes.

"My name is Jason Gould," the man said. "I own the Missouri Pacific Railroad."

"Heard of you," Pritchard said.

"Really?" Gould said. "What have you heard?"

"That you're a common horse thief who fancies himself a robber baron. Folks say you're a man who'd pry the silver out of his own ma's teeth iffen he could get away with it."

"People don't usually talk to me that way, Marshal Pritchard."

"You asked me what I'd heard," Pritchard said with a shrug, "and I told you. Ain't my fault it sours your ears."

"Charles," Brody said to the valet over his shoulder, "fetch Mr. Marsh and Mr. Finchum at once."

The man in the white coat bowed slightly and wordlessly vanished through the door at the far end of the car. Major Duncan motioned for the two soldiers to depart as well. They saluted and followed the servant from the car.

"Please, gentlemen," Pritchard said. "Don't let me hold up your meetin'. Go on about your business."

"Not in your presence," Brody insisted.

"Something you don't want me to hear?" Pritchard said.

"Nonsense," Brody said. "This is a private meeting concerning railroad, state, and military interests, and none of your business."

"People from this county and my town are dead or maimed," Pritchard said, his pleasant demeanor evaporating. "Other towns, too. Some of those towns are now without their mayors. That's my business."

"I see no harm in the Jackson County Sheriff participating in our meeting," Gould spoke up, "nor the Atherton town marshal, even if they're the same person. We've nothing to hide, do we, John?"

Brody glared at Gould, while Coleman continued to fidget nervously. Major Duncan remained impassive.

"Very well," Brody conceded. "You may stay, Marshal Pritchard." He gestured toward a vacant seat.

"Thank you," Pritchard said. He sat down, placing his wide-brimmed Stetson on his lap.

"Please continue your briefing, Major Duncan," Brody said, resuming his seat.

"As I was saying," Duncan said, reading from a small notebook, "there were ninety-two people on board the train. Eighty-eight were passengers, and the rest were railroad employees; the engineer, fireman, conductor, and mail guard. The death toll at this hour currently stands at fifty-three. I'm told by the surgeons there may be several more fatalities to add to that total by morning."

"Good lord," Coleman said. "What a terrible tragedy."

"What caused this 'tragedy,' Major?" Gould asked, lighting a cigar. "I'd very much like to know your thoughts, especially since it was one of my trains that was wrecked."

"The wreck was caused by the deliberate removal of a section of track leading up to the Rock Creek Bridge," Duncan went on. "It would appear the train was derailed so the robbers could gain access to the safe in the mail car. According to your accountants, Mr. Gould, the safe contained over forty-thousand dollars in cash."

"A heinous criminal act," Brody said, shaking his head. "Fortunately, thanks to Major Duncan's diligent investigation, we know who perpetrated this despicable crime."

"We do," Duncan affirmed. "A survivor told of a dozen or more riders in the raiding party, led by none other than Jeremiah Rupe. Rupe and his men apparently made no secret of their identities."

"This is unquestionably Jeremiah Rupe's handiwork," Brody said. "It's exactly like what he did on the Platte Bridge during the war."

"What's being done to apprehend these trainwreckers?" Gould asked.

"We've notified all military posts and civilian authorities in the territory," Duncan said. "There are army patrols and sheriffs' posses searching the countryside as we speak. Rest assured, Mr. Gould, we'll find Arkansas Jem Rupe and his outfit before long."

"How soon before the rail line is restored?" Coleman asked. "The governor will want to know."

"We hope to have it repaired and operating by tomorrow," Brody said, "the day after at the latest. An inoperative rail line costs everyone money. It's in all of our interests to get the trains running again, right, Jason?"

Gould only nodded, exhaling cigar smoke.

"Which explains why rival railroad bosses are sippin' finical brandy together like two bugs in a wool rug," Pritchard said.

"Jason and I, despite leading different railroad companies, have a number of common interests," Brody said defensively. "We are by no means enemies."

"Iffen you say so," Pritchard said. Gould said nothing.

"Very well," Coleman said, clapping his hands together

and standing up. "It sounds as if all that can be done is being done. Your respective railroads, and the army, appear to have everything well-in-hand. If you'll excuse me, I'll take my leave. I still have to prepare a telegram to brief the governor before I retire. In light of the regional mayors' meeting in Kansas City being canceled on account of this terrible train wreck, Governor Hardin will want to know how things are progressing. Thank you, gentlemen, and good night."

Brody, Gould, and Duncan also rose, signaling the end of the meeting.

"That's it?" Pritchard said, still seated. "That's all you boys have to say about the matter?"

The others turned to look questioningly at Pritchard. Coleman still wore his nervous expression, Brody appeared even more irritated, Gould seemed interested, and Duncan's eyes narrowed.

"What else is there to say?" Brody said.

"I can think of a few questions," Pritchard said, "that folks might be inclined to ask."

"Such as?" Brody said, rolling his eyes.

"Why was it necessary to wreck an entire train just to rob it?" Pritchard said. "Plenty of mail cars get robbed without wreckin' the train pullin' 'em."

"Jeremiah Rupe likes to wreck trains," Duncan said. "He proved as much during the war."

"Maybe," Pritchard conceded. "There're other questions. Such as, why did the robbers kill all the mayors? I examined the bodies myself. Every single town mayor on that special car who wasn't killed in the derailment was headshot."

"Not all the mayors were killed," Duncan pointed out.

"Your friend wasn't, and there were others besides mayors on the train who were shot."

"You're wrong about that, Major," Pritchard countered. "The only one of more than a dozen mayors not killed in the wreck or headshot by the bandits, my friend Ditch, looked like he was gonna die anyway. The only other person shot on the train beside the mayors was the mail guard, who put up a fight. Every other passenger who expired died because of injuries they got in the wreck. Nobody else but a dozen mayors and a mail guard took a bullet. That doesn't seem a mite odd to you boys?"

"I find no oddity," Brody argued. "Robbers are savages. Men of low character who think nothing of shooting defenseless men. What more explanation do you need?"

"Then why not kill everybody?" Pritchard asked. "Why only the politicians in one particular car? Why leave any survivors at all to identify 'em to the law?"

"Perhaps," Coleman suggested, "while the bandits are clearly men of low morals, as Mr. Brody mentioned, their character wasn't so low that they would stoop to the murder of women and children?"

"Who are you kiddin'?" Pritchard said. "You're tellin' me they'd wreck a train, murder everyone who survived in one car, but not harm the passengers in the other?" He shook his head. "It doesn't make sense. And why would any of 'em, much less their leader, give up so much as a hint as to who he was?"

"Pride, perhaps," Brody said, "or the arrogance of vanity? Maybe Arkansas Jeremiah Rupe wanted people to know this carnage was his handiwork? Or maybe he didn't intend to disclose his identity, and somehow revealed it inadvertently?"

"It don't figure that way," Pritchard said. "My friend Ditch told me Rupe gave his own name. He believes Rupe let him live purely to point the finger at him."

"What, exactly, are you getting at, Marshal?" Gould asked.

"Only that it's mighty fishy to me why a man like Arkansas Jem Rupe, if he's even still alive, would let anyone know it was him what done this murder and robbery? Rupe's a feller who's been successfully hidin' out from the law for more'n ten years, ever since the war, iffen he ain't already dead. Why pop his head out of his hidey-hole now?"

"I don't presume to understand the motives of vicious killers and brigands, Marshal Pritchard," Brody said. "You, as a killer of men yourself, might be more inclined towards such insight. All I know is this Jeremiah Rupe character, along with a dozen of his men, wrecked my good friend Jason Gould's train, robbed it, murdered its passengers, and disrupted rail service to both our lines, which deeply affects commerce throughout Missouri and beyond. I, for one, intend to see that justice is done. This Jeremiah Rupe will be hunted down, tried, and hanged. Towards that end, I am posting a fifty-thousand-dollar reward for his capture."

"I'll match it," Gould said.

"One-hundred-thousand dollars," Major Duncan whistled. "That's a very generous bounty. You'll bring every gunman and bounty hunter from all over the territory."

"That is my intent," Brody said loftily. "No price is too steep in the pursuit of justice."

Pritchard looked down at the hat on his lap, clucked his teeth, and shook his head.

"Something troubling you, Marshal?"

"Why, yes," Pritchard said, "'troubling' is just the word I was looking for. I find it troubling as hell that so many of the murdered passengers just happened to be on the way to a meetin' in Kansas City with you, Mr. Brody."

"Are you insinuating something, Marshal Pritchard?" Gould asked.

"Nope. Just makin' an observation."

"Will you be joining the search for Jeremiah Rupe, Marshal?" Duncan asked.

"I'm on the trail of the men who wrecked this train," Pritchard said, "if that's what you mean?"

"Then you're going after Jeremiah Rupe," Brody said.

"Didn't say that," Pritchard answered. "I told you I'm on the trail of them that wrecked this train." He looked up and met the eyes of the four men standing over him. "When I find 'em, and I will, you can bet they're a-gonna know it."

The door to the train car opened abruptly and two men wearing suits entered. One was a stocky man of medium height with a handlebar mustache and wearing a bowler, and the other an extremely tall man, even taller than Pritchard, with a wide-brimmed hat and sporting a drooping mustache. Both wore belted pistols. The man in the bowler wore a .44 caliber Smith & Wesson Russian revolver, and the taller man a pair of Colt Army Models in tied-down holsters.

"You wanted to see us, Mr. Brody?" the man in the bowler asked.

"Yes," Brody said. "I'd like you to meet Sheriff Samuel Pritchard, from Jackson County. He's also Atherton's town marshal." The two newcomers appraised the seated lawman.

Brody smiled smugly. "Marshal Pritchard, allow me to introduce two of my most trusted and loyal employees; Railroad Detectives Earl Marsh and Asa Finchum. Both, like you, are veterans of the late troubles. Also, like you, they are no strangers to violence."

Marsh, in the bowler, and Finchum, in the wide hat, both looked down at Pritchard. He was the only man in the passenger car still seated.

"I've heard the name Pritchard bandied about before," Marsh said to Finchum. "Name of a man who used to be known as Smokin' Joe Atherton, they say. It's rumored he's quite the gun hand."

"You never can tell what folks'll gossip about," Pritchard said.

"I heard Atherton was the fastest gun still above ground," Finchum said out of the side of his mouth. His voice carried the deep tone of the heavy smoker.

"That's what they say," Marsh repeated.

"The marshal," Brody told the newcomers, "has worn out his welcome and needs to be escorted from this train. Please see to that, would you?"

"With pleasure," Marsh said.

"Our meetin' is over?" Pritchard asked innocently.

"It most certainly is." Brody smiled, brimming with confidence now that Marsh and Finchum were present.

"I wonder how fast he is?" Marsh asked Finchum. He parted his coat behind the butt of his holstered Smith & Wesson.

"Was wonderin' the same thing," Finchum said, as he tucked his coattails behind his dual guns.

Major Duncan's face tightened. Lieutenant Governor Coleman's face paled, and his eyes darted instinctively for the door. Gould bit down on his cigar, but otherwise his expression didn't change. Brody haughtily tucked both thumbs into his vest and rocked back and forth on his heels.

"What do you have to say for yourself now, Marshal Pritchard?" Brody taunted.

"Do you fellers know who has the fastest draw?" Pritchard asked Marsh and Finchum.

"Who?" Marsh said.

"The feller who already has a gun in his hand," Pritchard said. He lifted the hat from his lap with his left hand, revealing a Colt .45, with the hammer back, levelled at a spot midpoint between the two men standing before him.

When Brody sent his servant from the car, Pritchard discretely drew his right-hand gun and silently cocked it beneath the concealment of the Stetson on his lap.

Marsh's eyes flashed. Finchum's dull eyes showed nothing.

Pritchard slowly stood up, put on his hat, and drew his other gun while keeping his Colt steadily leveled. Neither of the men facing him moved even slightly.

"Don't just stand there," Brody demanded of Marsh and Finchum, "do something."

"Can't," Marsh said flatly. "He's got the drop."

"But there're two of you?" Brody whined.

"Makes no difference," Finchum said.

"Put those lead-pushers on the table," Pritchard ordered, "butt-first, and real slow. And don't think I ain't heard of the Road Agent's Spin, neither."

Both Marsh and Finchum complied. Pritchard lowered his revolvers' hammers, holstered them, and picked up the three guns from atop the map table.

"Tell me somethin', Mr. Brody?" Samuel said. "Are these two the best you've got?"

"I thought so," Brody said, scowling at Marsh and Finchum. He was no longer haughty and smiling.

"I were you," Pritchard said, "I'd see about gettin' me some better ones." He backed toward the door.

"What about our guns?" Marsh asked.

"You'll find 'em outside," Pritchard answered, "in the creek." He tipped his hat. "Good night, gentlemen."

"I'll be joining you, Marshal," Gould said, following Pritchard out of the car. "The evening"—he looked derisively at Brody, Marsh, and Finchum—"and the company, seems to have digressed." Lieutenant Governor Coleman and Major Duncan exited the car directly behind them.

Once the others left, Brody turned to Marsh and Finchum. "I am not pleased," he said. "I don't pay you two to get buffaloed."

"It won't happen again," Marsh said.

"You're right," Brody snapped. "Because if it does, you'll both be seeking employment elsewhere. Where's the payroll money from Gould's train?"

"It's stashed in the livery car," Marsh said. "We didn't want to risk moving it until after dark."

"That's the first intelligent thing I've heard you say," Brody said. "See that it's brought to my private car tonight. I want it in my safe as soon as possible."

"As you wish," Marsh said. "There's nothing to fret about, Mr. Brody." He turned to his tall partner. "We'll deal with the marshal, won't we, Asa?" Finchum merely nodded.

"Nothing to fret about?" Brody mimicked, as his face turned crimson. He pointed his finger at the two men like a pistol barrel. "Marshal Pritchard was personally responsible for the death of my friend Dominic Quincy and the ruination of his empire. I will not stand idly by and have him do the same to me and my railroad. Are we clear?"

"Clear as glass," Marsh said. "Pritchard's nothing but a small-town sheriff."

"Maybe so," Brody argued, "but he's no fool. He suspects. You two morons didn't hear the questions he raised. Questions the governor's office and the army heard him ask. For a small-town sheriff, Pritchard's got a bloodhound's nose."

"Don't you worry," Marsh assured Brody. "He'll soon find his nose lopped off."

"I don't want to know what you do," Brody said, pouring himself a glass of brandy with shaking hands. He didn't offer a drink to Marsh or Finchum. "But whatever it is"—he downed the brandy in one gulp—"do it soon and make it permanent. I've grown weary of Marshal Samuel Pritchard."

Chapter 10

Pritchard spent the next hour searching for a wagon to take Ditch back to Atherton with little success. Night had fallen, the wind had picked up, it was beginning to rain, and few drivers were willing to trade the light and warmth of one of the many tents at the campsite for the soggy darkness of a twelve-mile, nocturnal journey back to Atherton.

He eventually got lucky and ran into Simon Tilley, Atherton's undertaker, and his adult son Seth. They'd arrived in the late afternoon, each driving a wagon. Simon drove their hearse and Seth a covered wagon filled with food and blankets to contribute to the relief effort. They unloaded the supplies from the wagon, then loaded up the bodies of several Atherton residents into the hearse. These included the corpse of nine-year-old Donnie McKitchern, who'd been traveling on the train to visit his grandparents in Kansas City when he met his untimely demise. His grieving father rode up front, alongside Simon.

When Pritchard explained Ditch's situation, Simon and Seth readily agreed to immediately return to Atherton.

They also refused any payment from the marshal. A weak and feverish Ditch was loaded into the back of the covered wagon, along with Dr. Mauldin, who announced he'd done all he could for those at the wreck. He wanted to continue to attend to Ditch for fear the young mayor would contract pneumonia if he remained at the wreck site any longer.

Pritchard had just grained and watered Rusty and was preparing to mount, when a man in a suit he didn't recognize approached. "Marshal Pritchard?" he asked.

"That's right."

"I represent Jason Gould, of the Missouri Pacific Railroad. Mr. Gould would like a word with you."

"I'm fixin' to depart," Pritchard said, nodding to the two wagons.

"Please, Marshal," the man implored. "Mr. Gould said it was a most urgent matter, and insisted I bring you along. I'm sure he won't take up much of your time."

"Go on ahead," Pritchard said to Simon and Seth Tilley. "Get Ditch home. I'll catch up."

The father-and-son undertakers waved an acknowledgment and got their respective wagon teams moving east.

Pritchard allowed himself and Rusty to be led to the train on the east side of the Rock Creek Bridge. He tied the big Morgan to the rail of the passenger car, went up the steps, and entered. The man in the suit, now soaking wet, did not enter with him.

Pritchard found the interior of Gould's private train car even more opulent than Brody's. In addition to a larger bar, Gould's car had a fireplace, which was blazing. Pritchard removed his hat, but not his sodden slicker, as Jason Gould stood to greet him.

"Thank you for coming, Marshal," Gould said.

"No thanks are necessary," Pritchard said. "What can I do for you, Mr. Gould? Your man said you wanted to speak with me."

"You don't like me, do you?"

"Don't know you."

"But what you've heard isn't good?"

"I usually take what I hear with a grain of salt."

"And Mr. Brody? How do you feel about him?"

"He once parlayed with a man who tried to end me and my little sister. I can't say it plainer than that." A smirk lighted Pritchard's face. "Don't think I didn't see you twitch back there in Brody's private car when he called you his 'good friend.'"

"That obvious, was it?" Gould said. "If I may ask, what are your feelings regarding Mr. Brody's railroad?"

"Much as I'd like to remain in this warm, dry car and chew the fat with you," Pritchard said, "my feelings are personal, and frankly, I've got business elsewhere. I'm escorting my wounded friend back to Atherton."

"At this hour? In this weather?"

"Got no choice," Pritchard said. "Doc says he needs to be indoors. Another day in a tent, in this damp, could be the death of him."

"I see," Gould said. "I'll get right to it, then." He put out his cigar in a shiny brass ashtray. "You said some things back at Brody's train which led me to believe you have suspicions about who's responsible for the derailment."

"I have my doubts," Pritchard said.

"I have similar suspicions," Brody said. "I was hoping you might elaborate on yours."

"Nothin' to elaborate on," Pritchard said. "I don't know anything yet, and I generally ain't inclined to speculate on what I don't know."

"Perhaps not," Gould said, "but I happen to know you were a Texas Ranger. Even your speculation is of value to me."

"All I know, Mr. Gould, is that a dozen riders leave a lot of trail. That nobody, not the army nor any posse, has picked up that sign is a bit of a puzzlement, ain't it?"

"It is indeed," Gould said. "You previously voiced concerns about the motive for the derailment as well, didn't you?"

"A forty-thousand-dollar payroll in a mail car's safe will draw men of bad intention," Pritchard said, "ain't no doubt about that. Maybe even a feller like Arkansas Jem Rupe and a dozen armed riders. But why the mayors were gunned bedevils me. Almost seems like somebody knew they were gonna be on that train, don't it?"

"It certainly does. And you intend to sort it out?"

"Sort it out?" Pritchard said. His smirk widened. "Is that what you high-falutin' railroad barons call it?"

"How would you characterize it?"

"A nine-year-old boy from my hometown lost his life, along with scores of innocent passengers. My best friend is short one leg, and may yet expire, and that don't count the dozens of others injured and maimed. If by 'sort it out,' you're referrin' to me puttin' my guns or a rope to each and every son-of-a-bitch who had a hand in that deviltry, then you're damn right, Mr. Gould, I'm sure as hell a-gonna 'sort it out.' Now if you'll excuse me, I've got a pair of wagons to catch."

Pritchard wordlessly donned his hat and left the car. Gould tugged a bell cord along the wall and lit another cigar. Before he had it fully going the man in the suit entered through the car's door.

"Take a message to the telegraph operator," Gould said, exhaling smoke. "Have him send out a wire to all of our offices. Get me Laird Bonner."

Chapter 11

The rain increased in intensity, and the spectacular lightning was interrupted by correspondingly severe peals of thunder. Simon Tilley had no trouble keeping the hearse on the road, thanks to the lightning, but he was beginning to worry about the impact of the extra weight of so many corpses as it progressed along the increasingly soggy path. Behind him, the Conestoga driven by his son Seth was making similar trudging progress. In the rear of that wagon was Doc Mauldin, attending to Ditch Clemson by lantern. Ditch had been made as comfortable as possible in a makeshift bed of straw and blankets. The wind had picked up considerably, driving the rain into the small caravan. The four-horse teams pulling each wagon were becoming skittish in response to the storm.

Simon Tilley occasionally peered around the corner of the hearse, searching behind the wagons for Pritchard in the split-second visibility the lightning flashes provided. Visibility was limited, and he saw nothing except darkness and rain. They'd been on the road back to Atherton from the camp for more than two miles, and he hoped the marshal would catch up by now. Tilley wasn't afraid to admit he felt better with the young lawman in their company, especially with train robbers still at large somewhere in the countryside.

"This wasn't part of the deal," the Big Man said, as he and his men stripped off their work clothes inside the boxcar.

"The deal was," Marsh said, "you and your men get paid to do as you're told."

"Maybe so," the Big Man protested, "but we never agreed to go galivantin' off into the night in the middle of a toad-strangler. Especially after you worked us all day on the damn tracks like common railroad hands. Not to mention makin' us eat the same slop as all them other railway diggers. We ain't even had a drop of whiskey."

"I already told you," Marsh said, "you and your boys have to lay low. That's why we blended you in with the other laborers. It's for your own good."

"Iffen we're supposed to 'lay low,'" the Big Man said, as he slipped into the clothes and boots he'd worn earlier that morning, "why are we goin' out on horseback now? Ain't that a-gonna ruinate your plans to blend us in?"

"Don't worry," Finchum said. "No one will find out. We already had the liverymen take your horses off the train. They're stashed behind the caboose. In the dark, in this storm, ain't nobody goin' to see you. Everybody's hunkered down in their tents tryin' to stay dry and get themselves off to sleep."

"Which is what we should be doin'," the Big Man grumbled. He accepted his revolver and checked the cylinder to ensure it was filled with five cartridges. "Don't see why we can't do this tomorrow?"

"Are you done whining now?" Marsh asked.

"How much?" the Big Man said, holstering his gun and putting on his top hat with the snakeskin band and turkey feather.

"How much what?"

"How much extra are we gonna get for findin' and buryin' this one-legged mayor and marshal for ya?"

"Don't worry," Marsh said. "You'll be adequately compensated."

"That's what you said the last time I asked about our pay," the Big Man in the top hat said. He looked around at his men, who were now dressed, armed, and ready to go. "And I got the same nonsense outta your mouth for an answer. I asked you a question, Marsh. How much extra?"

As he spoke, the Big Man put his beefy hand on the butt of his holstered revolver. All twelve of his men followed his lead and did the same, parting their dusters and gripping their holstered guns.

"I know you and Finchum are professional gun hands," the Big Man said, "but there's a dozen of us. Quote us a price or we're goin' back to bed. If you don't like them two choices"—he grinned—"we could always settle the account with our guns."

That's when the Big Man and his men noticed Marsh's and Finchum's holsters were empty.

"Speakin' of guns," he asked, "where are yours?"

Marsh's face reddened around his handlebar mustache. Finchum's face remained stolid.

"Don't worry about our guns," Marsh said. "Just do as

you're told. Find and finish that mayor and marshal, and it'll be an extra two-hundred dollars for each of you."

One of the men whistled. The others grinned and smiled. "That's more like it," the Big Man in the top hat said. "We know who the mayor is, but what does the lawman look like?"

"He's a big lad," Marsh said, "nearly as tall as Asa but twice as broad. Wears a Texas-style head case and a pair of revolvers. He was riding east atop a healthy-sized Morgan on the main road to Atherton about ten minutes ago. He'll be with the wagon that's toting the mayor."

"I heard of that feller," one of the riders spoke up. "His name's Pritchard. I saw him earlier today, walkin' along the tracks."

"I heard of him, too," another spoke up. "He ain't just no town marshal, neither. Heard he rode with Witherspoon's Rangers during the war, under the name Atherton, as part of Shelby's Iron Brigade. After the war, it's said, he spent ten years killin' men for the Republic of Texas. Killed more men than the pox, they say."

"I also heard of him," a third man chimed in. "They say he's the Devil's Right Hand with a hog leg." Others nodded in agreement.

"He's only one man," Marsh said. "They're thirteen of you. It's dark, it's raining, and he doesn't even know you're riding after him. It'll be the easiest two-hundred dollars you'll ever make."

"Iffen it's so easy," the Big Man in the top hat said, "whyn't you two professional pistoleers ride out in the rain in the middle of the night and do it yourselves?"

"We can't leave camp," Marsh said. "Folks would notice us gone. Besides that, we crossed words with the marshal earlier. We'd be suspected if he fell to a bullet. Also, this needs to be done quietly."

"You two bein' suspected if the marshal comes to a bad end wouldn't have anything to do with your missin' pistols," the Big Man asked Marsh and Finchum, "would it? Could it be the marshal had a hand in disarmin' you?"

"That's none of your business," Marsh shot back defensively.

"I suppose it ain't," the Big Man chuckled. "Nonetheless, it seems mighty convenient at the same time you want this marshal gunned, you two boys seem to have misplaced your barkin' irons." The other men laughed.

"Every minute we stand in this boxcar gabbing," Marsh said, as his face got even redder, "Marshal Pritchard and those wagons get farther away. Do you want the job, or not?"

"We'll take the job," the Big Man in the top hat said. His smile vanished. "Two-hundred dollars is two-hundred dollars, ain't it?"

Chapter 12

Rusty shook his head from side-to-side, snorted, and tugged the reins in Pritchard's wet hands. The rain came down in torrents, punctuated by tremendous flashes of lightning and resounding peals of thunder.

"Easy," he said, patting the side of the big Morgan's neck. "Nothin' to be afeared about, Rusty. Lord knows we've ridden storms before."

Pritchard wasn't exaggerating. He and Rusty had been a team more than a dozen years, since he and Ditch fled Atherton as seventeen-year-old boys. He'd ridden the big, chestnut-colored horse through every kind of weather, on countless raids and battles during the Civil War, throughout ten blood-soaked years as a Texas Ranger, during a cattle drive from Taylor County, Texas, to Abilene, Kansas, and for his short tenure as a Missouri lawman.

Pritchard and Rusty knew each other as well as man and horse could. Thus, he was a bit perplexed when the Morgan displayed such discomfort in riding through a mere rainstorm, despite its intensity.

Pritchard wasn't overly concerned about the storm. He knew the Tilleys' wagons couldn't be too far ahead of them on the trail. If he didn't catch up to them on the road, it was only a dozen miles to Atherton. He'd meet with them at Ditch's and Idelle's place, or in Atherton, within a couple of hours.

Thunder roared and Rusty reared, turning in a circle. Pritchard, surprised at the horse's uncharacteristic fit of temper, reined him down. As he calmed Rusty, another long flash of lightning erupted, illuminating the surrounding countryside.

In the lightning's glare Pritchard sensed movement. As thunder again resounded, and another flash of lightning ensued, he spotted the silhouettes of a dozen or more riders approaching at a gallop. They were less than fifty yards away.

That's why Rusty was having fits! It wasn't the storm that made him skittish—his more attuned senses detected the approaching riders!

Pritchard spurred the Morgan to a run as the sound of a dozen gunshots rang out. The reports were muffled by the rain and drowned out by another thunderclap.

Many more muted shots went off as Pritchard and Rusty fled together. The lawman felt several bullets whiz past, something he'd experienced many times before. One grazed his left arm, tearing his slicker. Another sizzled past his ear.

Accurate firing with pistols from horseback was difficult at best, particularly at night in a heavy rainstorm, but Pritchard knew from his days as a partisan guerilla and Texas Ranger that sheer volume-of-fire could make up for lack of accuracy. Fire enough bullets, and a lucky shot could find its target as easily as one that was deliberately aimed. With a dozen guns firing at them, Pritchard knew the odds were against him and Rusty.

Rusty had taken them perhaps a quarter of a mile through the rain and darkness when the big Morgan suddenly pitched forward, ejecting Pritchard from the saddle. The lawman found himself rolling head-over-heels in the Missouri mud.

When he finally came to rest and stood up, minus his hat and on unsteady feet, Pritchard realized, courtesy of another brilliant lightning flash, that Rusty lay motionless on his side behind him. He ran back to the downed animal, his heart sinking.

The next flash of lightning confirmed Pritchard's worst fears. Rusty's left foreleg was shattered, and blood was freely flowing from his mouth and nose. At least one of the bullets chasing them had found its mark in the horse's flank, and the stalwart Morgan had broken his leg as he collapsed.

Pritchard knew his horse was in mortal agony, but had little time for the niceties of a solemn good-bye. He drew a revolver, knelt, and ended Rusty's suffering with a shot to the head.

Looking up he saw the riders, still shooting, and approaching in more-or-less a perpendicular line. This was the only way they could advance while firing and not inadvertently strike one another. The formation confirmed Pritchard's suspicion that his attackers had military training or experience as horseback cavalrymen or raiders.

Pritchard plucked his 1873 Winchester from its scabbard with one hand, and with the other snatched the box of .44-40 cartridges from within the saddlebag. He emptied the entire box of fifty cartridges into the right-hand pocket of his sodden duster and knelt behind Rusty, using the big animal's carcass as cover.

Like most horsemen bearing saddle rifles who weren't fools, Pritchard kept his weapon stocked with fifteen cartridges in the tube magazine and an empty chamber under the hammer to prevent unintentional discharge while jostling on horseback. He levered a .44-40 cartridge into the breech, stuffed a fresh round into the loading gate, shouldered the Winchester, and awaited the next flash of lightning.

He didn't have long to wait.

Thunder crashed, and the dark and rain were again briefly traded for light. He saw about a dozen riders, only yards away. They'd slowed their mounts to a walk, and were scanning the horizon for their quarry.

Pritchard was able to fire, lever, and fire again before the burst of lightning faded. In the electrified light of the crackling flash, he could easily make out his rifle's front sight, rear sight, and most important, his targets. Two riders fell from their saddles.

He levered his rifle again and waited for the next bout of lightning as thunder rumbled, using the pause to stuff another two cartridges into the Winchester. A few shots fired back at him, but they weren't even close.

Pritchard knew why the incoming fire had diminished to a trickle. He noted during the last bout of illumination that the riders seemed to be armed with only pistols. Not as accurate as rifles, handguns nonetheless provided his attackers with rapid firing capability at close range. But he surmised that most of them had expended their weapons' loads during their initial charge. The bulk of his antagonists' guns were now empty.

Re-charging a revolver first required its owner to extract the empty cartridge cases, then insert fresh cartridges, one-by-one. This was an intricate maneuver under ideal conditions, but these gunmen were currently struggling to reload their revolvers on horseback, in the dark, with cold, wet, hands and in the midst of a gunfight with a competent rifleman who was shooting from behind cover.

Lightning flashed. Pritchard, already hunkered over his rifle with little more than a portion of his bare head and Winchester exposed over the bulwark of Rusty's carcass, fired twice. He hit his two intended targets and was gratified to note that when struck, both riders were hunched over their pistols trying to reload. He saw them flop from their saddles, and their horses flee, before darkness again overtook the landscape.

Thunder reverberated as Pritchard topped off his Winchester with two more cartridges and waited for the next burst of lightning.

"Where is he?" he heard a voice call out from the rain and gloom. There was a hint of panic in it.

"Don't know," another voice replied. "Can't see a durned thing in this storm."

"Find him!" a deep voice boomed.

"I think he's on the ground," still another voice added. "Over yonder."

"Where the hell is 'over yonder'?" another voice, also tinged with panic, called out.

"Dismount, you fools!" the deep voice, clearly belonging to the rider in authority, ordered. "Advance on foot! Find him and finish him!"

"How're we supposed to find him?" another nervous voice pleaded.

"Look for his gun flashes, you idjits!" came the angry reply.

The driving rain prevented Pritchard from hearing the men dismount, but he knew they were doing as told and getting themselves unhorsed. He also knew that most, if not all, had by now reloaded their revolvers. Though he couldn't hear them, and without the lightning couldn't see them, he could almost sense the gunmen moving in closer. During the last flare of lightning, they weren't but a dozen yards away.

"Iffen you boys want to see gun flashes," Pritchard muttered to himself, "I'll be happy to oblige."

Lightning once again sparked. Pritchard began firing.

What the men advancing on Pritchard in the dark didn't know was that long before he'd ever held a pistol he was one of the finest rifle shots in Jackson County, Missouri. He and Ditch had grown up hunting in the dense woods between the Missouri and Little Blue Rivers, using a .54 caliber Hawken rifle belonging to Ditch's pa.

While his skill with firearms of the one-handed variety was what made his reputation, both as Smokin' Joe Atherton and Marshal Samuel Pritchard, his proficiency with long-arms was no less remarkable.

This time, in the split-second surge of lightning, Pritchard fired much faster and got off four shots. He traversed rapidly between his targets and watched three men fall flat and a fourth drop to one knee. Their close proximity helped. Their horses, which they'd been leading by the reins, took off.

A barrage of return fire instantly broke out as darkness resumed and thunder exploded. Pritchard ducked behind Rusty and plugged four more cartridges into the Winchester. He heard and felt a hail of bullets *thwap* into the dead horse's body. They'd found him, but it cost several of his attackers their lives.

Seconds later, when the next landscape-alighting crackle of lightning broke out, Pritchard rose again to one knee, shouldered his rifle, and commenced firing. This time he fired as rapidly as he could, triggering, levering, and triggering again. He swung the muzzle from left and right, back and forth, squeezing off shots at the half-dozen men standing before him. Even after the illumination of the lightning faded, he continued to fire. Within a few seconds he'd expended all sixteen shots in his rifle.

Pritchard was rewarded with several screams. Some revealed fear, others pain. He ducked again behind Rusty, drew one of his revolvers, and propped his rifle against the saddle. Keeping his pistol aimed out into the storm with one hand, he reloaded the Winchester from the stash of cartridges in his duster's pocket with the other. It took longer to recharge his lever-gun in this manner, but during that time no shots were fired at him from out of the darkness.

When lightning again flashed after he'd reloaded his rifle, Pritchard holstered his revolver and peered over the parapet of Rusty's carcass. In the split-second glare he hastily counted at least nine men on the muddy ground. He also saw several riderless horses trotting away. He spotted no more standing men, but could just make out a couple of mounted men fading away in the downpour.

Pritchard waited for several minutes, and several more bouts of revealing lightning, before becoming convinced the surviving attackers had fled. It wasn't lost on him that they retreated west, back toward the camp at the site of the train wreck.

Pritchard retrieved his hat, then slowly approached the men lying motionless out on the muddy prairie. There were ten. One by one he examined them. It took a while, as he had to wait for successive flashes of lightning.

He learned little. In addition to each stopping at least one of his bullets, the men had several other things in common. Every one of them had been of age to have fought in the war, but none had money or papers on them. All were armed with only revolvers, and all but one was fully expired. The last man he checked, despite having been shot through the upper chest, was lying face up. He gagged and blinked, coughing and moaning.

"Help me," the man groaned. He looked up at Pritchard, looming over him with his rifle.

"Tell me who you are?" Pritchard said, kicking the man's pistol away into the dark, "and why you're ridin' with Jem Rupe."

"Who's Jem Rupe?" the man asked.

"Who set you against me?"

"I ain't a-gonna tell you nuthin'," the man said. "Not unless you help me."

"Why should I help you?" Pritchard said. "You and them boys you rode with killed my horse."

"Please," the man pleaded. "You can't just leave me out here on the cold ground. It ain't Christian."

"And ridin' up on a feller in the dark to backshoot him is?"

"I can't feel my legs."

"Then I reckon I won't have to worry about you comin' after me, will I?"

In the next lightning flash, Pritchard noticed one of the

horses which had run off during the shooting had circled back. The animal stood forlorn in the rain.

The horse, a medium-sized quarter, let Pritchard approach and take his reins. He walked the horse back to Rusty's body, where he replaced his rifle in the scabbard. He then removed the quarter horse's saddle and replaced it with Rusty's.

"At least give me some water," the man said, as Pritchard lashed Rusty's bridle to the pommel.

"Plenty of water fallin' from the sky," Pritchard said. "Help yourself."

"You're just gonna leave me here in the mud to die?" the man challenged, spitting blood. "What kind of lawman are you?"

"The unforgivin' kind," Pritchard said.

"Then put a bullet to me. Ease my sufferin'?"

"Nope. Not a-gonna."

"Why not?" the man demanded, outraged. "You did it for your horse, didn't you?"

"I liked my horse. Can't say the same for you."

"Go to hell," the man cursed.

"After you," Pritchard said, mounting up.

Pritchard contemplated riding west, after the survivors of the mob that attacked him but quickly decided against it. Had he been aboard Rusty, he wouldn't have hesitated. As things were, at night, in a storm, and on a horse of unknown reliability, such a course of action was out of the question. Besides, Ditch, the Tilleys, Doc Mauldin, and the grieving Mr. McKitchern were up ahead on the trail, on the way to Atherton in a pair of wagons. What if they were being attacked as he was by another group of marauders?

As much as Pritchard wanted to exact retribution for the attempt on his life and the loss of his beloved Rusty, he knew where his duty lay.

He waited for another flash of lightning to show him the road, then spurred the quarter horse east.

Chapter 13

"I see the camp," the gunman, whose name was Gilbert, said. He had to shout to be heard over the torrential rain and the squishy *clop* of the horse's trotting in the mud. "Over yonder," he pointed. "I can see the trains, too."

"So can I," the Big Man in the sodden top hat said. He pulled his horse to a halt and dismounted.

"What are we stoppin' for? Bundy is gutshot all to hell. We need to get him to the camp doctors."

"We're stoppin' here," the Big Man said, "for a minute. Get Bundy off his horse."

"How come? We ain't but a quarter mile from the camp? Why not go on?"

"Because I said so," the Big Man said. His tone implied he expected no further argument.

"Iffen you say so," Gilbert grumbled.

The Big Man in the top hat, and the only two riders left in his dozen-man party, Gilbert and Bundy, had fled their botched ambush beneath a hail of .44-40 gunfire. He held the reins of all three horses as Gilbert eased Bundy, who'd intercepted one of the bullets from Pritchard's Winchester, from his saddle to the ground. Bundy instantly crumpled to his knees, bending at the waist with both hands clutched over his blood-soaked belly.

"It hurts," he moaned. "It hurts somethin' awful."

"Ain't surprised," the Big Man in the top hat said. "Fact is, I expected you'd have bled out by now and expired more'n a mile back."

"Huh?" Bundy said, squinting up at the Big Man through the rain. He spit blood.

"You heard me," the Big Man said.

"I don't understand?" Gilbert said.

"Hold these horses," the Big Man told Gilbert. The confused gunman dutifully accepted three sets of reins.

"I surely am sorry," the Big Man addressed Bundy, who was kneeling at his feet, "for your misfortune. Luck of the draw, I'm afraid. Catchin' that blue whistler in the belly was low card, that's fer sure."

As he spoke, he drew a Bowie knife from under his coat and thrust it, hilt deep, into the kneeling man's neck. Bundy fell on his face, twitched, and died.

"What the hell?" Gilbert exclaimed. His right hand held three sets of reins. His gun was holstered on his right side, under his slicker, or he would have drawn.

"Had to be done," the Big Man said matter-of-factly. He wiped his knife on the dead man's coat and sheathed it. "He couldn't be seen in camp after bein' stomach-shot. It'd raise too many questions the folks who're payin' us don't want asked. If Bundy didn't want to get stuck, he shoulda had the good sense to expire on the trail. As it is, we're already in a heap of trouble with Marsh and Finchum."

"You didn't have to knife him, did ya?" Gilbert complained.

"You challengin' me?" the Big Man said, drawing his

revolver. He cocked the hammer back, but held the weapon down at his side.

"I ain't challengin' nobody," Gilbert said. "Just want to know why Bundy had to get butchered like a seasoned hog?"

"We're close enough to camp someone might hear a pistol shot," the Big Man explained. His eyes narrowed. "You got a problem with how I run this outfit?"

What outfit? Gilbert thought to himself. *Ain't no outfit left. There's just me.* "No, boss," he replied, "I ain't got no problem."

"If you want to stay healthy," the Big Man said, "and keep ridin' with me, you'd best keep it that way." He lowered the hammer on his revolver and holstered it. "Help me lash Bundy to his horse. We'll head downstream a mile or so and dump him in the creek. After that we can circle back and get aboard the train without bein' noticed."

"Sure," Gilbert said. "Whatever you say."

"One more thing," the Big Man said. "When we get back to the train, you keep your pie hole buttoned. You let me do the talkin', you hear?"

"Whatever you say," Gilbert repeated.

Chapter 14

By the time Pritchard arrived at the Clemson home, the storm had abated. Replacing the clouds, thunder, rain, and lightning was a waning moon and starlit sky. He walked the quarter into the barn, removed the saddle and bridle, put the horse into a vacant stall, and made sure it was fed before retrieving his rifle and trudging across the yard to the big, two-story, brick house.

The Clemsons' stately home was built on what had been the Pritchards' land before it was "commandeered," as Burnell Shipley declared it, for the "Great Cause" more than a decade prior. The original house was burned to the ground by Shipley's men, and the new one had been rebuilt by Ditch as a wedding present to Idelle.

The land adjacent to the Pritchards' had once belonged to Ditch's deceased father, a hardscrabble horse rancher. The combined properties, through his marriage to Idelle, were now one of the largest and most beautiful estates surrounding Atherton.

Pritchard didn't see the Tilleys' hearse or Conestoga on the property and concluded they must have gone on into town, a little more than a mile away. He noticed the chimney was smoking, which was unusual for the Clemson household after midnight.

The door opened, and Pritchard found Tater Jessup at the door with his shotgun across his chest. A roaring fire burned in the hearth inside the main room. Behind him, Idelle came into view. She looked as beautiful as ever, though exhausted, and her eyes were red and swollen from crying.

"It's Samuel!" Tater exclaimed, lowering his weapon. "Good Lord, you look like a catfish that got dredged up from the bottom of the Missouri!"

Pritchard handed his rifle to Tater and removed his soaked duster and hat. The mud he'd been covered with had long since been washed away in the torrential rain during his journey to his sister's home.

"Where've you been?" Idelle asked. "Simon Tilley said you were supposed to come along with him. I was worried sick."

"Sorry I'm late," Pritchard said, removing his boots and handing them to Tater along with his cartridge-laden gun belts. "Got waylaid about ten miles back."

"Waylaid?" Idelle asked.

"Gunmen. They shot Rusty." He pointed to his slicker, torn where a bullet grazed. "Durn near got me."

"Who was it?" Tater demanded.

"Don't know," Pritchard said.

"Come on inside," Idelle insisted. "You're soaked. Get yourself warmed up by the fire. I'll wake Constance and have her make you some hot food."

Constance Randle, and her husband Ike, lived on the property in the servant's cottage. Constance served as housekeeper and cook for the Clemsons, and Ike as liveryman and groundskeeper.

"Don't bother," Pritchard said. "Let Mrs. Randle sleep." He looked into his sister's red-rimmed eyes. "How's Ditch doin'?"

"He's feverish," Idelle said, "but sleeping. Doc Mauldin left for town with the Tilleys about an hour ago. Said he'd be back in the morning to check in on Ditch. So far, thank the Lord, there's no sign of infection in his leg. Doc says to keep him warm and get plenty of hot fluids into him." She looked up at her towering brother. "Thank you, Samuel, for bringing him home to me. Doc said he wouldn't have lasted long, in his condition, out on the prairie in a tent."

Idelle suddenly rushed into Pritchard's arms, her sobs releasing in a torrent as if from a collapsed dam. "Oh, Samuel," she cried. "They nearly killed him and they took his leg. Why would anyone do such a thing to my Ditch?"

"Don't know yet," he said, patting her back. "But little sister, I aim to find out. Where's Baby Sam?"

"He's in his crib," she said, stepping from her brother's arms and composing herself just as quickly as she'd fallen apart. She wiped her eyes, took in and let out a deep breath, and within a moment was again herself. Pritchard had deliberately invoked her child, his nephew, knowing her maternal instincts would kick in and override her grief.

"You'd best get yourself off to bed, too," Pritchard said. "You look plumb done in."

"I doubt I could sleep," she said.

"You must," Pritchard admonished her. "You've got to rest, Idelle. You have to be strong. Not just to take care of

Ditch, but to care for the baby and yourself. Iffen you're frazzled to a nubbin you ain't no good to anyone."

"I suppose you're right," she conceded. "Good night, Samuel. Good night, Tater." She gave the rotund deputy a hug. "Thank you for coming out to deliver the news. I'm glad I heard it from you and not someone else. And thank you for staying here with me until Samuel arrived."

"No thanks necessary, Miss Idelle," Tater said. "I just wish I hadn't brung such sorrowful tidings. But I wasn't a-gonna leave your side; not until Samuel got here."

Though he knew she was technically "Mrs. Clemson," Tater had known Idelle since a baby and always referred to her as "Miss Idelle." She disappeared into the house.

"Any whiskey handy?" Pritchard asked, once Idelle departed. "I could use a snort."

"I'll fetch it," Tater said, "while you get over to that fire and get out of those wet clothes. Mrs. Randle left some fresh duds out for you."

Pritchard stripped and put on a dry set of clothes. He owned little in the way of wardrobe, but what attire he didn't keep at his room in the marshal's office he stored at Ditch and Idelle's place.

He'd just finished dressing when Tater returned with a bottle of Kentucky whiskey and two glasses. He poured both half-full with amber liquid and handed Pritchard a glass.

"Here's to not repeatin' this infernal day," Tater said. They clinked glasses and drank. Tater set Pritchard's boots, duster, and hat by the fireplace, while Pritchard went into the study. He came back with a rag, a rifle rod, a tin of oil, and two boxes of .44-40 cartridges from Ditch's supply of ammunition. He also had Ditch's

Winchester rifle and Colt .45, identical to Pritchard's revolvers in that it sported a custom, five-and-one-half-inch barrel. Ditch had purchased it at the same time Pritchard won his pair in Kansas. The pistol was nestled in a holster and belt slung over his shoulder.

"I'll be echoin' what Idelle had to say, Tater," Pritchard said. "I'm powerful glad it was you, and not someone else, who brung her the news about Ditch's train." He placed the items on the table.

"Sorely wish I didn't have to," Tater said. "The news hit her like a chargin' bull. And not knowin' if Ditch was alive or dead was dreadful hard on her. Can't tell you how relieved we all was when the Tilleys rode up in them two wagons with Ditch and Doc Mauldin inside. I practically started singin' hymns." He looked solemnly into his glass. "Until I saw Mr. McKitchern, and learned about his boy ridin' in the back of Simon Tilley's hearse."

"A right terrible thing," Pritchard said. "And somethin' somebody's gonna account for." He changed the subject. "How'd Idelle handle Ditch's . . . injury?"

"She acted like him missin' a leg weren't nothin' at all," Tater said, staring into his glass. "Hustled him into the house and doted on him like he had little more'n a common cold. But I could see in her eyes she was tore up somethin' fierce. That sister of yours is made of stern stuff, Samuel, and then some. Ditch Clemson is one lucky feller."

Pritchard's face tightened and his blue eyes deepened. Tater saw something pass over the marshal's features. Something he'd seen before. Something dark, ominous, and hungry.

Tater poured them both another jolt. "Tell me more

about them riders you encountered?" he asked, taking his turn to change the subject.

Pritchard unloaded his rifle, disassembled it, and began to clean and oil the weapon. "A dozen or more of 'em, armed with pistols." He looked up from swabbing the Winchester's bore. "They rode in on me from the direction of the train wreck."

"Now there's a coincidence," Tater remarked, tugging on his whiskers. "I stopped by John Babbit's office on the way out here, after I got the townsfolk off to the wreck like you told me. He said it was goin' out all over the telegraph wire that the train had been wrecked and robbed by a dozen-or-so armed riders. The wire claimed the wreckin' party was led by none other than Arkansas Jem Rupe."

"That's what I was told," Pritchard said.

"You believe it?"

"Don't rightly know," Pritchard said.

"Ole Jem ain't been heard of since the end of the war," Tater mused. "Honestly, Samuel, most folks figured he was dead and buried. Hell, I'm one of 'em."

"Can't say many folks would have thought his passin' was a loss."

"Jem was a trainwrecker, all right," Tater said. "He done some right nasty work durin' the war. You gotta admit, dead or alive, this derailment today sure looks like his handiwork."

"Don't it just?" Pritchard said.

He finished cleaning his Winchester, wiped it down with a coating of oil, and reloaded it. "Take this," he said to Tater as he offered Ditch's rifle, identical to his.

"Already got my two-eyed blunderbuss," the portly

deputy replied, pointing to his double-barreled, 12-guage coach gun leaning against the door. "Why on earth would I need Ditch's rifle?"

"Them dozen horsemen I met up with weren't out ridin' herd," Pritchard said, setting down the rifle and retrieving his revolvers. "Not at night, in the middle of a Missouri toad-strangler. They was ridin' after me, them two wagons, or both."

"You think they were goin' after Ditch again?"

"Can't say fer sure they weren't."

"Lucky they didn't get you," Tater said.

"It weren't luck," Pritchard said. "Me, Rusty, and my Winchester left ten of 'em face down in the mud."

"I reckon them night riders bushwhacked the wrong marshal," Tater said, slapping his thigh. "Sounds like it cost 'em plenty. I doubt they'll want to tangle with you again."

"I don't," Pritchard countered. "The plain truth is, Tater, they were set upon me and Ditch. That means somebody must've done the settin'. Likely by now whoever that is got word his murder party weren't successful. Might be, he'll send another."

"And you think they'll come here?" Tater accepted Ditch's Winchester. "To Ditch's home?"

"We can't set the possibility aside," Pritchard said. He unloaded his revolvers, removed the cylinder pins and cylinders, and began to clean and oil the individual components.

Pritchard was meticulous about his weapons. He'd learned, in the crucible of military, professional, and personal combat, to care for his guns as if his life depended on their reliable operation. There were too many instances where such circumstances had come to pass.

"Ditch is known in these parts," Pritchard explained. "He's also the only mayor on that train who survived the wreck. Likely he survived only because the trainwreckers, who put bullets into the noggins of all the other mayors, believed he was soon to expire on account of his crushed leg. Now that they know different, they might want to finish the job."

"Why'n hell would somebody want to kill a passel of Missouri mayors?" Tater said. "It don't make no sense?"

"Don't know," Pritchard said, as he reassembled his revolvers and reloaded them. "Like I told Idelle, I aim to find out."

"Iffen I know you, Samuel," Tater said, "you'll be doin' more than educatin' yourself. You're a-gonna be a-holden' them responsible to account, ain't ya?"

"I reckon so," Pritchard said. "Meantime, I want you to stay here and keep watch over the family." He handed Ditch's revolver, and a box of cartridges for the Winchester, to the deputy.

"I'm better'n a fair shot with a rifle," Tater protested, "but you know I ain't no good with a belly gun. And Ditch's pistol belt sure as hell ain't a-gonna fit around me." He patted his sizable tummy.

"Maybe so," Pritchard said, "but you keep that revolver handy just the same. And when Ike wakes up, you give him Ditch's Henry rifle and the both of you keep a sharp eye out. Anyone who comes a-ridin' onto this property that you don't know is to get shot out of the saddle with your rifles, and anyone who comes uninvited into this home is to get a load from your scattergun or a pill from

Ditch's Colt. I mean it, Tater. Don't you fellers hesitate. Not for a second."

"You ain't gonna have to remind me not to dawdle when it comes to ministerin' a gunpowder welcome to them who ain't," Tater scoffed. "You're forgettin' I ended Cottonmouth Quincy on the front steps of this very house." He checked the Winchester's load and looked up at his boss. "Don't you fret none, Samuel. Anyone comin' here with intentions to harm Idelle, Ditch, or Baby Samuel is a-gonna find out the hard way that Deputy Tater Jessup's bite is a damn sight worse'n his bark."

"I don't doubt your grit," Pritchard said, resting a hand on Tater's shoulder. "Never did. That's why I'm trustin' you with the lives of my family."

Tater's chest puffed out. "I won't let you down. Neither will Ike. Where're you goin'?"

"Back to Atherton," Pritchard said, as he slipped on his damp boots, belted on his pistols, and grabbed his rifle and hat. "I'll be back, along with Doc Mauldin, before noon."

"If you're comin' back in the mornin' anyways," Tater asked, "why not just spend the night here?"

"Can't," said Pritchard, as he shrugged into his duster. "I've got to prepare Atherton for what's to come."

"What's a-comin'?" Tater asked.

"Trouble," Pritchard answered.

"Trouble?" Tater echoed. "How much trouble?"

"Iffen my hunch is right," Pritchard said, donning his hat, "a trainload."

Chapter 15

The first rays of dawn's light were breaking the horizon at the site of the train wreck. On both sides of the creek hordes of people from two different railroad companies' separate work camps were awake and tending to their duties. Fires were being lit, food was being cooked, and mobs of laborers were busily preparing for the day's grueling work.

Earl Marsh knocked on the door of John Brody's private car. When Brody's manservant, Charles, opened the door Marsh entered first, followed by the Big Man in the top hat, who was no longer wearing his top hat, and finally Asa Finchum.

Brody was seated at a linen-covered table. The servant poured coffee from an expensive silver set into a china cup while a cigar burned in a tray at his elbow. His fat body was clad in a silk robe and what was left of his hair was combed, but he otherwise looked like he'd just been awakened.

"I'm not pleased," Brody said, scooping spoonful-after-spoonful of sugar into his coffee. "Not pleased in the slightest."

"I know it looks bad," Marsh began. "If you'll allow me to explain—"

"What's to explain?" Brody interrupted. "You imbeciles have once again let Marshal Pritchard make fools of you, and in doing so, make a fool of me."

"If you think I planned for things to turn out the way they did," Marsh said, "you're mistaken."

"I'm not sure you planned at all," Brody snapped. "I enlisted you, and your partner, to do a job. Your reputations implied I was hiring competent men who could deliver the services they were contracted for. In this case, those services involved completing a simple and discrete task. When I pay someone to do a job, I expect results. That's how you run a railroad, Mr. Marsh."

Brody paused to take a sip of his heavily sugared coffee. "But instead of results," he went on, "what I bought was incompetence and failure. A poor investment on my part, wouldn't you agree?"

"Not entirely," Marsh argued. "We got the lion's share done. We wrecked Gould's train, didn't we?"

"Yes," Brody conceded, "that portion of your assignment was completed handily enough. But you were supposed to dispense with those troublesome mayors. That was the most critical part of the venture."

"We did that," Marsh insisted.

"No," Brody corrected him, "you didn't. Your men," he pointed his cigar at the Big Man with his coffee cup, "allowed one of them, who happens to be one of the most popular and influential politicians in the region, I might add, to survive."

"I'll admit," Marsh said, looking over his shoulder

harshly at the Big Man who'd led the raid, "that was a mistake. Give us a chance and we'll correct it."

"Like you did last night?" Brody mocked. "The way I heard it, a dozen of your men rode out into a rainstorm after a sick, one-legged, man laid up in a wagon. A man who was guarded by a single lawman. I understand only two of your men returned." He angrily ground out his cigar. "Tell me exactly, Mr. Marsh, how you'll correct your mistake?"

"Hear me out," Marsh insisted. "Once you listen to what I have to say, I believe you'll agree that what happened last night isn't nearly as bad as it seems, and might actually work in your favor."

"I'm listening," Brody said.

"As we speak," Marsh began, "Major Duncan and his troops are being led out to the place where those men put to rest last night by Marshal Pritchard lay."

"Are you insane?" Brody gasped, his face reddening. "You're leading the army right to the evidence?"

"Don't worry," Marsh said. "Nothing can be connected to you or your railroad. Gilbert already sounded the alarm earlier this morning at my direction. I instructed him, acting as one of our railroad workers, to claim he was out hunting for meat and chanced upon the bodies. He reported it to the army. He's leading Major Duncan and a platoon of cavalry there now."

"Won't the major be suspicious?"

"Not at all," Marsh said. "Major Duncan and his men will undoubtedly believe, just like everyone else, once word gets out, that those bodies belonged to Jem Rupe's gang. I had Gilbert plant some of the trinkets and personal effects taken from the passengers during the train robbery on the bodies. It'll be presumed Marshal Pritchard ended them, which isn't untrue. Not only will the law and the army then stop searching for them, but it now means that you, Mr. Brody, will no longer have to pay them."

Brody's anger suddenly subsided, his face returned to its normal color, and one eyebrow lifted. "Not bad," he said.

"I shouldn't have to remind you that in addition to less money out of your pocket," Marsh said, "they'll now be fewer loose mouths to worry about, as well."

"What about Marshal Pritchard?"

"He'll be hailed as a hero for cleaning out most of Rupe's gang," Marsh explained, "which works to our advantage."

"How?" Brody asked, gesturing toward the Big Man in work clothes standing between Marsh and Finchum. "Aren't you forgetting about Arkansas Jem Rupe?"

"It'll be presumed Rupe went south," Marsh said, "and took the forty-thousand-dollar payroll from the train robbery with him. But that's not how it's going to play out."

"How's it going to play out?" Brody said.

"Once the news gets spread about the hero lawman who was responsible for clearing out his gang," Marsh said, elbowing the Big Man next to him, "it won't be a surprise to anyone, will it, if ole Jem Rupe decides to seek out Marshal Pritchard for a little payback?"

"No surprise at all," the Big Man said.

"When Pritchard is killed," Marsh said, "it'll be attributed to Rupe's revenge." He nodded to Finchum and the Big Man. "We'll make certain of it."

"What you propose," Brody said, "is a rather clever

solution to a problem that shouldn't have arisen in the first place. I confess, not having to pay your men is an unexpected and welcome bonus. Clearly you and Finchum have your own reasons to be looking for a bit of payback; no doubt on account of the ease with which Marshal Pritchard disarmed and rendered you both, supposedly top gun hands, as defenseless as newborn babies."

"It won't happen again," Marsh said through his teeth.

"It surely won't," Finchum echoed.

"If it does," Brody said, "presuming you two survive the encounter, none of you will remain in my employ." He pointed at the Big Man standing between them. "And that goes double for anyone in your employ."

"Don't worry," Marsh said, "there's only two of our hired men left. Him"—he jerked his thumb at the Big Man standing between him and Finchum—"and Gilbert. Between the four of us, we'll soon have no more trouble with Marshal Pritchard."

"That remains to be seen," Brody said. "What about the surviving mayor? Clemson is his name, from Atherton."

"Another piece of luck," Marsh said. "Rumor has it, Mayor Clemson is related to Marshal Pritchard. Brother-in-law, so I'm told."

"So what you're saying," Brody said, "is—"

"—two birds can be had with one stone," Marsh finished the sentence. "And both can be pinned on Arkansas Jem Rupe."

"I'm still displeased," Brody said, "but I must admit, you've successfully assuaged my concerns for now." He pointed a chubby finger at Marsh. "See to it that you don't raise any more."

"You can count on us," Marsh said. The Big Man smiled, and Finchum merely tipped his hat.

"Perhaps," Brody said. "But just in case, I've telegraphed our office in Topeka for more men of your unique profession. They're already en route, and hopefully of much higher quality than you. They should be here in a day or two."

"Are they reliable men?" Marsh asked.

"That's rather comical," Brody said, dismissing the trio with a wave of his hand, "coming from you. Get out."

"That went better than expected," Marsh said, once the three men had departed Brody's private train car.

"Ya think?" Finchum grunted. "Sounds like Brody's fixin' to replace us."

"He won't get the chance," Marsh said, fiddling with his handlebar mustache. "We'll end that one-legged mayor, deal out Pritchard, pin it all on the legendary Arkansas Jem Rupe, and get our payday." He slapped the Big Man on the back as he spoke.

"I imagine the real Jem Rupe is rollin' over in his grave," the Big Man said.

A pair of railroad workers approached. Both were soaking wet and each was bearing at least one pistol.

"Found your guns, Mr. Marsh," one of the workers said. He handed a Smith & Wesson .44 Russian to Marsh, and a pair of Colt Single Action Army revolvers with the standard, seven-and-one-half-inch barrel, to Finchum.

"Took us a while to find 'em," the worker explained, "on account of the creek bein' so swolled-up due to last night's rains. Say, how'd your shootin' irons end up in the creek, anyways?"

"Get out of my sight," Marsh said, handing each of the laborers a dollar. The pair scurried hastily away.

"Yeah," the Big Man asked, "I'd kinda like to know myself how your pistolas ended up takin' a swim? Seems I just heard Mr. Brody mention somethin' about Pritchard disarmin' you?"

"Mind your tongue," Marsh said, examining his revolver. "This Pritchard business is all your fault. That colossal lawman would be nothing but another grieving mourner if you'd done your job and finished off all the mayors like you were supposed to."

"You told me to leave somebody alive to tell folks it was Jem Rupe?" the Big Man said, repeating his earlier protest.

"Not one of the mayors, you moron," Marsh shot back. "I told you that already."

"He had one leg gone and the other foot in the grave," the man insisted. "How was I supposed to know that particular mayor was of a tougher stripe and gonna live? It were an honest mistake."

"What about last night?" Marsh said. "Was that an 'honest mistake'? One lawman took out eleven of your men and sent you packing like a frightened schoolgirl."

"That lawman's aim was the work of Satan. It didn't hurt him any that he was forded up with a rifle behind an animal carcass and we were all out in the open, on horseback, armed only with revolvers, in the middle of a storm. You'd have run, too, or else been beefed like the rest of my men who're now feedin' worms in the Missouri mud."

"None of that matters anymore," Marsh said. "All that

matters, is that we do like we told Brody and clean this mess up."

"I, for one," Finchum said, as he shook water from his revolvers, "am lookin' forward to meetin' up with the marshal again."

"I wouldn't be so cocksure," the Big Man said, "if I were you. By the look of them soggy guns, I'd say that lawman got the bulge on you two boys easy enough. And he had no trouble shooting a dozen of my boys to hell and gone and stiverin' me and Gilbert off."

"Are you afraid to face him again?" Marsh asked.

"Ain't sayin' that. All I'm sayin' is this Pritchard feller might not be as easy a knot to tie as you made out to Brody."

"Pritchard may fancy himself a big, tough, hombre," Finchum said, "with a man-killin' reputation, but he'll drop like any other man when he runs into a lead plumb."

"I reckon we'll see about that," the Big Man said, "won't we?"

Chapter 16

"You wanted to see us, Samuel?" Judge Pearson said, as he entered the marshal's office. He wasn't alone. Undertaker Simon Tilley, his adult son and business partner, Seth, Dr. Mauldin, newspaperman/telegraph operator John Babbit, and Manfri Pannell, the leader of the town's Romanichal community and owner of the Sidewinder Saloon, all entered the office directly behind the judge. These five men represented the Atherton Town Council, along with Mayor Ditch Clemson.

"Thanks for comin'," Pritchard said, acknowledging the group as they filed in.

It was early morning, and Pritchard was busy packing. Into his saddlebags he was stuffing extra clothing, jerky, whiskey, and boxes of ammunition. He packed .44-40s for his Winchester, .45s for his pair of Colts, and .44s for his pair of 1863 Remingtons, which had been converted to fire metallic cartridges by a Dallas gunsmith.

"You going on a trip?" Judge Pearson asked.

"I am," Pritchard said.

"Looks like a hunting trip," Simon Tilley said.

"I reckon so," Pritchard said.

There were no prisoners in the jail. Deputy Strobl handed out tin cups all around, and began to pour from the pot on the stove. Once everyone had a fresh cup of coffee, Judge Pearson spoke.

"What's on your mind, Samuel?"

"Trouble's a-comin'," Pritchard said, "and it's comin' to Atherton."

The men looked at each other and then back at Pritchard. "Go on," the judge said.

"As you all know," Pritchard began, "I was at the wrecked train yesterday. While I was there, I discovered that the wreck weren't no mere robbery."

"Not a robbery?" the judge said. "Rumor has it, the train was derailed in order to rob it. That's what everyone is saying, anyway."

"Not true," Pritchard corrected him.

"But it was all over the wire yesterday," Babbit said, "that Jem Rupe and a dozen riders robbed the train. In fact, it was the army who put out the telegrams."

"The army's wrong," Pritchard said, as he blew over the surface of his coffee. "The robbery was only part of it. The other part was the deliberate murder of a dozen Missouri mayors. If I ain't mistaken, that was the main part."

That's a very serious charge," Babbit said. "Can you back that up?"

"I can," Dr. Mauldin interjected. "I was there, too. The only people shot, besides the guard who was posted inside the mail car, were the mayors. They were in a special train car reserved just for them. Who would have known that? And every one of the mayors who was gunned was done in with a head shot. Like the marshal said, that's about as 'deliberate' as it gets."

"But Ditch didn't get shot," Seth Tilley pointed out. "He survived."

"I believe he was allowed to live solely to identify Jem Rupe," Pritchard said, "and because it was expected he'd expire due to the grievous nature of his wounds." He gave a nod to Mauldin. "Thanks to the good doctor, that didn't come to pass."

"Why would anyone want to murder Mayor Ditch," Manfri Pannell asked in his British accent, "and a dozen other Missouri mayors?"

"I don't know," Pritchard said. "All I know is that Ditch told me he and the other mayors were on their way to a pow-wow in Kansas City with John Brody, head of the Brody Railroad."

"What was the meeting about?" Simon Tilley asked.

"Don't know that, either. So last night, I invited myself into a meetin' on John Brody's private railroad car. Jason Gould, who's the head of the Missouri Pacific Rail Line and Brody's main competitor, was there, along with an army major and the lieutenant governor."

"They allowed you to sit in?" Babbit asked.

"I didn't ask permission," Pritchard said.

"What did you find out?"

"I picked up a few things. I learned it was one of Gould's trains that was wrecked and his payroll that got nicked. I also learned the governor knew about the meetin' in Kansas City beforehand. And I learned that John Brody was awful eager to pin the wreck and robbery on Jeremiah Rupe, even though ole Arkansas Jem ain't been seen or heard from in more'n ten years."

"Interesting," Judge Pearson said.

"It got even more interestin' as the night wore on," Pritchard said. "Brody tried to buffalo me with a coupla' his hired guns, and Jason Gould let it slip that he had his own suspicions about who wrecked and robbed his train. But it wasn't until after I left camp to escort Simon, Seth, Doc Mauldin, Mr. McKitchern, and Ditch back to Atherton that things got really interestin'."

"By the way," Simon Tilley asked, "what the heck happened to you last night? We waited for you, and kept looking behind us on the road, but we couldn't see anything. We figured you must have elected to stay back at one of the railroad camps on account of the storm."

"I didn't abandon you," Pritchard said. "I got waylaid."

"Waylaid?" Simon Tilley exclaimed.

"I was jumped on the trail by a dozen or more riders. They came at me from the direction of the train wreck. Only thing that saved me was the dark, the storm, and my Rusty."

"Good heavens," Judge Pearson said. "I think I can speak for everyone here when I say I'm greatly relieved you survived."

"Thank you, Your Honor." Pritchard smiled. "I appreciate the sentiment." His smile vanished. "They got my horse though. Had to put Rusty down and leave him out on the prairie."

"Those bastards," Seth Tilley said. "Shooting a man's horse. They oughta be strung."

"What of the riders?" Manfri Pannell asked.

"I left ten of 'em out on the prairie," Pritchard said, "feedin' the worms along with Rusty."

"Good heavens," Judge Pearson repeated.

"Serves 'em right," Seth Tilley said.

"I didn't bring you all here without your breakfast to hear my tale of woe," Pritchard continued. "I brung you here to give you a warnin'."

"A warning?" Judge Pearson said.

"That's right," Pritchard said. "I don't know if them riders who came up behind me was goin' for me or for Ditch? Maybe they was set upon both of us?"

"It sounds like Jem Rupe and his boys were likely the ones who attacked you?" Babbit said.

"Perhaps," Pritchard said. "Maybe it was Jem Rupe, maybe not? If so, where did he and his boys come from? They had to be close. How did a band of horsemen that size avoid the dozens of army patrols and posses scourin' the countryside all day? And most important, how did they know me and Ditch were gonna be on the trail to Atherton at that time of the night, in the middle of a storm?"

"The marshal's right," Simon Tilley said.

"Undoubtedly," Babbit said.

"Which leads me back to the warnin'," Pritchard said. "I believe whoever came after me and Ditch will likely try again."

"Good heavens," Judge Pearson said a third time.

"Given what the marshal just told us," Seth Tilley said, "I'd have to agree."

"It certainly stands to reason," Manfri Pannell said.

"Even if not," Deputy Strobl finally spoke, "we cannot take the chance, can we?"

"My thoughts exactly," Pritchard said.

"Ditch is out at his place with Idelle and the baby. Tater and Ike Randle are armed and watchin' over 'em, but one plump deputy and one old groundskeeper ain't gonna stave off an attack by a force larger than a couple of riders."

"What do you propose?" Pearson said.

"With your permission, fellers, I'd like to fetch Ditch and his family and bring them here into town where they can be better protected. They can stay at the hotel." He met the eyes of every man in the room. "I want to start up the Vigilance Committee."

"Are you making a formal motion, Marshal?" Judge Pearson asked.

"I am," Pritchard said.

"Very well," Pearson said, clearing his throat. "Marshal Pritchard has made a formal motion to activate the Atherton Vigilance Committee. All in favor?"

"Aye," John Babbit said.

"By all means," Simon Tilley said.

"I'm for it," Seth Tilley said.

"Yes," Manfri Pannell said.

"Absolutely," Dr. Mauldin said.

"I will add my enthusiastic 'aye' as well," Pearson said. "The 'ayes' have it. The Atherton Vigilance Committee is hereby activated." He turned to Babbit. "Can you make the necessary notices, John?"

"All able-bodied townsmen on the list will be notified by noon," Babbit assured, "and I'll officially record it in the *Athertonian*. We'll have at least a dozen armed men patrolling the streets at all times, and with the ringing of the church bell plenty more on the way if need be."

"I thank you," Pritchard said. "Hopefully, we won't have need. But whatever this abominable train wrecking is all about, those responsible for it thought nothin' of maimin' and killin' innocent women and children, and murderin' defenseless men, to advance their aims. I reckon we oughta be prepared for anything. Especially with me bein' gone."

"Where're you going?" Pearson asked.

"I'll be leavin' the defense of this town in the able hands of the Vigilance Committee," Pritchard said. "As Atherton's marshal, I aim to bring to account them that murdered young Donnie McKitchern and maimed our mayor. Done swore myself an oath."

"Understood," the judge said. "Don't you worry, Samuel. Atherton, and your family, will be safe while you're away."

"Of that I'm certain, Your Honor."

"If you'll excuse us," Simon Tilley said, "I've got a young boy to prepare to bury, a family to console, and Seth and I need to ready our guns." The undertaker patted his son's shoulder. "But we'll stand our watch true, just like everybody else."

"Durn tootin'," Seth said.

Pritchard shook the Tilleys' hands, along with each of the others, one-by-one. "I'll be going out to fetch Ditch and Idelle now," he announced.

"I'd like to go with you," Dr. Mauldin said. "I'd planned to go out to the Clemson place to check in on Ditch this morning."

"Glad to have you," Pritchard said. "Let's all meet back at the Atherton Arms Hotel in an hour or two. I want to get Ditch and his family safely tucked away."

"You may want to delay your departure a day," Simon Tilley said. "If you can, that is? Young Donnie McKitchern's funeral is tomorrow."

"A day won't matter," Pritchard said. "Of course, I'll stay. Wouldn't be right to miss the burial."

"I figured as much," Simon Tilley said. "After the boy's been properly buried you can get on the trail of those trainwreckers."

"Correction," Deputy Strobl said to Tilley. "We can get on the trail."

"You don't have to accompany me," Pritchard told Strobl. "Might be best, with your extensive military experience, for you to remain here in town and supervise the Vigilance Committee?"

"Nonsense," Strobl said, nodding to the others in the room. "More capable men do not exist. As your deputy, I belong at your side. A child of Atherton has been murdered, and Mayor Clemson and his family, who are my friends, are under mortal threat. The good men of Atherton, in the form of the Vigilance Committee, stand ready to defend the town. I, Florian Strobl, of the Vienna Strobls, will therefore be standing with you, Marshal Pritchard, when the men who are responsible for these foul crimes are brought to account. This I declare, upon my honor."

"Right proud to have you along, Florian," Pritchard said.

Chapter 17

". . . as we commend the body of Donald Bertrand McKitchern, taken long before his time, to the earth from whence it came. His eternal soul now rests in the Kingdom of Heaven, where he sits beside the Almighty Father and the angels who serve him. Amen."

"Amen," the large crowd of mourners said in unison. The pastor, a solemn-looking man named Donaldson, nodded to the four men standing with their heads bowed at the grave.

Seth Tilley, Manfri Pannell, John Babbit, and Donnie McKitchern's heartbroken father slowly lowered the small casket into the ground by rope. The boy's mother quietly sobbed, along with countless other women in attendance. Men stood solemnly, their hats in their hands, as the box descended. All were dressed in their Sunday best. None of the men wore guns.

"Let us now lift our voices," Pastor Donaldson called out to the crowd, "to guide the soul of the departed on his journey to the Gates of Heaven." He'd presided over enough funerals in his time to know that without the uplifting and unifying notes of a soothing hymn to occupy their minds, only the sounds of sadness and loss would reign over the assembly. "Who will join me?"

As the good people of Atherton began a tearful chorus of *Gather at the River,* mourners filed past the grave. The women released flowers, and the men a handful of dirt, into the hole. The first to do this was Mr. McKitchern, whose tears fell along with the soil in his trembling fingers. The second was Pritchard, and the third was Mayor Ditch Clemson, helped along by his wife Idelle on one side and by Dr. Mauldin on the other.

Ditch Clemson had insisted on attending. Though pale, gaunt, missing a leg, and wearing a bandage over his head and with his right arm in a sling, his appearance and health had nonetheless improved significantly during the past twenty-four hours. This was in no small part due to the expert treatment of Dr. Mauldin and the loving care of his wife. Like the mayor, most of the town had turned out for the burial, which was held at the Churchyard. Simon Tilley's hearse, the Clemsons' buckboard, and countless other wagons were parked along the road.

Atherton's main cemetery, a tree-filled glade commonly referred to as the Churchyard by the locals, sat on the high side of town overlooking the river valley. During the war it had expanded greatly, with sections divided by familial affiliation, religious connotation, and by allegiance to either North or South.

Situated slightly below the Churchyard, close to Atherton's main road and separated from the larger cemetery by a wrought-iron fence, was Sin Hill. This resting place was reserved for those deemed unfit to lay in repose among decent folk. Sin Hill contained the remains of former mayor Burnell Shipley, Sheriff Horace Foster, Marshal Elton Stacy, deputy and gunslinger Eli Gaines, and Cottonmouth Quincy, as well as several-dozen other men of bad character and violent deed put down by Marshal Pritchard or his deputies.

It was no accident Sin Hill sat closest to the road. The tainted cemetery acted as a warning to those entering Atherton bearing ill intent.

Two men on horseback rode up to the edge of the Churchyard and halted their mounts before the funeral assembly. One was stocky, of medium height, and sported a handlebar mustache under a bowler. The other was freakishly tall, extremely thin, and had dull eyes and a drooping mustache beneath a wide-brimmed hat. His horse looked puny underneath him.

"Hallo there," Earl Marsh called out to the crowd, ignoring the fact people were engaged in singing a hymn. "Any of you folks know where I can find Marshal Samuel Pritchard?"

No one answered. The assemblage continued to sing.

"I asked you all a question," Marsh called out, even louder than before. "I said, where can I find Marshal Pritchard?"

"Can't you see?" Pastor Donaldson replied, as the hymn raggedly dissolved. "We are in the midst of a burial."

"Who died?" Asa Finchum rudely demanded.

"My son," Mrs. McKitchern said through her tears.

"I'm sorry for that," Marsh said insincerely, "but we've got important business with the marshal and are pressed for time."

"What sort of business warrants the interruption of a

family's grief at the repose of their child?" the pastor fumed.

"Railroad business," Marsh said smugly. "Where's the damned marshal?"

"Right here," Pritchard said, emerging from the crowd. He stood a full head taller than anyone else.

"John Brody wants to see you," Marsh said bluntly.

"I don't care," Pritchard said. "What you just done, interruptin' this burial, was uncalled for."

"When I've got business," Marsh said, turning his head to spit, "I attend to it. Don't much care whether it's a wedding, a funeral, or a church social going on around me while I conduct it."

A murmur of outrage spread throughout the townsfolk. An enraged Mr. McKitchern started to rush forward, but was restrained by several fellow townsmen.

"Whoa there, feller," Marsh laughed, wagging a finger at McKitchern. "Pull in your horns, before they get shot off."

"You've right poor manners," Pritchard said, as he stepped closer to the two horsemen. "Disturbin' the bereaved at a funeral." His eyes darkened. "I'll be attendin' to that directly."

"Mighty ambitious," Marsh said, as he swept his coat behind the butt of his holstered Smith & Wesson, "for a man who isn't wearing an iron." Finchum also tucked his coattails behind his twin revolvers.

"I see you boys found your guns," Pritchard said. "Did it take you longer to swim for 'em, or to dry 'em out?"

"He's awful confident for a feller who ain't heeled," Finchum remarked to Marsh.

"Don't need no firearm to teach you curs a lesson."

"Oh yeah," Marsh scoffed, hooking a thumb in his belt near his holster. "How that's going to happen?"

"Like the marshal said," Deputy Strobl announced as he stepped from behind Simon Tilley's hearse, "he doesn't need a gun. I've got one."

Strobl had both of his Chamelot Delvigne revolvers out of their shoulder holsters. The hammers were back, and each gun was leveled at one of the two horsemen. "Actually," he said, in his Austrian accent, "I brought two."

"You think you can get us both?" Marsh said, his smile vanishing. "You might get one of us, Fritz, but one of us will sure as hell get you."

"Perhaps," Strobl conceded with a shrug. "Or perhaps you'll be cut in half by a shotgun blast before you can draw?"

"What shotgun?" Marsh said. "You're bluffing, Deputy. I don't see any scatterguns about."

"Yoo-hoo," Tater said, stepping from behind the Clemsons' wagon. His double-barreled coach gun was up at his shoulder, and aimed at a point midway between the two mounted men. A skilled winged-game shooter, Tater could swing the weapon to either Marsh or Finchum in an instant. Both of the weapons' hammers were locked to the rear.

"Touch them guns," Tater said, "and they'll be pickin' up chunks of you boys in the next county."

"I always heard you were fearless," Marsh said to Pritchard. "Seems I heard wrong, since you're hiding behind your men. What's the matter, Marshal? Afraid to handle your own business?"

"When I told you I'd be addressin' your manners directly," Pritchard said, removing his coat, "I meant what

I said. Keep 'em covered," he told Strobl and Tater, "while I fetch my irons."

"As you wish," Strobl said.

"With pleasure," Tater said. "Take your time, Samuel," he continued. "I'm a-hopin' one of these boys'll get twitchy while you're occupied getting heeled. I'd like nothin' more'n to blast 'em outta their saddles."

"I'll be with you fellers momentarily," Pritchard said.

He went to Ditch's buckboard and retrieved his revolvers from within its bed. He buckled them on as several hundred Athertonians watched from the Churchyard. Once he had his pistols belted on, he strode back to where Marsh and Finchum still sat on horseback.

"Which of you is the better gun hand?" he asked.

"That'd be me," Finchum said. He spat at Pritchard's feet.

"Get unhorsed," Pritchard said, "and face me." He gave a nod to Strobl and Tater and they lowered their guns.

"I wouldn't pull on Asa, Marshal," Marsh said with a laugh. "He's got more than twenty notches."

"Mind your mouth," Pritchard said. "I'll tend to you presently."

Finchum dismounted and handed the reins of his horse to Marsh. He stepped to the center of the road, rolled his shoulders once, cracked his neck, wrung his hands, and grinned at Pritchard.

"Any time you're ready, Marshal."

"After you," Pritchard said.

"Look at the bright side, Marshal," Marsh taunted. "We're already at the boneyard. You won't have far to go."

"I told you once already," Pritchard said. "Mind your mouth."

Finchum drew.

Pritchard knew what Marsh and Finchum were doing. By engaging him in a verbal exchange, Marsh was attempting to create a distraction. A diversion designed to slow Pritchard's reaction time just enough to give his partner an edge in the draw.

Finchum never even touched his guns. One instant, Pritchard's large hands were hanging loosely at his sides with his Colts in their holsters. The next instant, both his .45s were in his fists and leveled at Finchum with the hammers back. There seemed, to the observers watching, to be no perceivable transition between the two points.

Finchum's eyes widened, and his hands dropped. Still in the saddle, Marsh cursed under his breath and deflated.

"Go on," Pritchard said. "Finish your draw."

"If I do," Finchum said, "you'll kill me."

"That's a righteous possibility," Pritchard said. He lowered the hammers of his revolvers and re-holstered them.

"You wanna try again?" Pritchard said. "This time, without your partner's mouth tryin' to interfere with my draw?"

"No," Finchum said. "Ain't no point. You'd edge me again. We both know it."

"All right, then," Pritchard said. "Unbuckle that belt and drop them pistols." Finchum complied.

Pritchard walked over to Finchum, who stood an inch taller than his own six-foot-six-inches in height, and landed a haymaker directly onto the gunman's jaw.

Finchum's hat flew off, his head snapped back, he

stumbled backward, and fell unconscious to the ground. Pritchard picked up his revolvers and handed them to Tater.

"Hang on to these, Deputy Jessup," he said.

Pritchard turned to Marsh, who by now had gone pale in the face. "Unhorse yourself," he commanded.

"Wait a minute," Marsh said. "Let's talk about this. There isn't cause to—"

"Get off that horse," Pritchard cut him off, "or by God, I'll unhorse you myself."

"Samuel," Pastor Donaldson called out, "remember what the Good Book says? Vengeance is mine, saith the Lord."

"I've heard that verse before," Pritchard said. "I believe today I'll give the Lord a rest."

Marsh got off his horse and held his hands out in front of him. "There's no need for you to get riled," he said nervously, as Pritchard approached him. "You're a man of the law, remember?"

"There was no need for you to come to this cemetery and insult those who're grievin' over a child cut down by the greed of them who pay your wages," Pritchard said. "What you and your partner done today is as foul a thing as a man can do." His expression hardened. "I already done told you I'd be tendin' to it." Pritchard's voice got flat and hard. "Draw," he said.

"I can't," Marsh whined. "You'll kill me."

"That's my intention."

"I won't," Marsh said. He unbuckled his belt and let his gun drop to the ground.

"Suit yourself," Pritchard said. He stepped forward and punched Marsh a roundhouse left that would have dropped him if he hadn't caught the gunman before he fell. Pritchard held him upright by the collar and punched him once more, this time letting the unconscious man crumple to the ground like a rag doll.

Pritchard picked up Marsh's Smith & Wesson and tossed it to Strobl. "For your collection," he said. He grabbed the canteen from Finchum's horse and poured the contents onto the slack faces of Marsh and Finchum. Both men awakened, sputtered, and sat up.

Finchum's jaw was broken. He spat blood and held it in place with both hands. Marsh's nose and lips were shattered. He shook his head and spat teeth.

"The both of you," Pritchard began, "are gonna march up that hill and apologize to Mr. and Mrs. McKitchern, and the pastor, for what you done here today at this funeral."

"I . . . c-can't . . . t-talk," Finchum mumbled, as blood burbled from his lips.

"Then Marsh will do the talkin' for the both of you. Do it, or I'll give you back your pistols and we'll commence what we started."

Marsh and Finchum struggled shakily to their feet, picked up their hats, and stumbled toward the congregation. "We apologithe," Marsh lisped through his missing teeth. A steady stream of blood trickled from his broken nose. Mr. McKitchern glared silently at them while his wife wept into her kerchief.

"Be off with you," Donaldson said. "Your transgression today may be forgiven, but it will not be forgotten."

Marsh and Finchum took the reins of their horses and mounted. Finchum removed his hat and tied his jaw in place with his neckerchief. Pritchard addressed them.

"That's two times you boys have braced me," he began. "The first time I disarmed you. The second time, I disarmed and thumped you. If I see either one of you fellers a third time, it'll be the last time anybody sees you walkin' this earth. And you can tell your boss, Mr. Brody, that I'll be a-comin' to see him when I'm right good and ready. Now git."

As the two railroad gunmen turned their horses and rode off, Strobl, Tater, and Dr. Mauldin half-escorted, and half-carried, Ditch to his buckboard. He was weak, pale, sweating profusely, and nearly exhausted from the exertion of attending the funeral.

"Those were Brody's men?" Ditch asked, as he was placed onto the buckboard. Idelle climbed aboard and took the reins.

"They were," Pritchard confirmed.

"Why's Brody got gun hands on his payroll?" Ditch said. "And why did he send 'em around here?"

"Right good questions," Pritchard said.

Chapter 18

"Mr. Laird Bonner to see you," the servant announced. He stepped aside, and a tall, lean man in a black suit and black Boss of the Plains entered the car past him.

Gould came from behind his imposing desk and extended his hand. "Thank you for coming, Mr. Bonner," he said. "I'm Jason Gould. My friends call me Jay."

"Nice to meet you," Bonner said, as he shook Gould's hand.

"You arrived earlier than expected," Gould said, gesturing for his guest to be seated.

"I happened to be passing through Saint Louis on business when I got your telegram."

"Hunting someone?"

"That's my profession," Bonner acknowledged. "Seems a pair of competing railroad companies, yours being one of them, have put up a bounty on a former Confederate partisan named Jeremiah Rupe. Biggest bounty I've ever heard of, and I've been doing this awhile."

"Do you know why Rupe is wanted?"

"It's claimed that he and a dozen men riding with

him wrecked the train I saw being dismantled and hauled away out yonder."

"You doubt that claim?"

"One-hundred-thousand dollars is an awful lot of money for one man's head. Too much money, actually. Enough to make me think the people putting up the bounty don't actually expect they'll have to pay it out."

"It's of interest to me how you'd reach that conclusion," Gould remarked. "If you had doubts about the bounty's authenticity, why did you respond to my telegram?"

Bonner answered Gould's question with one of his own. "Why are you here, Mr. Gould?"

"One goes where one must when duty calls," Gould said.

"Seems to me," Bonner said, as he removed his hat, "supervising a train derailment would be something an underling could attend to. Would a single train wreck normally require the attention of the president and owner of the Missouri Pacific Railroad?"

"This particular train wreck is quite unique," Gould said.

"So I've heard," Bonner said, as he adjusted his pair of 1872 Open Top Colts. He wore one revolver on his right hip, and the other cross-draw over his left.

"May I offer you a drink?"

"Whiskey, if you have it?"

The servant stepped forward and poured a healthy portion of amber liquid from a leaded decanter into a crystal glass for Bonner. For Gould he poured brandy into a snifter.

"Do you mind if I smoke?" Bonner asked.

"I'll join you," Gould said, as he produced a cigar from

an ornately engraved box on his desk. "I'd offer you one, but I happen to know you only smoke your own."

Bonner smiled, and lit a dirty-brown cheroot he withdrew from an inside pocket.

"What exactly," Gould began, once both men got their tobacco burning, "if you don't mind telling me, have you heard about this particular train wreck?"

"Only that one of your trains got derailed, robbed, and that passengers died. Heard some local politicians on board died, too, but scuttlebutt says it wasn't from the wreck."

"You're very well informed."

"Not really. Hundreds of laborers have been here for the past couple of days working to repair the bridge and tear apart the train, not to mention a detachment of soldiers and a few reporters. Folks tend to talk."

"And you've obviously heard about Jeremiah Rupe's involvement?"

"Yeah," Bonner said with a dry laugh. He sipped bourbon. "I heard about that, too. And the bounty, of course."

"You find something humorous?" Gould asked.

"Not humorous," Bonner said. "Peculiar."

"Peculiar?"

"Yeah, peculiar. Last anybody heard or saw of Arkansas Jem was ten years ago, at the war's end, and nobody's seen or heard from him since. Suddenly he reappears, out of nowhere, to wreck this particular train?"

"Stranger things have happened," Gould said.

"Perhaps," Bonner said, as he exhaled smoke. "But why now? And why haven't any of the posses or army patrols picked up his sign? More importantly, with a one-hundred-thousand-dollar price on Rupe's head, why hasn't one of his own men turned him in? The kind of men riding with a fellow like Jem Rupe would turn in their own mother for a five-dollar gold piece." He chuckled again. "Back in Indiana, where I hail from, this Rupe situation is what we'd call 'peculiar.'"

"I'm from New York," Gould said, "and I also find it peculiar."

"I doubt we're alone," Bonner said.

"We're not," Gould said. "There's a Missouri lawman who shares our reservations about Rupe's involvement. He used to be a Texas Ranger. His brother-in-law is the mayor of a nearby town who nearly perished in the wreck. As it was, the poor fellow lost a leg. As you can imagine, this lawman is rather upset about the derailment, to put it mildly. He has, in my very presence, sworn to bring those responsible to account by bullet or noose."

Bonner cocked his head and ground out his cheroot. "This particular lawman wouldn't be blond-haired, blue-eyed, six-and-a-half-feet-tall, built like a lumberjack, and sporting a bullet scar on his forehead, would he?"

"As a matter of fact," Gould said, "you've described him perfectly. His name is—"

"Samuel Pritchard," Bonner finished Gould's sentence for him. He shook his head and exhaled heavily as he spoke the name. "Used to go by the alias Joe Atherton when he was wearing a star for Texas."

"You know him?"

"I do," Bonner said. "Know his brother-in-law, too. His name is Clemson. Mayor Ditch Clemson. His wife, Pritchard's sister, is named Idelle. I've dined at their house."

"What can you tell me about Marshal Pritchard from

the standpoint of someone in your profession?" Gould asked.

"All I can tell you about Samuel Pritchard," Bonner said with a hard grin, "is that right about now, the last person on earth I'd want to be is whoever wrecked your train."

Chapter 19

Pritchard sat at a table in the restaurant inside the Atherton Arms Hotel and cradled his nephew. His sister Idelle sat next to him, and seated across from them was Dr. Mauldin.

Mauldin was drinking whiskey, Pritchard a beer, and Idelle a glass of white wine. Deputy Strobl was stationed in the lobby, smoking a cigarette and reading a newspaper through his monocle. His Henry .44 rifle, which once belonged to Pritchard, was leaning against his overstuffed chair. Deputy Tater Jessup was in the hotel kitchen with his double-barreled shotgun, minding the back door.

When Pritchard asked Tater which post he'd rather stand, the hotel lobby or the kitchen, Strobl merely laughed and headed for the lobby. Tater cursed as Strobl left, but happily ambled off to the kitchen.

"How's Ditch doin'?" Pritchard asked Mauldin, once the waitress departed with their dinner orders. Little Samuel cooed and chortled in his massive arms.

"As well as can be expected," Mauldin said. "The injury to his scalp wasn't a fracture, thank goodness, and only required a few stitches. He's got a broken collarbone, but that'll heal up in no time; I've been treating Ditch Clemson's broken bones since he was knee high to a grasshopper and busting broncs alongside his father. His leg," Mauldin smiled reassuringly at Idelle, "is showing no signs of infection. That has as much to do with the care he's receiving from his wife as my professional ministering. All he needs now is plenty of fluids and red meat to replace the blood he lost, and lots of rest."

"That's why he couldn't join us for dinner," Idelle said. "Going to the funeral earlier today nearly did him in. But you know Ditch; he insisted. Once we got back to the hotel room, he flopped on the bed and has been sawing logs ever since."

"That's good," Mauldin said. "Let him sleep. Sleep is when the body heals."

"He'd sleep a lot better," Idelle said, "in his own bed. When can we go home, Samuel?"

"I can't rightly say," Pritchard answered, nuzzling Samuel. "Not until I get back."

"Get back?"

"I'll be leaving at first light with Florian to hunt down Jem Rupe."

"How long will that take?" Idelle complained.

"It'll take how long it takes," Pritchard said. "This ain't gonna be no springtime frolic."

"I know that," Idelle sighed. "Don't mind me, big brother. I realize you're only doing what's best for us and the town."

"Protectin' my family, and Atherton, is only part of it," Pritchard said. "Somebody's gonna pay for what they done, and I'm a-gonna be collectin' the bill."

John Babbit entered the hotel, nodded to Strobl, and

strode past him into the restaurant. Judge Pearson was with him. In addition to his usual visor and apron, Babbit wore a holstered Navy Colt. Pearson also wore a firearm, but his was inside the full-flap crossdraw holster he wore as a Union officer during the war. The military pistol belt looked odd under his fancy suit.

"Good evening," Babbit greeted the diners. "I just got a telegram I thought you should see directly, Samuel." He handed a piece of paper to Pritchard, who handed off Baby Samuel before accepting.

"What is it?" Idelle asked.

"It's my appointment," Pritchard said, as he perused the document.

"Appointment?" Idelle said.

"At your brother's suggestion," Judge Pearson began, "I telegraphed the governor and requested appointments for Samuel and Florian Strobl as U.S. Marshals."

"That way," Pritchard explained, "when Florian and I travel about, we won't be limited in our authority as peace officers."

"A wise move," Dr. Mauldin said.

"Thank you, Your Honor," Pritchard said, folding the telegram and tucking it into his pocket.

"Won't you join us?" Idelle asked the newcomers.

"Thank you kindly," Pearson said, "but we have important duties to attend to. Now that the Vigilance Committee has been activated, we must regularly check the watchmen's posts at each end of town, and the train and stage depots, and make sure the street patrols are kept up." Both tipped their hats. "Good night."

"They're taking this Vigilance Committee thing pretty seriously," Idelle said, once the duo had departed.

"As they should," Pritchard said. "There've already been two attempts on Ditch's life, and one on mine."

"But you routed them," Idelle argued, "out on the prairie between here and Rock Creek? That's what Tater told me. The threat is over, isn't it?"

"Not by a long shot," Pritchard said. "Anyone who can go the big figure to rustle up a baker's dozen gun hands can surely round up a dozen more."

Seth Tilley entered the restaurant with his hat in his hand. "Evenin', ma-am," he said to Idelle. "I got word you wanted to see me."

"That's right," Idelle said, handing Samuel over again to her brother. "I have it right here."

"Have what?" Pritchard asked, as he happily took receipt of his nephew.

Instead of answering, Idelle dug into a carpetbag at the foot of her chair. From it, she withdrew one of her husband's boots; the left one.

Tilley, in his late thirties and skeletally thin like his undertaker father, held the boot at arm's length and examined it.

"Shouldn't be no trouble at all," he announced. "Gimme a few days, Mrs. Clemson, and I'll have it ready for him."

"I'm grateful," Idelle said. She extended several bank notes. "This should cover it."

"Oh no," Tilley said, showing her his palm. "I wouldn't think of charging you."

"But you must," Idelle insisted. "Ditch is the mayor. I have to pay you, otherwise it'll appear as a gratuity."

"I'm not sure I know what the word 'grat-too-it-tee' means," Tilley said, "but I won't be taking your money.

No ma'am. Grat-too-it-tee or not, Ditch is my friend." He put on his hat, tipped it, and left.

"What was that all about?" Pritchard asked.

"Seth Tilley is the best woodsmith in Jackson County," Idelle said.

"Oh," Pritchard said, suddenly making the connection between the undertaker, who was also a coffin maker and woodworker, Ditch's left boot, and his missing leg.

Pritchard, Mauldin, and Idelle had just ordered their food when Deputy Strobl entered the restaurant.

"Marshal Pritchard," he said, bowing slightly and removing his hat, "I apologize for the interruption. There is a couple in the lobby demanding to see you."

"Who are they?" Pritchard asked. "What do they want?"

"They refused to disclose," Strobl said in his Austrian accent, "and insisted on speaking with you immediately. The woman claims it's a matter of 'life and death.'" The eyebrow above his monocle lifted. "Your life or death."

"Then I reckon I'd best attend to it," Pritchard said, handing over the now slumbering Baby Samuel to his sister once more and rising from his seat. He followed Strobl into the hotel lobby, where a young man and woman stood expectantly.

The man was over six feet tall, thickly built, and a few years younger than Pritchard's twenty-nine years. He had a broad face, strong jaw, and dull eyes. He was wearing a suit and tie, which he looked uncomfortable in. He had the tanned complexion and calloused hands of someone who made his living outdoors.

The woman, who wasn't much older than Idelle, was striking. She was extremely petite, and couldn't have weighed more than one-hundred pounds. She had short, auburn, hair, large brown eyes, and very prominent breasts, despite her lean frame.

"Are you Marshal Pritchard?" the woman asked, as he and Strobl approached.

"Who else would he be?" the man snorted derisively. "He's wearin' a badge, ain't he?"

"Anybody can pin on a badge, Carl," the woman retorted.

"Look how tall he is, fer criminy sakes?" he countered. "Everybody we asked said Atherton's town marshal is as tall as a tree."

The woman turned irritably from her companion to Pritchard.

"I'm Marshal Pritchard," he said, settling the dispute. "What can I do for you?"

"Forgive my friend," the woman said, casting a disapproving glance at the man with her. "My name is Dorothy Greaves. This," she gestured to the man standing next to her, "is Carl Ewell. We hail from Wapello County, Iowa."

"Seems I've met someone else recently from Wapello County," Pritchard said. "If I ain't mistaken, his last name was Greaves, too?"

"My little brother, Delbert," she said. "I'm very concerned about him. You say you've already made his acquaintance?"

"I have," Pritchard admitted. "He was here a coupla days ago, as a guest of our jail."

"He was arrested?" she said. "What for?"

"Waving a pair of pistols in the street and makin' a nuisance of himself, mostly," Pritchard said.

"I was afraid of that," Dorothy Greaves said. "For

weeks before he left home, he claimed to anyone who'd listen that he was going to Missouri to gun down a famous Texas Ranger and gunfighter named Smokin' Joe Atherton. Like everybody else, I thought Del was idly bragging." She looked up at Pritchard with weary eyes. "Delbert often says boastful things. Nobody takes him seriously."

"He was pretty serious when I met him," Pritchard said. "He called me out. Would have drawn on me, too, iffen my deputy hadn't conked him on the noggin."

"So it's true?" she said. "You're Smokin' Joe Atherton?"

"I was," Pritchard said, "once. I use my given name, now: Samuel Pritchard."

"Mighty suspicious," Ewell said with a snort, "iffen you ask me? A man who uses two names ain't a man to be trusted, whether he's wearin' a badge or not."

"Hush up, Carl," Dorothy said. "Nobody's asking you."

"Don't have to," he said. "Got a right to my opinion, don't I?"

"Then have the good sense to keep it to yourself," she said. "I apologize, again, for Carl's inexcusably rude behavior, Marshal."

"No need to apologize for your boyfriend's mouth," Pritchard said. "Like he said, he's got a right to his own opinion."

"Oh, Carl's not my boyfriend," Greaves blurted, a bit too rapidly. She stepped closer to Pritchard. "He lives on the farm down the road from ours. He agreed to accompany me to Missouri so I wouldn't be a woman traveling alone, that's all." She gave Ewell a contemptuous glare. "There's nothing whatsoever between us."

"Hey," Ewell protested. "Now just wait a gosh-durned minute, Dorothy. I thought—"

"You thought wrong," Greaves cut him off. She spoke over her shoulder while batting her eyes up at Pritchard. Pritchard smiled down at her. Ewell's face reddened.

"Do you know where your brother is now?" Pritchard asked.

"I was hoping you could tell me," she said. "He sold one of our horses without telling the family a couple of weeks ago and left, and we haven't seen him since. I made some inquiries among the layabouts and lunk-heads he calls friends, and learned of his desire to shoot you. I came here to find Delbert and to warn you."

"Warn me?"

"My little brother is very skilled with guns, Marshal, and he's desperate to become a big shot. I think he believes if he bests you, he will somehow acquire your reputation. That people will then respect and fear him."

"He wouldn't be the first," Pritchard said.

"All he ever does is practice drawing and shooting," she went on. "Night and day. When he gets a bur under his saddle, like he has with you, he won't let it go. If he's taken a mind to shoot you, I can assure you he'll do it or at least try. He's always been small, weak, picked on, and pushed around. But ever since he took up a gun, something changed inside him. He struts about waving pistols and threatening, bullying, and picking on others as was done to him, only worse. I'm afraid he's entirely forgotten his Christian upbringing."

She looked directly into Pritchard's eyes. "I don't want to see harm or trouble befall my little brother, but I certainly don't want to see him shoot you, either. I came to Atherton to do two things, Marshal: to warn you, and to beg you not to kill him."

"I had my chance to do that already," Pritchard said, "and spared him, but only because I could. Happenstance gave me the opportunity to have my deputy buffalo him with a pistol before he was able to pull on me."

"Mighty cowardly way to settle a gunfight," Ewell grunted, "iffen you ask me? Sounds like you was a-scared of Del, and had your deputy stop the gunfight before it began on account of you wanting to save your own neck?"

"Carl!" Dorothy Greaves gasped.

"The next time your brother braces me," Pritchard continued, ignoring Ewell's insult, "neither of us might be so lucky. I can only promise you, Miss Greaves, that I'll do everything within my power to keep from shootin' him, as I do with all folks I encounter in the course of my peace officer duties. But you'd best know that sometimes shootin' someone is the proper course and ain't avoidable. The only person who can decide whether your brother gets shot is Delbert himself."

Pritchard's smile vanished. "I've been shot before, ma'am; more'n once. It ain't no fun. If I can avoid shootin' your little brother, I'll do it. You have my word on that. But iffen I can't, and it's him or me, he'll be shot. That's the best I can do."

"I suppose that's all I can ask for," Greaves said. She held out her hand. "Thank you, Marshal Pritchard.

"Please," Pritchard said, holding her hand, "call me Samuel."

"Hey," Ewell protested weakly. "What's goin' on here?"

"Hush up," Dorothy Greaves snapped at him, still smiling at Pritchard. "I'm busy talking with the marshal."

Chapter 20

"You are familiar with Arkansas?" Strobl asked.

"Ditch and I enlisted in the Confederate cavalry here," Pritchard said. "Spilt my share of blood, and had mine spilt, in Arkansas. I reckon you could say I'm familiar with the place."

Pritchard and Strobl were in Fort Smith, having spent the better part of two days traveling from Atherton by rail. They'd just disembarked, and were off-loading their horses from the livery car.

Strobl brought along Schatz, his medium-sized quarter horse. With Rusty gone and Pritchard without a mount, Ditch insisted he take one of his best horses; a big roan named Soldier.

Ditch Clemson was a horse breaker by trade, having learned his craft from his father and older brother while growing up on their family's modest ranch. Now wealthy, he kept an impressive array of horseflesh in the stables he'd built on what was once his father's property, down the road from the stately home he shared with Idelle. One of Pritchard's favorites was Soldier.

Soldier, Like Rusty before him, was birthed and raised

on the Clemson ranch. Also like Rusty, Soldier stood well over eighteen hands tall. This was a requirement to haul around someone of Pritchard's stature. Unlike Rusty, who was a chestnut bay, Soldier was a roan with a white mane and tail. At three years old he possessed a staid disposition, largely due to the firearms training Ditch and Pritchard put into him. As former Confederate guerillas, both men valued strong animals who wouldn't spook at gunfire.

While Strobl saddled their horses, Pritchard got directions to the courthouse from the station agent. People at the railroad depot stared at the strange duo as they mounted and rode off.

Strobl sat atop Schatz in polished European riding boots, jodhpurs under a tweed jacket and ascot, and wearing a Homberg and half-cape. His Henry .44 was in the scabbard on his saddle, and belted around his waist were Earl Marsh's .44 Smith & Wesson and Asa Finchum's pair of Colts. Concealed beneath his jacket were his Chamelot Delvigne revolvers in their twin shoulder holsters.

Pritchard was no less distinct in appearance. The giant lawman straddled his giant horse clad in spurs, Texas-style boots, denims, button-front shirt, and a wide-brimmed Stetson. His ever-present pair of Colt .45s were holstered in twin belts laden with cartridges. Hidden under a vest, which he typically didn't wear, rode his pair of 1863 Remington .44s in custom-made shoulder holsters patterned after Strobl's. His .44-40 Winchester was sheathed in the saddle.

Both horses' saddles featured bedrolls, bulging saddlebags, and dual canteens, and both men atop them wore circle-and-star badges that read *United States Marshal*.

"Fort Smith certainly is an eclectic place," Strobl commented, as they took in the sights during their ride.

"Not sure what that word means," Pritchard said.

"It means," Strobl explained, "filled with many different things."

"Can't argue that," Pritchard said.

The streets were indeed bustling. Both sides of the main thoroughfare were littered with hotels, gambling halls, brothels, and saloons. The throng of men on the street was a mixture of cowhands and clerks, former slaves and livestock barons, soldiers and muleskinners, miners and shopkeepers; an equal blend of those who slept indoors and those who slumbered on the prairie.

The women in Fort Smith were just as varied as the men in their appearance, and ranged from common folk such as housewives, negresses, painted ladies, squaws, and shop gals, to those wealthy enough to be decked out in attire more suitable to the finer haunts of Kansas City or Saint Louis. Virtually all the males in view were armed. Countless hard cases roamed the streets, their hungry eyes scanning their surroundings for predators and prey alike.

Despite the diversity of folk inhabiting Fort Smith, few failed to notice Pritchard and Strobl as they navigated the streets. They ended up at the Federal Courthouse, housed within what was once a large, brick barracks on the former military post.

Pritchard and Strobl were challenged by a pair of men carrying rifles and wearing similar badges as they dismounted.

"Who are you," one of the men demanded, "and what's your business?"

"Deputy U.S. Marshals Pritchard and Strobl, from Missouri, to see Judge Parker. He's expectin' us."

"Wait here," one of the men said, before disappearing into the building.

"Folks seem a mite jittery around here," Pritchard remarked.

"Is this your first trip to Fort Smith?" the remaining deputy marshal asked.

"Ain't been in these parts since the war," Pritchard said. "Was a downright unhealthy territory in them days."

"Not a helluva lot's changed," the marshal said, spitting tobacco. "Place was already bad enough, between a dozen different tribes constantly on the warpath and every rustler, claim-jumper, highwaymen, and killer in the Territories hereabouts. But then we had to get ourselves a brand-new judge this month, which only spurred on the general lawlessness. And if them apples ain't sufficient to keep a feller frettin' over his scalp night and day, there's the biggest bounty anybody ever heard of been placed on a wanted man hailin' from around these parts. That damned reward is drawin' every scalp hunter, gun slick, and bounty killer on both sides of the Mississippi to Fort Smith like flies to a church picnic. I've never seen the like."

"Who's this wanted feller?" Pritchard asked, though he already knew.

"A Reb holdout named Jeremiah Rupe. Goes by the name of Arkansas Jem. His family hails from Booneville, near Coal Creek. It's a day's ride from here."

"What do you know about this Arkansas Jem feller?" Pritchard said. "If you don't mind me askin'?"

"Not much." The deputy marshal shrugged. "He's a

big man, they say; maybe not as big as you, but plenty large. It's said he committed an atrocity durin' the war; wrecked a train. Folks are split about even as to whether Arkansas Jem is still alive or not. Most believe him dead. Every once in a while, though, somebody claims to have seen him out in the Territory, which keeps his legend breathin'. Whether he really is above the snakes, nobody can say fer sure."

"Evidently," Strobl said, "the bounty hunters infesting the area around Fort Smith must believe Mr. Rupe is still among the living, or else they wouldn't be here."

"Hell"—the deputy marshal grinned, revealing blackened teeth—"for one-hundred-thousand dollars, most of them boys would go huntin' for Abraham Lincoln."

"One-hundred-thousand?" Pritchard said, feigning ignorance and surprise.

"Yep," the deputy marshal said. "Like I told you, it's the biggest bounty anybody ever heard of. Pair of railroads put up the reward, supposedly on account of Jem wreckin' and robbin' a train up in Missouri, recently." He squinted at Pritchard and Strobl. "Say," he went on, "didn't you boys say you was from Missouri?"

"We are," Pritchard said, "and we've heard of Jem Rupe and his train wreckin'. I wasn't tryin' to pull your leg, Deputy, nor insult you. I just wanted to find out how far and fast word about Arkansas Jem wreckin' that Missouri train had spread?"

"Word's spread like a prairie fire," the deputy said. "There's already been a shootin' or two in town between competin' gun hands in seek of that bounty. There're more pistoleers on the prod in Fort Smith right now than I've ever seen, even countin' durin' the war, and I've lived here all my life."

"I'm obliged for the information," Pritchard said.

"Long as we're tradin' information," the deputy marshal said, "ain't you Joe Atherton? Smokin' Joe, they used to call you? Can't be two fellers who look like you walkin' about."

"Judge Parker will see you now," the second deputy announced, emerging from the building. "Follow me."

"Name's Pritchard," he said in answer to the first deputy's question. "Not Atherton."

"Iffen you say so," the deputy said, as Pritchard and Strobl went inside.

Pritchard and Strobl were led through the old brick building, past a courtroom, and into an office behind the bench. There they found a surprisingly young man in a suit. He couldn't have been more than a few years older than Strobl, who was in his early thirties.

"I'm Judge Isaac Parker," the man said, extending his hand. "I received word you might be heading this way in search of Jeremiah Rupe."

"Word travels fast," Pritchard said, shaking his hand. After the introductions, all three men took seats.

"You got notice from Governor Hardin?"

"Yes," Parker said. "But only after I'd already received word about your mission from the president."

"The president?" Pritchard said.

"Yes," Parker confirmed. "He has shown great interest in the search for Jeremiah Rupe."

"The railroads must have a powerful lot of pull," Pritchard said to Strobl. "More'n I sussed, that's for sure."

"They do indeed," Parker said, "but I believe President

Grant's interest in Rupe is somewhat more personal. I presume you are both veterans of the War of the Rebellion?"

"You mean the War of Northern Aggression?" Pritchard corrected him. "I am."

"I too, am a veteran," Strobl said in his Austrian accent, "but did not fight in your American Civil War. I fought against Garibaldi in the Italian Alps."

"Did you fight in the war?" Pritchard asked the judge.

"I did not," Parker said, with only a hint of defensiveness. "I was a corporal in the Home Guard. I saw no action."

"What's the president's interest in Rupe?" Pritchard said.

"Are you gentlemen familiar with the Platte Bridge Atrocity? It was early in the war, when Confederate guerillas derailed a train over the Platte River, near Saint Joseph?"

"I am not," Strobl said.

"Only vaguely," Pritchard said. "I was only fourteen years old. All I remember about it was Union troops burning Platte City to the ground in retribution."

"Allow me to educate you both," Parker said. "Rebel bushwhackers, by all accounts led by a murderous spy named Jeremiah Rupe, sabotaged the Platte River Bridge. This caused a train owned by the Hannibal Railroad to plummet into the waters below. Twenty people were killed, and over a hundred were badly wounded. It was a cowardly act committed by the foulest of criminals."

"Iffen I recall," Pritchard said, "such acts were committed by both sides durin' the war."

"The Platte Bridge Train Wreck was a barbaric act

of deliberate cruelty committed by murderous rebels," Parker insisted. "Not a lawful act of war."

"Funny, ain't it?" Pritchard said. "How a train gettin' wrecked, or a civilian town gettin' pillaged, or women gettin' raped, or unarmed men gettin' executed, is 'barbaric' when committed by your enemy? But when them same acts are committed by those fightin' on your side, wearin' the same color uniform, they're called a 'lawful act of war'?"

"I'm not going to debate the morality of war with you," Parker said smugly.

"I wouldn't either," Pritchard said, "iffen I was a feller who ain't never fought in one."

Parker's face flushed and he changed the subject. "To answer your question about the president's interest in Jeremiah Rupe, at the time of the Platte River Derailment, Brigadier General Grant was the Union Officer in charge of guarding all U.S. railroads. He took the incident very personally, and vowed to bring those responsible to justice."

"If that's true," Pritchard said, "I reckon President Grant didn't forget the name Arkansas Jem Rupe?"

"He did not," Parker said. "Like many, I suppose, President Grant presumed Rupe dead since he hadn't been heard from since the war. But when the president learned of the recent train wreck in Missouri, and of Jem's involvement, he became incensed. He also became most interested in the outcome of the hunt for the fugitive trainwrecker."

"Then you know why I'm here?" Pritchard said.

"I know a great many things about you, Marshal Pritchard," Parker said. "I know that you and your family suffered during the war. I know how you got that unique scar on your forehead. I know of your war record, and why you assumed an alias afterwards. I know of your history as a lawman for the Republic of Texas under that assumed name. I know of your reputation as a gunfighter and mankiller. And I know of your doings as a lawman since returning to Missouri and resuming your family name."

"You're mighty well informed," Pritchard said. "Did you also know folks from my hometown were on the train that was wrecked over Rock Creek? A nine-year-old boy from Atherton lost his life. My best friend, the mayor, lost his leg."

"I heard," Parker said. "I presume it's one of the reasons you're hunting Jeremiah Rupe?"

"You reckon I need another?"

"I don't know," Parker said. "The question I keep asking myself is if your allegiance to a former fellow Confederate soldier outweighs your oath as a lawman?"

"Judge Parker," Pritchard said without inflection, "if you ever say anything like that to me again, judge or not, I'll beat you like a rented mule."

Parker's eyes widened. "Are you threatening me, Marshal?" he asked incredulously.

"Not in the least," Pritchard said. "I'm just explainin' what'll befall you the next time your mouth runs far enough ahead of your brains to insult my honor to my face."

"I could call in a dozen marshals right now and have you arrested," a flustered Parker said.

"Sure you could," Pritchard said, "iffen you want to see

a lot of your marshals get hurt. Best know there ain't a one of 'em who can put your teeth back into your head."

"You would really strike me?" Parker said.

"Believe me," Strobl interjected, "he would."

"Judge Parker," Pritchard began, "I don't court trouble. I respect you, and the office you hold. But I don't wantonly insult others. And I don't tolerate others, magistrate or not, who assail my character with uncalled-for insults. Ain't nothin' personal, Your Honor; that's just the way I was raised."

Parker's features softened and his shoulders slumped. "You are right," he said. "I had no cause to express doubts about your character. Even if warranted, and admittedly they are not, it was uncalled for. I forget sometimes, like many in these parts, that the war is long over. I sincerely apologize."

"No apology necessary," Pritchard smiled. "I reckon you've a lot on your plate. Such things can frazzle a feller."

Parker accepted Pritchard's conciliatory words. "You are correct, Marshal. I am indeed 'frazzled,' as you put it. I've been the district judge here only a couple of weeks and have already overseen a half-dozen trials, sentenced several men to death, which I despise doing, experienced numerous threats on my life, had a score of my deputies desert their posts, and in the past few days watched the town become overrun with gunmen and bounty hunters looking for Jem Rupe. Not to mention the Indian troubles seemingly always ready to boil over in the Territory, and not counting the rampant criminality plaguing Fort Smith in general. In truth, it has been a rather daunting month."

"I can imagine."

"What, if anything, can I do to assist you, Marshal?"

"What I need," Pritchard began, "is to find someone who knows Jeremiah Rupe? I've never seen him myself, and don't know what he looks like. A relative, or a feller who rode with him? Somebody who can identify him and swear to it in a court of law?"

"I may know of such a man," Judge Parker said. "After I got the president's telegram, I made a similar inquiry among my staff. I was told of a local man named Hoke Rupe. Evidently he used to be a deputy here in Fort Smith. He's Jeremiah Rupe's brother."

"Where can I find him?"

"I understand he worked in the jail," Parker said. "He was let go a couple of years ago on account of his drinking. You'll find him down at the Horseshoe. It's the largest saloon in town. You can't miss it."

"I appreciate your help," Pritchard said, taking his feet. Strobl joined him.

"You might want to be cautious in approaching Hoke," Parker said. "Quite a number of bounty hunters have infiltrated Fort Smith ever since the railroads put up that infernal bounty a few days ago. Most have taken up residence in the hotel above the Horseshoe. They'll have their eyes on him."

"We'll tread lightly," Pritchard said. "I only want to talk to this Hoke Rupe feller, not end him. Same for Jem, iffen he's still above the snakes."

"No offense," Parker said, "but that is not your reputation."

"None taken," Pritchard said, shaking the judge's hand.

"I'm somewhat confused," Parker said, as they shook. "The price on Rupe's head is payable whether he's brought in dead or alive. Again, no offense, Marshal, but with your reputation, and knowing what Rupe did to your friend and town by wrecking that train at Rock Creek, not to mention the lucrative bounty, I assumed you'd be collecting your reward over his carcass?"

"Not entirely a wrong-headed assumption," Pritchard conceded. "But you're assuming two things, Your Honor: first, that Arkansas Jem is still alive. And second, that if he is alive, he was the feller who wrecked that train."

Chapter 21

"This isn't fair, Mr. Brody," Earl Marsh protested. "We were each promised ten-thousand. That was the deal. You promised Asa and I five-grand apiece to wreck Gould's train, and another five each to cash out the mayors riding on it. That's what we agreed on, and that's what we did. Seems to us you're trying to crawfish."

Asa Finchum nodded in agreement with his partner. It was all he could do with his jaw wired shut.

"You fulfilled the conditions of the first part of your contract," Brody said. "That's why I'm paying you each five-thousand dollars. But you failed to fulfill the second part. Not only did you leave one of the mayors alive, in violation of our agreement, your repeatedly bungled attempts to take corrective action not only didn't eliminate the surviving mayor, but have aroused the suspicions, and ire, of a very dangerous lawman—a former Texas Ranger who has a well-documented history of personal crusades—as well as the governor's ear. My sources in Jefferson City inform me that he's been appointed a federal marshal. As we speak, he is in Arkansas hunting for Jeremiah Rupe."

"Pritchard isn't going to find Rupe," Marsh said.

"That's my point, you imbecile," Brody snapped. "Marshal Pritchard's already publicly expressed doubts Rupe had anything to do with the derailment, robbery, and murders. When he doesn't find Rupe, or worse, uncovers evidence that Rupe is long dead, where do you think he'll look next?"

Marsh didn't immediately answer. He was busy wiping snot and blood from his handlebar mustache with a handkerchief. Pritchard's fist had left him with a shattered septum and missing an upper, and lower, front tooth.

"What about our other two men?" Marsh finally asked. "They need to get paid, too."

"Pay them out of your share," Brody said. "They're your men. Their failure is your responsibility."

"That isn't right," Marsh said. "Eleven of our boys were cashiered by Pritchard. That ought to count for something?"

"That's right," Brody smirked. "It counts as further proof you and the men you hired couldn't get the job done. It also counts, as you once said, as eleven men I don't have to pay."

"Be reasonable, Mr. Brody?" Marsh pleaded. "It's not like the money's coming out of your pocket? You've got over forty-thousand dollars from Jason Gould's payroll tucked away in your safe. Money that me, Asa, and our boys took from his railroad for you."

"And have been paid for," Brody said. He placed two stacks of five-thousand dollars in one-hundred-dollar bills on the table before Marsh and Finchum. "There's your money. Take it or leave it, but it's all you're going to get from the Brody Railroad."

Marsh and Finchum grudgingly scooped up the bills.

A knock sounded, and Brody's manservant, Charles, entered the car. "A Colonel Odom to see you," he said.

"Send him in," Brody commanded. Charles disappeared. Brody turned to Marsh and Finchum.

"This transaction concludes our business. I presume you gentlemen know what would happen to you if either of you decided to divulge anything of our previous dealings?"

"We're not fools," Marsh said.

"A debatable issue," Brody sneered. "Know this: should either of you, or the two remaining men in your employ, breathe a word out-of-turn to anyone I will spare no expense in my retribution, which will be final. Is that understood?"

Marsh and Finchum only nodded.

Brody dismissed them. "Good day."

Passing the two battered and gunless gunmen on their way out of Brody's private car was a medium-sized man in his mid-forties with a full head of closely-cropped white hair and a sculpted beard. He wore a riding suit, and removed a narrow-brimmed hat as he entered.

"Colonel Odom, I presume?" Brody asked, extending his hand.

"Walton Odom," the man introduced himself. He shook Brody's hand and closed the door behind him.

"Thank you for coming on such short notice," Brody said.

"Your telegram," Odom said, "and your generous retainer fee, made it hard for me to refuse."

"You come highly recommended," Brody continued.

"By whom?"

"A former friend and colleague," Brody said, gesturing to the bar. Odom nodded. "Dominic Quincy, God rest his soul."

"I rode with Cottonmouth Quincy during the war," Odom said. "I was only a captain, then."

"I know," Brody said. "Your exploits on behalf of the Union are well known." He poured brandy into two snifters from a recently re-filled decanter.

"What we did wasn't always for the Union," Odom said, accepting a glass.

"I know that, too," Brody said. "I also know you're a man of great repute."

Odom merely raised his glass and sipped.

"Most of your work now is for cattlemen, isn't it?"

Odom nodded. "Me and my boys spend the bulk of our time driving off sheepherders, tearing down fence, evicting squatters, and stringing rustlers." He shrugged. "It's a living."

"Ever work for a railroad before?"

"Not yours."

"You are now," Brody said. "How many men do you have with you?"

"I brought six of my best," Odom said. "Who do you want brought in or put down?"

"Two men. A one-legged Missouri mayor and a federal marshal. And I don't want them 'brought in.'"

"Understood," Odom said. "That marshal wouldn't be a former Reb who used to gun folks under the name Atherton and now wears the name Pritchard, would he?"

"He would," Brody said. "Is there a problem with that?"

"The mayor's no problem," Odom answered. "A federal marshal, who also happens to be an ex–Texas Ranger, is something altogether different."

"Can you do it," Brody asked impatiently, "or not?"

"Sure. Anybody can be ended. It's only a matter of how much grief if takes to get it done. Ending Pritchard will cost you extra, Mr. Brody. Bringing down a lawman of his reputation will bring other lawmen to avenge him. That's extra grief. Extra grief means it'll cost you extra."

"I'm willing to pay whatever it takes," Brody said.

"I like the sound of that."

"I'm also paying for your discretion, of course," Brody quickly added.

"Of course," Odom said. "All my employers do. Wouldn't be making much of a living in this business if I weren't discrete, would I?"

"So true," Brody said. "When can you get started?"

"Can I finish my drink?" Odom said.

Marsh and Finchum met up with Gilbert and the Big Man behind the caboose, well back of the main Brody Railroad Company's camp.

During the past several days, massive teams of horses led by hundreds of workers from both railroad companies had dismantled and pulled the damaged train cars from the creek, repaired the bridge spanning it, and replaced the tracks over it. The rapidity with which the derailed train was cleared spoke to the lost revenue for both railroads. In another day both camps would be broken, the workers ferried away, and little evidence of the tragedy at Rock Creek would be left in their wake.

"How much did you get?" the Big Man asked Marsh.

"Only a thousand dollars apiece," Marsh lied. "Which means we each get five-hundred."

"The hell you say," the Big Man fumed. "I was promised a thousand for the train job, another two-hundred for ridin' out into that storm, and expected a bonus on account of Brody not havin' to pay them ten boys Pritchard left bleachin' out on the prairie."

"Brody won't pay the full amount," Marsh said, "because he claims we didn't finish the job."

"And you let him buffalo you like that?" Gilbert demanded.

"What were we supposed to do?" Marsh said.

"Apparently not much," the Big Man spat, "seein' as how you both lost your guns again, and have been beaten like red-headed stepchildren."

Finchum's eyes flashed and Marsh's face reddened, yet neither had any choice but to take the Big Man 's verbal abuse. Both were, in fact, unarmed, and in no physical condition to engage in fisticuffs with either him or Gilbert.

"Maybe you and me oughta take it up with Mr. Brody ourselves?" Gilbert suggested to the Big Man.

"It wouldn't do no good," the Big Man grumbled. "We've done been replaced."

"Whaddya mean?" Gilbert said.

"He's right," Marsh cut in. "That fellow who just entered Brody's private car? It's Walton Odom. He's a former army colonel and professional killer from up north. And those six gun hands with him? You think Walton brought them along to churn butter?"

"He only brought six gun hands?" the Big Man scoffed. "Hell, Pritchard ended eleven of ours."

"Maybe Odom has better men?" Marsh said.

"Don't matter who they are," the Big Man said. "They're on the Brody payroll now, and we're not. That's what matters."

"So we're supposed to take this lyin' down?" Gilbert protested. "Give up what's owed us, and our jobs, to some old Union bounty hunter and his half-dozen gun hands?"

"What do you propose we do?" the Big Man retorted. "There's seven of them, countin' Colonel Odom and only four of us." He glared at Marsh and Finchum. "And two of us ain't even heeled."

"I know a way we can get paid what we're due," Marsh spoke up, "and get back at Brody at the same time."

"Shut up, Earl," the Big Man said. "I've had a belly full of your grand ideas."

"Let him speak," Gilbert said. "Iffen Earl's got a way to collect what's comin' to us, I wanna hear it."

"Aren't you boys forgetting the payroll we robbed from that train we wrecked?" Marsh said. "Forty-thousand dollars, if I recall?"

"Who's 'we,'" the Big Man challenged, "and what of it? That money's locked in a safe in Brody's private railroad car. A train car which happens to be surrounded by railroad guards armed with Winchester rifles."

"I know where it is," Marsh said. "I'm the fellow who put it there, remember?"

"Just how do you propose we get the payroll out?" the Big Man said.

"There's always a way," Marsh said. "Right, Asa?"

Finchum nodded and grinned as much as his damaged jaw would allow.

"Whatever you got planned for that forty-thousand," Gilbert said, "you'd best get it done quick. By the look of things in camp, both railroads will be pullin' out of Rock Creek tomorrow."

"That's what I'm planning on," Marsh said.

Chapter 22

When Pritchard and Strobl entered the Horseshoe Saloon, which was more than crowded, silence erupted like a cannon shot. The pianist stopped playing, the bartender stopped pouring, and the raucous conversation abruptly ended. All eyes were fixed on the six-and-a-half-foot-tall lawman in the wide-brimmed Stetson and his oddly dressed companion.

Patrons instinctively gave way as Pritchard strode across the sawdust-covered floor with Strobl in his wake. A large number of those imbibing inside the saloon wore guns and appeared to be newcomers to Fort Smith, just like he and Strobl.

When Pritchard got to the bar, he tilted his hat back on his head, revealing the bullet scar. He smiled at the bartender, who was a robust-looking fellow in his mid-fifties.

"I'll take a short beer," Pritchard said, tossing coins on the bar, "and whatever my friend is havin'."

"A brandy would do nicely," Strobl said, tipping his hat.

The bartender turned to fill the orders. Hushed murmurs broke the silence. Pritchard turned, placed both elbows on the polished bar, which required him to slouch considerably, and grinned at the sea of curious and hostile faces staring back at him.

A large man with a deep scar across one cheek and wearing a battered Boss of the Plains adorned with an eagle feather stood from where he was playing cards and approached the bar. He was wearing a pair of low-slung Army Colts.

"You're Atherton, ain't ya?" the man demanded.

"Nope," Pritchard said. "Name's Pritchard."

"You're a-lyin'," the man challenged. "I seen you gun a feller in Laramie 'bout five years after the war. You was a Ranger named Atherton, then. Smokin' Joe, they called you."

"I recall," Pritchard said.

"The feller you gunned," the man said, "was Dakota Pete Buchalter. He was a friend of mine."

"My condolences," Pritchard said.

The man turned his head and spat. "I don't like it, you shootin' my friend."

"Maybe your friend shouldn't have pulled on me," Pritchard said casually, "from behind my back?"

"Pete never was too smart," the man said, "nor particular fast with his iron." An oily smile spread across his scarred face. "Me, I'm plenty fast."

If the room was quiet before, one could now hear a pin drop.

"Your drinks," the bartender said, setting a mug of beer and a brandy on the bar. After he set the drinks down, he backed nervously out of the line-of-fire.

Pritchard turned around, picked up the drinks, and handed the brandy to Strobl. He kept his beer in his left hand as he raised his glass. Strobl did the same. Both men drank.

"Don't you turn your back on me," the man said. He thumbed off the leather loops restraining the hammers of his holstered revolvers.

"Not a bad lager," Pritchard said to Strobl, ignoring the man behind him. He wiped his mouth on his sleeve. "Cold, too."

"The brandy isn't anything to write home about," Strobl said, "but it 'wets the whistle,' as you Americans like to say."

"Hey," the man said. "I'm talkin' to you, Atherton."

"I done told you," Pritchard said over his shoulder, "my name ain't Atherton. Best leave me be."

"I'll leave you face down in the sawdust," the man said, "that's what I'll do. Turn yourself around and face me like a man."

All those standing near Pritchard and Strobl scooted hastily away.

Pritchard shook his head in annoyance. "It's hard for a feller to have himself a quiet drink around here," he remarked to Strobl.

"Tragic," Strobl acknowledged, "but true."

"Turn around, Atherton," the man said again. Both of his hands were poised over the butts of his holstered revolvers. "Turn around and take what's comin'."

"Can I finish my beer first?" Pritchard said over his shoulder.

"TURN AROUND!" the man shouted. His oily smile had been replaced with fury.

"Suit yourself," Pritchard said.

Faster than most would expect a man of his great size

to move, Pritchard wheeled around to face his challenger. In the same split second, he tossed the contents of his mug in the man's face and drew his right-hand Colt.

But instead of thumbing back the hammer and firing, Pritchard executed a reverse Road Agent's Spin and brought the weapon's butt crashing down on the man's head. The scarred man in the hat with the eagle feather collapsed to the floor without ever touching either of his guns.

Another split second later, Pritchard had his left-hand gun out and leveled alongside his right, which he had put into firing position with another Road Agent's Spin. Both pistols now had their hammers back and were aimed at everyone, and no one, in the room.

Strobl, without seemingly being noticed, had dropped his brandy, drawn both of his Chamelot Delvigne revolvers, and was also covering the room. Since his weapons were double-action in design, he hadn't bothered to thumb back their hammers.

"I'm a-gonna order me and my friend another drink," Pritchard announced to those assembled in the saloon, "on account of this feller spillin' our first ones. Next feller who interrupts our sippin' ain't gonna get a lump on the head; he'll be gettin' blue whistlers outta our guns. Any questions?"

Nobody spoke. Pritchard lowered his guns' hammers, holstered, and bent down to remove the two revolvers from the man lying unconscious at his feet. He set them on the bar, along with a roll of cash he found in the man's vest pocket.

"Drinks are on him," he said to the bartender, pointing his thumb at the snoring man on the ground. The piano started up again. The crowd began to whoop and holler as they rushed the bar.

Pritchard and Strobl ducked from the path of the thirsty mob. Pritchard approached a saloon girl who'd been pushed aside in the rush for free drinks.

"What's your name, handsome?" she cooed, as she looked up at the tall lawman. She batted her eyes, patted her hair, and sidled up. "My, but you're a big one." She was a petite brunette with an hourglass figure and wearing a lot of makeup. "My name's Mimi."

"I'm Samuel," Pritchard said, "and I'm lookin' for somebody."

"Aren't we all," Mimi said. She stepped in closer, pressing her breasts against Pritchard's abdomen. "I'm somebody," she smiled. "Why don't you find me?"

"Actually," Pritchard said, "I'm lookin' for a feller named Hoke Rupe? Heard tell he waters himself here."

"Figures," she harrumphed. "Everybody's been lookin' for that old drunk lately." She pointed to a bearded man sitting round-shouldered over a bottle at a table in one corner of the saloon.

"Obliged," Pritchard said, as he tipped his hat.

"If you want anything else," Mimi offered, as he and Strobl headed across the saloon, "you know where to find me."

Pritchard and Strobl approached the seated man. He looked to be in his late forties, was tall, and had a deeply lined face and scraggly beard. He wore simple, clean, clothes that looked new. One hand was wrapped around a bottle and the other held an empty glass.

"Are you Hoke Rupe?" Pritchard asked.

"Been asked that more times in the past few days than

I've been asked in my whole life," the man said without looking up. "Who wants to know this time?"

"U.S. Marshal Samuel Pritchard. This here's Deputy U.S. Marshal Strobl. We're from Missouri."

"I've heard of you," the man said. "You fought for the South, just like me and my brother Jem, didn't you?"

"I did."

"I'm Hoke Rupe, all right," he admitted. "Folks say you're a helluva gun hand, Pritchard. A pure killer. That you'll shoot a man down just for squintin' in the noonday sun." He gestured with his empty glass at the unconscious man lying on the saloon floor. "Guess them folks are wrong."

"Folks say a lot of things," Pritchard said. "Like Jeremiah Rupe is dead, for instance."

"Lemme guess? You're looking for Jem, ain't you?"

"That's right."

"You and everybody else on both sides of the Mississippi," Hoke grumbled. "I make most folks buy me a drink or two before I tell 'em what I'm gonna tell you, Marshal Pritchard. But since I just watched you spare a man's life that you could've surely ended, I'll tell you for nothin.' My brother Jem is under the snakes. That's where his is, all right. Shot dead and buried, nigh on ten years ago. No matter what bedtime stories you've been told, dead men don't walk around. And they damn sure don't wreck trains in Missouri."

"Ain't so sure about that," Pritchard said. He sat down across from Hoke without being invited and removed his hat, revealing the bullet scar over his right eye. "I've been shot dead, Mr. Rupe. Was buried, too, as a matter-of-fact. I'm still walkin' around, ain't I?"

Hoke looked up. His eyes met Pritchard's as he took in the scar on his forehead.

"I reckon so," he said.

"You'd best know," Pritchard said, "that unlike every other feller who's been houndin' you about your brother's whereabouts lately, I don't want any bounty money. And I don't want to kill him, either."

"Then what do you want?"

"To clear his name."

"Huh?" Hoke said. "You wanna clear Jem's name?"

"You heard me. Iffen your brother is still alive, and I ain't sayin' he is, I don't believe he wrecked that train in Missouri."

"Why not?" Hoke said. "From what I hear, durn near everybody else believes he did. It's why there's a bounty on him bigger than the one Pontius Pilate put up on Jesus. It's why every gun from here to Mexico is in Fort Smith askin' me where he is. And it's why I'm gettin' drinks bought for me like I was the virgin belle of the ball. Tell me, lawman, why don't you believe Jem wrecked that train?"

"Because a very powerful man is tryin' too hard to convince everybody he did," Pritchard said.

Hoke stared at Pritchard through bleary eyes for a long minute before he spoke again. "What would you do iffen you found him?" he finally said.

"If Jem's dead, I wanna see his bones for myself," Pritchard said. "If he's not, I want to speak to him. I wanna look him in the eye and hear him tell me in his own words whether he wrecked that train or not."

Hoke poured the last remnants of the bottle into his glass, downed it, and wiped his mouth on his sleeve.

"Let's get out of here," he said. He stood on shaky legs and put on his hat. "Too many ears are perked up in this saloon."

"We're right behind you," Pritchard said, resuming his feet. He and Strobl followed Hoke Rupe from the saloon under the watchful eyes of dozens of armed patrons.

Chapter 23

"You shouldn't be up," Idelle scolded. "You're going to make yourself sick again."

"I can't lay around in bed forever," Ditch answered, as he balanced himself on his new crutch. "After all, I am the mayor. Somebody's got to run this town."

Ditch was hobbling across the lobby of the Atherton Arms Hotel on a crutch made for him by Seth Tilley, who promised to have his wooden leg finished within the week. Ditch told the undertaker and woodworker to take his time, since the wound below his left knee was still raw. It would likely be several weeks before the site of the amputation would be sufficiently healed to support an artificial limb.

In the meantime, Ditch asked Tilley to construct the crutch to tide him over until he was ready to strap on the wooden leg. He was determined to get out of bed and become ambulatory as soon as possible. The fact that he was a skilled horse breaker meant he already possessed uncommonly acute balance, even on one leg. But he was still weak from the recent loss of so much blood and had yet to fully regain his strength or color. Sweat broke out over his face as he hobbled back and forth across the lobby floor.

Idelle held Baby Samuel, who giggled and squirmed as she followed in Ditch's footsteps and fretted. Deputy Tater Jessup sat in one of the plush chairs by the hotel doors, sipping a cup of coffee. He wore Ditch Clemson's holstered revolver around his substantial belly, held in place by a belt he had made at the tannery only the day before.

Due to Tater's girth, the belt was constructed large enough to facilitate loops for a full box of fifty .45 Colt cartridges. His double-barreled messenger gun rested against his chair, and the pockets of his overalls were stuffed with 12-gauge shells.

"Gonna be a right nice day today," Tater commented. "Good plantin' weather."

"If my husband doesn't take it easy," Idelle retorted, "the only thing that's going to be planted around here is him."

"Don't worry," Tater said. "Your husband ain't gonna be planted anytime soon. He's as tough as they come, ain't ya, Ditch?"

"Sure, I am," Ditch huffed, as he hobbled over to the chair across from Tater and plopped heavily into it. "Tough as hickory bark, that's me." He looked at Tater and wiped his brow. "Is that my revolver?"

"It surely is," Tater confirmed. "The holster, too. The belt ain't yours, though," he said sheepishly. "Your belt weren't long enough."

"I've never known you to wear a short gun," Ditch said.

"I generally don't," Tater agreed. "But Samuel . . . er . . . Marshal Pritchard, gave me strict orders. He told me to protect you and your family. He also told me to wear this pistol and to keep my scattergun handy at all times. He was right particular about it, Ditch, and when Marshal Pritchard gives me an order, I carry it out."

"I know that, Tater," Ditch said. "And I'm grateful. Not just to you, but to all the men on the Vigilance Committee who are lookin' out for me and my family."

Tater poured coffee for Ditch. "Heck," he said, "we don't need Marshal Pritchard to order us to look out for you, Miss Idelle, and Baby Samuel. That's what men do. And besides, I'm a deputy town marshal." He tapped the badge on his chest. "Says so right here. I got me a proper duty to carry out."

"Yes, you do," Ditch said. "And a deputy of your caliber shouldn't be performin' his duties with a borrowed pistol. I'll tell you what, Tater. After lunch, you're goin' down to the mercantile and see Wynn Samples. You tell him to pick you out a new Colt's revolver and a holster to carry it in. Then I can have mine back, and you'll have one of your own."

"I couldn't do that," Tater protested. "I cain't afford no brand-new Colt's pistol. Them guns cost twenty dollars each, which is half my monthly wages."

"The hell you can't," Ditch said. "You ain't payin' for it. I, as Mayor of Atherton, am purchasing the firearm to arm one of my deputies—that's you. It's an official town purchase. And I ain't takin' no for an answer. I'm your boss in Samuel's absence, and I'm orderin' you to get yourself a pistol. That's my final word on the matter."

"Iffen you put it that way," Tater said, scratching his head.

The hotel doors opened and in came Judge Pearson and John Babbit. Both still wore holstered revolvers, the judge's beneath his suit coat and the newspaperman's over his ink-stained apron. They tipped their hats to Idelle.

"We got word you wanted to see us?" Babbit said.

"That's right," Ditch said. "I have a request for you, John, as telegraph operator. It's official business, so I wanted Judge Pearson to bear witness. Normally, I'd convene a meeting of the town council but there isn't time."

"Sure," Babbit said. "What would you like me to do?"

"I want you to fire off a passel of telegrams," Ditch began. "One to Governor Hardin, and one each to all of the telegraph operators in all the towns in eastern Missouri, especially the towns who lost a mayor in the Rock Creek train wreck."

Babbit removed a pad and pencil from his apron pocket. "What shall I send out?"

"Tell everyone that I'm recommending all the communities band together. I want to forge an agreement in regards to that big railroad expansion Governor Hardin is brokerin' with the army and U.S. government. You tell 'em that Mayor Ditch Clemson, of Atherton Missouri, the lone surviving mayor of the Rock Creek Train Wreck, ain't gonna let Governor Hardin sign any contract with either the Missouri Pacific or Brody Railroad until Samuel's—I mean Marshal Pritchard's—special investigation is completed. I want the other mayors, and acting mayors, to join me."

"That's going to stir up a hornets' nest," Judge Pearson said. "John Brody and Jay Gould aren't going to take kindly to such a pact among the towns in Eastern Missouri. Not one bit."

"That's my intention," Ditch said. "Samuel's of a mind that one of those railroads, perhaps both in cahoots, is behind this mess. Until we know for sure, I ain't gonna allow the Town of Atherton, or Jackson County for that matter, to support any expansion agreement with either railroad."

"Can't the U.S. government and the army plow on ahead with their railroad 'spansion plans anyway?" Tater asked. "Whether local towns like Atherton object or not?"

"You're right, Tater," Judge Pearson said. "Legally, they can. But I see what Ditch is getting at. If Governor Hardin wants to get re-elected, he'd best not stand idle while the army and the U.S. government run roughshod over the objections of half the municipalities in his state. Hardin could march ahead against the objections of all the towns, but doing so would be political suicide come the next election and he knows it."

"Do you think most of the other towns will agree to Ditch's proposal?" Idelle asked.

"I'm certain of it," Babbit answered her. "Ditch is extremely popular in the region, as is Marshal Pritchard. The railroad companies—especially now, after the train wreck—are not. I'd be surprised if a single town or county doesn't agree to what your husband is proposing."

"I concur," Judge Pearson said. "Despite his youth, Ditch Clemson's name comes up as a potential gubernatorial candidate regularly. Don't think Governor Hardin doesn't know that, too."

"I'll get this telegram written up and sent out right away," Babbit said, "and see that it gets to the entire eastern half of the state. What would you like me to send to the governor?"

"Just send him a copy of the one you're sending out to

everybody else," Ditch said, "but add that I expect to hear from his office as soon as he knows any more about the train wreck and robbery. Because until I find out, I'm bringing his railroad expansion plans in Eastern Missouri to a standstill."

"Consider it done," Babbit said.

"May I make a recommendation?" Pearson said.

"By all means," Ditch said.

"I suggest John, as editor of the *Athertonian,* also write up an editorial explaining in detail our suspicions and reservations regarding the origin of the train wreck? He wouldn't have to draw any conclusions, since there are none to draw yet with Samuel's investigation still underway. But he could certainly express doubts, and the fact that there's an investigation at all will get most folks thinking. Tempers are hot right now, and sentiment was already leaning heavily against the railroads before the train wreck at Rock Creek. The editorial might put additional pressure on the governor to resist what I suspect are significant financial incentives being offered to him, under the table, of course, from the two competing railroads. Both Brody and Gould badly want that government contract for their own. A press campaign which makes the voting public aware of the potential for such a backroom deal would give Governor Hardin pause."

"I like it," Ditch said.

"Me, too," Babbit agreed. "After I print the editorial in the *Athertonian,* I'll make sure it gets circulated to the newspapers in Kansas City, Independence, Jefferson City, and Saint Louis. It'll be like tossing that hornets' nest

Judge Pearson mentioned into the middle of a church picnic."

"That's exactly what I aim to do," Ditch said. "Let the governor know that if he ain't careful, he's gonna get stung."

Seated in the hotel's restaurant, with a view into the lobby, sat two men. Both were innocuous-looking in appearance and wore ill-fitting city suits. They carried valises not unlike traveling salesmen and were enjoying lunch. They'd arrived in Atherton on the morning train.

"That's him, all right," the first man said in a low tone.

"Of course, it is," the second man replied. "The missing leg and busted arm kinda gives it away, don't-cha think?"

"Who's the prime article with him? His wife? She's a looker, ain't she?"

"I reckon so," came the reply. "Right handsome woman, I'll give her that. Cute kid, too."

"Don't get soft," the other man cautioned. "Didn't you notice that deputy who's never more than a few feet from all three of 'em?"

"That old tub-o-lard?" the first man chuckled. "How could I miss him? He ain't gonna be no trouble when the time comes."

"I wouldn't be too sure. You notice his shotgun?"

"I saw it. I also saw all those townies outside with rifles."

"I spotted 'em, too," the first man said. "None of 'em are gun hands. They look like shopkeepers, liverymen, and saloonkeepers, takin' up arms on account of their marshal bein' gone. Just a local vigilance committee, I'll bet," he scoffed in contempt.

"This job ain't gonna be hard," the second man said, looking warily around. "Not hard at all."

"Not hard," the first man agreed, "but likely messy."

Chapter 24

Pritchard, Strobl, and Hoke Rupe stopped for the night on the banks of a large creek. They'd ridden thirty miles from Fort Smith, and it was only another ten to Booneville, but darkness had fallen and Hoke suggested they cease their journey for the night. The effects of his last bottle seemed to be wearing off, and he wearily insisted they make camp. He led them to a spot he knew that was, in fact, a very nice campsite.

Once they stopped Hoke perked up. He gathered wood and built a large fire while Strobl tended to the horses and Pritchard unpacked their saddlebags, dug out the eating utensils, and prepared dinner. Soon the smell of sizzling venison strips, spiced beans, and boiling coffee permeated the camp.

"Somethin' smells mighty good," Hoke declared. Pritchard and Strobl were seated by the fire. Both still wore their hats and had their rifles across their laps.

"Supper's almost ready," Pritchard said. He pointed to the waterline. "You might want to wash up. You've got a scent about you like a liquor barrel."

"What's with the long arms?" Hoke asked. "You expectin' hostile company?"

"Could be," Pritchard said.

"Whaddya mean?" Hoke said.

"You were in no condition to notice," Strobl explained, "but when we left Fort Smith, quite a few interested parties observed our departure."

"We wouldn't be hard to track," Pritchard added.

"Everybody's lookin' for poor Jem," Hoke muttered, as he went off to the water's edge. "The fools." He removed his hat, knelt, and dunked his head.

"I suspect that creek is the only water Mr. Rupe has consumed in quite a while," Strobl said with a laugh.

"I suspect you're right," Pritchard said. He set his rifle against the log and loaded a plate with venison strips and beans. Strobl poured coffee into a tin cup. When Hoke returned, shaking water from his hair and beard like a wet dog, they handed the items over.

"Obliged," Hoke said, as he accepted his supper and coffee. "You wouldn't have any whiskey in those saddlebags, would you, Marshal? To season the coffee?"

"I've got whiskey," Pritchard confirmed. "Why don't you put somethin' else in your belly first? We'll enjoy a taste of the bottle after supper."

"Sure thing," Hoke said, though he sounded disappointed. He sat down and began to eat. "You really think some of those durned bounty killers might've followed us all the way out here?"

"One-hundred-thousand dollars is a lot of money," Pritchard said, as he served Strobl. "But they shouldn't bother us tonight."

"Why not?" Hoke asked around a mouthful of beans.

"No reason to, yet," Pritchard said. "If they're smart, they'll wait until we lead 'em to your brother to make their play."

"But I already done told you," Hoke said. "Jem's dead."

"Doesn't seem like many folks believe that," Pritchard said, filling his own plate, "does it?"

"I reckon you don't, leastways," Hoke said.

"How exactly did your brother die?"

"Jem came home to his wife and daughter after the surrender, a wounded, hunted, man. Since he'd refused to lay down arms and give up, the Union put a price on his head. Wouldn't have made no difference iffen he had given himself up. He'd already been labeled a war criminal after the Platte Bridge affair. Iffen Jem had surrendered he'd have been strung, just like Captain Marcellus Clarke. Everything Clarke did, just like Jem, was under lawful orders—General Sterling Price even said so—but they hanged him just the same."

"Those who win wars are called victors," Strobl commented. "Those who lose are called criminals. It is the way of all wars."

"What happened to Jem once he got back to Arkansas?" Pritchard asked. "It's rumored he was done in by a posse?"

"That's true," Hoke said, shaking his head. "He was up in the Ouachita's, hidin' from the government and starvin' through the winter. He had to hide out because even back then, bounty killers was keepin' an eye on his wife and little girl. Jem was a big feller—almost as tall as you, Marshal—and weighed over three-hundred pounds. But the last time I saw him, in the winter of sixty-six, he was nothin' but skin and bones. He got word his wife caught the typhus, and when he came outta the hills to visit her a couple of bounty men and some soldiers were waitin' for him. They shot him in Booneville, but he was able to ride off and they lost him. That's when I went off lookin' for him."

"You found him?" Strobl asked.

"His body, anyhow," Hoke said. He finished his food and turned his attention to his coffee. "He was layin' dead in a pine hollow. I buried him without no marker. Nobody but me knows where."

"What became of his wife and child?" Strobl asked.

"His wife died a week after he did. She's buried in the Booneville Presbyterian Church cemetery. His daughter was taken in by the pastor. She's all growed up now, and lives there still."

"Iffen you don't mind me askin'," Pritchard said, "why didn't you take your niece in and raise her yourself? After all, she's your kin?"

"Wish I could've," Hoke said. "I wasn't the man for the job. I weren't married, was drinkin' hard, even then, and at the time was wanted by the law myself." His eyes took on a faraway look. "Jem wasn't the only Rupe who did some guerilla fightin' for the Confederacy."

"I know what you mean," Pritchard said. "Done a fair bit durin' the war myself. Reckon if I hadn't joined the Texas Rangers, the government would've come after me, too."

Pritchard suddenly stood up, levered his rifle, and turned away from fire and into the darkness. Strobl did the same, but faced in the opposite direction so they were back-to-back. "Show yourself," Pritchard announced, "or we start a-shootin'."

"No need for gunplay," a man's voice called out from the darkness. "Just want to talk, Marshal, that's all."

Pritchard gestured to Hoke, who kicked dirt over the

fire. As darkness enveloped the campsite, Pritchard and Strobl moved to new locations, knelt, and shouldered their rifles.

"Weren't cause to put out your fire," the voice said. "Iffen we wanted to shoot you boys, you'd be shot already."

"What do you want?" Pritchard said.

"Same thing you do," the voice said. "To find Arkansas Jem and cash in. We know you don't believe he's dead, or else you wouldn't be trampin' around his old stompin' grounds with his drunkard brother."

"So find him yourself," Pritchard said.

"That's what we're doin'," the voice said. "Except we ain't gonna do the findin'. You're gonna do it for us."

"What makes you think I'm gonna do anything for you?"

"Cause iffen you don't," the voice said, "we'll end you. I've got enough boys with me to finish you, Marshal, and your deputy, too."

"Then do it," Pritchard said, "and spare us your boastin'."

"You're doubtin' we ca—"

The voice was cut short by a shot from Pritchard's Winchester. A second later came the dull *thud* of an adult man striking the earth from standing height. Pritchard had deliberately engaged the man in conversation and used the sound of his voice to locate him in the dark.

Pritchard moved several feet to his left. "Lie down flat," he ordered Strobl and Hoke in a whisper. An instant later a volley of rifle and pistol fire blazed through the camp. Pritchard guessed there were five or six guns, at most, that were aimed at where the muzzle flash of his Winchester had been a moment before.

Pritchard and Strobl immediately began returning fire. They fired, levered fresh rounds into their rifles, and fired again, aiming at the muzzle flashes blinking at them from the darkness. Each of their respective rifles, Pritchard's Winchester .44-40 and Strobl's Henry .44, held fifteen cartridges in their tubular magazines. Both men fired at least ten times before the gunfire coming at them stopped. In the silence that ensued after the shooting ended, they heard a man scream, another grunt, and the sound of several horses riding away.

"Come on back tomorrow mornin'," Pritchard called out into the darkness after the retreating attackers. "Breakfast is served at sunup."

"That certainly added a bit of excitement to dinner," Strobl said, as he and Pritchard stood up, "although very little to my digestion."

"I reckon they've had enough for tonight," Pritchard said. "But I'm fairly sure we ain't seen the last of 'em."

"I concur," Strobl said. "I'll sleep with one eye open, and my rifle in hand, if I sleep at all."

"We can take shifts on watch," Pritchard agreed, as both men reloaded their rifles. "How about you, Hoke? You ready for that drink now? I reckon all three of us could use one."

There was no answer from Hoke, who remained prone and motionless on the ground.

"Hoke?" Pritchard said. He still didn't move or answer. Pritchard and Strobl rushed to his side.

They found him conscious, but just barely. He'd been shot in the stomach, and he was groaning and clutching the whiskey bottle from Pritchard's saddlebags. They rolled him gently onto his back.

"He must've decided to stand up and go for the bottle in our saddlebags when the shootin' commenced," Pritchard said to Strobl, "instead of gettin' down flat like he was told."

"Imprudent," Strobl said, "at best."

"Gimme a slug of that whiskey," Hoke sputtered. His voice was hoarse and weak.

"That's not a good idea," Strobl said, as Pritchard tore away Hoke's shirt and examined his wound. He met Strobl's eyes and silently shook his head. Both men had seen enough gunshot wounds to know the assessment was irrefutable.

"Sure it is," Hoke said. "I'm gutshot. We all know what that means. I'm goin' goslin' shortly. Ain't no reason to go on the journey thirsty, is there?"

"I reckon not," Pritchard said. He uncorked the bottle and poured some down Hoke's throat.

"Thank you, Marshal," Hoke smiled. A moment after he swallowed, he winced in agony.

"I gotta know," Pritchard said, "is Jem alive? These are near your dyin' words, Hoke. I'll have no more fairy tales about findin' your brother's carcass and buryin' it un-awares. If I'm to bring those who wrecked that Missouri train to account, and clear Jem's name, I must have the truth."

"Take me into Booneville," Hoke began, as his voice grew weaker, "and I'll introduce you to his daughter. Maybe she'll tell you what became of her father? I won't. I swore an oath, and I ain't a-gonna break it, deathbed or not. That's the best I can do, Marshal."

"It'll have to do," Pritchard said. He turned to Strobl. "Saddle up the horses, Florian. We ain't got much time."

"I don't expect you do," Hoke agreed. Blood dribbled from his mouth. "There's something else I want you to know, Marshal."

"I'm listenin'," Pritchard said.

"I done what I done for Jem because he's my brother," Hoke said, grabbing Pritchard by the shirtfront. You'd have done the same, iffen your brother was bein' hounded by a lynchin' party."

"I reckon so," Pritchard said, remembering his father's lynching.

Chapter 25

Pritchard, Strobl, and Hoke Rupe arrived in Booneville a little after midnight. The ten-mile ride into town took longer than expected, due to Hoke's fragile condition. Pritchard rode ahead of him, and Strobl behind, fearing the wounded rider would fall from his saddle. But Hoke did not, and a couple of hours later they reached the town limits. They were met on the main road by two men armed with rifles and a lantern. Both wore badges.

"Whoa there!" one of the men called out. "Who are you, and what's your business in Booneville?"

"Deputy U.S. Marshals Samuel Pritchard and Florian Strobl," Pritchard answered from horseback. "We've got an injured man here. He's been shot and needs a doctor."

"The doctor's busy fixin' up a troupe of fellers who come ridin' in a little while ago," the other Booneville deputy said, as both lowered their rifles. "Three men, all shot to hell."

"I'll wager those are the lads who attacked our campsite," Strobl offered.

"What's left of 'em, anyhow," Pritchard agreed. "Where can I find the doc?" he inquired.

"Don't bother with the doctor," Hoke said, his voice tight with pain. He was leaning over the pommel, his face was ashen, and he appeared near collapse. "Even if a sawbones could do anything for me, which he can't, I ain't got much time left. Get me to the Presbyterian church."

"Sure enough," Pritchard said.

"The church is at the far end of town," one of the deputies said. "Biggest one in Booneville. You can't miss it."

"Obliged," Pritchard said. "Is Bob Blevins still the sheriff here?"

"He is," the deputy answered. "You know him?"

"I do," Pritchard said. "Iffen I could impose on you fellers further, would you get word to Bob that Samuel Pritchard is down at the Presbyterian church?"

"Bob's likely fast asleep at this hour," the other deputy said.

"He'll get his britches on for me," Pritchard said, reining his horse toward the church.

The Presbyterian church was as big as the deputies had described it. It was almost a quarter-mile out of town, but clearly visible by virtue of the steeple, which made it the tallest building in or around Booneville.

When they got to the church, Pritchard helped Hoke from the saddle while Strobl tied their horses to the hitching post. The trio mounted the steps with the two deputy marshals holding the wounded man upright between them. Strobl pounded on the door.

After a minute, which Hoke spent spitting blood, the large double-doors opened. Greeting them was a very tall, lean man in a nightshirt holding a candle. He had thick, muttonchop whiskers and an eyepatch over his right eye.

"I'm right sorry to bother you at this hour," Pritchard

began, "but this feller's been gutshot. He asked us to bring him here. His name is—"

"Henry," the large man said, as his shoulders slumped in recognition. "Henry Rupe. I know him well. I'm Reverend Oliver Winfield. Bring him inside."

Hoke collapsed as he started forward and Pritchard caught him. He carried the now barely conscious man as Winfield led them through the nave to the rear of the church where the pastor's quarters were located.

Suddenly a young woman appeared. Her hair was up, and she was dressed in a robe. "What's going on?" she asked, clearly having only just awakened.

"It's your Uncle Hoke," Winfield said. "He's been shot."

"Oh no!" the young woman exclaimed. She started to rush forward.

"No." Winfield halted her. "Go inside and boil some water. Bring it, and some whiskey, into the bed chambers."

The woman disappeared. Winfield opened a door and motioned for Pritchard to place Hoke on a bed in the center of the room as he lit a pair of kerosene lamps.

Hoke lay on his back, his hands clasped across his blood-soaked stomach. His face was gray, he was trembling, and he was sweating profusely, though it was not a warm night. He gazed up at the towering reverend with eyes rapidly losing focus.

"I promised . . . to bring the marshal . . . to meet Tess," he gasped, speaking through spasms of pain, "iffen he . . . brung me . . . here."

"I understand," Winfield said.

"I kept . . . my oath," Hoke said, as Winfield sat on the

bed and gently pulled his hands apart. "I never . . . said . . . nothin'. Not . . . never. I swear."

"I know," Winfield said. He opened Hoke's bloody shirt and examined the wound. After seeing the injury, he closed his only eye, sighed, and nodded once to himself in resignation.

"Whiskey?" Hoke said, His own eyes closed, and the tension in his body slackened.

Winfield opened his eye, looked at Pritchard, and nodded. Strobl handed the reverend the bottle. He started to press it to the wounded man's lips, but stopped when he realized it was too late. Hoke Rupe was dead.

Reverend Winfield made a sign of the cross and touched Hoke's forehead. As he was standing, the young woman entered. The reverend blocked her view of the bed with his body.

"The water is still boiling," she said. "How's Uncle Hoke?"

"He's gone," Winfield said softly. "Your uncle is at peace now."

The woman, who looked to be no more than twenty years old and was quite pretty, put her face in her hands and began to cry. Winfield embraced her, and held her as her crying became sobbing. Pritchard signaled Strobl, and both discretely made their way from the room.

Pritchard turned back to look as he crossed the doorway. In the dim light of the kerosene lamps, he saw a single tear trailing from the reverend's unpatched eye.

Chapter 26

A distinguished-looking man stepped off the Atherton train platform, then turned and extended his gloved hand to the woman stepping off behind him. The man sported a thick head of closely cropped white hair, a matching beard, and was wearing an expensive suit, gloves, and a Homburg. The woman accompanying him, clad in an equally expensive dress and hat and holding a parasol, was very attractive. Behind them followed a burly servant carrying their luggage.

The man was Colonel Walton Odom, and an engraved Richards-Mason .41 caliber Colt revolver rested in a holster beneath his jacket under his left arm. The woman was a prostitute he'd hired for the day as his consort, and the couple's baggage carrier was one of Odom's burlier gun hands. A pair of Remington .44s were tucked in his belt under his coat.

"I beg your pardon," Odom asked the station agent, "but could you direct us to the Atherton Arms Hotel?"

"Sure," the agent said around his wad of tobacco. "Tall, fancy, building in the town square, right across from the new courthouse. Gotta big ole sign. Cain't miss it."

Odom tipped his hat, extended his elbow, and began strolling leisurely toward town with the woman on his arm. The baggage handler walked closely behind them.

"How'll we know him when we see him?" the handler asked in a hushed voice.

"He shouldn't be hard to spot," Odom said. "He's only got one leg, remember?"

"All I remember," the handler said, "is the two scouts you sent comin' back and tellin' us he's got a deputy with a scattergun who don't leave his side. I don't fancy a belly full of buckshot."

"That's what you're here for," Odom said calmly. "You'll take out the deputy, and I'll dispatch Mayor Clemson. It's as simple as could be."

"But the scouts also said there was a Vigilance Committee about," the handler argued. "Men with guns, lurkin' around the mayor and his family."

"Don't worry," Odom reassured him. "From what our boys reported, this Vigilance Committee is nothing but shopkeepers and farm hands. Marshal Pritchard is out of town, remember? There's likely not a true pistoleer among them. Besides, we're ready for them. Don't forget, our other five men are already in town, over at the saloon. They'll be watching, and when they see us approach the hotel, they'll move in to back our play."

"I'm scared," the woman suddenly blurted. "I didn't know there was gonna be gunplay."

"You weren't too scared," Odom reminded her, "when I gave you that fifty dollars, were you?"

"You didn't say nothin' about no guns," the woman protested.

"I didn't have to," Odom said. "Why else would I be

payin' a two-dollar whore fifty dollars? Now be silent and act like what you're supposed to be, an obedient wife."

The trio walked in silence for the remainder of their short journey into the heart of Atherton. As they strolled down the main street, Odom took in the sights. He spotted the stately Atherton Arms Hotel exactly where the station agent said it would be. Across the picturesque town square, at the Sidewinder Saloon, he recognized one of his men standing outside. The man was dressed as a cowhand, and making an elaborate gesture of checking one of the six horses tied to the hitching post in front of the saloon.

Odom gave a slight nod to the cowhand, and got a nod in return. The man then waved to another, similarly dressed, man standing just inside the Sidewinder's swinging doors. A minute later, just as Odom, his consort, and their baggage handler reached the steps of the Atherton Hotel, four men emerged from the saloon. All, like the man outside they joined, were dressed as cowhands and armed with at least one pistol. They strode in a single group across the square toward the hotel.

Deputy Tater Jessup held the hotel room door for Idelle, who was carrying Baby Samuel. Her husband Ditch followed behind her. He was getting proficient on his crutch, despite the short amount of time he'd been on it, and was determined to get even more proficient before he transferred to his wooden leg in a few weeks. Tater fell in behind them. Around Ditch's waist was belted his Colt revolver, because around Tater's waist was his new one.

Acting on Mayor Ditch Clemson's orders, Tater had

dutifully gone to see Wynn Samples at the Atherton Mercantile. He'd obtained, at city expense, a spankin'-new Colt Army Model .45 revolver with the seven-and-one-half-inch barrel, along with a holster to carry it. He wore it high, above his sizable belly, in a belt stoked with fresh cartridges.

In addition to his new sidearm, Tater carried his double-barreled coach gun. It was mid-morning, and Ditch noticed the portly deputy eyeing the big clock down in the hotel lobby as they descended the stairs.

"Late for an appointment?" Ditch asked.

"Just noticin' the time, that's all," Tater replied.

"I know what time it is," Ditch chuckled. "It's halfway between breakfast and lunch."

"Aw, Ditch," Tater grumbled, "taint my fault my gullet is always gnawin' at me and watchin' the clock. You wouldn't understand, bein' such a slim feller."

"I understand," Ditch laughed, as he carefully conquered the stairs, one-at-a-time, on his good leg and crutch. "I'm only joshin' with you, Tater. Truth be told, I'm already gettin' a hankerin' for lunch myself."

Idelle, with Samuel in her arms, frequently paused and looked back to ensure her husband was all right on the stairs. She smiled when she heard him mention he was hungry. The return of his appetite was a sign his body was healing.

Just as Tater, Ditch, Idelle, and Baby Samuel reached the bottom of the stairs, a distinguished-looking and well-dressed man with white hair and a white beard, escorting a very comely and much-younger woman, entered the hotel. Trailing behind them was a tall, burly, man lugging a pair of suitcases.

Idelle and Ditch had no sooner smiled a silent greeting to the newcomers when the burly man with the suitcases abruptly dropped them. He swept open his coat and drew a pair of revolvers from his belt.

At the same time, the distinguished-looking man elbowed the woman he was escorting aside and thrust his right hand inside his coat.

Tater started to bring his shotgun up, but stopped halfway. He was behind Ditch, Idelle, and the baby, and they stood directly in the line-of-fire between him and the two gunmen. He dare not fire.

Ditch released his crutch and went for his pistol.

Tater moved laterally, as fast as his bulk would allow, to give himself a clear shot at their attackers. He wasn't fast enough.

Before Tater could get a clear angle, and Ditch could draw his Colt, the burly baggage-handler stepped forward and pressed one of his pistol barrels against Idelle's temple. He cocked the hammer back with a pair of audible *clicks*. His other revolver, also cocked, he aimed at Tater.

Tater and Ditch both froze. There was nothing else they could do. Idelle gasped, and clutched her baby tighter to her bosom.

The distinguished-looking man drew his Richards-Mason .41 from beneath his coat and pointed it directly at Ditch's face.

"Drop your gun, Mayor Clemson," the man said. "You too, Deputy. Both of them. If you don't, my associate will open up your wife's head, just like your fellow mayors on the train at Rock Creek."

"Okay," Ditch said. "Take it easy. We'll do what you

want. Just tell your friend not to point that gun at my wife."

"Not until you lose those guns."

Ditch opened his hand and let his revolver drop to the floor. He nodded to Tater, who reluctantly lowered his shotgun to the ground, then slowly drew and dropped his revolver.

"We ditched our irons," Ditch said. "Now take that gun off my wife."

"I think not," the distinguished-looking man said. "That gun on her will keep you and the deputy from heroic notions. Though I'm not sure what harm a one-legged politician and a fat, old, lawman could do?"

Tater's face reddened in fury and his expression twisted into a scowl. "You yeller, bushwhackin', scum," he hissed. "What kind of varmint points a gun at a woman and a helpless little baby?"

"A well-paid varmint," the distinguished-looking man said. He stepped forward and shoved Ditch, who was struggling to balance himself on his one leg. Ditch instantly fell to the ground onto his back as Idelle cried out. She started to move toward him, but the burly gunman kept her in place with a prod to her forehead from his revolver barrel.

"Mayor Clemson certainly doesn't look very mayorly," the distinguished-looking man said to his female companion, "down there on the floor, does he?"

"What are you doin'?" the young woman demanded. Her face was contorted in fear and anger. "Why is he pointin' that gun at a woman and child? What is this?"

"This," the distinguished-looking man said, "is how I make a living."

"Who's payin' you for doin' me in?" Ditch asked, looking up at the man standing over him. "Brody or Gould?"

"Will it matter when you're dead?" the man replied.

"Why are we jawin'?" the burly baggage-handler said to his white-haired partner. "Get on with it. Plug him and let's vamoose."

"No!" Idelle begged. She was afraid to move but couldn't hold her tongue. "Don't shoot. Leave him be."

"I'm sorry ma'am," the distinguished-looking man said. "But I've got to do what I'm paid to do. That's just the way it is."

"You're both gutless bugs," Tater spat, "without a lick of manhood 'atween you. If I still had my scattergun in my mitts, I'd—"

"But you don't have your gun," the distinguished-looking man taunted, "do you, Deputy?" He slowly swung his pistol from Ditch to Tater. Tater stared defiantly back at him. Idelle began to cry.

"I've got a gun," a voice from across the room said. "A pair of 'em, in fact."

Chapter 27

Though only mid-morning, the sun overhead Booneville was already hot and promised an unseasonably warm spring day. Pritchard and Strobl were in the Churchyard behind Reverend Winfield's Presbyterian church. They were nearly finished digging.

Pritchard and Strobl had risen early, at Winfield's request, to prepare the grave. They took turns as one lawman stood watch with his rifle and the other dug. After the campsite attack that resulted in Hoke Rupe's death, the duo were taking no chances. Especially after hearing from the watchmen as they entered Booneville the previous night that several of their attackers, though injured, had preceded them into town.

Reverend Winfield remained inside the church, praying over Hoke's sheet-wrapped body with Tess.

"Did you know," Strobl said, as he labored, "despite the war, and all the killings I've experienced, this is actually the first grave I have ever dug?" He was hatless, wearing his dual shoulder holsters over his undershirt, and speaking around a cigarette.

"Is that so?" Pritchard said. He stood shirtless over the

grave with his Winchester cradled in the crook of one arm and both of his Colt revolvers belted around his hips.

"Indeed," Strobl affirmed. "Officers of the Austrian army do not perform those duties. We have underlings for such menial tasks."

"Dug plenty of graves, myself," Pritchard remarked. "Hell, two of 'em were mine."

Reverend Winfield and Tess emerged from the church. She wore a simple but elegant dress, which couldn't conceal the contours of her excellent figure, and her hair was combed and down. She looked quite beautiful. Strobl stared up at her, his cigarette falling from his lips. Tess's eyes flashed briefly, as the slender, aristocratic, deputy hastily stamped it out.

"Is the grave ready?" Winfield asked.

"I reckon it's deep enough," Pritchard said. He extended a massive hand and helped Strobl from the hole. Once out, the Austrian quickly brushed himself off and stood erect, keeping an eye on Tess. Despite her obvious sorrow, Pritchard thought he saw the makings of a tiny smile crack her lips as she observed Strobl from the corner of her eye.

"Tess has prepared food," Winfield said. "Why don't you gentlemen wash up? We'll eat, and then put Hoke's remains to rest." Tess returned to the church.

"As you wish, Padre," Pritchard said. As the trio were walking back to the church, a lone rider approached. He was a tall, heavy-set man in his fifties with whiskers and a wide-brimmed hat. A rifle lay across his pommel, and a Navy Colt was holstered at his side.

Strobl started to draw one of his Chamelot Delvigne revolvers when he was halted by Pritchard.

"Howdy, Bob," Pritchard called out.

"Howdy yourself, Samuel," the rider called back. "Mornin', Preacher."

"Good morning, Sheriff Blevins," Winfield greeted. "I gather you two know each other?"

"We surely do," Pritchard said, as Blevins dismounted and they shook hands. Pritchard introduced Blevins to Strobl. "We've tracked down a few lawbreakers together."

"Got word you were in town," Blevins explained, "and were out here at Reverend Winfield's church, but I couldn't get out to see you till now. Spent most of the night sortin' out trouble over at the doc's place. Seems a trio of fellers come a-ridin' in all shot to hell and gone. One' of 'em already done expired."

"There's a couple more of 'em lyin' out on the trail between here and Fort Smith," Pritchard said. "They expired last night, too."

"With a bit of help from our rifles," Strobl added.

"I figured as much," Blevins said. "A passel of shot-up gun hands showin' up in town and Samuel Pritchard comin' in on their heels can't be a coincidence."

"We left Fort Smith in the company of Hoke Rupe," Pritchard explained. "Bounty hunters trailed us. They jumped us at camp last night."

"Serves 'em right to get filled up with holes," Blevins said. "Ever since those damned railroads put up that King Midas bounty on Jem Rupe, the county's been teemin' with pistoleers and bounty killers. I hear tell they've been houndin' Hoke somethin' fierce in Fort Smith. Plyin' him with drinks and tryin' to get him to spill the beans on what became of his brother."

"They'll hound him no more," Winfield said. "Hoke is dead."

"What?" Blevins said. "Hoke dead? How?"

"He caught a blue whistler when those bounty killers jumped us," Pritchard said. "He passed during the night."

"Poor old Hoke," Blevins said, shaking his head. "He just never could shake his demons from that damned war."

"Some demons ain't so easy to shake," Pritchard said solemnly.

"How's his niece takin' it?"

"Hard," Winfield said. "Hoke was the only family Tess had."

"You sure about that?" Blevins asked, staring hard at the reverend.

"I'm sure," Winfield said, averting his eye.

Reverend Winfield invited Sheriff Blevins to breakfast and he accepted. The men walked to the church, and to the attached cottage where Winfield and Tess resided. Blevins tied and tended to his horse while Strobl washed up at the pump. Once Winfield, Strobl, and Blevins went inside Pritchard began washing.

While he was toweling off his face, Tess Rupe emerged unseen from the cottage. She startled him when he looked up from his towel to find the beautiful, but red-eyed, young woman standing beside him.

"I apologize for my disrespectful appearance," Pritchard said. "I didn't realize you were standin' there."

"No apology necessary," she said, as she looked up at the towering lawman. She took in his thickly muscled torso, forged from a youth spent cutting and hauling wood at his father's lumber mill. She also noticed the patchwork of gunshot, blade, and surgical scars crisscrossing his chest.

"I wanted to ask you something, Marshal," she said.

"Ask away," Pritchard said, as he shrugged into his shirt.

"Uncle Hoke spent his last hours on earth with you, didn't he?"

"He did."

"Did he," she looked at the ground a moment, hesitating, "tell you anything?"

"Only his dying wish. That he wanted me to speak to you."

Tess's eyes widened. "Speak to me? About what?"

"Your father," Pritchard said, tucking in his shirt.

"My father is dead," she blurted.

"I ain't sayin' he ain't," Pritchard said. "All I'm sayin' is I can understand why a gal would have reason to keep folks believin' that her pa, iffen her pa was Arkansas Jem Rupe, was dead and buried. Especially iffen that pa was the only kin that gal had left in the world."

"What do you know about it?" Tess replied hotly. "That badge of yours might make it legal, but for all your fancy talk you could be nothing but another bounty hunter trying to make a fortune on my father's name. That's likely why you brought Uncle Hoke back here in the first place—you were hoping he'd birddog my father for you."

"You'd be wrong about my intentions," Pritchard said.

"I'm supposed to believe that?"

"Believe this: My own pa was lynched before my eyes when I was nothin' but a boy. I know what it's like to live under the shadow you live under now. Scorned, hunted, ashamed, and afraid to use my own name. I had to change my name—take up a false one—just to survive, and to protect what was left of my family."

The truth in Pritchard's words was undeniable. Tess could see it herself in the lawman's face. Her anger subsided.

"And there's something else you'd best know," Pritchard continued. "You're right about one thing. I did come here looking for your father, but not for the reason you think. I don't know whether your father is alive or dead, Tess, but I do know this. Dead or alive, he didn't wreck that train in Rock Creek."

"Is that what you'd have me believe?" Tess said, though the fire was gone from her tone. "That you're the one lawman on either side of the Mississippi who believes Arkansas Jem Rupe, the notorious Trainwrecker of Platte Bridge, is innocent?"

"Your Uncle Hoke believed me. That's why he agreed to bring me here to meet you."

"Why do you care who wrecked that train, anyway? Without the bounty on Pa's head, which you claim you're not interested in, what's it to you?"

"Folks from my hometown died in that wreck, and my best friend lost his leg. If I'm a-gonna bring those responsible to account, and I swore to do just that, I've got to prove that train weren't derailed by a ghost from the war who ain't been seen in ten years."

"I don't understand?" Tess said.

"The men who wrecked that train pinned it on your father because they know he had a history of such acts during the war, and because they believed him dead. Ghosts can't defend themselves from charges of train robbery and murder. But a living, flesh-and-blood man can. Those money-grubbin' carpetbaggers who run the railroads wouldn't have put up such a richsome bounty on your father if they actually believed they'd have to pay it. That's what gave 'em away; their greed."

"What, exactly, are you planning to do if you find my father, Marshal?" She crossed her arms and tilted her head. "If he was alive, that is."

"If your father were to suddenly appear, alive and well, and testify in Fort Smith before Judge Parker with an alibi that proves he didn't wreck that train in Missouri," Pritchard said, "he'd clear his name."

"It would clear his name all right," Tess conceded, "but how does that help you?"

"It would prove somebody else wrecked the train at Rock Creek, and framed up a conspiracy to pin on Jem to keep the finger offen himself. The only man who'd benefit from such a plot, and who has the money and influence to do such a thing—"

"—owns a railroad," Tess finished his sentence. "That might be so, but it still won't save Pa from a rope. He's a wanted war criminal, remember? If he suddenly reappeared, even if cleared of the Rock Creek train wreck, the government would still arrest and string him, sure as sunrise, for Platte Bridge."

"Maybe not," Pritchard said. "I can ask the governor of Missouri to petition President Grant on your father's behalf." He looked down at Tess with one eyebrow raised. "Assuming he's alive, that is."

Tess looked down at her feet.

"We can request a pardon," Pritchard went on. "The war's long over. What your father did in the war, just like me and every other soldier, was done under orders from higher-ups. It weren't his fault, no more than mine, that he fought on the losing side. If he's a war criminal, I'm a war criminal, too."

"If that's true," Tess asked, "how did you keep from the gallows yourself?"

"I did my penance in ten years of man-killin' for the Texas Rangers."

Tess nodded to herself, stepped closer, and put her hands on Pritchard's arm. "I want to trust you, Marshal. I truly do. But we both know I can't. Uncle Hoke trusted you, and he's going into the ground today."

"Fair enough," Pritchard said, "but you may not have a choice."

"What do you mean?"

"Those five bounty hunters my deputy and I encountered last night ain't gonna be the last ones makin' their way to Booneville. Fort Smith is crawlin' with 'em, and more are arrivin' every day. One-hundred-thousand dollars will do that. When they find you, and they will, they won't be askin' you, as I am, for the truth about your father. What they want they'll be pluckin' from you at the business end of a red-hot brandin' iron."

"You're trying to scare me, aren't you?"

"I am not," Pritchard said. "Your Uncle Hoke knew those bounty hunters would be a-comin' for you, Tess. I think that's the real reason he agreed to bring me out here to meet you. He sat in a saloon drinkin' whiskey every day and watched Fort Smith fill up with gunslingers and bounty killers, knowin' they'd eventually end up at your doorstep. He loved you, feared for your safety, and knew he couldn't protect you alone."

"And you figure Hoke reckoned that you, Marshal Samuel Pritchard, was the man to protect me?"

Pritchard looked around. "You see anybody else willin' to take on the job?"

Tess was silent for a moment. "Can I ask you something else, Marshal?"

"Of course."

"Your deputy," she began tentatively, "the man with the strange accent. I didn't get a chance to formally meet him last night. With Uncle Hoke's death and all, I must have forgotten my manners."

"Think nothing of it," Pritchard said. "I'm sure he understands."

"If you don't think it indiscreet," she said, her voice lowering to almost a whisper, "may I inquire if he is married?"

"He is not," Pritchard said, biting back his grin. "His name's Florian Strobl. He's Austrian nobility, of some sort. A right solid feller, too."

"Thank you, Marshal," Tess said. She turned on her heels and left Pritchard grinning and scratching his head.

Chapter 28

Marsh and Gilbert crawled on their bellies in single file atop the roof of the railroad car. It was mid-morning, already plenty warm, and neither man was particularly comfortable in their heavy coat, gloves, and burlap mask. Their hats were cinched firmly on their heads by stampede strings to prevent them from flying off, and their revolvers were tucked tightly into their belts. The train, John Brody's private special, was moving westward at almost fifteen miles per hour.

"I don't know why we couldn't have done this when the train weren't a-movin'," Gilbert complained. He wasn't worried about anyone inside the car hearing his voice due to the roar of the engine. "We're like as not to fall offen this steam wagon."

"We couldn't do it while the train was stopped, you moron," Marsh replied, "because the only time the train isn't surrounded by armed guards is when it's moving."

"Oh," Gilbert said.

Marsh gritted his cracked teeth and continued to crawl. He wished he was accompanied by Finchum, or even the Big Man, whom he disliked immensely. Both were infinitely more reliable and intelligent than Gilbert, who was merely the Big Man's only surviving gun hand. But Finchum, by virtue of his extraordinary height and slenderness, and the Big Man, by virtue of his significant height and great bulk, would have both been easily recognized by their distinct physiques, even if masked. That left only him and Gilbert, both medium-sized men of non-descript build, to tend to the task at hand.

Marsh and Gilbert had crawled along the railroad track during the darkness of the previous night, beneath the cars of Brody's private train and beyond the eyes of his guards standing watch surrounding it. There they huddled until the changing of the guard just before dawn. The switch of sentries allowed them a moment to emerge from beneath Brody's private luxury car and clamber up to the roof, where they lay unseen for another hour before Brody finished his breakfast, the guards boarded a passenger car, and the train got underway. It was widely known that Brody felt the motion of the train interfered with his digestion, a fact Marsh also knew, which provided a general idea of approximately what time the train would depart from Rock Creek.

"It's time," Marsh said to Gilbert. "Follow me." The two men carefully climbed down from the roof onto the platform of Brody's private car. All the guards, Marsh knew, were in the car behind them, napping, smoking, drinking, and playing cards. There was no need for them to stand vigil on a moving train. In the unlikely event that robbers or brigands should attack, the engineer would blast the whistle, alerting them to action.

Marsh and Gilbert drew their pistols, opened the door, and stepped into Brody's car, immediately closing it behind them. Brody, who was seated and being shaved by his elderly servant, Charles, looked up in astonishment at the two masked men wielding guns.

A long moment of awkward silence transpired before Marsh elbowed Gilbert harshly in the ribs. It had been previously agreed that Gilbert would do the talking, since he had never spoken to Brody before. The railroad boss would have surely recognized Marsh's voice.

"You know what this is," Gilbert said, cocking his revolver and pointing it at Charles. "Drop that razor, and git your hands up."

Charles immediately complied. Brody's face revealed fear but his voice was calm.

"Do you know who I am?" Brody asked.

"I do," Gilbert said. "And I know you've got a safe in this here fancy car, right behind that bar over yonder. You're a-gonna open it up."

Marsh tucked his gun back into his belt and produced a length of rope and a kerchief from his pocket. He busied himself binding Charles's hands behind his back and gagging him.

"And if I don't," Brody replied with a shaky voice, "you'll shoot me? Is that it?" He tried his best to exude bravado. "At the sound of a gunshot, my men will swarm this car and shoot you both down. Neither of you will live to spend a penny of this railroad's money."

Neither Brody, Charles, nor Marsh could see Gilbert's smile under his mask as he bent down and picked up the straight razor the servant had dropped. He wiped the shaving soap residue off on his sleeve and held the gleaming blade before Brody's now widened eyes and gaping mouth.

"Who said anything about shootin' you?" Gilbert said.

The .44 Henry rimfire bullet fired from the 1872 Open Top Colt in Laird Bonner's right hand struck the burly baggage-handler holding Idelle Pritchard and her infant son Samuel at pistol-point directly between his mercenary eyes. His head snapped back, his knees buckled, he dropped his gun, and he collapsed. He was dead before he hit the ground.

The distinguished-looking and well-dressed gentleman started to swing his fancily engraved, Richards-Mason, .41 caliber Colt revolver from where he'd been previously pointing it—at Tater—toward Bonner. He stopped halfway when he found the merciless black tunnel of the 1872 Open Top Colt in Bonner's left hand staring him in the face.

"Hello, Walton," Bonner said casually. "Been a while."

"Laird?" Odom declared incredulously. "What're you doing here?"

"Seeing that you don't line your pockets by harming my friends," Bonner said. "Drop the pistol."

"This is a very rare, expensive, firearm," Odom said. "Dropping it on the floor may damage its finely engraved finish. How about I just put it away?"

"Drop it, Colonel," Bonner said flatly, "or I'll drop you." Odom shrugged irritably and complied.

Tater reached down and grabbed his own revolver from the floor, cocking it and aiming the weapon at Odom. Idelle rushed to help Ditch to his feet, balancing Samuel in one arm. Bonner holstered his left-hand Colt after lowering its hammer, and automatically began reloading his other. Odom's consort fell to her knees and covered her face, sobbing.

"Howdy, Laird," Ditch said, as Tater handed him his crutch and he got upright. Tater began collecting the other firearms scattered about the floor. "You can't rightly know how good it is to see you." He wiped his brow with his good arm and shook Bonner's hand.

"Sure, I can," Bonner said. "It's always good to see you, Ditch." He tipped his hat to Idelle. "Mrs. Clemson." He nodded.

"I reckon I'm pretty durned happy to see Laird, too," Tater chimed in, "seein' as how this dandified coward was fixin' to plug me just afore he arrived." He pumped Bonner's hand vigorously.

"Be cautious who you call a coward, hayseed," Odom said loftily to Tater. "I've killed far better men than you for far less. Mark my words, Deputy, these tables will turn."

"A coward is what I called you, and a coward is what you is," Tater said. "Any man fixin' to shoot down an unarmed feller in front of his own wife and baby son is a coward in my book, and I can't even read."

Tater pulled a cloth from a nearby hotel table and covered the dead man, who was clearly less of a baggage-handler and more of a gun-handler, from further public view. "And as far as this gutless varmint with you is concerned," he spat, nudging the body with the toe of his boot, "what Laird gave him was lettin' him off easy. Pointin' a gun at a woman and a baby! Hell and tarnation! I'd like to resurrect this cur and shoot him myself!"

"Bold talk from a worthless deputy," Odom scoffed. "Had not Bonner intervened, you'd be the one on the floor."

Tater retrieved his shotgun, handed Ditch his gun, holstered his new revolver, and approached Idelle, who was busy giving Bonner a grateful hug and wiping the tears of relief from her eyes.

"Pardon me, Miss Idelle," Tater began, "but you might want to turn yourself and Baby Samuel away. I don't want either of you seein' this."

"Seeing what, Tater?" Idelle asked, confused.

"This," Tater said, as he slammed the butt of his shotgun into Colonel Walton Odom's gut. Odom folded at the waist and collapsed to all fours, explosively vomiting as he went down.

John Babbit, Judge Pearson, Manfri Pannell, Seth Tilley, and several other members of the Atherton Vigilance Committee suddenly burst into the hotel lobby with rifles and pistols at the ready.

"We heard a shot," Judge Pearson declared. "What happened? Is everyone okay?"

Ditch held up his hand. "It's all over," he said. "Thanks to our good friend Laird, we're all just fine."

Tater leaned over and grabbed Odom by his white hair. "You are under arrest," Tater said, "whoever the hell you are." He yanked him to his feet.

"His name is Colonel Walton Odom," Bonner announced to all present. "He's a former Union army officer and professional killer-for-hire. I encountered him a while back in the Dakotas. He shoots unarmed Indians and peaceful sheep farmers at the behest of wealthy ranchers. He usually travels in a pack of about five or six gun hands, so there may be more of his boys about. One thing's for sure; he wouldn't be here if he wasn't getting paid."

"Who paid you to kill Mayor Clemson?" Judge Pearson demanded.

"Wouldn't you like to know?" Odom smirked.

"I'll tell the rest of the Vigilance Committee to keep a lookout for strangers in town," Seth Tilley said, heading back out of the hotel. "And I'll bring the hearse from Pa's shop."

"I can't believe you're doing this," Odom said to Bonner, wiping vomit spittle on his sleeve. "We're in the same profession, you and me. You're going to let these hicktown regulators take me in? Where's the professional courtesy?"

"What's been done to you," Bonner said, "you did yourself. And we sure as hell aren't in the same profession."

"Of course, we are," Odom argued. "You're a professional gun hand, just like me. You had no right to interfere in my business."

"You call this business?" Bonner retorted. "Sure, I track men for money. But unlike you, every man I ever tracked, or gunned, was wanted by the law, armed, and facing me. I've never put a gun to a woman, armed, wanted, or not, and I sure as hell never pointed a pistol at an infant. You're filth, Odom, and you've backshot your last victim. The only reason I didn't shoot you down like your partner lying at your feet was because I'm looking forward to watching you hang."

"Hang?" Odom said smugly. "I won't hang. I didn't kill anyone. What can I hang for?"

"Conspiracy to commit murder," Judge Pearson said, as he holstered his revolver, "and murder. Under the law, you, Colonel Odom, are responsible for this man's," he pointed to the sheet-covered body on the hotel floor, "death."

"That's ridiculous," Odom said. "I didn't shoot him. Bonner did."

"That's correct," the judge agreed, "except that the commission of your criminal act, in concert with this deceased man as your confederate, directly led to his death. In the eyes of the law, you are guilty of his murder, not Bonner, who fired in the lawful defense of another."

Tater pointed to the woman, still on her knees, who'd come in with Odom and his partner. "Suppose we ask this little lady what she's got to say about all this?"

"An excellent idea, Deputy Jessup," Pearson said. He helped the woman to her feet and escorted her to a chair. "Tell us about him," the judge began, gesturing toward Odom. "And know that if you lie to me, as a duly-appointed magistrate, you may share his fate."

"I don't know these fellers," the woman said numbly. "I swear. They hired me out of a dance hall in Kansas City two days ago. Bought me a fancy dress, and told me I was to act as his"—she pointed to Odom—"wife. When I asked why? he said, 'So's we can get close to somebody in a place called Atherton who's bein' guarded round-the-clock,' or some such words. He paid me fifty dollars cash money, and we came in on the train." She rummaged in her purse and came out with a wad of bills. "I've still got forty-three of it, right here."

"There you have it," the judge declared. "Conspiracy

to commit the murder of our mayor, Ditch Clemson, plain as you please."

"You small-town rubes can't be serious?" Odom said, shaking his head. "You fools aren't going to take the word of a two-dollar whore over that of a former military officer and gentleman?"

Idelle walked over to Odom and slapped him hard. Both Tater and Bonner instantly moved in to prevent him from striking her back.

"Mind who you call fools and whores," Idelle said. "We'll be the ones watching you dangle from the gallows."

"I think not," Odom said dismissively.

"On the contrary," Pearson said. "I believe a jury of Atherton's finest citizens would have no trouble finding you guilty. In fact, I believe I'll convene the trial for this afternoon."

"I'll post a notice immediately," John Babbit said. "I've got a feeling getting a seat on this jury will be like winning a church raffle."

"And I can personally assure you," Pearson continued, "as the jurist who will be issuing your sentence upon being convicted, that under Missouri Law, capital punishment is more than appropriate."

Colonel Odom's complexion, already pale from expelling the contents of his stomach, grew paler.

"Is it really true," Manfri Pannell spoke up, trying to grasp what was transpiring, "what you all say? That these men came to Atherton to kill Mayor Ditch? And threatened to shoot Missus Clemson and her little baby?"

"'Tis a stone fact," Tater answered. "Seen it with my own two eyes."

"That's right, Manfri," Ditch said, staring directly at

Odom. "This professional gun-for-hire would have shot me down before my own wife and baby son."

"Holy Saints in Heaven," Pannell exclaimed, shaking his head and staring hotly at Odom. "Why bother with a trial?"

"My sentiments exactly," Tater said.

Chapter 29

After a wordless meal, which began with Reverend Winfield asking all to join hands while he gave thanks and blessed the food, Pritchard and Strobl carried Hoke Rupe's sheet-wrapped body to the Churchyard. Pritchard noticed, with some amusement, that during the meal prayer Strobl and Tess held each other's hands a few extra seconds after the praying ended.

Winfield read Bible passages as they lowered the deceased into the hole and began to fill it. Sheriff Blevins stood alongside the grave with a softly weeping Tess, his hat in hand.

"... amen," Winfield finished, closing his book.

"Would anyone like to say words?" Winfield asked. Blevins nodded and stepped up.

"Known Hoke Rupe, and the Rupe family, since I was a boy," he said. "Hoke was a drinkin' man, it's true, and some thought a ne'er-do-well. But he was a soldier of the Confederacy, a jailer in Fort Smith, for a time, and no man was ever truer to his word."

Tess stepped forward next. "Uncle Hoke was always kind to me, and brought me gifts and trinkets when I was little. I always knew he loved me, and looked out for me, and I hope he went to his reward knowing he was loved in return."

Pritchard looked directly at Reverend Winfield. "Only knew the feller a day," he began. "All I know about him was his dying act. Givin' his life to bring me here to meet his niece." He switched his gaze to Tess. "I believe Hoke was held prisoner by an oath. An oath he felt had outlived its time, but nonetheless believed was his duty to honor. Hoke Rupe was an honorable man." When he returned his scrutiny to the reverend, he found Winfield wouldn't meet his eyes.

The solemn group was walking back to the church when a rider appeared in the distance, approaching on the road from town. The horse was moving at full gallop.

"Get inside the church," Pritchard said to Winfield and Tess. He, Strobl, and Blevins automatically began checking their revolvers.

"Hold on," Blevins said, squinting at the incoming rider. "Relax. That's one of my two deputies, Jim Spears."

The horse pulled up in a cloud of dust, and its rider hastily dismounted. "We've got trouble, Sheriff," Spears breathlessly declared. Pritchard recognized him as one of the two watchmen who'd challenged them while entering Booneville the night before. "Plenty of it. And it's a-headin' straight for ya."

"Calm down, Jim, and tell me all about it," Blevins said.

"Twenty riders or more," Spears began, removing his hat and wiping his brow, "every one of 'em armed to the teeth. They barn-stormed into town, asking where the doc's place was? Then they went straight there and collected them fellers who came into town last night all shot to pieces."

"Go on," Blevins said.

"Them boys went tearin' through town, bracin' anyone they ran into," Spears continued. "Askin' everybody they saw 'where's Tess Rupe?' Folks who wouldn't answer got a rap on the noggin with a pistol. They're as nasty a herd of polecats as I've ever seen, and they ain't makin' no secret of what they're after. They want that gosh-durned bounty, and they believe Tess Rupe is the way to get it. All I can tell you, Sheriff, is they found out she's out here at the church in right short order."

"Where's Deputy Johnson?"

"He lit out," Spears spat. "Took one look at that posse of bounty killers, took off his badge, dropped it in the street, and rode off."

"I always figured Johnson for lily-livered," Blevins grunted. "Reckon I was right. How'd you get out of town unmolested?"

"I was in the livery, tendin' to my horse. I knew you'd come out here to Reverend Winfield's earlier this mornin', and figured it'd be healthier for both our scalps if I rode out here myself, unseen, to warn you instead of tryin' to brace twenty or more of 'em all by my lonesome in town."

"Right sound figurin', Jim," Blevins said. He turned to Winfield and Tess. "Gather your things," he told them. "Me and Jim'll hitch up your buckboard. You'd both best light out of here before that pack of mongrels arrives."

"I'm not going anywhere," Winfield said. "This is my church. I'll not abandon it."

"An admirable notion, Reverend," Blevins said. "But

notions don't stop bullets. Besides, you need to get Tess outta here and pronto."

"I won't go," Winfield said.

"We must go," Tess said, taking Winfield's arm. "You heard the sheriff?"

"It's too late to go," Pritchard said, pointing off in the distance. A cloud of dust was visible in town, on Bonneville's main road. It was the kind of cloud twenty or more mounted horses riding in a group would create.

"Marshal Pritchard's right," Blevins said. "They're practically here. There's no way we could outrun 'em now."

"Get Tess inside the church," Pritchard said once more to Winfield. "Florian, get our rifles and saddlebags." He turned to Blevins and Spears, who were already retrieving rifles from their own horses. "How do you want to play this hand, Bob?"

"I reckon they'll come straight at us, Samuel, in a great, big, pack," Blevins said. "They'll be overly confident in their numbers, and will probably march right up to the church's front doors. Once the shootin' commences, they'll split up, surround the church, and lay siege. Wouldn't surprise me if they try to burn us out, especially if we down enough of 'em during the initial salvo."

"I agree," Pritchard said, as he accepted his saddlebags and rifle from Strobl. He immediately opened the bags and began donning the dual shoulder holsters containing his 1863 Remingtons. He covered them with a vest, also taken from inside his bags, and stuffed its pockets with .44 and .45 Colt cartridges.

"Why'n't you take charge," Blevins offered. "I may be

the sheriff of Booneville, but we both know you've got a helluva lot more battle experience than me. Between the war and the Texas Rangers, I'm bettin' this type of fracas ain't your first rodeo?"

"You'd be right," Pritchard agreed. "If you boys have no objections," he went on, as he added a sixth cartridge to the cylinder of each of his four revolvers, "I'd like to put Deputy Strobl up in the steeple. A finer rifle shot, and a cooler hand under fire, you ain't a-gonna find." Strobl clicked his heels and bowed slightly. He had his Henry rifle, and two boxes of .44 Rimfire, cradled in his arms.

"Suits me," Blevins said. "Where do you want us?" He also had a Henry rifle and a box of fifty cartridges.

"I want you, Bob, at the front doors of the church. You're the law in this town, and if anyone is gonna convince those fellers to ride off peaceable-like, it'll be you. It'll also make the killin' legal and proper iffen they don't obey." Pritchard grinned. "Besides, I happen to know how you prefer to fight: out in front, and right down the bastards' throats."

"You know me pretty well," Blevins chuckled, "don't you?"

"What about me?" Spears said. He was armed with a Smith & Wesson revolver and luckily an 1873 Winchester like Pritchard's. Pritchard handed him a box of .44-40 cartridges from his saddlebags.

"You'll have to be the Johnny-on-the-spot inside the church," Pritchard explained. "You'll need to cover the rear door, and both the windows on both sides, to fend off any of 'em tryin' to gain entry."

"Are only two men inside the church, and one on top,

going to be able to stave off attacks from all sides?" Winfield asked.

"You could help them," Pritchard said, extending his Winchester.

"I am a man of God," Winfield said, refusing the offered rifle. "I will not take up arms."

"It hasn't always been that way with you," Pritchard challenged, "has it, Reverend?" Tess's face reddened, and Winfield turned away.

"The reverend does have a point," Blevins said. "Even with me and Jim inside the church together, and Strobl in the steeple, our three guns won't be enough to stop a force as large as theirs if they launch a proper attack."

"I don't think it'll come to that," Pritchard said. "After the majority of those bounty hunters see a few of their compadres shot down tryin' to get in, they'll back away and try to pick you off piecemeal. But that won't work for 'em either; not with Florian in that bell steeple sharp-shootin' 'em to pieces. That's when they'll get frustrated and try to burn you out."

"How're we supposed to defend against that?" Blevins said. "We'll be trapped in the church and surrounded on all sides?"

"I reckon that's where I come in," Pritchard said.

Chapter 30

Twenty-three horsemen rode up to the church and halted in a cloud of dust at the front steps. At the head of the pack was the large man with the scar on his cheek Pritchard had clobbered at the Horseshoe Saloon back in Fort Smith. He'd evidently retrieved his pair of Navy Colts, and was still wearing his battered Boss of the Plains adorned with a feather.

The riders with him were just as rough-hewn as their leader. Whether clean and town-bred, or dirty, unshaven, and sons of the prairie, the nearly two-dozen horsemen shared two things in common: all wore hardened, hungry, expressions, and all were armed.

The doors to the church opened and Reverend Winfield's large, heavy, body stepped into view. He held his Bible across his chest and surveyed the mob of gunmen before him through his one good eye.

"There are no services at the church at this hour," Winfield announced.

"We didn't come to pray," the scar-faced man said, amidst a chorus of laughter within the ranks behind him.

"Who are you, then," Winfield demanded, "and what do you want?"

"Who I am ain't important," the man said. "What we want is Hoke Rupe and his niece, Tess, and we want 'em now."

"What's your business with them?"

"None of yours, Padre. Send 'em out. We know they're in that church."

"Hoke is dead," Winfield said. "One of your number shot him last night. He's buried out yonder." He pointed to the fresh grave in the Churchyard.

"Then send out the girl."

"I will do no such thing," Winfield said. "What gives you the right to take someone against their will? Especially an innocent young woman?"

The scar-faced man drew one of his Navy Colts. "This here pistol is what gives me the right," he said with a grunt. "That gal is worth a hunnerd-thousand dollars. Send her out, or by God we'll come in after her. Iffen we have to do that, Padre, you're eatin' a bullet and your church is gonna get burned to the ground. Is that what you want?"

"What I want does not matter in the eyes of the Lord," Winfield said. "This church is a holy sanctuary. I will not turn Tess Rupe over to a band of murderous criminals."

"Suit yourself," the scar-faced man said. He cocked his pistol, aimed it at Winfield, and was just starting to press the trigger when the .44 caliber bullet launched from Deputy Florian Strobl's Henry rifle entered the top of his head. It was fired at a sharply downward angle, from the steeple of the church above. The scar-faced man toppled from his saddle.

As twenty-two, still-mounted, gunmen all began to draw their pistols, Sheriff Blevins and Deputy Spears suddenly came into view from opposite sides of the church's doorway. Blevins shouldered Reverend Winfield roughly aside as he and Spears began firing their Winchesters.

Deputy Spears knelt, and Sheriff Blevins stood over him, as both aimed into the densely packed mob of horsemen clustered at point-blank range before them. Squeezing off shots in rapid-fire as fast as they could, the two Booneville lawmen levered new cartridges into the chambers of their rifles just as rapidly as they fired.

A half-dozen bounty hunters fell from their saddles to Blevins and Spears' fusillade before even one of them could get off a shot of their own. Four more dropped from the precision fire of Strobl's Henry rifle, above them.

Men screamed in fear and panic. Horses reared and bucked. Those in the mob able to remain atop their mounts returned only sporadic and ineffective fire, unable to take proper aim in the maelstrom of dying men and spooked animals swirling around them.

"Dismount!" one of the gunmen shouted to his comrades, struggling to be heard over the cacophony of gunfire, braying horses, and shrieking men. "Dismount, and get yourselves into the woods! We'll re-group there and burn 'em out!"

A dozen gunmen, all that was left standing of the twenty-three in number who had originally rode up to the church, left their horses and raced to the woodline, fifty yards away. Strobl picked off one, and Blevins another, as they fled for their lives.

As the remaining ten bounty hunters approached the woodline, most in a state of fury or panic, Pritchard emerged to greet them. He stepped from behind a tree with a Colt in each hand and began systematically firing.

As skilled a marksman with his left hand as he was with his right, a trait deliberately acquired through more than a decade of daily dry-fire pistol practice, Pritchard began dropping men one-by-one as he walked steadily toward them.

He fired rapidly but with precision, oblivious to the hastily fired pistol-shots being directed at him. When his Colts clicked empty, he smoothly holstered them and drew his pair of 1863 Remingtons from the dual shoulder-holsters beneath his arms. A gift from Ditch, and converted to fire .44 Henry rimfire cartridges, these were the guns Pritchard used throughout most of his tenure as a Texas Ranger. The familiar weapons were almost extensions of his arms. The last remaining gunmen fell before him.

Before Pritchard could empty the Remingtons, it was over. He swept his guns over the ground before him, ensuring none of the downed bounty killers were still in the fight. A stark silence, created by the sudden cessation of gunfire, was punctuated only by the sound of hoofbeats as terrified horses fled the area.

Satisfied there were no further threats, Pritchard holstered his Remingtons and reloaded his Colts. He'd holstered them, and was reloading the Remingtons, when Blevins and Spears walked up. Both were still carrying their Winchesters at the ready and going from body to body to make certain there were no gunmen playing possum.

"Anybody hurt?" Pritchard asked them.

"Deputy Strobl got nicked by a splinter from up in that bell tower," Blevins said, "but otherwise we're all okay." He prodded one of the dead gunmen, a half-breed with a LeMat revolver still clutched in his lifeless hand. "Can't say the same for these fellers. All but one or two are done in, and those that ain't will be shortly."

"Helluva fight," Spears remarked. "Your plan worked like a charm, Marshal. There's dead men scattered over this Churchyard from here to Christmas."

The trio walked back to the church where they found Strobl, Tess, and Winfield. The Austrian deputy was being attended by Tess, who was bandaging a slight gash on his forehead, obtained when a bullet ricocheted near him in the steeple. He didn't seem averse to the attention.

Winfield was kneeling over one of the downed bounty hunters. The man had been chest-shot, and was sputtering and spitting blood. The reverend held his Bible in one large hand, the dying man's bloody hand in the other, and quietly prayed.

"I wouldn't squander your prayers on him," Pritchard said. "If he'd had his druthers, you'd be the one shot and dyin', your church would be a-smolderin', and young Tess would be at the mercy of him and his ilk. Send him to hell without the comfort of prayers, says I."

Winfield stood up, an indignant expression on his face. "That's exactly what I would expect," he said angrily, "from a Godless savage like yourself." He swept his arm at the carnage before them. "Behold, Marshal Pritchard, the fruits of your murderous ways."

"Reckon it's better them than us," Pritchard drawled.

"I'd be a mite less inclined to condemn Marshal Pritchard," Blevins said, "iffen I was you, Reverend?

Without him and his deputy, we'd all be in the hereafter. Is that what you'd prefer? To see your church destroyed, and Tess taken, instead of these cowards and killers dead?"

"Don't lecture me, Sheriff Blevins," Winfield scolded. "You yourself are just as guilty in the eyes of the Lord for this carnival of killing as the marshal."

"I've always been right skeptical of men who claim to speak for the Lord," Pritchard said, standing face-to-face with Winfield. "And as far as the right or wrong of endin' those who try to end me, I ain't luggin' so much as a pinch of regret. Killin' fellers of such stripe is akin to steppin' on a scorpion or shootin' a rattler."

"It is not for us to judge these men," Winfield said haughtily, pointing at the corpses lying all around them. "That is God's place."

"But that's what you're doing," Tess suddenly spoke up, "isn't it? You're judging Marshal Pritchard, aren't you?"

"Silence," Winfield barked at her. "Those men came looking for you, Tess. This entire, bloody, affair is your fault."

"No, it isn't," Tess shot back at the reverend. Strobl stood and put his arm around her shoulder. "It's yours," she retorted hotly. "This is all your fault, and you know it."

Chapter 31

"Has the jury reached a verdict?" Judge Pearson asked.

"We have," announced Wynn Samples, the jury foreman. He owned and operated Atherton's General Store and Mercantile. The other jurors were all local businessmen, too.

It was late afternoon, and the remainder of the day had been consumed with hearing the sworn testimony of Mayor Clemson, his wife Idelle, Deputy Jessup, Laird Bonner, and a twenty-two-year-old dance hall hostess hailing from Kansas City named Mollie Brecken.

Colonel Walton Odom sat defiantly shackled in the defendant's chair, silently absorbing the accumulation of damning statements against him. When asked if he wished to testify in his own defense, he merely spat on the floor.

A little less than fifteen minutes after Judge Pearson sent the jury out to deliberate, they returned. No one in the courtroom appeared surprised.

"What is your verdict?" Pearson asked the foreman.

"Plumb guilty, Your Honor," Samples announced. "Guilty on all counts."

A loud murmur of satisfaction broke out among the spectators in the courtroom. Odom shook his head and grunted in disgust. Pearson banged his gavel a single time to restore order.

"Colonel Walton Odom," Judge Pearson began, once he'd regained silence in his courtroom, "you have been duly tried and fairly judged by a lawfully seated jury of your peers. Let the record show you have been found guilty of the crimes of conspiracy to commit the ambush killing of Atherton's mayor, and of taking his wife and baby son as hostages to facilitate that foul and murderous act. If not for the timely intervention of Mr. Laird Bonner, you may well have succeeded. As it was, the commission of your crime resulted in the shooting death of your equally guilty confederate, whose untimely end is laid to rest at your feet for an additional charge of murder."

Odom closed his eyes, rocked back his head, and laughed.

"Do you have anything to say to the court before you are sentenced?" Pearson asked. "The court would certainly like to know the identity of who commissioned you, a hired killer of men, to murder Mayor Clemson? I am compelled to advise you that the court will gladly consider your cooperation when issuing its sentence. It's only fair to tell you, that if you provide the name of the person or persons who hired you, your sentence could potentially be reduced from capital punishment to life in prison."

Odom suddenly stopped laughing and stared in contempt at the judge seated behind the imposing bench above him. "Go to hell," he said. "Wouldn't have much of a chance of survival if I did that, would I? If I gave up that name, he'd hire someone just like me to put me down."

"Very well," Pearson said. "You leave the court little choice. By the authority invested in me by the Town of Atherton, Jackson County, the State of Missouri, and the Government of the United States," Pearson continued, "I hereby sentence you, Walton Odom, for your willful and deliberate crimes, to hang by the neck until dead. The sentence is to be carried out tomorrow at sunrise. Court is adjourned."

"You bumpkins won't get the chance to see me swing from a rope," Odom shouted, as he was hauled to his feet by two members of the Vigilance Committee, Seth Tilley and Manfri Pannell. "My men will come for me. They'll burn this town to ashes before they let my neck get stretched. If you're smart, Your Honor, you'll turn me loose now while you still can. Spare the folks of Atherton a bloodbath, and the spectacle of watching their homes and businesses torched."

"Take him to the jail and lock him up," Pearson commanded. Odom was escorted from the courtroom.

Once Odom had been taken away, and the courtroom emptied of spectators and jurors, Pearson invited Ditch, Tater, John Babbit, and Laird Bonner into his chambers. Idelle and Baby Samuel were escorted back to the hotel by several armed citizens.

"What's on your mind, Judge?" Ditch asked, as he took a seat. His strength was returning, albeit slowly, but he needed to sit a spell. The rest of the assembly remained standing.

"I was thinking about Colonel Odom's threat," Pearson

said, as he removed his black robe and belted on his pistol. "I'd be lying if I said I wasn't concerned."

"Me, too," Ditch said. "Our new jail is as solid as they come. It's a stone building with a tin roof and only one door and window. But we don't know how many men Odom has or how close they are? The only thing we know about them is that they're killers like him."

"Likely they're already somewhere in town," Babbit observed. "A handful of gunmen wearing disguises, like the ones Odom and his accomplices wore, could easily blend in with the regular flow of out-of-town travelers, drovers, dock workers, ranch hands, lumbermen, and laborers passing through Atherton each day."

"Odom usually travels with a posse of about a half-dozen gun hands," Bonner said. "I'm sure the man I killed today wasn't the only one he brought."

"But how could the Colonel get word to them," Pearson asked, "if he's locked up in our jail?"

"He won't have to," Ditch said. "For all we know, one or more of 'em was in that courtroom watchin' the proceedin's firsthand."

"What do you think those backshootin' varmints of Odom's will do?" Tater asked.

"I know what I'd do if I were them," Bonner offered. "Create a diversion somewhere else in town, far from the jail. A fire, a shooting, a stampede, a robbery, something that would get everyone to come running. While everybody in Atherton was preoccupied and distracted by that ruckus, a force of armed men could easily storm the jail."

"Your military and professional expertise," Judge Pearson said to Bonner, "is both profound and appreciated. I concur with your tactical assessment."

"So what should we do?" Tater said.

"We could declare martial law?" Ditch suggested. "Have everyone close up shop, shutter their doors and windows, clear the streets, arm every able-bodied man in Atherton, and have them patrol the town along with the Vigilance Committee?"

"That would rile up the townsfolk somethin' awful," Tater said, "and put everybody on edge. Not to mention, we couldn't maintain such a posture indefinitely. By mornin', all the men who'd stood watch durin' the night would be tired, frazzled, and durn-near useless. Between guardin' Ditch and his family, and maintaining the guard at the jail, the Vigilance Committee is already stretched plenty thin."

"Couldn't we wire for help from the army?" Babbit asked.

"They wouldn't get here in time," Ditch said. "Besides, they're already busy searchin' the countryside for Arkansas Jem Rupe and his gang."

"I know one thing we could do," Bonner said. A hard grin spread across his lean face. "Eliminate the reason Odom's men have for attacking the town."

"What do you propose?" Pearson asked.

Bonner withdrew one of his dirty brown cheroots from an inside pocket and struck a match. "What I have in mind would not only keep Odom's men from assaulting the jail directly, but it's guaranteed to bring them out of hiding."

"Just how, exactly," Ditch asked, "do you plan on accomplishing those things?"

"Easy," Bonner said, lighting his smoke. "Don't wait

for sunup. String Odom now. If that doesn't bring his boys out into the open, nothing will."

"I'd be happy to fetch a rope," Tater eagerly volunteered.

"I'm afraid moving up the timetable for Colonel Odom's hanging is out of the question," Judge Pearson said. "I've already ruled, and my ruling stated the sentence was to be carried out at sunrise. To be legal, sunrise it must be."

"It was worth a try, anyhow," Tater said to Bonner. Bonner shrugged and blew a smoke ring.

Chapter 32

"What is Tess talkin' about, Reverend Winfield?" Pritchard challenged. "Or should I call you Arkansas Jem Rupe?"

"I am not that man," Winfield said.

"Sure you are," Pritchard argued. "You're Jeremiah Rupe. I'd bet my horse on it."

In answer, Winfield looked away from Pritchard.

"There's no point lying any longer," Tess said, as she turned to Strobl. To his surprise, she went onto his arms and began crying into his chest. "Uncle Hoke's dead," she sobbed. "All these bounty men are dead. We've nearly been killed." She looked up and her eyes met Strobl's, then turned their focus back onto Winfield. "No more killing, Pa. No more lies."

Winfield hung his head. "I reckon you're right, daughter. It's time for the lies to end." He looked again at Pritchard. "You're not wrong, Marshal. I'm Jem Rupe. Have been since the day I was born."

Pritchard turned to Sheriff Blevins. "How long have you known?"

"All my life." Blevins sighed. "I grew up around here,

remember? I've known the Rupe family since I was a boy. Hoke taught me to fish." He nodded his chin at the reverend. "And Jem here taught me to shoot."

"Huh?" Deputy Spears exclaimed. "You knew Reverend Winfield was Arkansas Jem Rupe all along, and you never said nuthin' to nobody?"

"It's nobody's business," Blevins told his deputy. "The war's long over. Everyone else who knew Jem Rupe is dead or moved on. Me, his daughter, and Hoke were the only ones hereabouts who knew the truth."

"Why didn't you tell anyone?" Spears blurted. "You could've made a bundle of cash?"

"Don't need a bundle of cash," Blevins said. "Besides, I reckon the Golden Rule applies. Figured Jem had as much right as anyone to put the war behind him, forget, raise his daughter, and live out the remainder of his life in peace. It's what I'd want, iffen I were him."

"And I'll always be grateful," Rupe said.

"Arkansas Jem Rupe," Spears whistled, "right under my nose all this time. Been attendin' his sermons since I was a kid. Don't that beat all?"

"Tell them," Tess said. "Tell it all." Her father nodded.

"I was a broken man," Rupe began, "when the war ended. I had a price on my head and the entire Union army on my trail, so I hid up in the hills. But when I got word my wife was sick, I knew I had to come home. The Union knew it, too, which was my undoing. Troops and bounty killers were waiting for me."

"I remember that night," Tess said, wiping her eyes and regaining her composure. She remained in Strobl's arms. "I was twelve years old."

"After my wife died, I was out of my mind with grief.

I let my guard down. That's when a Union patrol caught up to me. I killed most of them. They shot me all to hell—even shot out my eye—but I was able to get away alive. It was Hoke who found me, just this side of the grave, and got me back up into the hills. He hid me out and nursed me back to health."

"How'd you come to be the Reverend Oliver Winfield?" Pritchard asked.

"Hoke told everyone I'd been killed, which wasn't hard for folks to believe since the last time anyone saw me I'd been shot half-a-dozen times. He said he buried me up in the Ouachitas. When the army demanded he show them the grave, he claimed he was too drunk at the time to remember exactly where in the hills he planted me. They didn't believe him, of course. They whipped him senseless trying to get the truth, but he stuck to his story and kept my secret." He smiled at Tess. "Kept it until the day he died."

"A few months later," Rupe continued, "while still healing up and hiding out in the Ouachitas, I encountered a traveling religious barker named Oliver Winfield. He was very old, and near his end from consumption. He wintered with me, since we were both in no condition to travel further. During that time, we read together from the Bible every night. He passed the following spring and I buried him. I gave him a Christian planting as best I could."

"You must have missed your daughter?" Strobl said.

"Something powerful," Rupe said. "So I burned my fancy top hat with the turkey feather, shaved off my soup-catcher, patched up my missing eye, and came home in the Reverend Oliver Winfield's wagon full of Bibles as the Reverend Oliver Winfield himself. I looked mighty different, by then, on account of losing my whiskers, so much weight, and one of my eyes. I also took on the posture of being a man of God, which wasn't merely a disguise. I haven't touched a gun, nor acted in anger, in ten years."

"Hidin' in plain sight," Spears said.

"I've been living by the word of the Lord, and the Good Book, ever since I stopped being Jeremiah Rupe and became Oliver Winfield. Doing my best to raise my little girl and make amends for what I done in the war."

"A feller can't be blamed for that," Blevins said, patting Rupe on the shoulder.

"I thought Jeremiah Rupe was dead and buried," Rupe went on, "but he was resurrected, just like Jesus. As soon as I heard about that train wreck in Missouri last week, and that Jeremiah Rupe was the man who did it, I knew there'd be another bounty. What I didn't figure on was how big it would be. Once I learned it was a-hundred-thousand dollars, I knew lawmen and bounty killers would be coming from all over hell's half-acre to collect it." He looked out at the numerous bodies strewn over the church grounds. "I'd have to say, I was right."

Rupe aimed his eye directly at Pritchard. "Looks like you just got yourself one-hundred-thousand dollars richer, Marshal."

"I'll tell you what I told your brother Hoke," Pritchard said. "I ain't interested in any bounty money, nor in you, Jem, other than to find you, which I done, and prove you didn't wreck and rob that train. My only aim is them who did. I have no quarrel with you, and no reason to arrest you."

"I don't believe you," Rupe said. "One-hundred-thousand dollars isn't a bounty, Marshal, it's king's ransom. And if the money wasn't enough, you'd also have the honor of being the man who hunted down and captured Arkansas Jem Rupe, the infamous trainwrecker. If it isn't the money you're after, it's the fame, no matter what you claim. But since you and your deputy saved me and my Tess, I suppose you're entitled to collect that reward money, and all the glory, as much as any other bounty hunter. All I ask of you, and I know I don't have any right, is to let my Tess go? Nobody has to know she was here when you and your deputy caught me. Let her get away from here, change her name, and start a new life without the burden and shame of her father's sins upon her shoulders?"

"To hell with the damned bounty," Pritchard said. "I don't care a whit about reward money, and I damn sure don't give a hoot about fame nor glory. I done swore an oath to bring them who wrecked that train to account, and I aim to keep it."

"I still don't believe you," Rupe insisted.

"Marshal Pritchard is not lying," Strobl spoke up. "He is a man of honor. Of this I can swear, on my own honor, as well as my life."

"I can swear to his character as well," Blevins added. "I've ridden a few trails, and hunted a few outlaws, with Samuel since he became the Marshal of Atherton and the Sheriff of Jackson County. If Samuel Pritchard says he ain't interested in your bounty nor your hide, and he ain't a-gonna arrest you, you ain't a-gonna be arrested. That's as sure as sundown."

"I . . . I don't understand?" a confused Rupe said to

Pritchard. "You really don't want to collect the bounty on me?"

"For a learned Man of God," Pritchard said, shaking his head, "you're a mite thick-headed, Reverend. All I want is to know if you wrecked and robbed that Missouri train?"

"Of course not," Rupe said. "On the day that train was wrecked I was here in Booneville, three-hundred miles away. I haven't left town in months."

"It's true," Tess said. "We were here."

"Do you have any other witnesses who can bear that out?" Pritchard asked.

"The Reverend Winfield gives two sermons every day," Blevins said. "One in the mornin' and one in the evenin'. My wife's religious. I was at the mornin' sermon on the day of the train wreck. Me, and about two-dozen other folks in Booneville, can testify to that fact in any court of law. I can also swear to knowin' Jem Rupe all my life."

"Can you also swear to how long he's been missin' an eye?" Pritchard asked.

"Of course," Blevins said, confused. "He lost that eye only a few months after the war ended. What's Jem's missin' eye got to do with anything?"

"The witness to the train wreck," Pritchard explained, "never said nothin' about the man claimin' to be Arkansas Jem Rupe missin' an eye."

"I reckon that might make a difference," Blevins conceded, "in provin' Jem's innocence."

"I suspect it will," Rupe agreed.

"Would you, Mr. Rupe," Pritchard said formally, "and you, Sheriff Blevins, be willin' to accompany me to

Fort Smith and swear out your statements before Judge Isaac Parker?"

"He can't," Tess interjected, before either man could answer. "If my father goes to Fort Smith and reveals himself, he'll be arrested and hung for what happened at Platte Bridge. President Grant has sworn to it."

"That remains to be seen," Pritchard said.

"I won't let him go," Tess insisted. "I won't see my father hung for the crime of following orders during the war, something every other soldier did."

"I'll go to Fort Smith," Rupe said flatly. "It's high time I stopped hiding and faced my accusers."

"I'll be right there along with you," Blevins said. "We'll face 'em together."

"No!" Tess protested.

Rupe took his daughter gently from Strobl's arms and pulled her to him. "Tess," he said, hugging her tightly, "I took on a false name, and posed as someone else all these years, to protect you. But I've been discovered. That means you've been discovered. You're in danger now."

"Your pa's right," Blevins said.

"You're all grown now"—Rupe's eye met Strobl's and he nodded—"and don't need my protection any longer. So it's time for me to step out of the shadows and bring back honor to our family's name. To do that, I must walk into the light. I believe that's the path God wants me to walk, and why he allowed Marshal Pritchard and Deputy Strobl to find me first, instead of those bounty killers. It's time to cast aside the Reverend Oliver Winfield, and become Jeremiah Rupe again. I don't expect you to understand, my precious girl, but I do expect you to know that I must follow my conscience and do what's right. And to know that I love you."

Tess nodded, biting back her tears. Rupe turned again to Pritchard. "I leave my fate in God's, and your, hands, Marshal," he said.

"I reckon you could do worse," Blevins said.

"I'm ready to go," Rupe said. "I give you my word, Marshal, that you'll have no trouble from me."

"Don't expect I will," Pritchard said. "We'd best get mounted and ride out before any more fellers with visions of riches in their heads and guns in their hands come a-callin'."

"You and Tess pack what you need and hitch up your team to the buckboard," Blevins said to Rupe. "I'll get my horse."

"I'll ready our horses," Strobl said to Pritchard.

"No," Pritchard corrected his deputy. "I'll saddle our horses. You stay with Tess and her father."

"Afraid I'll run off?" Rupe said upon hearing Pritchard's order.

"Nope," Pritchard said. "You done gave me your word, didn't you? I want a solid gun hand near you both, in case we get any more unexpected visitors."

"Fair enough."

"What about me?" Deputy Spears asked Blevins. "You want me to go along with you?"

"Nope," Blevins said. "You're in charge of Booneville, Jim, until I get back. I want you to raise a party of menfolk to help you bury all these dead men around the church and round up their horses. Collect all their guns and valuables, too, and lock up all the swag in the jail. Then I want you to deputize and arm a posse to patrol the town in the event any more bounty killers come a-sniffin' around. Think you can you handle all that?"

"Sure I can, Sheriff," Spears said with a wounded look. "Why couldn't I? Anything else?"

"One more thing, Jim," Blevins said. "Get yourself to the telegraph office and send out a wire to Fort Smith. Let Judge Parker know that Marshal Pritchard and I will be bringin' in Arkansas Jem Rupe."

Chapter 33

"Shake a leg on those steaks!" Dady Perkins howled into the kitchen over the din. "Put a better crisp on the cheese taters! They're too soft! And while you're at it, check the scald on those yardbird stems! The chicken legs are comin' out like they could run away by themselves!"

Dady Perkins was a robust, handsome, blond woman in her early-forties with smiling eyes and a warm face. Widowed during the war and never remarried, she put all her energy into the business which was her livelihood. Despite her warm appearance, when in her diner in the middle of the suppertime scramble, she had a voice like a lumber crew foreman and the carriage of a ship's captain on rough seas.

Perkins's Diner was the largest, if not the best, eatery in Atherton. While there were a few fancier eating establishments in town featuring more elaborate menus, and certainly several more expensive ones, no restaurant offered better food at lower prices.

Consequently, Perkins's Diner was packed full of hungry customers every breakfast, lunch, and dinner. The eatery had originally been a lumber camp chow hall before the war, but as Atherton grew so did the diner. Capable of serving over two-hundred patrons at a time, and employing a staff of over twenty cooks, waitresses, and busboys, the diner, which occupied a large building adjacent to the General Store and Mercantile, was a popular mainstay of Atherton's daily life.

Deputy Tater Jessup, who received a healthy discount on his meals in exchange for rendering janitorial services to the diner after closing time, revered Dady and considered her diner the closest thing to heaven he'd ever experienced. The restaurant's most loyal customer, he was often the very first patron in line for breakfast when the doors opened at sunrise. Nicknamed as a youth for his physique and affinity for spuds, Tater was particularly fond of Perkins's blueberry pancakes. He had been seen by multiple, credible witnesses to have consumed more than thirty of the delicious, spongey, blue cakes in a single sitting.

Tater had just left the crowded diner carrying a basket containing a steak and potatoes dinner for the Atherton jail's only prisoner in one hand, and his shotgun in the other. He couldn't wait to get back to the Marshal's Office where mortician Seth Tilley had agreed to mind Colonel Odom while he fetched the condemned man's last meal. As soon as that chore had been tended to, Tater planned to amble straight back to the diner and get himself fed.

Tater had no sooner rounded the corner of a local law office, stepping past the alley separating it and a dress shop, when two men emerged from the shadows behind him. A pistol was discretely pressed into Tater's back. One of the gunman, a thin fellow dressed as a lumberjack, fell into step on one side of the portly deputy. His partner, a stouter man wearing the attire of a ranch hand, bracketed him on the other.

"Not a word, Deputy," the lumberjack said softly. Tater heard dual *clicks* as the revolver's hammer was thumbed past half-cock all the way to the rear. "Keep walking. Make a sound, or go for your guns, and we'll shoot you down right here in the street."

The ranch hand relieved Tater of his shotgun and re-volver. He quickly removed the two shells from the scattergun and handed it back. As they continued to walk, he extracted the five cartridges from Tater's Colt and stuffed it back into the deputy's holster.

"You're Colonel Odom's boys, ain't ya?" Tater asked, silently cursing himself for the gastrointestinal-induced absent-mindedness that allowed him to be taken with so little effort. He was keenly aware that neither Marshal Pritchard nor Deputy Strobl would have been caught un-awares so easily.

None of the other passers-by paid much attention to the trio of men, who appeared to be merely three acquain-tances engaged in casual conversation as they strolled the evening boardwalk together.

"That's right," the lumberjack said, prodding Tater with the barrel of his gun. "You're gonna walk us into that jail and fetch the Colonel out of his cell. If you don't get stupid, and do like you're told, you'll survive this night."

"As far as me gettin' stupid," Tater said out of the side of his mouth, "most folks hereabouts would argue that horse is already out of the barn." The men strolled past the just-completed gallows in the center of the town square. It was after sunset, and the crew was packing up their tools. One of the workmen gave Tater a friendly wave. He replied with a weak smile and a nod of his head.

"You'd best re-think your notion about springin' Odom," Tater said. "He ain't a-goin' nowhere. Whether you shoot me, or not, don't matter a whit. There's a feller inside the marshal's office with a fifty-two caliber Sharp's rifle. At the first sign of trouble, he's got orders to plug the Colonel outright."

"We figured you'd have something like that set up," the ranch hand said. "So we set up a little somethin' of our own. Take a gander behind you, Deputy, back at the diner."

Tater stopped walking and slowly turned around to examine Perkins's Diner, behind them in the square. Two men were standing in front of the closed front door. Both were dressed as common laborers, both wore revolvers, and both were smoking cigars. He could see their glowing tips. Between the men, set in front of the diner's entrance, was a five-gallon tin bucket Tater instantly recognized as the type sold at the Atherton General Store and typically used to contain kerosene. One of the men smiled and waved his lit cigar at Tater and his escort.

"Know what's in that pail in front of the diner?" the lumberjack asked Tater.

"Coal oil," Tater said, with dread.

"That's right, Deputy," the man said. "Evidently, you ain't as stupid as you look. There's two more of our boys with another pail just like it at the diner's rear door. If they hear a gunshot—it don't matter who fires it—they're gonna tip those buckets and light 'em off. How many folks you reckon are eatin' supper inside that diner tonight?"

"Why you filthy heeler!" Tater spat, his face reddening. "There's women and chilluns in there! They'd be cooked like pork fritters!"

"That's the idea," the lumberjack said. He jabbed Tater hard with his gun. "Keep your voice down, Deputy, or I'll plug you and set off the whole shootin' match."

"Any man who'd threaten to burn up innocent folks is nuthin' but a white-livered poltroon," Tater said through his teeth. "I oughta—"

"You oughta think, Deputy," the ranch hand cut off Tater's tirade, "before your mouth lets loose the reins on your sense and you do somethin' everybody in town is gonna regret. You're a lawman, ain't ya? Sworn to protect the citizens of Atherton? All you've gotta do, to honor your oath and keep everybody safe, is to walk us into that jail, turn the Colonel loose, and let us ride away. Nobody has to get hurt."

"Iffen I don't?"

"Atherton is gonna have itself a mighty big barbeque tonight."

Tater knew he had no choice. Even if he had the means to resist, which he did not, doing so would result in the agonizing deaths of countless of his fellow Athertonians, many of them, as he'd pointed out to his captors, women and children.

"All right," Tater said glumly. "You can have your damned Colonel. Take him and leave the innocent folks here be."

"That's the plan," the lumberjack said, as the trio reached the jail. "We know the marshal's office door is locked, because we watched you lock it when you left for the diner. Open the door, go inside, and we'll follow in behind you. No tricks. If you get heroic, Deputy, them citizens in the diner get scorched."

Tater nodded, handed the gunman dressed as a ranch hand the dinner basket, and unlocked the office door with a key from his pocket. He stepped inside to find Seth Tilley reading the *Athertonian* by lamplight at Marshal Pritchard's desk and Colonel Odom lounging on his cot in the nearest cell. Tilley's Sharps rifle was leaning against the desk.

The undertaker looked up in astonishment as Tater was pushed roughly aside and two men quickly entered the office behind him. The man dressed as a lumberjack stepped forward, leaned across the desk, and placed the barrel of his gun inches from Tilley's face. The man dressed as the ranch hand closed the door behind them.

"Touch that rifle," the lumberjack said to Tilley, "and die where you sit."

"I reckon so," Tilley said with no emotion. The ranch hand snatched up his rifle.

"About time," Odom declared, rising from his bunk in the cell to greet the newcomers. "I was beginning to think you boys were going to let these yokels hang me."

"We didn't forget you, Colonel." The lumberjack smiled. "You ain't paid us yet, remember?"

"I'm sorry, Seth," Tater explained mournfully. "They got the drop on me. Worse'n that, they've got boys with buckets of coal oil staged at both doors of the diner. Said they'd torch the place, with everyone inside, iffen I didn't let 'em spring the prisoner."

"No need to apologize, Tater," Tilley said, as he raised his hands and slowly stood up. "Ain't your fault. This is exactly what Laird said would happen."

"If Bonner told you that," Odom grinned, as the ranch hand found the keys and unlocked his cell, "you boys should have listened. Where is he, anyway? He's the only gun hand in this hick town we need to worry about."

"What do I look like," Tater snapped, "his minder?"

The lumberjack switched his gun from Tilley back to Tater. "Answer the Colonel's question, Deputy."

"No need to threaten nobody," Tilley said. "Ain't no secret. Bonner's at the hotel, eatin' dinner with the mayor and his wife."

"You wanna go get him?" the ranch hand asked Odom. "We can do him in at the same time we polish off Mayor Clemson. Ain't that what we came to Atherton for?"

"Forget it," Odom said. "Taking on the local Vigilance Committee is one thing. Taking on Laird Bonner is quite another. We'll make our exit and finish our business at a more opportune time. We can always come back to Atherton when the odds are more in our favor. Are the horses ready?"

"Staged outside of town," the lumberjack said. "Ready and waitin'."

"Put these two in a cell," Odom ordered, pointing to Tater and Tilley, "and let's go."

The gunman dressed as a lumberjack prodded Tilley and Tater toward the cells.

"Hold on a minute," Odom halted the gunman. He approached Tater.

"I recall mentioning during my trial," Odom gloated, "that you bumpkins weren't going to get the chance to see me swing."

"You'll swing, all right," Tater said. "Maybe not tomorrow at sunup, but you're a-gonna dangle, sure as

Jesus wears sandals. Marshal Pritchard will see to it personal."

Odom's smile vanished. He extended his hand, snapped his fingers, and the man dressed as the lumberjack handed over his pistol. It was already cocked when Odom put it to Tater's head.

"I didn't forget that you struck me with your shotgun this morning," Odom said.

"How could you?" Tater replied with a chuckle. "Ain't every day a feller gets to see a meal twice—before, and after, he's ate it. You shoulda seen yourself, down on all fours, barkin' up your breakfast? I declare"—he laughed—"I ain't never seen a feller puke that hard."

Odom's eyes flashed and his face reddened. Still keeping his weapon aimed at Tater, he stepped back, extended his arm, and placed his finger on the trigger.

"I wouldn't do that, boss, iffen I were you," the lumberjack said. "As it is, we can get out of town with nobody the wiser, slick-as-you-please. At the sound of a pistol shot, the boys'll light off the diner and every rifle in town will come a-runnin'."

"This is your lucky day, Deputy," Odom said, as his features relaxed and he lowered the pistol's hammer. He suddenly slammed the weapon down on Tater's skull, sending the lawman instantly to the floor with blood flowing from his hairline. Tilley started to move forward toward Tater to render aid, but was stopped by a jab from the ranch hand's gun.

"Lock them up," Odom commanded. "Tie them, gag them, and let's be off. I've grown weary of Atherton. For today, anyway."

Chapter 34

"This is a very good ale," Bonner said, wiping the foam from his upper lip. He clinked his mug with Ditch's.

"You can say that again," Ditch agreed, after downing a swallow. "Best beer in Jackson County."

"Manfri Pannell brews it," Idelle said, "over at the Sidewinder. I don't drink beer myself, but his wife told me he brought the recipe with him from England. He lets the hotel have a keg each week, as long as we don't charge less than the Sidewinder does."

"Wherever he got it," Bonner said after another sip, "you can bet I'll be sampling it again."

The trio, along with Baby Samuel, had just finished dining at the restaurant inside the Atherton Arms and were enjoying after-dinner libations. Idelle was sipping from a glass of red wine.

John Babbit entered the hotel with Judge Pearson on his heels. Babbit was holding a sheaf of papers, and both men were animated.

"Just got a reply from the governor's office," Babbit exclaimed excitedly. He thrust a stack of telegrams on the table. "Governor Hardin has agreed to host the meeting.

The army is going to be there, and both railroads, too."
He pointed at the telegrams. "See for yourself. Most of
the mayors and acting mayors have signed on. Your
gamble paid off, Ditch."

"I figured it would," Ditch said, scanning the telegrams,
"once the governor and the two railroad bosses realized
that no Missouri town, especially one without a mayor on
account of that train wreck, was gonna stand for Hardin
and his cronies decidin' which railroad company got
awarded that big, fat, federal contract without their say-
so."

"For such a young mayor," Pearson said, giving Ditch's
good shoulder a squeeze, "you exhibit uncommon political savvy."

"Don't have to be George Washington to know that
Governor Hardin wants to get re-elected," Ditch said.
"Any word from the president?"

"Haven't heard a word from Washington," Babbit said.

"We'll hear from Grant's office, all right," Pearson
said, "once he susses out that a major cross-country railroad expansion is dead in the water unless the State of
Missouri sorts out the squabble between the Brody Line
and the Missouri Pacific Railroad."

"That's what I was bettin' on," Ditch said, "when I had
you send out all those wires."

"Glad to do it," Babbit said. "I just hope your scheme
pays off."

"I'm a bit confused," Bonner admitted. "What scheme?"

"Immediately after Colonel Odom's trial this afternoon," Judge Pearson explained, "Ditch had John send
out a batch of telegrams to all the towns and villages in
Missouri announcing the second attempt on his life, by a

paid-for killer, and suggesting that until further notice they refuse to participate in any of the government's railway expansion plans. Ditch was betting that putting the brakes on the federal government's big railroad contract would send a clear message to the governor that unless he does something about the lawlessness associated with these railroads, his days as chief executive of the State of Missouri are numbered."

"Evidently Governor Hardin got the message," Idelle said, nuzzling Samuel.

"I'm sure John's editorial in the *Athertonian,*" Pearson added, "which was distributed to every newspaper in Kansas City, Independence, Jefferson City, and Saint Louis, had something to do with the governor's sudden epiphany."

"That was quite a piece of writing, John," Ditch complimented. "You really outdid yourself. While you didn't outright state it, you hinted that the real reason the train was wrecked had little to do with robbin' it and more to do with the competition between the Brody Line and the Missouri Pacific for the government contract. Anybody with a lick of brains readin' that editorial of yours would conclude that Hardin was allowin' John Brody and Jason Gould to fight it out amongst themselves, with the good folks of Missouri caught in the crossfire between 'em, purely to raise the stakes in their under-the-table, back-room deal with him."

"One of my better editorials," Babbit smiled, "if I may say so myself. But don't forget to thank Judge Pearson. He suggested it."

"What's this about a meeting?" Bonner asked.

"Ditch's telegrams also suggested a single meeting,"

Babbit said, "unlike the two separate ones which were originally scheduled between all the mayors in Eastern Missouri and the two individual railroads. Remember how those meetings got canceled on account of the train wreck?"

"No coincidence," Bonner said.

"This time," Babbit went on, "Ditch proposed that the meeting be an open invitation to all the mayors and municipalities in the State of Missouri. He further proposed that it be held in Jefferson City. Not only is Jefferson City the capital, and has several rail lines running through it, it's in the center of the state. It's the easiest place for everyone to get to."

"Ditch put Governor Hardin in a real bind," Pearson said. "Sandwiched him between the mayors, a mob of angry constituents, the army, the federal government, and the two railroads. If he wants to stay in office, he had no choice but to agree."

"That was very clever," Bonner said to Ditch. "You practically dared the governor not to host the meeting. When's the big pow-wow going to take place?"

Before Ditch could answer, the doors to the hotel burst open and Ronnie Babbit, John Babbit's eleven-year-old son, came running in. He skidded to a halt at Ditch's table, his face red and his chest heaving.

"What's wrong?" Babbit asked, recognizing the alarm in his son's features. "Take a breath, Ronnie, and tell us what's got you so riled?"

"Trouble," Ronnie breathlessly declared. "Down at the jail. The prisoner's gone."

"Colonel Odom's escaped?" Pearson exclaimed.

"That ain't all," Ronnie said. "Deputy Tater's been

hurt. I already fetched Doc Mauldin and sent him over to the jail."

The group wordlessly stood and headed from the Atherton Arms to the jail. Ditch insisted the others go on ahead, since he couldn't move as fast on his crutch, but Bonner refused. After the attempts on Ditch and his family, Bonner was reluctant to leave his side.

By the time they reached the jail, a crowd had already formed outside the marshal's office. "Make way!" Judge Pearson demanded, as he, Babbit, Ditch, Idelle with Baby Samuel, and Bonner pushed their way through the throng and into the marshal's office.

Tater was sitting up on the floor, with Mauldin and Seth Tilley tending to him. Mauldin was holding a bloody towel against the deputy's injured forehead. Tater looked up when Ditch, his wife and son, Pearson, Babbit, and Bonner entered. The expression on his face belied the shame and anger he felt.

"It's all my fault," Tater lamented. "I got taken by Odom's boys as easy as a coyote takes a lingerin' lamb. I'm right sorry, Ditch . . . er, I mean, Mayor Clemson."

"It ain't just Tater's fault," Tilley chimed in. "I was caught flat-footed, too. If there's any blame to be laid, at least half belongs to me."

"Nobody's to blame," Ditch insisted, "'cept Colonel Walton Odom himself." He turned to Mauldin. "How bad is he hurt, Doc?"

"Deputy Jessup will need a few stitches," Mauldin said, "and will likely have a headache for a spell, but otherwise he's going to be okay."

"Are you sure he'll be all right?" a concerned Idelle asked, as Tilley and Mauldin helped Tater to his feet. In response, Tater immediately bent back down to the floor and grabbed the basket containing what was supposed to be Colonel Walton Odom's last meal. Oblivious to all around him, Tater lifted the basket's lid, inhaled the content's aroma, and said, "I knew it; apple pie. I just knew Dady's Dutch apple pie was gonna be that varmint's dessert."

"He's all right," Ditch confirmed.

"Well," Idelle remarked, "if there's any good to come of this, at least we're rid of Colonel Odom. That man was evil."

"We're not entirely rid of the Colonel," Bonner contradicted. "I know Odom. Like any professional gunman, his livelihood depends on his reputation. He was paid to do a job, which was to end Ditch, and he didn't get it done. If he wants to get paid, and to continue working in the future, he's got to ensure that his reputation for completing a job remains intact."

"Which means," Ditch said, "he'll be a-comin' after me again, won't he?"

"That's a certainty," Bonner said with a smile. He withdrew one of his dirty brown cheroots from the inside pocket of his coat and lit it with a wooden match.

"No offense, Mr. Bonner," Babbit said, "but if you don't mind me saying so, you seem almost happy that Odom escaped."

"Not happy," Bonner said, "just grateful for the opportunity."

"Opportunity?" Idelle said in disbelief.

"Yep," Bonner said, exhaling smoke. "Now that Colonel Odom's escaped, I presume he'll have a bounty on his head, won't he?"

"He surely will," Judge Pearson said. "In addition to the charges for which he was already scheduled to be hung, I'm adding the crimes of assaulting an officer of the law and escaping from the Atherton Jail. That'll put his bounty at well over five-thousand dollars."

Bonner's smile widened. "Yes, Mrs. Clemson, I'm indeed grateful. A man's got to make a living, doesn't he? After all, I am a bounty hunter."

Chapter 35

"Mr. Earl Marsh and Mr. Asa Finchum to see you."

"Send them in, Charles," Brody said.

John Brody sat behind his massive desk in his opulent Kansas City office and did not rise when Marsh and Finchum walked in. Both men were wearing expensive suits, contrasted by their new holstered revolvers. Marsh's black eyes had faded, though the gaps where teeth used to be were still visible, and Finchum's wired-up jaw was discernible by the odd appearance of his clenched teeth. Finchum was carrying a paper-wrapped bundle under one arm.

"We're glad you finally agreed to meet with us, Mr. Brody," Marsh said.

"It appears I didn't have much choice," Brody replied. "Your telegram, though cryptic, suggested that I either meet with you immediately, or you would be meeting with Jason Gould in Saint Louis. Your threat to extort me was quite clear."

"You'll be glad you did," Marsh said. "You'll have to forgive me for speaking for Asa, but he's having a bit of difficulty talking these days. Difficulty eating, too, no thanks to Marshal Pritchard."

"I care nothing for your troubles," Brody said. "In fact, I recall, during our last, and what I presumed would be our final, meeting, warning you both what would happen if you opened your mouths about our previous dealings."

"You did indeed," Marsh said.

"What makes you think that warning wasn't to be heeded?" Brody stood up and puffed out his chest, which was largely unnoticeable due to the size of his stomach. "I will not be blackmailed by a pair of cut-rate gunmen. A word from me, along with the proper financial incentive, and the both of you would be dead within a week."

"Speaking of financial incentives," Marsh said, "how much would you be willing to pay to have us ended?"

"Does it matter?" Brody said dismissively. He nodded to Charles, who stepped forward with a decanter and a single snifter and began to pour brandy. He offered none to Marsh or Finchum.

"You two are nobodies," Brody said. "Any number of competent professional gunmen, unlike yourselves, would take the job for hundreds, not thousands, of dollars. I spend more on brandy and cigars each week than it would cost to see you both buried."

"You're wrong about that," Marsh said. "It would cost you more than forty-thousand dollars to have us gunned."

"Forty-thousand dollars?" Brody scoffed. "Hah! For that amount I could get President Grant shot."

"Forty-thousand is what it'll cost you," Marsh said. "Because that's how much money was in the canvas payroll bag which was taken out of your safe while you were getting your whiskers scraped."

Marsh elbowed Finchum, who unwrapped the parcel under his arm and tossed its contents on Brody's mahogany desk. It was a canvas payroll bag.

"You remember this satchel, don't you? It's the one you had us nick from Jason Gould's train after we wrecked it for you? It's marked *Property of the Missouri Pacific Railroad,* and even has a number stenciled on it which identifies it as the payroll bag from that particular train."

Brody's puffed-out chest deflated and his face went slack. "I suspected it might have been you two who orchestrated the theft. Who else would have known the payroll was in my safe besides the men who put it there?"

"A fair point," Marsh said, stepping forward. Finchum spread his coat apart, exposing his new pair of Colt revolvers. Both of their expressions hardened. "You're damn right we took it," he said. "After you crawfished on us, insulted us, and threatened to have us killed, what did you expect?"

"What do you want?" Brody demanded.

"First," Marsh said, "a drink. Then we can either sit down and talk business, like reasonable men, or Asa and I will go to Saint Louis and talk business with Jason Gould. We feel he'd be delighted to speak with us. He'd be even more delighted to get some of his money back and hear all about how we happened to come into its possession, don't you think?"

"Very well," Brody said, realizing he had no choice but to concede. He didn't become a railroad tycoon by refusing to recognize when he was cornered.

Brody waved to Charles, who appeared with two more brandy snifters. "It would seem we will be back in business together. Before we resume our working relationship, however, I need to know how much money is still in that bag?"

"Twenty-thousand," Marsh said.

"Twenty-thousand?" Brody exclaimed. "Why, there was over forty-thousand dollars in that bag when it was taken from my safe!"

"After you short-changed us the first time, we reckoned it might be better to hold on to our share, and not wait for you to pay us."

"But I already paid you five-thousand dollars each!" Brody argued. "I only owed you ten!"

"The other ten is for our troubles," Marsh said, "and for trying to cheat us."

"This hardly seems like the way to resume an honest business affiliation," Brody grumbled.

"Nobody ever accused you of being an honest man," Marsh said. "Do you want to do business with us, or not?"

"It seems I have little choice," Brody said. After Charles poured for Marsh and Finchum, Brody lifted his own glass, started to take a sip, but then stopped himself. "Before we drink to our newly rekindled business affiliation," he said, "there's someone else who would like to join us in our toast."

He motioned to Charles, and the servant walked over to an adjoining door and opened it. A medium-sized man in his mid-forties with a full head of closely cropped white hair and a sculpted beard entered. Charles handed the newcomer a snifter of brandy as he approached the trio at Brody's desk.

"Mr. Marsh and Mr. Finchum," Brody made the introductions, "meet Colonel Walton Odom. You'll be working together from now on."

Marsh and Finchum, who'd seen Odom briefly only once before but knew him by reputation, appraised the older man coolly. Odom merely smiled and nodded.

Brody raised his glass. "Gentlemen," he toasted, "here's to solving our mutual problems. Let's hope our joint business venture has more success in the future than it's had in the past."

"I'll drink to that," Odom said.

"Why not?" Marsh said.

The four men drank. Finchum winced as the brandy flowed past his wired jaw.

"I have a bit of news," Brody said, "which should make your jobs somewhat easier. Earlier today I received a telegram informing me that Marshal Pritchard has located the real Arkansas Jem Rupe."

"I thought Rupe was dead?" Marsh said.

"I did, too," Brody acknowledged. "I thought everybody believed him dead. It's why I chose Rupe as the scapegoat in the first place."

"Evidently Marshal Pritchard didn't believe Rupe was dead," Odom remarked.

"Evidently," Brody mimicked.

"This is bad," Marsh said. "Bad for all of us. If the real Rupe's alive, and he's got an alibi for the train wreck, then—"

"—the authorities," Brody interrupted him, "are going to be searching elsewhere for those responsible."

"You mean searching for us, don't you?" Marsh said.

"Speak for yourselves," Odom said bluntly. "I never wrecked any train."

"Perhaps not," Brody said. "But if I'm not mistaken, you allowed yourself to get caught in the act of trying to murder the only surviving mayor of that train wreck. As a result, you now have a death sentence hanging over your head. You're in this as much as any of us, Colonel Odom. Neck deep, I daresay, if you'll pardon the pun."

"What are we going to do?" Marsh asked.

"The answer should be obvious," Brody said. "Marshal Pritchard, and anyone else who could testify to Rupe's identity, must be silenced. The same goes for Atherton's pesky mayor."

"Clemson's no longer a problem," Odom said. "He's a one-legged nobody. I plan on dealing with him eventually, but there's no rush."

"You're wrong, Colonel," Brody said. "Clemson is not a 'nobody,' and time is of the essence. Apparently, he's got enough juice to bring the current Missouri railroad expansion negotiations I've worked so hard to influence to a standstill."

"How could he do that?" Marsh said.

"He buffaloed Governor Hardin. Made him call a meeting in Jefferson City, in only a few short days, which will be attended by the army, most of the mayors in Missouri, and myself, as well as my aggravating counterpart at the Missouri Pacific, Jason Gould, not to mention the President of the United States."

"That changes things," Marsh said.

"Sounds like we have our work cut out for us," Odom said.

"How many men do you have at your disposal?" Brody asked them.

"I've got six," Odom said, rubbing his whiskers. "Seven, counting me."

"Four," Marsh said, "counting Asa and I. That's eleven

guns, total. I'd prefer to have a few more hands, Mr. Brody, if we're going after Samuel Pritchard. Don't forget, he cleaned out nearly a dozen of my men all by himself."

"Perhaps you should ride with better men?" Odom said.

"Perhaps you should go to hell," Marsh said, parting his coat to reveal his Smith & Wesson revolver. Finchum took a step forward.

"Please, gentlemen," Brody intervened. "This is no time to argue. We must work together, and work fast, if we are to solve our mutual problems."

"You should all know," Odom said, "that it's not just Samuel Pritchard and Mayor Clemson we have to worry about. Laird Bonner is in Atherton, and he's dealt himself into Clemson's hand."

"Laird Bonner?" Marsh said. "On Clemson's side? Me and Asa saw him gun a pair of men in Stillwater a couple of years back. Shot them both down before they cleared leather." He shook his head at Brody. "We're definitely going to need more men."

"If eleven men is what you've got," Brody said, "eleven is all you're getting. I'm not bringing in any more men. Too many people already know too much."

"That's going to cost you extra," Odom said.

"Damn right," Marsh said.

"That's rich," Brody said, "coming from three men I already paid who didn't finish the jobs they were paid for." He waved his hand and motioned for Charles to re-fill their glasses.

"You want to dicker over price," Marsh said, "that's fine with me and Asa. Horse-trading takes time, Mr.

Brody, and that's one thing you haven't got. I'm willing to bet if that big meeting Mayor Clemson called with the governor and the other Missouri mayors goes through, you and your railroad stand to lose a fortune, and you know it. Take all the time you want, figuring out our fee."

Marsh turned to Odom. "You, too, Colonel. You take your time, too. Me and Asa already have thirty grand in our pockets, and neither of us are running from a rope. We've got nothing but time."

"Quit playing games," Brody said to Marsh. "You're in no better position than the Colonel and I. We have bigger problems to worry about now. If we don't deal with Pritchard and Clemson, we're all going to be marching up the steps to the gallows."

"Are you saying if you're nabbed, you'll give up Asa and me?" Marsh challenged.

"All I'm saying," Brody shot back, "is the best thing for all of us is to silence Clemson and Pritchard."

"The more time we spend here sipping and jabbering," Odom remarked, "the closer Pritchard gets to Fort Smith and the sooner Clemson attends that meeting with the governor." He stared evenly at Marsh and Finchum. "Do you two want to work or to haggle?"

"We'll work," Marsh said. "But how do you figure we're going to get to Fort Smith and take care of Pritchard and Jem Rupe," Marsh asked, "and then to Atherton to deal with Clemson and Bonner in just a few days? I'm telling you, Mr. Brody, without more men at our disposal, it can't be done."

"Sure it can be done," Odom said. "Who says we have to traipse all over Arkansas and Missouri to track down

Pritchard and Clemson? Wouldn't it be much simpler to have them come to us?"

"And how, exactly," Marsh said, "do you plan on accomplishing that?"

"Easy," Odom said. "When I was in Atherton, I noticed something."

"What's that?" Marsh asked.

"Mayor Ditch Clemson," Odom answered with a satisfied smirk, "has a son. A baby boy named after his Uncle Samuel Pritchard. Clemson's family is forded up at the Atherton Arms Hotel, being guarded by a Vigilance Committee composed of local shopkeepers and field hands. Imagine, if you can, how quickly we could command the attention of that child's father and uncle if we were to get our hands on that wee little child?"

"I like the way you think," Marsh said to Odom. He smiled at Finchum, who couldn't smile back. "Don't you like the way the Colonel thinks, Asa?" Finchum could only nod in reply.

"Well," Brody asked, "what are you gentlemen waiting for?"

Chapter 36

The .44-40 caliber bullet, fired from a Winchester rifle at a distance of approximately twenty-five yards, struck Pritchard full in the chest. He tumbled backward from the saddle, his hat flew off, and he fell to the ground. The big roan stopped, and slowly began walking circles around him as he lay prone and unmoving.

Pritchard had been riding in the lead of their little caravan. Jem Rupe and his daughter Tess were in the middle in their buckboard, closely escorted by Strobl on Schatz, with Sheriff Blevins bringing up the rear. It was approaching sunset, and the group had traveled three-quarters of the forty-mile distance to Fort Smith since departing Booneville. Pritchard was scouting near a grove of trees for a place to make camp for the night when the gunshot rang out.

Strobl and Blevins drew their rifles, and were trying to determine where in the grove the rifle shot emanated from, when another gunshot rang out, followed by a chorus of at least five more.

A voice came from the grove. "Drop them guns!" the man hollered. "We've got you in the open, with six rifles on you-all. Iffen you boys don't lose them guns, we'll shoot the woman right offen that-there wagon."

"Samuel's down," Blevins said to Strobl. "There's no guarantee they won't kill us, anyway, if we surrender our guns."

"I'm inclined to agree," Strobl said. "Better to die on our feet than to be cut down on our knees."

"Don't be fools," Rupe interjected. Tess had thrown her arms around her father, her eyes wide in terror. "You heard how many shots just went off. Whoever they are, they've got half a dozen guns aimed at us, it's nearly dark, they're behind cover, and we can't even see them. If you resist, we're all dead. If you yield, we at least have a chance."

"Jem's right, I reckon," Blevins admitted. "If they wanted to kill us, they could have done it already."

Strobl looked at Tess. "Unfortunately," he said, "they are right."

"We're dropping our guns," Blevins called out. He threw out his rifle, and then his revolver. Strobl followed suit, discarding his Henry rifle, the Smith & Wesson, and the pair of Colts belted around his waist. He and Blevins dismounted, tied their horses to the back of the buckboard, and along with Rupe, raised their arms.

Six men emerged from the woods and approached. All but one looked like farmers and were carrying rifles. It was dark enough to hide their features until they were but a few paces away. One of them, obviously their leader, stood out in front.

"Surprised?" Deputy Jim Spears asked.

"I thought I recognized that voice," Blevins said, shaking his head in disgust. "You're a lawman, Jim. How could you?"

"Wrong, Marshal," Spears corrected. "I was a lawman till this mornin'. I ain't one now. I quit the law the moment I found out Jem Rupe, a feller worth more cash money than King Midas, was right under my nose."

"And to think I trusted you," Blevins grunted.

"Evenin', Preacher," Spears said, turning to Rupe. He tipped his hat to Tess. "Or should I call you Jem?"

"I don't care what you call me," Rupe said. "You are damned. You just murdered Marshal Pritchard in cold blood from ambuscade."

"Yes, I did," Spears gloated. "I just done in the toughest gun alive, all by my lonesome. Almost in the dark, too. Pretty fair shot, iffen I say so myself. Now I'm not only gonna be rich, I'll be famous, too."

"You're a coward and a murderer," Rupe said, "and you'll pay for what you've done."

"Get paid is what you meant to say, ain't it?" He turned to Strobl and Blevins. "You can put your arms down, fellers." Blevins, Rupe, and Strobl complied. "Because if either of you move foolish"—he pivoted and pointed his Winchester at Tess—"she gets it first." The other riflemen kept their weapons trained on the three men.

Tess gasped, and Rupe started to step forward. Blevins took his arm and halted him. "Easy, Jem."

"That's right," Spears mocked, "take it easy, Jem." He switched his rifle to Rupe. "I'd hate to have to plug you, but I will. From what I read on that reward notice back in Booneville, the bounty on you gets paid whether you're dead or alive. We can toss your big ole lanky carcass into that-there buckboard and ride you into Fort Smith easy as pie."

"So you did send that telegram to Fort Smith like I told you?" Blevins asked.

"I sent three of 'em, actually," Spears said. "One to Fort Smith, like you ordered me, tellin' Judge Parker that Arkansas Jem Rupe had been captured and was comin' in. But I made one minor change. Instead of wirin' that you and Marshal Pritchard were bringin' Rupe in, I notified the judge that Deputy James Spears of Booneville had captured him. What do you think about that?"

"I think you ain't a dime's worth of dog meat," Blevins said.

"Don't you want to know where I sent the other two telegrams?" Spears laughed, ignoring the insults. "I sent one to John Brody, the head of the Brody Railroad Line, and the other to Jason Gould, the boss of the Missouri Pacific. They're the fellers who put up the reward money. Their names were on the bottom of that reward poster in your office."

"Not takin' any chances, are you?" Blevins said.

"Not with the money that's owed me," Spears said. "I want those two railroad chiefs to know who's bringin' in their trophy."

"You have it all figured out," Strobl said, "don't you?"

"You sure talk funny," Spears said. "And yeah, I got it figured. That's why I'm a-standin' here with the drop, and you boys are about to get bedded down."

"Hold on a minute," Rupe said. "There's no cause for any further killing. I'll go along quietly with you to Fort Smith and give you no trouble. But you must let

Sheriff Blevins and Deputy Strobl escort Tess back to Booneville. She's not a part of this."

"She's part of it, all right," a man behind Spears said. He was fat, smelled of pig-grease, and leered at Tess. "The best part."

"We'll give her an escort, all right," one of the other men behind Spears said around his wad of tobacco. He was a seedy-looking man in a tattered coat and a shapeless felt hat.

"We'll escort her right outta that-there skirt and knickers," another of the gunmen, a stubby man in overalls, added.

Strobl's eyes narrowed. Rupe's face reddened, and his eye flashed. Blevins remained impassive.

"You mean to let these animals have a go at Tess?" Blevins asked.

"Who're you callin' animals?" Spears grinned. He winked at Tess. "I'm a-goin' first."

"Let's get to it," another of the riflemen spoke up. His dirty face was lit with anticipation. "I don't care who's first, or who's last, as long as I get my turn."

A vein bulged in Rupe's neck. Blevins kept a firm hand on his arm.

"Got chores to do, first," Spears said. "Pick up all those guns, and put 'em in the back of the buckboard. Somebody go fetch our horses outta them woods. Fetch Pritchard's horse, too, and while you're at it, check the marshal's carcass. His guns are mine, but any money or baubles you find on him you can divide among yourselves."

Three men went off to retrieve their horses, fetch Soldier, who was still standing over Pritchard, and scavenge his body. The other two remained with Spears to watch over the prisoners.

"That's quite a posse you brought with you," Blevins said sarcastically. "Top hands."

"They ain't exactly parade soldiers," Spears admitted, "but they're my kin, every one of 'em. I can trust 'em."

"How'd you get your family to join you in this murder spree?" Blevins asked.

"Easy," he said. "I promised to pay 'em, and to let 'em have a poke at Tess." He winked at her again. "After I get my poke first, of course."

"I'm afraid I won't allow that," Strobl said.

"How're you gonna stop me?" Spears challenged.

"I'm going to kill you," Strobl said calmly, in his Austrian accent.

"Is that so?" Spears said with a chuckle.

"On my oath," Strobl said.

"We'll see about that," Spears said.

"I'm begging you," Rupe appealed to Spears. "Let Tess go. Don't let these brutes do harm to her. You don't have to do this. You were once a man of the law. She's an innocent girl, for heaven's sakes. In the name of God—"

"Shut up," Spears cut him off. "You've got no right to be invokin' heaven or God. I've been listenin' to your high-and-mighty sermons since I was a kid. What a fool I was? Turns out, you wasn't even a real preacher. I'll take no requests from a man who wrecks trains."

"It was a long time ago," Rupe said. "It was war. I was a soldier, acting under orders."

"Shut up," Spears repeated. "You'll be gettin' yours at the end of a rope in Fort Smith, unless I grow weary of your mouth beforehand. In that case, I'll quiet you with a bullet and still collect my bounty."

Rupe hung his head and silently began to pray. Soon the only sounds that could be heard were crickets, and Tess Rupe's muffled weeping.

Chapter 37

"One of you get our horses from the woods," the eldest riflemen ordered his two companions, "and the other can fetch that big roan."

"What're you gonna be doin' while we're gatherin' horses?"

"I'm a-gonna see what valuables that dead lawman's got on him," he replied.

"The horses can wait," the second man said. "Let's search him together."

"Why not?" the first man said. "Strike a match, will ya?"

A match was lit, and three men stood directly over Pritchard's body. "Hold my rifle," the eldest one said. He knelt down, removed the two Colt revolvers from the lawman's holsters, and handed them up to one of the men standing over him. He began to roll the body over.

"Lord, but he's a big one," one of the standing men commented. "Must be halfway to seven feet tall?"

"He's right heavy, too," the kneeling man grunted.

"Seein' how big a target he is," the other standing man said, "I ain't so impressed any more with Jim's shot. Missin' this feller would've been like missin' a barn."

When Pritchard's body was finally rolled over onto its back, its eyes opened.

"Howdy, fellers," Pritchard said.

"We know you're takin' Jem into Fort Smith," Blevins said to Spears, "and what you've got in store for Tess Rupe. Mind divulgin' what you have lined up for Deputy Strobl and me?"

"You're no fool," Spears said. "I already told you what's a-comin' your way. It'll happen as soon as the rest of the boys get back with the horses."

"Why wait?" Strobl asked.

"He has to," Blevins answered before Spears could. "All of 'em have to shoot us together, at the same time, like in a firin' squad. If everyone puts a bullet into us, none of 'em can ever tattle on the others because they'd all be equally guilty. For kin, who he claims to trust, he surely don't trust 'em very much."

"Cowardly," Strobl commented, "but smart."

"I told you I had it all figured," Spears said. "Keep 'em covered well, boys," he reminded the two men with him. "They know what's waitin' for 'em. Desperate men are prone to desperate acts."

"Just let 'em try," the grease-covered rifleman said. He aimed his weapon at Strobl, and his tobacco-spitting counterpart aimed his gun at Blevins. "Iffen they get frisky, we'll send 'em to hell before the others get back."

"Still think you're gonna kill me?" Spears goaded Strobl.

"Indubitably," Strobl replied.

"Huh?" Spears said. "What the hell does that mean?"
Strobl rolled his eyes.

That's when three shots went off.

Lying on his back, staring up into the astonished,
match-lit, faces of three men looming over him, Pritchard
fan-fired his Remington revolver three times. Each man
received a .44 rimfire cartridge in the center of his face.

Pritchard leaped to his feet, stuffed the 1863 Remington back into the empty holster under his arm, retrieved
his Colts, and was on Soldier in seconds. He drew his
Winchester from the saddle-scabbard as he spurred the
big roan to a full gallop.

At the report of three, rapid-fire, pistol shots behind
them, Spears and his two gun-wielding relatives instinctively turned their heads in the direction of the sound.
Neither Strobl nor Blevins hesitated.

Blevins snatched the barrel of Spears's rifle and thrust
it upward. The gun went off, triggered by Spears, but the
bullet sailed harmlessly skyward. Blevins then yanked the
weapon violently from his former-deputy's grasp and
butt-stroked him in the skull. Spears was down and unconscious before he had a chance to draw his revolver.

Tess screamed as Rupe moved to shield her.

In the same instant that Blevins moved, Strobl drew
the pair of Chamelot Delvigne revolvers from the dual
shoulder-holsters beneath his riding jacket. He repeatedly
fired both guns double-action, putting three, eleven mil-
limeter bullets into each of the two riflemen before him.

As they fell to the ground, still clutching their rifles, he took no chances. He fired a fourth bullet from each revolver into their heads.

"Grab your rifle," Blevins called out to Strobl, as he relieved the unconscious Spears of his revolver. "There's still three more of 'em out there in the dark."

"I'm not certain about that," Strobl said, but he nonetheless scurried to the buckboard and snatched his Henry .44 while Blevins grabbed his Winchester. Both levered cartridges into the breeches of their rifles, shouldered them, and knelt back-to-back.

"I hear a horse coming," Rupe announced. "Coming in fast."

"Halt or be fired upon!" Blevins called out into the darkness.

"Hold your fire," Pritchard called back. "I'm a friendly!"

"Come on in," the bewildered Blevins said. He and Strobl stood up.

Pritchard rode in, took in the scene before him, and dismounted.

"We got three of 'em," Blevins reported, but there're still three more armed men unaccounted-for. We'll need to find 'em before they circle back and jump us."

"Already found 'em," Pritchard said. "They're over yonder, fixin' to feed the buzzards breakfast."

"Those three shots we heard," Strobl said. "I surmised it was you who fired them." He gestured to the unconscious Spears and the two dead men lying at their feet. "I must compliment you on your timing, Samuel. Your shooting provided exactly the distraction Sheriff Blevins and I needed."

"Pardon me for askin'," Blevins said to Pritchard, "but why ain't you dead?"

"I watched you get shot from the saddle with my own eyes," Rupe said.

"Though not ungrateful," Strobl said, "I, too, would very much like to know why you still walk among the living?"

Pritchard parted his vest to reveal the dual shoulder-holsters containing his pair of 1863 Remington revolvers. He removed the pistol under his left shoulder and held it up for all to inspect. Strobl struck a match.

In the glow of the flame, a .44-40 bullet could be seen wedged between the revolver's cylinder and frame.

"Bullet struck me at an angle," Pritchard explained. "Only thing between it and my heart was one of my Remington forty-four's. The shot knocked me clean off my horse. The gun's ruined," he lamented, "but it saved my life one last time before it cashed-in. Got some sore ribs to show for the experience, but otherwise I'm right as rain."

"I'm grateful you're okay, Marshal," Rupe said.

"I could say the same for you-all," Pritchard said. "What happened hereabouts?"

"My deputy," Blevins said, pointing to Spears, "a man I trusted, bushwhacked us. He shot you, was gonna gun me and Florian down, and had lined himself and five of his kin up to deflower Tess. Most likely they'd have done her in, too, once they slaked their urges. All on account of that infernal bounty on Jem's head."

"He chose poorly," Pritchard said, "between his sworn

duty and blood money." He bent down, tore the badge from Spears's shirt, and handed it to Blevins.

Rupe stepped forward and shook Pritchard's hand. "I prayed for deliverance, Marshal. The Lord heard my prayers, and raised you from the dead to deliver us."

"I reckon he did," Pritchard said, "at that."

Rupe turned to Blevins and Strobl. "I'm indebted to both of you for saving my daughter." He extended his hand. "Again."

"Our pleasure," Strobl answered for all three lawmen as they shook. He helped Tess from the buckboard, and as Pritchard's eyebrows lifted, took her into his arms and kissed her. Rupe gave Strobl's shoulder a squeeze in paternal approval.

Spears groaned and sat up. Blood eked from his hairline. Blevins had already picked up the guns belonging to the dead men and put them into the buckboard. There he discovered his own revolver as well as the three belonging to Strobl.

After Blevins had re-holstered his gun, he handed Strobl, who begrudgingly released Tess, the Smith & Wesson and pair of Colts once belonging to Earl Marsh and Asa Finchum and which now belonged to him.

"It ain't fair," Spears grumbled, as he watched Strobl replace his firearms into their respective holsters around his waist. "How was I to know he had another pair of irons? Hell, we done relieved him of three. What sort of man carries five pistols?"

"A man who will live to see another day," Strobl answered. "Unlike you."

"What's that supposed to mean?" Spears said, as he rubbed the knot on his head.

"Do you not remember," Strobl asked, "that I swore an oath to kill you?"

"You ain't a-gonna kill me," Spears chuckled. "Not now, anyways. Sheriff Blevins, my ole boss, is too much the law-and-order type to allow that. He'll want to take me into Fort Smith, or even back to Boonville, for a proper trial."

"You'll still end up with a California collar around your turncoat neck," Pritchard said. "Ain't a judge in the territory gonna let you off the gallows after what you've done today."

"Who says I'll get to the gallows?" Spears taunted. "I've got plenty of kin in these parts." He folded his hands behind his head and lay back in the grass. "They ain't a-gonna let me swing. Ain't you heard? Prisoners get broke out of jail all the time." His chuckle became a laugh. "I ain't worried none."

"Perhaps you should be?" Strobl said, as he reloaded one of his Chamelot Delvignes. "I am a Strobl."

"I don't care who you are," Spears said. "To me, you're nothin' but a funny-talkin' foreigner that I should've plugged when I had the drop."

"Indeed, you should have," Strobl agreed, as he holstered his now-reloaded Chamelot Delvigne and drew the other. "For when a Strobl swears an oath," he said, as he cocked the pistol's hammer, "he honors it." He aimed the revolver down at Spears's face. "Any last words?" he asked.

Spears jumped to his feet, his mirth replaced by fear. Strobl tracked him upright with his pistol.

"Hold on," Spears protested, showing his palms. "Sheriff Blevins, you can't let this man shoot me! You know the law! I'm supposed to have a trial! This ain't proper!"

"Says the man who dry-gulched a U.S. Marshal," Blevins said, "and was gonna murder me and a deputy U.S. Marshal, not to mention lead the gang-rape of an innocent woman?" Blevins shook his head in disgust. "I reckon the law can turn a blind eye tonight."

"Wait!" a panicked Spears continued. "What about you, Preacher? You're a man of God? Would the Lord approve of lettin' this funny-talkin' foreigner shoot me down?"

"I'm not a preacher," Rupe said. "You said so yourself. I'm just an ordinary man. A man who was going to watch you kill my unarmed friends and defile my daughter." He, too, shook his head. "If you're looking for deliverance, young man, you'll have to look elsewhere."

While Spears was frantically pleading for his life, Tess walked to the rear of the buckboard. She picked up one of the Winchester rifles belonging to Spears's kin, which was placed there by Blevins.

"Tess?" Spears next turned to her. "Stop 'em, Tess!" he begged. Tears flowed freely down his terrified face. "They're gonna gun me down in cold blood!"

"I wouldn't fret about that," Tess said flatly. "I hear it's warm in hell."

"Finish him already," Pritchard said to Strobl. "We've got an appointment to keep in Fort Smith."

Spears dropped to his knees. "Please," he blubbered, "don't shoot me."

"Alas," Strobl said, "despite my oath, I cannot."

"Why not?" Pritchard asked. "We've strung many a murderer, rapist, and horse thief while ridin' together."

Strobl lowered his arm, and the hammer on his revolver. "I will not shoot down an unarmed man, even one as despicable as Mr. Spears. My code of honor does not allow it. I simply can't shoot him."

"Thank you," Spears babbled. Tears and snot ran down his face.

Tess stepped in front of Strobl, cycled the Winchester's lever, shouldered the weapon, and shot Spears in the head at point-blank range.

"I can," she said.

Chapter 38

Undertaker Simon Tilley, in his late sixties and arthritic, nonetheless insisted on standing his watch as a member in good standing of Atherton's Vigilance Committee. He patrolled the town square with his Sharps rifle in the crook of his arm and an old Colt Dragoon belted cross-draw over his narrow hips.

Accompanying him during his rounds was another member of the Vigilance Committee, Wynn Samples. Samples, a mild-mannered, bespectacled family man, owned and operated the general store. He was armed with a brand-new Winchester rifle from his store's stock and a bandoleer stuffed with cartridges across his chest.

It was an hour before midnight, and Atherton was quiet as a church. Even the Sidewinder had closed for the night, since it was a weekday. Other than the two Vigilance Committee members making their rounds, not another soul occupied the streets.

"Nights are getting warmer," Tilley remarked, as he drew his pipe from a pocket. "Gonna be full summer, soon."

"Sure enough," Samples agreed. "Those farmers who haven't commenced their plantin' by now had best start."

"Heard it's gonna be another hot June," Tilley said.

"Heat I don't mind," Samples said, "as long as there's the occasional rain. Don't want to see another summer of drought set in."

"Nobody does," Tilley concurred, searching for his tobacco pouch.

"If either of you touch your guns," came a voice from behind them, "or sound an alarm, you'll be shot dead where you stand."

Tilley and Samples slowly turned around to face the sound of the voice. They found nearly a dozen men had materialized behind them from the alleyways. All were holding guns, and several of those guns were pointed at the two vigilantes.

"I didn't hear no horses," Tilley whispered to Samples, "did you? Where'd they come from?"

"We didn't bring our horses," the speaker explained matter-of-factly. "We left them well outside of town." He was a medium-sized man with white hair and a sculpted beard. The others with him moved to disarm, bind, and gag Tilley and Samples.

"Here's what's going to happen," the man said calmly. "We know there are two more of your number inside the hotel guarding the lobby. You're going to escort us into the hotel. If you do as you're told, and give us no trouble, you have my word that no one, including yourselves, will come to harm. But if an alarm is raised, not only will we shoot you, we'll gun down anyone we find inside the establishment. Do you understand?"

Tilley and Samples nodded. "Let's go," the white-haired man said to his men. "You all know what to do."

The pack of gunmen split into two groups. One group,

led by the white-haired man, headed for the front doors of the Atherton Arms. The other, led by a very large, clean-shaven man, headed to the alley leading around to the back of the hotel. Tilley's eyes narrowed as he recognized two of the men in the second group; one medium-sized, with a handlebar mustache, and one very tall. They were the rude Brody Railroad messengers Marshal Pritchard disarmed at young Donnie McKitchern's funeral.

The white-haired man halted his group at the front doors to the hotel and pulled down Tilley's gag. "Before we go in," he asked them, "does your Vigilance Committee have a greeting, or a challenge and password, you use among yourselves?"

"Heck no," Tilley grunted disgustedly. "We're a Vigilance Committee, not a troop of Indian scouts prowlin' about the Nations."

"For your sake," the white-haired man said, replacing Tilley's gag, "you'd best be telling the truth."

The white-haired man cocked his pistol, opened the doors, and signaled for his men to push Tilley and Samples ahead of them into the hotel.

The group rushed in and found five people in the lobby. Two Vigilance Committee members, Manfri Pannell and his adult son Danior, were playing cards with their rifles leaning against the table within reach. The night clerk, prim Mort Ranier, was behind the registration desk and engaged in refereeing a heated argument between two hotel guests, Dorothy Greaves and Carl Ewell. Ewell appeared to be insisting Greaves was his girl; she was insisting not.

All those in the lobby looked up in astonishment as

the five armed men dashed in, waving their guns and herding the town's undertaker and storekeeper ahead of them.

"Nobody move," the white-haired man said calmly. Several of his men trained their guns on the two Romanichals, while others snatched up their rifles. Six more gunmen suddenly appeared from the direction of the hotel's back entrance, on the other side of the restaurant.

"There ain't nobody else downstairs, Colonel," the leader of the newcomers said. He was a very large man.

"What's going on here?" Ranier challenged. "What is this?"

"Shut up," the Big Man said. He moved over to the registration desk. The other men busied themselves searching and binding the Pannells, Ewell, and a wide-eyed Greaves.

"I'll ask the questions," the white-haired man said. "My associates and I have an appointment with the Clemsons, who are guests of this establishment. Please be so kind as to tell me which room they are residing in?"

"What do you intend to do to Mayor Ditch and his family?" Manfri Pannell demanded from across the lobby.

"None of your beeswax," the Big Man said. He tightened the gag around Pannell's mouth.

"I won't tell you which room they're in," Ranier said defiantly. "Hotel policy prohibits me from giving out that information."

Odom nodded to the Big Man. He smacked Ranier over the head with his revolver, but not hard enough to render him unconscious. The desk clerk fell to his knees, but was instantly yanked to his feet again. Blood streamed down his face.

"Here's my policy," Odom said to the bloodied clerk. "If you tell me which room the Clemsons are in, I will leave you and your other guests undisturbed. If you make me and my men search the hotel, I will not."

Odom placed the muzzle of his revolver against Ranier's temple. "I will find the Clemsons, with or without your assistance. As you can see, I brought enough men to do just that. Without your help, you are of no value. In that case, I will shoot you dead. Then I will have my men burn this hotel, and everyone in it, to ashes. Do you understand my policy?"

Ranier nodded meekly.

"I will ask only one more time," Odom said. "Which room?"

"Three-twelve," Ranier said groggily. "They're in the suite."

"Where's Laird Bonner staying?"

"He's in the room next door," a defeated Ranier said. "Three-ten."

"Fetch the keys," Odom ordered the clerk, as his men began ascending the stairs.

The sudden pounding on the door startled all three of the house's occupants. Ditch Clemson, John Babbit, and Judge Eugene Pearson looked up from the papers they were examining by lamplight. It was after midnight, and the trio had been at the judge's residence all evening preparing for Ditch's impending meeting in Jefferson City between Governor Hardin, the Missouri mayors, the army, and the two competing railroads.

"Who could that be at this hour?" Babbit asked. The insistent knocking continued.

"Let's find out," Pearson said. When he opened the door, he found Deputy Tater Jessup, Laird Bonner, and Mort Ranier, the night clerk at the Atherton Arms Hotel, standing on his doorstep. Ranier was holding a blood-stained towel to his head.

"I'm afraid we've brung some bad news," Tater said. "Miss Idelle," he began, pausing to swallow, "and Baby Samuel, are gone."

"Gone?" Ditch said, trying to contain the alarm in his voice. "What do you mean, 'gone'?"

"They've been taken hostage," Bonner said.

"Who took them?"

"Colonel Odom," Bonner said, "with at least ten men."

"Odom? What happened?"

"It looks like a pack of 'em snuck into Atherton on foot," Tater said. "They must've stashed their horses outside of town somewheres and crept in, Injun-style. They jumped Simon and Wynn outside the hotel, then got the drop on Manfri and Danior in the lobby." He pointed to Ranier. "As you can see, they thumped what they wanted out of Mort."

"I'm sorry, Mayor Clemson," Ranier said. "They said they'd shoot me, and burn down the hotel and everyone in it, if I didn't tell them which room you were staying in. They wanted to know Mr. Bonner's room number, too."

"I was caught flat-footed," Bonner said. "I heard a noise in the hallway, and when I came out to investigate ran smack into half-a-dozen guns waiting outside my room. I gather if they'd found you with your family, Ditch, they'd have killed you on the spot. Odom was furious that you weren't with them."

"It's a good thing you weren't," Pearson said.

"I wish I had been," Ditch fumed. "Then I could have done something to try and stop them." He put his face in his hands. "I wasn't able to protect my own family," he said through his fingers.

"If you'd been in that hotel," Pearson consoled Ditch with a hand on his shoulder, "you'd be dead right now, murdered in front of your wife and son. You'd be no good to anyone."

"He's right," Tater chimed in. "No matter how you feel, gettin' plugged full of holes wouldn't do nothin' to help your family."

"Did they hurt Idelle?" Ditch asked, lowering his hands and regaining his composure, "or the baby?"

"Not that I saw," Bonner said. "They bound and gagged us, and then hustled Idelle and the baby out of the hotel. Idelle looked scared, but was unharmed when I last saw them about an hour ago. We just got free of our bonds and came straight here."

"Did that bastard Odom say why he took them?"

"Yes," Bonner answered. "Odom told me to pass on a message to you. He claimed it was the only reason he let me live." His expression hardened. "He's going to regret that."

"What message?" Babbit said.

"He said," Bonner began, "'tell Mayor Clemson if he wants to keep his family healthy, go to that meeting in Jefferson City and convince the governor, the mayors, and the army that the Brody Line, and not the Missouri Pacific, is to receive the federal contract.' That's exactly what he said. He said if Brody gets the contract, you get your family back."

"And if I'm unable to convince the Governor and the other mayors?" Ditch asked.

"I posed the same question," Bonner said. "All Odom would say is, 'If Brody loses the contract, Mayor Clemson loses his family.'"

"So it was Brody behind the train wreck," Babbit said, "all along?"

"Stands to figure," Tater said. "Accordin' to Simon Tilley, at least two of the fellers with Odom tonight were that pair of Brody men Samuel thumped and run off from Donnie McKitchern's burial."

"Before tonight," Ditch said through clenched teeth, "despite our suspicions, Samuel and I couldn't be sure if it was Brody or Gould pullin' the strings. It's one of the reasons he went off to find the real Jem Rupe. He was hopin' to find answers."

"Now we know," Pearson said.

"The kidnapper said something else," Ranier spoke up. "He said if any of us reported what happened tonight and got the army, or any other authorities or law involved, he'd have Mrs. Clemson and her son shot outright."

"That gutless, white-livered, cur," Tater cursed. "That spit-faced, yeller-bellied—"

"Take it easy," Pearson cut off the deputy's tirade. "Any idea where Odom took them?"

Tater shook his head. "I sent Manfri Pannell and his son to scout around outside town for any horse tracks, but they haven't returned yet. It's awful dark, and there's a lot of ground to cover."

"Even if we located their tracks," Bonner said, "I

expect they wouldn't lead far. If I had to bet, I'd wager Brody had one of his specials parked a few miles west of town waiting to collect them."

"You believe Odom and his men put Idelle and my son on a train?" Ditch said.

"Why not?" Bonner said. "It's what I'd do, if I were Brody and had a private locomotive at my disposal. It's ideal for a kidnapper. A train would allow him to hide his hostages, move them at will, go in almost any direction, and would be hard to track and catch."

"Laird's right," Pearson said. "If you're John Brody, and you wanted to stage a kidnapping, a train is how you'd do it."

"How're we gonna find the train Idelle and little Samuel are on," Tater said, "much less catch up to it?"

No one answered. A long minute of silence ensued before anybody spoke. Ditch broke it.

"I don't know about you fellers," Ditch finally said, "but I ain't gonna sit idle while my family is snatched and murdered. I aim to find 'em, rescue 'em, and finish off anyone who had a hand in their takin', come hell or high water."

"I'm with you," Bonner said. "To hell it is, and then some."

"Damn tootin'," Tater said. "You boys ain't ridin' alone."

"No," Judge Pearson said, "you're not. We're all with you."

"Thank you," Ditch said solemnly.

"No thanks are needed," the judge said. "It's what men do."

"I surely wish Samuel were here," Tater said.

"Me, too," Ditch said.

"What's our next move?" Babbit asked.

"I don't rightly know," Ditch said, with no effort to hide his frustration. "I have no idea how to begin to find Brody's train."

"I don't know either," Bonner said, "but I know where Brody is going to be in two days."

"Of course," Ditch said. "He'll be at the meeting in Jefferson City! He has to be!"

"That's right," Bonner said. "And we'll be waiting." He turned to Babbit. "Can you send out a telegram for me?"

"Of course," Babbit said. "Right away. Who to?"

"My employer," Bonner said.

Chapter 39

"Do you honestly expect me to believe," Judge Parker said incredulously, "that this man standing before me is Arkansas Jem Rupe?"

"I do," Pritchard said, "because he is."

"But the picture on the wanted poster," Parker argued, "shows a much heavier man with a beard. And it certainly doesn't show, nor mention, Jeremiah Rupe having only one eye."

"Interestin', ain't it," Pritchard said, "how a few little things like losing a bit of weight, shavin' off one's whiskers, and bein' one-eyed can change a feller's appearance. Might have somethin' to do with Jem hidin' in plain sight for so long, huh?"

"I see your point," Parker said, "but I'm still skeptical. Every lawman and bounty hunter alive, as well as the army, has been hunting unsuccessfully for Arkansas Jem Rupe for over ten years. Yet you, Marshal Pritchard, who only recently began looking for him, were able to locate the fugitive in just a few short days? How did you find him, when so many others could not?"

"I looked real hard," Pritchard said.

"That," Strobl said, "is an understatement."

Pritchard, Blevins, Strobl, and Jem and Tess Rupe had arrived in Fort Smith that morning. Blevins suggested they push on the final ten miles into town during the night, but Pritchard insisted they make camp and rest. Everyone was exhausted, Tess was distraught, the horses were fatigued, and the small band was in no shape, after what they'd already endured that day, to fend off hostile Indians, road brigands, or any more bounty hunters they might encounter on the road in the dark.

Once in Fort Smith, they went straight to Judge Parker's courtroom. He canceled an in-progress court hearing to receive them.

"Can you explain how I got a telegram yesterday from someone claiming to be 'Deputy Spears,'" Parker asked, "from the town of Booneville, announcing he was bringing in Jem Rupe?"

"Deputy Spears will not be makin' that appointment," Pritchard said.

He introduced Sheriff Blevins, who was well-known to several of Parker's federal marshals. Blevins related, in detail, the sequence of events governing Rupe's "capture" and the fate of Deputy Spears.

"When you told me you, 'looked real hard,'" Parker said to Pritchard, after hearing the Booneville marshal's account, "you weren't kidding. Evidently all those tall tales I've been told about you, Marshal Pritchard, and your manhunting skills, aren't such tall tales after all."

"I assure you," Deputy Strobl said, "when it comes to the hunting of men, Marshal Pritchard is never 'kidding,' as you Americans say."

"You realize," Parker admonished Blevins, "if what you're telling me is the truth—"

"It is, Your Honor," Blevins interrupted, "on my oath."

"Then as an officer of the law," Parker continued, "you committed a crime yourself by knowingly harboring a wanted war criminal for over a decade? In the eyes of the court, you're just as guilty as Jeremiah Rupe. You could hang, right along with him."

"I reckon so," Blevins said.

"And you've come to my courtroom today," Parker said, "to turn yourself in? Knowing you could be sentenced to the gallows?"

"It was time for the truth to come to light," Blevins said. "War's long over."

"Perhaps the war is long over," Parker said, "but the memories of its atrocities live on in the eyes of the law."

"It's been my experience," Pritchard said, "that sometimes the law, and doin' the right thing, are on two different roads." He looked sternly at Judge Parker. "You don't have to charge these men. Their crimes can be forgiven. You have that authority, do you not?"

"What, exactly, are you asking me to do?" Parker said. "Turn a blind eye to the law and to these men's crimes?"

"No," Pritchard said. "I never said that. All I'm suggestin' you do, is take into account the extenuatin' circumstances which brung them here before you?"

"Extenuating circumstances?"

"Neither of these men, Jem Rupe nor Sheriff Blevins, had to come forward. Bounty or not, Jem had been successfully evadin' the law for over ten years, right here in Arkansas, and right under everybody's noses. There's no reason to believe he couldn't have continued to do so indefinitely, and no reason for Sheriff Bob Blevins, who's known the Rupe family all his life, to stick his neck out nor come forward to verify Rupe's identity."

"But they have come forward," Parker said, "haven't they?"

"Do you know why Jem chose to come forward, at great risk to his life and the life of his only daughter, and face the gallows?"

"I'm listening," Parker said.

"Jem did this foolhardy thing," Pritchard said, "because he was bein' accused of wreckin' a train in Missouri which he didn't wreck. Sheriff Blevins, and half the population of Booneville along with him, can prove it."

"There is no question," Parker said, "that these two men are to be commended for their courage in coming forward. But my hands are tied, Marshal Pritchard. Jeremiah Rupe wrecked the train at Platte Bridge. He must answer for that."

"Rupe wasn't alone when he wrecked that train," Pritchard said. "It was wartime. He was under command from General Sterling Price."

"I'm certain the court will be interested in those details," Parker said, "and I'm sure they'll come out during Rupe's trial."

"Maybe you should be less interested in a train wrecked under lawful orders during wartime more than a decade ago," Tess spoke up, "and more interested in bringing those who wrecked that Missouri train a few weeks ago to justice?"

"She's right," Pritchard said. "Jem Rupe wasn't framed-up for no reason. Those who set him up, believin' him dead when they did it, thought nothin' of wreckin' a train to achieve their aims. They killed and maimed scores of innocent folks to cover-up the murder of a passel of Missouri politicians—small town and big city mayors—who stood between a railroad baron and a fat government contract."

"I know all about the competition between the Brody and Gould Railroads," Parker said. "and how much is at stake. That federal railroad contract stands to impact not only Missouri, but Iowa, Arkansas, and many other states and territories in the region."

"Then you understand why one of those railroad bosses went to the trouble of framin' a dead man," Pritchard said, "to erase his tracks. What he couldn't know, and didn't count on, was that the man he framed, Jeremiah Rupe, was still above ground."

"That's why Jem Rupe came forward," Blevins said, "even though he didn't have to. To clear his name, and help Marshal Pritchard bring the real trainwreckers to account. Anybody with a lick of sense could see it was in his interest not to. But Jem's a man of honor, Judge, no matter what Yankee lies have been told about him since the war. Doesn't turnin' himself in count for somethin'?"

"That's not for me to judge," Parker said.

"If not you," Tess said, "then who? My pa and I were livin' in peace, by God's grace, not harming a soul. All we wanted was to run our church and be left alone. And now my father stands before you, facing a death sentence, after coming forward to right a wrong. A crime, according to Marshal Pritchard, which has already ruined dozens of lives and stands to ruin many more."

"I sympathize with your father's plight," Parker said.

"I truly do. But regardless of my personal feelings, I've sworn an oath to uphold the law."

"I swore an oath, too," Pritchard said. "I swore I'd bring those who wrecked that train in Rock Creek to justice. To do it, I had to convince Jem Rupe to come in. I didn't have to manacle him neither. He came in of his own accord."

Pritchard stepped forward and leaned over Parker's desk. The six-foot-six lawman, even taller in his boots and Stetson, loomed like a towering specter over the judge.

"We're both lawmen," Pritchard said to Parker, "and we both took oaths. I'll take another, right here and now, before you. I ain't a-gonna stand idle while Jeremiah Rupe, nor Sheriff Blevins, swing from no rope for the crimes of a cross-grained, Missouri, trainwrecker. You can take that as my final word on the matter."

"I understand how you all feel," Parker said, looking over his desk at the faces staring back at him. "But even if I agreed with you, I'm afraid President Grant might have something to say about it."

"I don't care a continental what Grant has to say," Pritchard said. "He may be the President of these here United States, but he ain't in this room decidin' these men's fates. You are."

"Are you threatening me, Marshal Pritchard?"

"Nope," Pritchard said. "Just takin' an oath."

"I see," Parker said, unconvinced. "I'll have to contemplate this awhile. There's much to consider. That's all I can promise at this time, Marshal."

"You do that," Pritchard said. "You're a good man, Judge Parker. I trust you'll come to the right decision."

"In the meantime," Parker said, "I'll have to insist that

Mr. Rupe and Sheriff Blevins remain here in the custody of the marshals until this gets sorted out."

"I understand," Rupe said.

"Of course," Blevins said.

"No!" Tess exclaimed. Strobl restrained her as she rushed toward the judge. "Please? My father's not a criminal? He doesn't deserve to be locked up!"

"I'm sorry," Parker said. "There's no other way."

"He's right," Rupe said, giving his daughter a hug. "We have to stay. You go with Deputy Strobl and Marshal Pritchard. They'll see no harm comes to you. Me and Bob will stay right here as guests of Judge Parker and catch up on our checker game."

"May I make a suggestion, Your Honor?" Marshal Pritchard said.

"By all means."

"I reckon it might not be a bad thing to keep Rupe's bein' here in Fort Smith under our hats. At least for a while?"

"I'm not sure I understand?" Parker said.

"Everybody else who knows Jem is alive, except us in this room, is dead. It would surely save you and your marshals a wagon-load of grief iffen nobody else knew. And it might give me some breathin' room to get my hands on the feller who posed as Rupe. If it gets around that the real Rupe has been caught, the poser might run to ground."

"That ain't a bad idea," Blevins said.

"Very well," Parker said. "I will keep Rupe's identity, and the fact that he is in custody here in Fort Smith, a secret for now. But I'm only doing this in the interests of advancing your investigation into the Missouri train wreck, and will only do it for three days. After that, I will have no choice but to report Jeremiah Rupe's arrest to the federal government where it will become public knowledge."

"That's more than fair," Pritchard said. "I thank you."

A knock sounded on the door and one of Parker's federal marshals entered. "Got a telegram for Marshal Pritchard," he announced. "It came in early this morning. I forgot all about it, but when I saw the marshal come into your courtroom I remembered."

Pritchard accepted the envelope. "Who's it from?" Strobl asked. "Mayor Clemson, back in Atherton?"

"No," Pritchard said, as he read. His features darkened. "It's from Jason Gould."

"The owner of the Missouri Pacific Railroad?" Parker said.

Pritchard didn't answer. All in the room watched a pallor befall the big lawman's countenance. His eyes hardened, his jaw tightened, and both of his hands contracted into fists.

"My apologies, Your Honor," Pritchard began, "but I've got to take my leave immediately."

"Is something wrong?" Parker asked.

"You could say that," Pritchard said through clenched teeth.

"I'm sorry," Parker said, "but I can't allow you to depart quite yet. I need to obtain your sworn statement, and a more detailed account of Rupe's arrest."

"Another time," Pritchard said. "I've got urgent business in Missouri."

"It'll have to wait," Parker said sternly.

"It won't," Pritchard said. "The lives of my family are

at stake. I'm a-leavin' now, and anyone who tries to stop me is gonna have themselves a real bad day. I'll return to give you my sworn statement as soon as I can."

"Now see here," Parker said, rising from behind his desk.

"C'mon Florian," Pritchard said to his deputy, ignoring the judge and heading for the door. "I need to send off a telegram, pronto."

"You can send it from here," Judge Parker called out. "There's a telegraph operator in this building."

"Thank you, Your Honor," Pritchard said over his shoulder. "I'm obliged."

"Just don't forget to return and give me that statement."

"I won't," Pritchard said. "I done gave you my word."

"Where are we going after we send the telegram?" Strobl asked, as he struggled to keep up with the long-striding Pritchard.

"We've got a train to catch."

Chapter 40

"I trust you are comfortable with the accommodations?" Brody asked.

"Are you addle-headed?" Idelle answered. "A cage is a cage, whether a cow town hoosegow or a gilded train car. I'm being held against my will, and so is my baby, and you have the nerve to ask me about the accommodations?"

Idelle and her son were in Brody's private car, on his private train, which was halted east of Kansas City near Sugar Creek, not far from where the train was wrecked at Rock Creek. Brody insisted on stopping while he dined on his mid-day meal, for it was commonly known the movement of locomotives interfered with his digestion. He was lunching on roasted duck and champagne. Despite his invitation, Idelle refused to join him.

In the car along with them was Charles, Brody's ever-present valet, Colonel Odom, Earl Marsh, Asa Finchum, and a very big, husky, man who leered hungrily at Idelle.

"I could have you and your son kept in the livery car," Brody said smarmily, "with the horses, if it would better suit you?"

"Do as you will," Idelle said defiantly, "while you can, Mr. Brody." She held little Samuel, who was nursing, tightly to her bosom. "Because when my husband and brother get their hands on you, and they will, your days of wrecking trains, murdering innocent folks, and kidnapping unarmed women and defenseless infants will come to an end along with your miserable life."

"Bold talk," the big, husky, man said, "from such a pretty young lady." He made no effort to conceal his lustful glances. "Your husband is a lucky man." His leer widened. "A lucky, one-legged, man," he chuckled.

"Go to hell," she said, "whoever you are."

"Your husband knows who I am," the Big Man said. He reached into his pocket and withdrew a watch. Idelle's eyes widened as she recognized it as the one she'd given Ditch as a wedding present. She also noticed Ditch's wedding ring threaded onto the chain. The man dangled the timepiece before her. "He and I are old friends. Hell," he mocked, "I was there when he surrendered his leg."

"Whoever you are," Idelle repeated, as her eyes narrowed, "my husband is going to kill you."

"What's he gonna do," the man laughed, "clobber me to death with his crutch?"

Brody and Marsh laughed at the insult. Finchum tried to, but only managed a grimace on account of his broken jaw. Odom, and the valet, Charles, remained impassive.

The Big Man opened the watch and examined the picture of Idelle inside the cover. "Right-good likeness, iffen I say so myself."

"I know who the rest of these curs are," Idelle said to Brody, scanning the faces of the men in the car surrounding her. "That's the man who tried to murder my husband," she pointed to Odom, "and those two," she pointed at Marsh and Finchum, "are the pigs my brother thrashed in Atherton. But who is this," she gestured to the Big Man, "gutless, greasy, tub-o-lard?"

"Wes Childress is my name," the Big Man said, as he snapped the watch shut and replaced it back into his pocket. His face reddened, and his lustful mirth changed to anger. "It's a name you'd best remember. I've killed more men than consumption, Little Missy, so you might want to be careful who you're insultin'."

"Or what?" Idelle said. "You'll kidnap me? Hah!"

"Mind your tongue," Childress scolded, "or I'll—"

"Thump a woman and a nursing baby?" Idelle cut him off. She shook her head in disgust. "You're a real curly wolf, Wes Childress. A genuine hard case."

"I'll tell you what I'm gonna do," Childress said, taking a step toward her. "After I end your one-legged husband and piss on his grave, I'll be puttin' you into my bed. Iffen you ain't real nice to me, under the covers, I'll give that baby boy of yours away to the Comanches."

"If you think you're going to lie next to me," Idelle said, "you're even stupider than you look. I'd rather bed down with a hydrophobic polecat than a barn-sized bag-of-guts like you."

Marsh snickered at Idelle's jab. Childress's face reddened further, and he started toward the seated woman.

"That's enough," Odom said, halting Childress. He turned to Marsh. "If you can't keep your dog on a leash, put him outside with the other animals."

"I don't take orders from you," Marsh said.

"Neither do I," Childress said.

"Gentlemen," Brody said, around a mouthful of duck. "We agreed to work together, remember?"

"You'll need to stick together, all right," Idelle said. "With Samuel Pritchard coming for you. You're going to need all the help you can get."

"Your brother doesn't even know where we are," Brody sneered. "As much as you might fantasize about being rescued, he has to find us, first."

"He'll find us," she said.

"He won't have to," Brody said. "Mrs. Clemson, if your husband does what he's told at the meeting in Jefferson City, there will be no need to be rescued. Once my railroad is awarded the federal contract, you will be released, unharmed, into his grateful arms."

"I'm supposed to believe that fairy tale?" Idelle said. "You already tried to kill him, twice, remember? And if he'd been in that hotel when your pack of gunmen showed up last night, he'd surely be dead now. So you'll have to forgive me if I don't trust you, Mr. Brody."

"It's true I once wanted your husband dead," Brody said. "He is a popular and influential politician in western Missouri, and I feared he would use that popularity and influence against me in favor of my rival, Jason Gould. I couldn't let that happen."

"Which is why you murdered all the other mayors," Idelle accused, "and maimed a bunch of innocent train passengers, to hide the deed?"

"One does what one must," Brody said dismissively. "But Mayor Clemson's death is not necessary, now. Thanks to the Colonel's quick thinking in taking you, I no longer have to end your husband. With his family as my guests, he's of more use to me alive than dead. If he ever wants to see you and his son again, he'll have no choice but to use his popularity, influence, and well-known oratory skill to convince Governor Hardin to award the Brody Line that juicy federal contract."

"You're a vile man," Idelle said. "It's little wonder you were a friend of Cottonmouth Quincy's. Look where he ended up?"

"Dead at your feet," Brody said, "if I recall."

"That's where you'll end, too. Except you'll be dangling above me."

"You really should be nicer to me, Mrs. Clemson," Brody said. "You and your husband are alive only through my good graces."

"Don't hold your breath," Idelle said. "You took his leg, and it wasn't for lack of trying you didn't take his life."

"All that can be put behind you, and your family, if your husband does as he's told."

"And if Ditch refuses to go along with your scheme? Or the governor and the army decide to award the contract to the Missouri Pacific Railroad, despite his arguments on your behalf?"

"Let's hope for your sake," Brody said, slurping champagne, "that doesn't happen. As you may have already noticed, I'll do whatever it takes to get what I want."

"You give my husband too much credit," Idelle said, adjusting the blanket to keep her nursing son, and her breasts, hidden from view. Childress craned his neck in an attempt to overcome her efforts. "He's only a small-town mayor. What makes you think he has the power to persuade the governor?"

Brody stuffed a forkful of roast duck into his mouth. "I have confidence in Mayor Clemson," he said with his mouth full. "Your husband's powers of persuasion are impressive. He persuaded you to marry him, didn't he?"

Childress laughed. "He's certainly got enough incentive to be persuasive now, with you and his son on this train."

"What will happen to me and my son in the meantime?" Idelle said.

"You'll both continue to enjoy my hospitality," Brody said, "of course. Soon I'll be joining your husband, among others, in Jefferson City, in the governor's mansion. In the meantime, you may relax in this luxurious train car. My servant, Charles, is at your disposal and will see to you and your son's every need."

"We'd rather stay in a barn," Idelle said under her breath.

Brody was amused by Idelle's defiance. He held up his glass. "Are you certain I can't interest you in some champagne?" he taunted her. "It's from my private stock."

"Choke on it," Idelle said.

Chapter 41

Ditch hobbled up the steps of the governor's mansion. A film of sweat had broken out over his face. While he was getting much better at maneuvering around on his crutch, the act of walking, especially upstairs, required greater effort. He still didn't have one-hundred percent of his strength back since the injury, and to make matters worse, it was very warm outside. May had become June the day before, and Jefferson City, Missouri, was in the throes of a late-spring heatwave.

Walking on either side of Ditch, as he mounted the steps, was Judge Eugene Pearson and Newspaperman/Telegraph Operator John Babbit. He had elected to bring them along to the meeting as his aides-de-camp. Though none of the other mayors brought aides with them, Ditch figured, as the person who'd proposed the meeting, that he was entitled, among other reasons.

Dozens of other Missouri mayors, and acting-mayors, since many of the towns who'd lost their executives in the Rock Creek Train Derailment had yet to hold special elections, joined Ditch, Pearson, and Babbit as they filed into the mansion. Once inside, the group was escorted, en masse, to a large stateroom where rows of chairs had been set up. At the head of the array of seats, a group of men waited expectantly.

Ditch recognized Governor Hardin, Lieutenant Governor Coleman, Major Duncan, Jason Gould, and John Brody. Some, like him, had aides with them. Duncan, now wearing the rank of colonel, was accompanied by a pair of junior officers. Gould had a stern-looking man by his side, and Brody had Colonel Odom at his elbow. Ditch was gratified to see President Grant, flanked by a pair of army officers, also in attendance.

Brody and Odom approached Ditch, Pearson, and Babbit. From across the room, Gould took notice.

"I trust you received my message?" Brody said quietly, ensuring the gaggle of people entering the room around them didn't overhear.

"I did," Ditch said, balancing himself on his crutch and wiping his face with a handkerchief.

"Then you know what to do," Brody said, lowering his voice even more, "if you want to see your wife and child again. Convince this assembly, and Hardin, to award me the contract."

"What makes you think I've got enough pull to do that?"

"Don't insult my intelligence," Brody snapped. "You called this meeting. Everyone here knows you're the voice of the Missouri mayors, and that Governor Hardin will not act to award the contract without their consent."

"You'd best not have harmed Idelle or my boy," Ditch said through clenched teeth.

"I haven't," Brody said, "yet. If you want to keep it that way, you'd best do as you're told."

"No tricks, either," Odom added. "I have the ability, within minutes, to communicate with the men holding your wife and child." He pointed to the window. "Take a look."

Ditch, Pearson, and Babbit went to the window. Across the property's expansive lawn, where buckboards and horses were parked, stood a number of liverymen. One of them appeared to have his attention riveted on the very window they were observing him from.

Odom removed a red silk handkerchief from his pocket and waved it once. The liveryman produced a similar handkerchief and waved back.

"I'll be seated by this window while you give your speech," Odom admonished. "One wrong word from you, and a wave of a scarf from me, and you're a widower."

"Not very honorable, Mr. Brody," Pearson said. "Black-mailing a man by threatening his woman and baby."

"I do what I must," Brody repeated his personal motto, "to get what I want. And don't think I won't remember you, Your Honor, when this is all over."

"I have a feeling you're going to remember me well," Pearson said.

"Don't forget me, either," Babbit spoke up.

"Believe me," Brody said, turning to Babbit, "I won't. You're that fellow who spread all those lies about me in the newspapers, aren't you?"

"John Babbit," the newspaperman said, tipping his hat, "of the *Athertonian,* at your service."

"I'll remember your name, all right."

"Would you all please take your seats?" Lieutenant Governor Coleman announced.

Brody leaned in toward Ditch. "Choose your words

carefully," Brody whispered. "Your family lives, or dies, on what you say." He returned to the front of the room, leaving Odom to take his seat by the window.

Once all the guests had been seated, Governor Hardin stepped forward and held up a hand for silence.

"Let's call this meeting to order, shall we?" he declared.

Gilbert took his hat off, wiped his brow on a forearm, and silently cursed the heat. It was near midday, the blistering sun was almost directly overhead, and where he was stationed, along with the animals hitched in front of the governor's mansion, there was no shade.

Despite Gilbert's protests, he'd been assigned by Childress to act as a signalman. He'd been forced to shave, get a haircut, and dress in the uncomfortable wool suit of one of Brody's railroad detectives, where he was posted on the street outside the governor's mansion. Ostensibly there to attend to the horses, as well as Brody's carriage and team, his true purpose was another job entirely.

Gilbert had already seen Odom wave to him once through the window, confirming their line-of-communication and notifying him that the next glimpse of red cloth would be his cue to act.

If Gilbert saw another flash of red cloth through that window, he was to immediately mount his horse and ride to the telegraph office only a few blocks away. There he would hand the telegraph operator the envelope he'd been given by Mr. Brody. He had instructions not to depart the telegraph office until the wire had been sent.

Gilbert wiped his brow again, and cursed himself for not having the foresight to fill the canteen on his horse. He also cursed Childress.

Ever since Childress had hired him, and the other eleven men, to wreck that train, Gilbert had been promised much and received little. All of the other men in the crew were dead, and he was forced to continue to work with Marsh and Finchum, whom he despised. If that weren't bad enough, he and Childress found themselves outnumbered by the slick Colonel Odom and his half-dozen professional guns, who seemed to have won Brody's favor.

And instead of guarding Mrs. Clemson and her son in the comfort of Brody's luxurious private locomotive, parked less than a mile away, Gilbert found himself wearing a starched collar and standing on a Jefferson City street corner under the blistering noonday sun, tasked with staring at a window until his eyes hurt.

What looked like a welcome respite to Gilbert's dilemma arrived in the form of a pushcart, which featured a large umbrella. The cart, being operated by two men, rolled to a stop in front of him.

"'Ello, Guv'ner," one of the men greeted him. He was a swarthy, muscular, man in his early fifties, who looked like a gypsy to Gilbert yet spoke with a distinct British accent. "Care for a shoeshine?" The other man, in his late twenties, resembled the first enough to have been his son.

"Nope," Gilbert said, as he momentarily basked in the glorious relief of the cart's umbrella. "My boots is fine."

"How about a sandwich?" the older man asked. "We have roast beef and pork?"

"Not hungry," Gilbert said, as he realized the cart, and

its large umbrella, had stopped directly between himself and the governor's mansion. It completely blocked his view of the window where Colonel Odom was stationed.

"Are you in need of having your knife sharpened?" the Romanichal said. "I can grind your blade to a razor's edge for only a penny?"

"I've no need for anything you've got," Gilbert said irritably. "Move that cart, will ya?"

"Do you have a match?" the Romanichal asked.

"No," Gilbert barked, "I ain't got no matches."

"We do," the older man said, as the younger man with him reached into the cart and came out with a bucket. He wordlessly dumped the contents, which turned out to be kerosene, over Gilbert's head.

Gilbert blinked, gasped, and sputtered as the pungent liquid soaked him. A moment later, when he was able to open his eyes and see, he found the two Romanichal men still standing before him. The younger man was holding a lit match, the older one a revolver.

"Stand still and be silent," Manfri Pannell said, prodding Gilbert with his pistol. He motioned to his companion with the lit match. "If you move, or raise an alarm, my son Danior will set you afire. Do you understand?"

The terrified Gilbert nodded as Danior searched him. He relieved the drenched gunmen of the pistol under his coat and an envelope he found in one pocket. He stashed both guns in his cart and produced a shoe-shine kit.

Manfri Pannell lit a cigar. "Care for one?" he mocked Gilbert. Gilbert shook his head vigorously.

"What are you gonna do to me?" Gilbert asked.

"If you answer my questions honestly, merely shine

your shoes." Manfri shrugged and blew a smoke ring. "If not, today will become a much hotter day for you."

"I don't wanna burn," Gilbert said, with no effort to hide his fear. "I'll tell you whatever you want to know."

"The train?" Manfri said, as his face hardened. He held the glowing tip of the cigar inches from Gilbert's horrified, kerosene-dowsed, face. "Where is the train?"

Chapter 42

"We all know why we are here," Governor Hardin began, "and unless anyone objects, I see no need to waste time with further discussion about expansion of the existing transcontinental rail lines running through Missouri. Everyone in this room already knows that these lines are vitally important to the future of not only this state, but the entire nation."

A murmur of agreement rippled through the audience. "Also," Hardin continued, "as I'm sure you're all well-aware, congress has approved funds to facilitate this nationwide expansion in the form of a federal grant to states, like ours, which figure geographically into those plans. Furthermore, everyone here knows full-well that two competing railroad companies, The Brody Line and the Missouri Pacific Railroad, seek these funds."

Hardin put his hands behind his back. "President Grant, under his executive authority, has decided to let the governors of each state determine which railroad company receives the federal grant in their jurisdictions. In keeping with my longstanding tradition of listening to the voices of the people I serve before making important decisions which will affect every citizen, I have decided to hold this meeting and obtain a consensus from the mayors."

"Those mayors who're still alive!" someone called out from the back of the room. A chorus of jeers broke out.

"Please, gentlemen," Hardin said. "The accident at Rock Creek was indeed a tragedy, but we must—"

"It weren't no accident!" another voice interrupted.

"Order!" Hardin said. "I will not have this meeting devolve into a mob. Each of you, should you choose, will have an opportunity to speak. The heads of the two railroads, John Brody and Jason Gould, will also be given an opportunity to address the attendees. After a reasonable amount of time to contemplate, I will then render my decision."

As he spoke, Hardin looked behind him. President Grant gave him a silent nod of encouragement.

"We don't need to turn this powwow into a washerwoman gabfest," one of the mayors shouted. "Ditch Clemson, of Atherton, will do the speakin' for us!"

A chorus of applause, whistles, and cheers erupted as Ditch stepped forward. He hobbled through the raucous assembly to the front of the room as all the mayors rose from their seats and thunderously applauded.

In the confusion, no one noticed John Babbit filter his way through the crowd to an empty seat adjacent to where Colonel Odom sat by the window.

"Why aren't you clapping?" Odom asked with a laugh. "Clemson's your mayor, isn't he?"

"Figured I'd join you here at the window," Babbit said, "and take in the sights." He pointed outside. "Nice day, isn't it?"

Odom looked out to find a street vendor's pushcart, replete with a large umbrella, completely obscuring his view of Gilbert.

Odom watched as a swarthy man with a stout physique stepped into view from around the umbrella. He smiled and waved.

"You think you and your Vigilance Committee friends are pretty clever," Odom said to Babbit, "don't you?" The fury in his whispered voice was clear. "Well," he continued, "you're not. All you've done is delay me by a moment or two. I only have to walk to the telegraph office myself, and Mayor Clemson's family is finished." He started to rise from his seat.

"Sit down," Babbit said, jabbing the barrel of his .38 caliber Navy Colt discretely under his arm and into Odom's side. "You aren't going anywhere."

"You won't shoot me," Odom scoffed. "You're a newspaperman and a wire operator, not a gunman. Besides, you can't very well put a bullet into me in front of all these people? It would be suicide, with the president here."

With two clicks of the hammer, Babbit's revolver was cocked. "Try me," he said. "To keep you from harming Idelle Clemson and her baby boy, I'd gutshoot you in church at midnight on Christmas Eve."

"I believe you would," Odom found himself saying, as Babbit relieved him of his pistol.

"Now you just sit there," Babbit ordered, jabbing the barrel of his gun again into Odom's ribs for emphasis, "and behave yourself. And start clapping."

* * *

Idelle Clemson removed Samuel's soiled diaper.

"Lord have mercy," one of the two men guarding her said, as he held his nose. He was one of Colonel Odom's gun hands. "That boy smells worse than a hog pen in July."

"I'm sure you smell just like a rose bush," Idelle said, "when your nappies are loaded."

The other guard, Childress, laughed. "She sure as hell put you in your place," he said.

"I'm going outside for a smoke," the irritated Odom man said. "Anything's better than the stench coming from that little monster."

"Mind who you call a monster," Idelle scolded.

"Take your time," Childress said to the other guard. "Smoke a couple stogies, if you've got 'em. I don't mind spendin' some alone-time with Mrs. Clemson."

"Best keep your hands to yourself," the Odom man said over his shoulder, as he opened the train car's door. "Remember what Mr. Brody and the Colonel told us. The woman ain't to be molested unless they give the word."

"Who says I'm gonna molest her?" Childress asked with feigned innocence. "Me and Atherton's first lady are merely gonna get ourselves better acquainted, ain't we?" He blew a kiss at Idelle. She cringed in revulsion.

The Odom man left the car, unwilling to engage in an argument with the gargantuan Childress. He was supposed to mind the woman, not his fellow guard.

He'd grown weary of his assignment. Colonel Odom had tasked him with minding Idelle Clemson and her squealing, pooping son, in Brody's private train car. The other men on the train were housed in the only other passenger car, the caboose, which was not nearly as luxurious as Brody's personal one. He'd rather have been in the less-fancy passenger car, away from the woman, the baby, and the bully Childress. At least in the caboose, crowded and smoky though it was, he could play cards and enjoy an occasional sip of whiskey. The fact that he shared the chore of guarding the hostages with the arrogant Childress, who made no effort to conceal his lust for the woman they were supposed to be guarding, didn't make his assignment any easier.

Brody's private train had been stopped since the night before on a section of railroad track less than a mile west of Jefferson City. The location was not chosen at random. The train was on a railroad switch turnout, parallel to a little-used section of track, but adjacent to a telegraph line. A copper wire stretched from the roof of Brody's private car to the line, where it had been spliced in. Charles, Brody's valet, was also a skilled telegraph operator.

Odom's man had no sooner left the car when Childress moved in to grab Idelle.

"It's just you and me, now," he said, as he took her by one arm and drew her closer. He looked her up-and-down, his eyes bright with arousal. "I reckon I have time to get what I want from you before he finishes his smoke."

"Get your filthy hands off me," Idelle demanded.

"Or what?" the huge Childress said with contempt.

In answer, Idelle stabbed Childress in the left eye with the safety pin she had only a moment before been in the process of affixing to her son's fresh diaper.

Childress let out an agonized roar, released Idelle, and stumbled clumsily backward with both hands clasped over his injured eye. He followed his roar with a guttural howl of pain.

"You bitch!" he shrieked. "You blinded me!"

"You asked 'or what,' didn't you?" Idelle said, scooping up Samuel and hastily retreating to the opposite end of the train car. "Well, that's 'what.'"

Childress lowered his hands, revealing blood and fluid streaming from his eye, and drew his revolver.

"I was gonna rut with you before I killed you," he snarled. "Now I'm just gonna kill you."

Idelle instinctively turned her back to Childress, in a desperate attempt to protect her baby from the impending bullet, when the door to the train car flew open. The other guard rushed in, followed by Earl Marsh and Asa Finchum. All three had their guns drawn.

"Lower that pistol," Marsh ordered Childress.

"I will not," Childress said defiantly. "Look what this trollop did to my eye? She's half-blinded me! She's gonna pay for it!"

"Lower that pistol," Marsh repeated, "or we'll shoot you." For emphasis, he, Finchum, and the Odom man cocked their revolvers and aimed directly at Childress.

Childress cursed but holstered his weapon. The others lowered theirs.

"What goes here?" Marsh asked Idelle. "Why did you see fit to stick Wes?"

"Why don't you ask him?" she said. Childress said nothing.

"I reckon I know why," the Odom man said. He pointed his revolver at Childress again. "You meant to have the woman when I went out for a smoke, didn't you?" He shook his head in disgust. "Couldn't help yourself, could you? Hell, I only just lit up."

"Get out," Marsh said to Childress. "Go to the passenger car with the others and have somebody tend to your eye. Asa and I will watch over Mrs. Clemson from here on out."

"You've got no right," Childress griped.

"And you had no right to disobey orders," Marsh said. "Get moving, before I put you off this train."

Childress placed his kerchief over his eye and left the car, cursing under his breath as he went.

"Thank you," Idelle said to Marsh. "I believe that maniac was actually going to shoot me before you came in."

"Don't thank me yet," Marsh said, as he holstered his gun. "If that telegraph set up in the caboose goes a-clickety-clack the wrong way, I'll be the one putting a bullet to you. Your baby, too."

Chapter 43

Ditch looked out at the sea of faces before him. Though he was offered a seat on account of having only one leg, he chose to stand. Behind him sat a smug John Brody, an impassive Jason Gould, Colonel Duncan, Lieutenant Governor Coleman, Governor Hardin, and the President of the United States of America, Ulysses S. Grant.

The mayors had finally concluded their applause and taken their seats. They waited expectantly for the speech of their designated spokesman, Mayor David "Ditch" Clemson, of Atherton, Missouri, to commence. Judge Eugene Pearson sat in the front row and gave Ditch two thumbs and an encouraging nod.

Before he started to speak, Ditch made eye contact with John Babbit. He was seated in the back of the room by the window, next to an uneasy-looking Colonel Odom. Babbit smiled confidently, and also gave a thumbs-up sign.

At Babbit's signal, Ditch took in a deep breath and exhaled.

"President Grant," he began, "Governor Hardin, Lieutenant Coleman, fellow mayors, and honored guests, I'm

Mayor Ditch Clemson, of Atherton. I was nominated by the assembled Missouri mayors before you to speak today, on behalf of all of 'em, about which railroad company, the Brody Line or the Missouri Pacific, should get awarded the big government contract everybody's so all-fired flustered about."

Ditch turned to look behind him and met Brody's arrogant gaze. The corpulent railroad baron waited expectantly for Ditch to utter the words that would ensure his railroad prevailed.

Ditch turned his attention back to the crowd before him. "But instead of givin' a speech," he said, "I figured I'd tell you a story. It's a helluva tale, actually. A rip-roarin' yarn about a wrecked train, a herd of mayors murdered by a man posin' as a long-dead Confederate soldier, a couple of attempts on my life, and the kidnapping of my wife and child, who at this very minute are bein' held hostage in an effort to force me to sway all of you to convince Governor Hardin to award that big government contract to one railroad over the other."

The room erupted into bedlam. The mayors all rose to their feet, shouting and pumping their fists. The president, governor, and lieutenant governor stood as well, expressions of bewilderment and confusion on their faces. Brody also took to his feet, but his expression belied barely suppressed fury. He took out his handkerchief and waved it, at the same time looking expectantly across the room at Colonel Odom. Odom merely shrugged impotently and tilted his head at Babbit, who sat grinning next to him. Only Jason Gould, wearing a satisfied smile on his face, remained seated.

At a nod from Governor Hardin, Colonel Duncan and

his aides restored order in the assembly hall. When all in the room had calmed and retaken their seats, the governor warily approached Ditch.

"You realize, Mayor Clemson," Hardin said, "that you are making very serious allegations?"

"I ain't makin' any allegations," Ditch said flatly. "What I'm about to tell you is the stone truth. I'd swear to it on the lives of my wife and son, but their lives are already at stake."

"I certainly hope you can substantiate your outrageous claims, young man," Grant said.

"Listen and learn, Mr. President," Ditch said.

Chapter 44

U.S. Marshal Samuel Pritchard, Deputy U.S. Marshal Florian Strobl, Atherton Deputy Marshal Toby "Tater" Jessup, and Bounty Hunter Laird Bonner sat astride their mounts and surveyed the scene below. Their horses were halted on a small rise overlooking John Brody's private train, which was parked on a deserted railroad switch turnout several hundred yards away. It was early afternoon, and the sun over central Missouri burned hot.

"It's right where Gould said it would be," Pritchard said to Bonner.

"Mr. Gould told me there're only a couple of places near Jefferson City Brody could stash a private train," Bonner explained, "that could provide him both concealment and access to telegraph lines."

"How do you suppose Gould knew for sure Brody's fancy-pants, private, train would be here?" Tater asked.

"I presume it helps to have a fancy-pants, private, train yourself," Bonner answered.

Danior Pannell had departed the quartet only moments before. He'd ridden from Jefferson City to Pritchard's location on the outskirts of town as fast as the horse he'd "borrowed" from Gilbert would take him. Pannell reported to the marshal what transpired outside the governor's mansion, and then received more instructions from Pritchard. He immediately headed back to Jefferson City at a gallop.

Pritchard dismounted, removed his canteen from his saddle, filled his hat, and presented it to his horse. Soldier lapped as Strobl, Tater, and Bonner unhorsed themselves and did the same. Strobl watered Schatz, his coal-black quarter horse, Bonner his sturdy brown quarter, and Tater the stout paint he'd borrowed from the Atherton Livery.

Once the horses were watered, Pritchard tended to his guns while the others wordlessly followed suit. He checked his Winchester, ensuring its tubular magazine was fully stocked with .44-40s, and added a sixth cartridge to each of his three remaining revolvers: the .44 Remington and his two .45 Colts.

Bonner topped off his pair of Open Top Colts with .44 Henry rimfires, charged his Shiloh Sharps with a single .50-90 cartridge, and stuffed the pockets of his black coat with more of the large rounds.

Tater added another .45 cartridge to his new Colt Cavalry Model, checked the load on his double-barreled, 12-gauge, coach gun, and jammed the pockets of his overalls with spare shotgun shells.

All three watched with interest as Florian Strobl first verified his Henry .44 rifle was loaded, then topped off his five revolvers: the two Chamelot Delvignes under his arms, the two Colt Cavalry Models once belonging to Asa Finchum on each hip, and the Smith & Wesson .44 stuffed in his front buckle holster.

"You sure you got enough guns on ya'?" Tater asked sarcastically. "Six irons may not be enough."

"I have learned many useful things since coming to America," Strobl said around his cigarette. "Many of them from Marshal Pritchard." He winked at Tater. "One such useful thing I learned, is that when going into battle you can never have too many guns or too many bullets."

"Amen," Bonner said.

Once he'd finished checking his weapons, Pritchard climbed aboard Soldier and tightened the stampede string on his Stetson tightly under his chin. Strobl, Bonner, and Tater mounted up as well.

"What's your plan?" Tater asked expectantly.

"I ain't rightly sure you could call what I'm a-gonna do a plan," Pritchard answered. "If I had my druthers, it'd be dark, moonless, and I'd creep up on that-there train Injun-style. I'd use my knife, and before half of them spineless curs knew I was there I'd have the other half of 'em gutted."

Pritchard shielded his eyes and looked up at the sun. "But you play the cards you've got, boys, not the ones you're a-wishin' you held. I ain't a-waitin' any longer to play this hand."

He lowered his eyes, turned in the saddle, and met the steady gaze of the trio of horsemen before him. "I'll tell you what I'm a-gonna do," Pritchard said. "I'm fixin' to trot down there, simple-as-you-please, and free my sister and my baby nephew. And any of those hostage-takin' sons-of-bitches who so much as lift a finger to vex me, I'm gonna send to hell across the lots."

"Sounds like a right-square plan to me," Tater said with a set jaw.

"It's only fair to warn you fellers," Pritchard said, "that after all that's been done to me, mine, and the folks of Atherton, I ain't of a mind to extend considerations of mercy. Far as I reckon, anybody on that train played a part in what Brody's done, and has a reckonin' a-comin'. If that don't sit with you, and you don't wish to accompany me on this particular saddle-charge, I want you to know I understand, and won't hold it against you."

"Ditch Clemson," Bonner began, "whom I consider my friend, had his wife and child taken while I was tasked with their safety. By God, I aim to make that right. I'm going with you, Samuel, whether you want me to, or not. If you think I have a problem with blasting those who took them to hell and gone, you, my friend, are badly mistaken."

Strobl spoke next. "I have sworn to fight by your side since the day you spared my life," he said. "It is my distinct honor, as a nobleman and former officer in the Austrian army, to fight alongside you once more. And as far as granting quarter to men who kidnap women and children," he angrily tossed his cigarette, "none should be expected this day from Florian Strobl, for none shall be granted."

"I don't know much about honor," Tater said, "nor about the grantin' of quarter. All I know"—he cradled his shotgun in the crook of his arm—"is them filthy, bushwhackin', train wreckin', kidnappin' sons-of-tenpenny-whores took Ditch's leg, and took Miss Idelle and Baby Samuel. That's plenty more'n enough for me to murderate every last, white-livered, one of 'em where they stand, sit, or crawl. So iffen you boys are finished jawin', I suggest we get ourselves on down to that-there train and commence the murderation."

"You heard Deputy Jessup," Pritchard said, as he spurred Soldier. "Let's ride!"

Chapter 45

Four determined riders spurred their horses toward the stationary locomotive at full gallop. At one-hundred yards' distance, it appeared no one on Brody's private train had noticed their impending arrival.

At fifty yards, that changed. One of Brody's railroad detectives stepped out onto the rear platform of the caboose to have a smoke. The caboose was linked directly behind Brody's fanciful private car and served to house the locomotive's crew and most of the gunmen. Hearing the approaching hoofbeats, he looked up to find a quartet of riders closing in fast. Each rider had guns in his hands and blood in his eyes.

He tossed his unlit cigarette and re-opened the door. "We've got company!" he hollered to the others lounging inside. "Lawmen!"

"Game's up!" Pritchard shouted to the others. "They know we're a-comin'! I'm goin' for Brody's car. That's where they'll have Idelle!"

"I've got the engine!" Bonner shouted back. They all knew the locomotive mustn't be allowed to leave with Idelle and little Samuel aboard.

"Tater and I shall take the caboose!" Strobl called out, nodding to the deputy riding beside him. He received a grim nod of acknowledgment from Tater in return. Since the caboose served as the only other passenger car on the small, private, train, it was believed the bulk of Brody's railroad detectives and Odom's gunmen would be located there.

Bonner rode to the front of the train as Pritchard leaped from Soldier's back onto the rear platform of Brody's private car. Strobl and Tater skidded their horses to a halt at the caboose. The two Atherton deputies grabbed their long arms and dismounted as men with pistols began to appear in the windows.

Bonner re-holstered his revolvers and executed a leaping dismount similar to Pritchard's. He grabbed the edge of the engine's roof and swung himself into the driver's compartment. A pair of engineers and the fireman already occupying the cab looked up in astonishment at the newcomer's abrupt arrival. Their astonishment lasted only an instant, however, as they quickly recognized the interloper as a threat. One of the engineers started to draw a pistol from inside his overalls, the other snatched up a large wrench, and the fireman, shirtless and soot-covered, raised his blackened shovel.

"Go!" Strobl yelled to Tater, as the deputy ran for the rear door of the caboose as fast as his short legs and hefty body would allow. "I shall cover you!"

As he spoke, Strobl rapid-fired his Henry rifle as fast as he could work the lever and squeeze the trigger. He raked a volley of fifteen shots laterally across the row of windows, forcing those inside the train car who were about to engage Tater with their revolvers to retreat and seek cover amidst the shower of bullets, splintered wood, and shattered glass.

Bonner drew both of his Open Tops simultaneously, handily beating the engineer with the pistol to the draw. He put a shot into the man's chest with his right-hand pistol, but had his left-hand gun smacked from his grasp by a blow to his forearm with the wrench held by the second engineer.

He had no time to acknowledge the agonizing pain in his arm as he was forced to throw himself backward and duck at the same time. The blade of a coal shovel passed less than an inch over the top of his skull, knocking Bonner's Boss of the Plains from his head and leaving him on his back in the cramped compartment.

Wes Childress was lying on his back in one of the berths in the caboose, gulping vigorously from a nearly empty bottle of whiskey which was full when he started drinking. Charles, Brody's valet, had bandaged his gouged eye before returning to attend to the woman and baby. Unfortunately, the servant had done nothing for Childress's pain, or the growing well of rage building inside him.

Suddenly Childress heard someone shout from outside the car. All he could make out was the word, "Lawmen!" and the frantic tone of the shouter.

There were nearly a dozen men sharing the car with him: a half-dozen of Colonel Odom's gun hands and a handful of Brody's railroad detectives. All dropped what they were doing, whether playing cards, reading, or napping, grabbed their revolvers, and scurried to the windows.

Childress, who was beginning to feel the effects of the whiskey he'd slugged down, started to sit his massive body up and see about the commotion. But he threw himself to the floor instead, as a barrage of bullets came crashing in through the caboose's windows.

Childress saw three men get hit. Two of Odom's hired guns suffered minor flesh wounds.

Childress didn't know how many lawmen were outside and wasn't of a mind to poke up his head, look out the window, and count. He drew his pistol, rolled over, and began to crawl toward the opposite door—the one leading to Brody's private car—as the interior of the caboose devolved into chaos.

Pritchard kicked in the rear door of Brody's private car, then immediately stepped back around the edge of the doorway as three gunshots rang out. Had his colossal body remained framed in the doorway after the kick, it was unlikely any of those shots would have missed him.

When Pritchard dashed into Brody's private car with his Colts in his fists a split-second later, the sight that greeted him was an alarming one. Across the opulently furnished train car stood Earl Marsh and Asa Finchum. Both men were holding their guns, which were cocked, and both were hiding behind others.

Marsh stood behind Idelle with one arm around her neck and the barrel of his brand-new Smith & Wesson against her temple. Finchum, however, couldn't hide his freakishly tall, skeletally thin body behind his hostage as

Marsh had done, because his hostage was only a baby. He held little Samuel in the crook of one arm, and kept one of his new Colt Cavalry Models pointed lightly against the infant's chest with the other. A demonic smile emerged from his wired-up jaw as the baby innocently played with the revolver's barrel.

Idelle's eyes belied the terror she felt; not for herself, but for her infant son. She couldn't speak, as Marsh had his arm tightly cinched around her throat.

"Drop those guns, Marshal," Marsh commanded. "If you don't, your sister and nephew die."

"Go to hell," Pritchard said flatly.

Chapter 46

Tater Jessup mounted the steps to the caboose two-at-a-time and kicked open the rear door. He dashed in, a snarl on his lips and his scattergun at the ready, but tripped on something as he stepped forward and fell flat on his face. As he landed, the shotgun slipped from his grasp.

When he looked up a moment later, Tater found nine men standing in the car above him. All wore furious expressions and had guns in their hands. A tenth man, with a bullet hole in his forehead, lay dead on the floor behind him. He was the reason Tater had tripped.

"Looks like you flummoxed yourself, lawman," one of Odom's gunmen said with a mirthless laugh. "Now we're gonna settle your hash right proper."

"Settle this," Strobl said, as he suddenly appeared in the doorway. He'd no sooner materialized than the Chamelot Delvigne revolvers in each of his hands spoke.

Since the Chamelot Delvignes were double-action in design, and didn't need to have their hammers manually cocked, Strobl was able to fire at an extremely rapid rate.

He fired twelve times, in the span of only seconds and at point-blank range, at the gunmen hovering over Tater.

The sounds of men screaming in pain and terror resonated within the car, along with the ear-splitting din of many gunshots. Gunsmoke filled the cabin as men fell. Some went down seeking cover, others when struck by Strobl's withering fusillade of pistol fire.

Tater wasted no time getting into the fight. He retrieved his shotgun and rose to one knee, just as both of Strobl's Chamelot Delvigne revolvers clicked empty. The Austrian deputy dropped the useless guns and went for the Colt Cavalry Models on each hip, leaving him momentarily vulnerable.

One of Odom's gunmen, who was unhurt and who'd taken cover, was crouched behind a nearby seat. He spotted Strobl through the thick fog of gunsmoke, extended his arm, and aimed his Remington .44 from only a few feet's distance. Strobl saw him and winced, knowing that he'd never get the long-barreled revolvers out in time to thwart the shooter.

Instead of the single pistol shot he expected, Strobl heard a tremendous "boom." Tater blew off most of the gunman's head, giving him both barrels, before he could fire.

Tater rose from his knee to stand shoulder-to-shoulder with Strobl as another gunman, this time one of Brody's detectives, also stood and aimed his revolver. Strobl fired twice, once from each Colt, and the man fell.

Tater quickly drew his own Colt and shot a man he spotted lying gutshot on the opposite side of the car, but who was nonetheless still able to wield his pistol. Then he holstered his gun, broke open his shotgun, extracted the empty shells, and re-stocked the weapon with a pair of fresh ones from his overalls pocket. He also stuffed another pair of shotgun rounds into his teeth and nodded at Strobl.

"Anyone else care to try their hand against us?" Strobl called out. "If so, consider this." He nudged Tater, who fired both barrels of his shotgun into the roof of the caboose. The sound was deafening, added immensely to the already heavy haze of burnt gunpowder filling the cabin, and rained splinters of wood down into the car.

No sooner had Tater fired, then he again broke open the shotgun, popped out the expended shells, and re-stoked it with the two rounds he held in his teeth. The entire reloading sequence took him only a second or two.

"Hold your fire, lawmen," a voice meekly called out from somewhere in the pea-soup of smoke within the caboose. "We surrender."

"Very well," Strobl said. "You are all under arrest. Show yourselves, with empty hands, or die where you are."

A solitary Odom man stood tentatively up with his hands in the air. He was wounded in the right arm. Strobl covered him while Tater cautiously searched the car. All others within the caboose were dead.

Bonner shot the fireman in the forehead as he raised his coal shovel for another swipe at the downed bounty hunter. He collapsed, dead at Bonner's feet. The second engineer instantly dropped his wrench and raised his hands.

Bonner slowly regained his feet, his broken left arm

hanging uselessly at his side. He placed the muzzle of his Open Top .44 on the tip of the surviving engineer's nose and thumbed the hammer back.

"Please," the man begged, "don't kill me?"

"Can you operate this locomotive?" Bonner asked.

"I can," the man said.

"Then it's your lucky day," Bonner said, "because I won't shoot you."

"Thank you," the engineer gasped.

"It isn't because I don't want to," Bonner said. "You're going to take this train back to Jefferson City."

"What did you say?" Marsh asked incredulously.

"You heard me," Pritchard answered. "I said, 'go to hell.'"

"If you believe I won't shoot your sister," Marsh said, "or that Asa won't shoot her baby, you are so very, very, wrong, Marshal."

"You ain't a-gonna," Pritchard said.

"And what makes you think that?"

"Because you," Pritchard said, "and that tin-jawed weasel you ride with, are both already dead. You just don't know it, yet."

"Is that so?" Marsh said.

"It is," Pritchard said. "The last time I saw you boys, at young Donnie McKitchern's funeral, I told you both if I ever saw either of you again, it'd be the last time you'd walk this earth. Those acquainted with me know I ain't prone to blusteration."

"Well, Marshal," Marsh said, "if you think we're scared—"

Earl Marsh's sentence was cut off by a gunshot. Actually, it was a pair of gunshots. The first, from Pritchard's right-hand pistol, launched a .45 caliber bullet into Marsh's right eye socket. He elected to drift leftward a hair, since Idelle was in the line-of-fire.

The second bullet, fired in sync with the first, struck Asa Finchum in the dimple on his upper lip. Both men were dead before they began to collapse. Pritchard didn't wait to move again.

He let Marsh, and the nearly unconscious Idelle, fall to the floor as one. Before Asa could fall, however, Pritchard instantly dropped his revolvers and rushed in to pluck his nephew from the gangly gunman's lifeless arms.

Baby Samuel was crying, as the twin gunshots had startled him. Pritchard knelt beside Idelle, and brought her around from her stupor. Then he helped her to a sitting position, where she took in gulps of air. After collecting herself, she gratefully took her son from her brother's arms.

Suddenly Pritchard drew the Remington from under his arm, cocked it, and aimed at the curtains behind Brody's fancy desk.

"Come out, you," he ordered.

"Don't shoot," Charles said, as he slinked from where he'd been hiding behind a curtain. "I'm no threat."

Pritchard grabbed him by the collar and jammed his revolver into the valet's throat.

"No, Samuel," Idelle said, as her son calmed. "Don't hurt him. He was kind to Samuel and me, and cared for us while we were held here against our will."

"Maybe so," Pritchard said, "but he stood silent while

you and Samuel were taken. He never lifted a finger to help you escape nor signaled for rescue."

He brought the valet's face close to his own, lifting the man almost off his feet. "Far as I'm concerned, you oughta hang alongside Brody. But I'll give you a choice: testify against your boss, and go to prison awhile or keep silent. But if your mutton hole stays shut, you'd best know if the law doesn't hang you, I'll dangle you myself. That's a Texas promise. What's it gonna be?"

"I'll testify," Charles gulped, "and I can give you something better than my word."

"What would that be?"

Charles pointed to Brody's safe. "Twenty-thousand dollars of the payroll taken from the train wrecked at Rock Creek is locked in there," he said. "The other twenty went to Marsh and Finchum. It's still in the Missouri Pacific Railroad's money bag it was stolen in."

"Do you know the combination to Brody's safe?"

"Of course," the valet said indignantly. "I've watched Mr. Brody open it a thousand times."

Pritchard smiled and lowered the trembling valet.

Chapter 47

Wes Childress, who'd polished off almost an entire bottle of whiskey before the lawmen arrived, crept clumsily from the caboose only seconds before Tater stumbled in. His injured eye no longer hurt as badly, but the vision in the other was beginning to blur. He heard the orchestra of gunfire behind him, which followed his hasty exit, and was glad he'd elected not to stay.

Standing on unsteady feet outside the train, Childress watched through the window of Brody's private car as Pritchard confronted Marsh and Finchum. For a brief moment, he contemplated sneaking into the car behind the big marshal and executing him with a backshot.

But when he saw Pritchard gun down both men in the blink of an eye, as they hid behind hostages no less, he abandoned any notion of going up against the lawman, especially in his intoxicated state. In all his time as a gun hand, Childress had never witnessed such pistol work, and it was at that moment he concluded flight was his best option.

But when he saw Pritchard embrace a sobbing Idelle and place her baby back into her grateful arms, he suddenly remembered his ruined eye. The feeling of rage that had been building within him, exponentially magnified by the whiskey, overwhelmed his self-preservation instinct. Childress drew his revolver, squeezed his massive body underneath the train car, and lay flat on the tracks, waiting for the comely young mother to emerge.

The survivors of the gunfight on John Brody's private train each made their way outside into the warm sun for different reasons. Idelle and her child because it was the first time they'd been allowed out of the dungeon of Brody's private car in days, and because she didn't want the baby to breathe in the powder fumes lingering inside.

Bonner, favoring his damaged left arm, came out herding the only three surviving members of Brody's and Odom's gangs: Charles, the valet; a nervous-looking engineer; and one of Odom's gunmen, who was only slightly wounded. Everyone else employed by either John Brody or Colonel Walton Odom, more than a dozen men, had been killed in the battle.

After Pritchard and Tater searched the train to ensure there were no holdouts, he sent the deputy to round up their horses and put them into the livery car. Once that task was complete, everyone would re-board the train and return to Jefferson City with all due haste.

Strobl fashioned a sling from his neckerchief, and was tying it around Bonner's neck and arm, when Idelle suddenly screamed. Everyone instinctively looked to her, and found a very large, clearly drunk, man had crawled from beneath the train. He wore a bandage over one eye, had risen to one knee, and was aiming a revolver at the woman and child.

"You took my eye, you witch!" the big gunman slurred, seemingly unaware that once he shot Idelle he would be shot to pieces by multiple guns. "Now I'm a-gonna take your life!"

Just as Pritchard, Strobl, and Bonner were going for their pistols, Tater materialized from between two train cars. Swinging his shotgun like a lumberman plying his trade, he clobbered Childress on the side of his head. The big, drunk, gunman slumped forward on his face like a felled tree and lay still.

"I reckon when we searched the train," Tater said to Pritchard with a satisfied grunt, "we plumb forgot to check under it."

"Who is that fool?" Bonner asked, as they contemplated the unconscious man.

"He's the one who posed as Jem Rupe," Idelle said. "He led the crew that wrecked the train at Rock Creek."

"He's a' dead ringer," Strobl remarked, "as you Americans say, for the real Jeremiah Rupe. Even down to the patched eye."

"You don't say," Pritchard said, rubbing his chin. "That gives me a notion. C'mon, Tater. Help me load this feller onto the train."

Chapter 48

"You don't seriously expect any of us to believe your fantastical tale, do you Mayor Clemson?" Brody said.

He'd taken the floor after Ditch spent the better portion of an hour addressing the assembly in the governor's mansion. Brody had risen from his seat, stuck his thumbs into his vest, and stood confidently at the front of the room.

"I don't care what you believe, Mr. Brody," Ditch said. "I spoke the God's-honest truth."

"You are contending," Brody challenged, "that I, John Brody, head of the Brody Railroad Line and a man who has never been so much as cited for spitting on the sidewalk, much less a serious breach of the law, am the corrupt mastermind of a criminal enterprise which employs gunmen and trainwreckers?"

"I am," Ditch confirmed.

"And you further contend," Brody continued in a mocking tone, "I orchestrated the derailment of the Missouri Pacific train at Rock Creek? Killing and maiming dozens of passengers, allegedly for the purposes of besmirching the reputation of the Missouri Pacific Railroad

Company and to murder a group of mayors on that train who would have influenced Governor Hardin against my railroad company in a bid for a government contract?"

"I do," Ditch said.

"If these delusions of yours aren't farcical enough," Brody chuckled, "you also claim I sent hired assassins to kill you? And that these same men kidnapped your wife and child? Am I missing anything? Have I got all that right?"

"Correct on all counts," Ditch said.

"Clearly," Brody said, switching from incredulity to solemnly addressing the assembled politicians, "the recent injuries Mayor Clemson suffered in the tragic train accident, which as you can all see by the scar on his forehead included a head wound, has had an unfortunate impact on his reasoning. I suggest, as good Christian men, we take into consideration his debilitation, and not hold any of these lunatic ravings against him. Perhaps, in time, with the proper care and our devout prayers, his full mental faculties will return?"

"I ain't of unsound mind," Ditch said. "What I said today was Simon pure. Why don't you fess up, Brody, and acknowledge the corn?"

"I cannot confess to a fantasy," Brody said smugly.

"Do you have any evidence to support your claims, Mayor Clemson?" Governor Hardin asked.

"At this time," Ditch admitted, "I do not."

"Looks like your plan to take down Brody has failed," Colonel Odom whispered to Babbit. "How's it feel to lose?"

"Shut up," Babbit said.

"I suggest," Brody said, "in light of Mayor Clemson's

obvious mental handicap, that he be excused from further deliberations associated with the awarding of the government railroad contract?"

"Hold your damned horses," Pritchard boomed, as the doors to the assembly room burst open and a group of people stormed in. With Pritchard was Strobl, Bonner, Tater, Idelle, Baby Samuel, and their four prisoners from the Brody train, as well as Manfri and Danior Pannell, who were on each side of a manacled, and kerosene-scented, Gilbert. The party was escorted by a quartet of U.S. Marshals bearing Winchester rifles.

"You want evidence?" Pritchard said. "Here's your evidence." He tossed a canvass bag, clearly marked with the words, *Property of the Missouri Pacific Railroad* on it and stenciled with a serial number, on the floor at Brody's feet.

"Guess where I found that?" Pritchard asked, as he shoved Gilbert, Charles, Childress, and the other prisoners forward. Then he scanned the room and found Babbit waving to him from the crowd.

"Arrest that man," Pritchard commanded a marshal, as he pointed out Odom. Two marshals rushed to comply. The Colonel was dragged forward to join the other prisoners.

"These men," Ditch announced, as the assembled mayors settled down from responding to the newcomer's unexpected and raucous entrance, "all work for John Brody. They participated in his plot. Each will confirm my story, if they don't want to hang, and lay proof to all I've claimed."

"I don't want to hang," Charles spoke up. "I'll tell you

what Mr. Brody has done. I was at his side at all times. I heard everything."

"I don't want to hang, neither!" Gilbert howled. "I'll talk! I was at the train, and among them who tried to bushwhack Mayor Clemson out on the prairie! Marshal Pritchard done killed most of us in a rainstorm!"

Jason Gould smiled. John Brody's face went ashen.

"And this man," Ditch jabbed Childress with his crutch, "is the man who wrecked the train at Rock Creek."

"His name is Arkansas Jeremiah Rupe," Pritchard suddenly said, as gasps of astonishment broke out. "The infamous trainwrecker of Platte Bridge."

Strobl looked quizzically at Pritchard, who gave the Austrian deputy a "trust me" wink.

"Can you prove this?" President Grant, who had been silent through the meeting until now, asked Pritchard. "Can you prove this man," he aimed his cigar at Childress, "wrecked the train at Rock Creek? And that he is indeed Jem Rupe, a criminal I have been waiting to bring to justice for over a decade?"

"I can," Idelle spoke up before her brother could answer. "Take a look in his pocket."

Governor Hardin signaled to Colonel Duncan, who began searching Childress. A moment later he held up an engraved pocket watch, with a man's wedding ring dangling from its gold chain. Duncan handed it to the governor.

"Look inside," Idelle told him.

Governor Hardin opened the watch and his eyes widened. He held it aloft, for all to see the picture of Idelle Clemson within it.

"He's Jem Rupe, all right!" Hardin declared. "This

proves it! This man," he pointed an accusing finger at Childress, "wrecked the train at Rock Creek! And if he wrecked that train—"

"—he wrecked the one at Platte Bridge!" Pritchard finished the sentence.

"Wait!" Childress protested. "I ain't Jem Rupe! Sure, I wrecked the train at Rock Creek! Brody's man, Earl Marsh, paid me to do it! But I never wrecked no other trains! I swear! My name's Wes Childress! I ain't Arkansas Jem Rupe!"

"Take them all away," Hardin ordered the marshals. "And arrest John Brody along with them." The marshals dutifully began to hustle the prisoners off.

"Wait—" Brody pleaded, as he was roughly grabbed by a marshal.

"I will not," Hardin cut Brody off. "I've heard enough."

"So have I," Grant said to Hardin. "I presume there is no further discussion needed on which railroad will be awarded the federal contract?"

"None whatsoever," Hardin said. He turned to Gould. "Congratulations, Mr. Gould. It would seem the Missouri Pacific Railroad has won the day."

A chorus of cheers, whistles, and rebel yells filled the hall.

"Mr. Brody!" a marshal's voice shouted above the din. "Something's wrong with Mr. Brody!"

Brody was lying on the ground, on his back, clutching his chest. His face was blue and his eyes were bulging. A marshal was bent over him.

"His ticker's gone south," the marshal said. "Somebody fetch a doctor!"

Pritchard shouldered his way through the crowd and

knelt at Brody's side. "You owe me fifty-thousand dollars, Mr. Brody," he said for all to hear. "Just 'cause you were the one who hired Jem Rupe, doesn't get you off the hook for payin' the bounty you put up yourself for bringin' him in."

"It won't get you off the gallows, either," Ditch added.

Moments later the governor's physician rushed in, along with a nurse, and were led to the supine Brody.

"Marshal Pritchard brought Rupe in," Governor Hardin confirmed, "so he collects the bounty." He extended his hand, which Pritchard shook. "Well done, Marshal Pritchard. Very well done indeed."

"I had help," Pritchard said, nodding to Tater, Strobl, and Bonner.

"It seems I owe you fifty-thousand dollars," Gould said to Pritchard, stepping forward. He also extended his hand. "When you told me you were going to 'sort it out,' you weren't kidding."

"I figure that one-hundred-thousand dollars," Pritchard said, shaking Gould's offered hand, "split up between the families of them who died and was maimed in that train wreck, might go some distance to easin' their sufferin'."

"I believe you're right," Gould said. "A noble idea, Marshal. I'll make it happen."

The marshals loaded Brody onto a stretcher. He was still gasping and sputtering as they carried him out of the hall.

"Is he going to die?" Idelle asked, balancing Samuel on her shoulder.

"I hope not," Ditch said, hugging his wife. "I want to see him swing."

"There has to be a trial first," Hardin said, "before sentence can be passed. I'll see to it at once."

"Begging the governor's pardon," Judge Pearson said, "but I have something to say about the trial. If I'm not mistaken, I believe the Rock Creek train wreck, the attempts on Mayor Clemson and Marshal Pritchard's lives, and the kidnapping of Mrs. Clemson and her son, all occurred in Jackson County?"

"You are correct," Hardin said, realizing where Pearson was going.

"Which means," the judge continued, "I will be presiding at the trial in Atherton, which is the Jackson County seat."

"I trust you will see that justice is done," Hardin said.

"I presume," President Grant said to Pearson, "that with you presiding over the trial of Arkansas Jeremiah Rupe for the train wreck at Rock Creek, which is a death penalty offense, there will be no need for the federal government to conduct a trial for the Platte Bridge wreck during the war?"

"You presume correctly," Pearson said. "I assure you, Mr. President, the gallows in Atherton works just as well as the one in Washington."

"That's good," Grant said. "Because I swore Jeremiah Rupe would hang. I don't break promises, especially to myself. See to it, will you?"

"With pleasure," Pearson said with a bow.

While everyone in the crowded hall was busy thanking Ditch, offering congratulations to Hardin and Gould, hugging Idelle and doting on her son, and pouring celebratory drinks, Pritchard discretely signaled for Strobl to meet him in a remote corner of the room.

"I must confess," Strobl began, once they were alone, "I was a bit perplexed by your actions? You told everyone that Childress is Jeremiah Rupe, when in fact, the real Jeremiah Rupe is currently inhabiting a jail cell in Fort Smith, Arkansas, along with Sheriff Blevins, as a guest of Judge Parker."

"You know that," Pritchard said, "and I know that. Ain't no need for any others to know."

"What about Judge Parker?"

"He was already skeptical," Pritchard reminded Strobl. "I've got a job for you, Deputy Strobl."

"By your command," Strobl said.

"Find John Babbit. Take him to the nearest telegraph office, and have him send a wire to Judge Parker at Fort Smith. Relay to Parker that Marshal Pritchard was wrong about the identity of his prisoner, and that the real Jem Rupe has been arrested in Jefferson City and will be brought to trial in Atherton. Be sure to have John mention in the telegram that Rupe's identity was verified by none other than President Ulysses S. Grant himself."

"I will do this at once," Strobl said.

"There's one more thing I need you to do," Pritchard said.

"What's that?" Strobl asked.

"Get on the next train to Fort Smith," Pritchard smiled, "and escort the Reverend Oliver Winfield and his daughter, Tess, to Atherton."

"I get it," Strobl said, snapping his fingers. "With Childress hung as Rupe, the real Jeremiah Rupe would be free, would he not?"

"You mean the Reverend Oliver Winfield, don't you?" Pritchard said. "I reckon the reverend and his rather pretty daughter, which I done noticed you noticin', might be interested in helpin' out Pastor Donaldson with his ministry here in Atherton? We could always use another pastor in town, couldn't we?"

"I am not a churchgoing man," Strobl said, "but I know a young lady who may soon have something to say about that."

"I was thinkin' the same thing myself," Pritchard said with a grin. "Now git goin', Deputy. You've got a journey ahead of you."

Chapter 49

Atherton, Missouri. June, 1875.

The massive crowd completely filled the town square. Folks had been streaming into Atherton for days in anticipation of the big event. They came from rural villages, small towns, and big cities in a dozen states and territories. Reporters from two-dozen newspapers, some as far away as California and New York, had also arrived to report on the extraordinary proceedings.

The trial of John Brody, the former owner of the Brody Railroad, Colonel Walton Odom, a former Union officer and professional gunman in his employ, and Jeremiah Rupe, the infamous Trainwrecker of North Platte, as well as the man responsible for the derailment at Rock Creek, lasted only three days.

Charles, Brody's valet, and Gilbert testified against the defendants in exchange for leniency during their own criminal trials. Each received a lengthy prison sentence, but had their lives spared. It was Idelle's testimony, however, which was the most dramatic and which sealed the defendants' fates.

At one point in Idelle's testimony, when describing how Brody's men pointed guns at her infant son, most of the male members of the audience in the courtroom appeared ready to skip the formality of a trial in favor of a tall tree and a short rope.

At the conclusion of the trial, Judge Eugene Pearson read the unanimous jury verdict. John Brody sat mute in his wheelchair as Pearson issued their sentences, while Odom cursed under his breath. Jeremiah Rupe, who repeatedly insisted his name was Wes Childress, cried.

Execution of the sentences was delayed seventy-two hours to give Seth Tilley, Atherton's best carpenter, time to construct a special gallows capable of hanging three men at once. This also gave Seth's father Simon, Atherton's undertaker, time to make preparations of his own.

The hanging was scheduled for noon. At a quarter till, Pritchard led the three condemned men, single file, from Atherton's jail through the rapt and silent crowd. The manacled Odom and Childress walked, with Strobl behind them, while Tater pushed Brody along in his wheelchair. He had suffered a stroke, and one side of his body was paralyzed.

Strobl searched the throng of faces until he saw Tess and her father. She smiled and waved, causing the Austrian to blush. Pritchard, scanning the crowd carefully for potential threats, grinned when he noticed his deputy fluster at the sight of the pretty young woman from Arkansas.

Pritchard also noticed another pair of familiar faces. Dorothy Greaves, looking as stunning as the day he'd met her, was standing near the front of the crowd, closest to the gallows. Behind her stood her sullen and unrequited suitor, Carl Ewell, who refused to make eye contact with the tall marshal.

Also standing at the front of the crowd, nearest the scaffold, was Mayor Ditch Clemson, his wife Idelle, Laird Bonner, and most of Atherton's Vigilance Committee, as well as the parents of Donnie McKitchern.

"I told you I'd see you swing, Colonel," Bonner said to Odom as he was led past the bounty hunter.

"That you did," Odom retorted. "I'm just glad you didn't get the bounty posted on me."

"John Babbit was awarded that," Bonner acknowledged, "and I'm happy to thank you for him. But don't worry; I was very handsomely paid by Jason Gould."

"Go to hell," Odom said.

"After you," Bonner said, tipping his hat and pointing to the gallows.

Odom mounted the gallows steps with his head erect, while Pritchard and Strobl had to drag the whimpering Childress up to the platform. Tater, with Pritchard's help, carried the heavy Brody up, leaving his wheelchair behind.

"Burn in hell, John Brody," Donnie McKitchern's mother hissed, as the invalid railroad baron was hefted up the steps past her.

Brody refused to look her in the eye as he was placed on a simple wooden chair on the platform. Ditch, carefully balancing himself on his crutch, hobbled his way up the steps to the top of the gallows last.

Strobl and Tater descended the steps, leaving Pearson, Pritchard, and Ditch as the only persons, beside the three condemned men, on the platform. Pritchard fixed a noose around each of their necks. Brody closed his eyes, Childress sobbed, and Odom grunted in disgust as the ropes were tightened.

Once each of the condemned was properly noosed, Pritchard nodded to Ditch, who limped over to the lever that released the scaffold floor from beneath them. He had asked Judge Pearson for permission to be the one to pull the lever, and it had been granted.

The swollen mass of people gathered in the town square below the gallows looked up, as Judge Pearson stepped forward to speak. It was quiet enough to hear a pin drop.

"Do any of you have final words?" Pearson asked the three condemned men.

Brody shook his head, still staring down at his feet.

"I won't give you the satisfaction," Odom said, also shaking his head.

"I ain't Jem Rupe!" Childress wailed. "You've got the wrong feller!"

Pearson turned to Pritchard. "Do you have anything to say, Marshal?"

"I do," Pritchard said, taking off his hat. "When I went to visit my friend, Mayor Ditch Clemson, at the train wreck at Rock Creek which took his leg, and saw all them bodies, and all those maimed, I swore me an oath. I swore those who done such a foul deed would come to account by gun or rope." He replaced his hat. "Today, with the help of God and the brave men of the Atherton Vigilance Committee, I make good on that pledge."

Judge Pearson gave a single nod, and Ditch Clemson placed a hand on the lever.

"I want you to know," Ditch whispered, as he stared directly at Childress, "I didn't forget what you said you were gonna do to my wife. I'm gonna enjoy pullin' this lever and sendin' you to your reward."

"Wait!" Childress blubbered. "Ain't you supposed to give us blindfolds?"

"Not today," Pritchard said. "After what you boys done, I want you fellers lookin' into hell's mouth on the way down."

"To hell with you all," Ditch said, as he pulled the lever.

Chapter 50

Despite the macabre events of earlier in the day, by evening Atherton was in a festive mood. The hotels, restaurants, and saloons were packed, the streets were filled with revelers, and the atmosphere in town was more akin to a harvest festival than a three-rope hanging.

Pritchard left the hotel restaurant where he'd dined with Ditch, Idelle, and his nephew, who occupied his lap while he ate, and headed for the jail. He wanted to relieve Tater, who was awaiting his return so he could make a beeline for Perkins's Diner and the jumbo-sized steak and spuds dinner awaiting him.

When last he saw Strobl, his Austrian deputy was strolling arm-in-arm with Tess Winfield. They were taking in the sights and seemed oblivious to anyone else in the swarming streets around them.

"Atherton!" a familiar voice called out from behind him, just as Pritchard reached the middle of the main street. "Smokin' Joe Atherton! Time to face me you yellow, backshootin', son-of-a-bitch!"

Pritchard turned slowly around to find Delbert Greaves standing in the street at fifteen paces. The would-be gunfighter was just as small and scrawny as when he saw him last and was wearing a newly acquired pair of Colt revolvers, slung low and tied down to his thighs.

Pedestrians on all sides of Pritchard and Greaves scattered.

"I told you once I was gonna put you in the bone yard," Greaves said. "That was before you took my guns and locked me up. Now I've really got a score to settle."

"You did those things to yourself," Pritchard said, "when you broke the law."

"I didn't come here to talk," Greaves said. "I came here to end you. Delbert Greaves is gonna be the one to bury Smokin' Joe Atherton. Folks are gonna remember my name."

"Don't do this, Delbert," Pritchard warned. "It ain't gonna end the way you think."

"Draw!" Greaves barked. "Draw, you yellow bastard!"

"I won't," Pritchard said, "unless you make me."

"Suit yourself," Greaves said, as he went for both of his guns.

Pritchard had both of his own revolvers out, the hammers back, and the barrels leveled steadily on Greaves before the young gunman's fingers even touched the walnut stocks of his guns. He froze without a chance to even start his pull.

"Enough," Pritchard said. "There'll be no more gunplay from you, young Greaves. This time, I ain't gonna run you out of town for tryin' to provoke a gunfight. You're old enough to account for your deeds, and you're under arrest. We'll see if a couple of years in The Walls doesn't convince you to change your ways."

"Drop your guns, Marshal," a woman's voice behind

Pritchard said. "I'm not going to let you take my little brother in."

"Do as she says," a man's voice joined the woman's. "Drop 'em, or I swear I'll shoot you down."

Pritchard looked over his shoulder to find Dorothy Greaves only a few feet behind him, aiming a short-barreled Webley at his back. Standing next to her was Carl Ewell, with an Army Colt also pointed at his back from point-blank range.

Out of the corner of his eye Pritchard saw Delbert, now wearing a maniacal grin on his face, drawing his guns.

Caught in a crossfire between four guns wielded by three different shooters, Pritchard realized his chances of survival were almost nil.

He had a split-second decision to make; which threat to address first? Delbert, though undoubtedly the better shot, was much farther away than his sister and Ewell, who would be unlikely to miss him from only a few feet away.

With no time for contemplation and no ideal options, Pritchard acted. He pivoted and dropped onto his back, firing both revolvers simultaneously. A .450 bullet from Dorothy Greaves's Bulldog and a .44 from Ewell's Colt sailed through the space he'd occupied only an instant before.

Both of Pritchard's .45 bullets found their mark. Dorothy Greaves took hers high in the breastbone, and Carl Ewell received his in the throat. Each dropped their gun and collapsed, folding into one another.

No sooner had Pritchard fired than he rolled. He knew Delbert Greaves's guns would be clear of their holsters and their barrels moving toward him. He automatically re-cocked his guns, bringing them to bear on Greaves, but halted the squeeze of the triggers when he saw the gunman before him.

Greaves had dropped his revolvers and was rushing, empty-handed, toward his downed sister. The kill-lust expression on his face had transformed into tear-filled dread.

"Dorothy!" he cried out, falling to his knees and taking her into his arms. Ewell, lying next to her, was already dead.

Dorothy tried to say something to her brother as he sobbed hysterically, but too much blood bubbled up into her mouth from inside her. All she could produce was her death rattle, a sound Samuel Pritchard, once known as Joe Atherton, had heard far too many times to forget.

THE END

Acknowledgments

I wish to express my heartfelt gratitude to the following individuals for their support in the writing of this novel:

Gary Goldstein. My friend, Editorial Director at Kensington Publishing, and the fellow who first prodded me into writing Westerns. I only wish I could write a character as wise, salty, and true as him.

Scott Miller. My friend, literary agent at Trident Media Group, and a man of honor who fights the good fight and keeps the faith.

The fine folks at the Western Writers of America, who welcomed me so generously.

The Calaveras Crew. Sidehackers all, and men to ride the river with.

The Usual Suspects, whose support is deeply appreciated. If it takes a village, ours is the "Village of the Damned."

Lastly, and most important, my wife Denise, daughter Brynne, and son Owen. They are the greatest blessings ever bestowed on a fellow. I am humbled every day. Today, tomorrow, and forever; you know the rest.

TURN THE PAGE
FOR AN EXCITING PREVIEW!

When the legend becomes fact, kill the legend.

**The saga of gunfighter Samuel Pritchard continues
in this violent story of blood and bullets from
acclaimed Western author Sean Lynch.**

THE DEVIL CAME DOWN TO IDAHO

As both a former Confederate guerilla and Texas
Ranger, and now a U.S. Marshal, no one knows the
dangers of the frontier and cow towns like Samuel
Pritchard. A couple of wagon trains traveling the
Oregon Trail have vanished, and Pritchard's got miles of
bad road across hostile territory to investigate.
But he must also reckon with a price on his head.
Bounty hunter Captain Laird Bonner is the greatest
manhunter throughout the West—and he's as ruthless
as he's relentless in pursuing his prey.

Then the trail for both Pritchard and Bonner ends in an
Idaho mining town named Whiskey Falls. Ruled by a
man who earned his stripes in Andersonville, the town
is a literal hell for everyone who lives there, slaving and
dying to satiate their captor's lustful greed.
To escape, Pritchard and Bonner must declare an
uneasy truce and take on an army of gunmen.

This is the story of Samuel Pritchard. A frontier-town
peacekeeper who left many outlaws dead in the dust . . .

THE BLOOD OF INNOCENTS
The Guns of Samuel Pritchard

BY
SEAN LYNCH
Author of *Death Rattle* and *Cottonmouth*

On sale now, wherever Pinnacle Books are sold.

Chapter One

East of Lawrence, Kansas. August, 1874

"They're not more'n a couple of miles ahead of us," Pritchard said, as he stood. He'd dismounted his big chestnut-colored Morgan, Rusty, and knelt to more closely examine the horse droppings left by a trio of riders he and his deputy had been tracking for the past two days.

"Will we overtake them before they get to Lawrence?" Strobl asked, in his Austrian accent.

"Likely," Pritchard replied. "We've still got a few hours of daylight left. I'd surely prefer to brace 'em afield. If we have to take 'em in town, it could get a mite messy."

Strobl nodded his assent. Both men had seen far too much innocent blood spilled during their lifetimes. As a result, each fervently wished to avoid gunplay near non-combatants whenever possible.

Atherton, Missouri, town marshal Samuel Pritchard, who was also the sheriff of Jackson County, and Deputy Marshal Florian Strobl were tracking three saddle tramps who'd passed through earlier that week.

Atherton was a booming lumber-town, bustling Missouri

River port, busy stopover on the Chicago, Burlington and Quincy rail line between Kansas City and St. Louis, and certainly not unfamiliar with horseback transients. But the three trail-dust-covered men who rode in were evidently unaware the town of Atherton was marshaled by Samuel Pritchard—formerly known as Smokin' Joe Atherton. Had they known, it's unlikely they'd have chosen Atherton as the place to do what they'd done.

Assuming the alias "Joe Atherton" as a teenager after he survived being headshot and buried prematurely in a shallow grave, Pritchard fled his hometown, went on to fight for the Confederacy as a horseback guerilla, served ten years as a Texas Ranger, and earned a reputation as the most lethal gunfighter on the frontier. The fact that Pritchard also stood six-and-a-half feet tall, was heavily muscled from a youth spent hauling lumber at his father's mill, and sported an ominous bullet-hole scar on his forehead over his right eye, did little to diminish his fearsome reputation.

When he finally returned home to Atherton last autumn, three years shy of his thirtieth birthday, Pritchard resumed his true name. He also avenged his murdered parents, and along with his childhood friend Ditch Clemson, wiped out the ruthless gang of murderers and thieves who'd ruled Atherton like Pharaohs since before the war.

In the months following the Battle of Atherton, as it became locally known, Pritchard had also been forced to stave off an onslaught of bounty-killers in a brazen attempt to wrest control of his family's considerable assets from his younger sister, Idelle, the town's acting-mayor. This became known as the Second Battle of Atherton.

The spring of 1874 had been a particularly bloody time

for the citizens of Atherton. Like most towns straddling the one-time border between North and South, its citizens were still suffering from the lingering after-effects of the Civil War almost ten years later.

As a lawman, Pritchard fought hard to bring a measure of peace to war-weary Atherton, and his determined efforts were finally beginning to bear welcome fruit. In the short time since he'd resigned his post as a Texas Ranger and pinned on a town marshal's star, Atherton had become a relatively safe place. Despite the First and Second Battles of Atherton, thanks to his fists, guns, and even-handed skill at enforcing the law, it was once more safe to walk the streets.

His loyal friend Ditch, in addition to marrying his sister, had been elected to replace her as mayor. Ditch's shrewd business acumen, acquired as a successful Texas cattleman in the years following the war, greatly contributed to the community's prosperity.

Fighting alongside Pritchard to bring peace and justice to Atherton was Florian Strobl, a European duelist who'd originally arrived among the flock of gunmen who'd come to collect a bounty on his head before the Second Battle of Atherton. A disgraced Austrian Count exiled to America, Strobl had switched loyalties after Pritchard spared his life. He subsequently joined the marshal as his deputy, and in that role set out with his boss after a trio of kidnappers and murderers two days previously.

Three strangers rode into Atherton, an otherwise unnoteworthy occurrence, and settled in at the Sidewinder, a restaurant and saloon operated by a local clan of Romanichals. After dining on steak and consuming two bottles of whiskey, the newcomers, claiming to be cowhands hailing from the Oklahoma Territory but whose hands suspiciously lacked the callouses of working men, took particular notice of the buxom, teenaged, waitress serving them dinner.

When one of the drunken men, none of whom were less than thirty years old, grabbed the fifteen-year-old girl, clamped a filthy hand over her mouth to suppress her screams, and proceeded to drag her out into the alley behind the Sidewinder, his two companions kept the other patrons at bay with drawn pistols. They also helped themselves to another bottle of whiskey as they followed their companion and his struggling captive out through the back door. Needless to say, no effort was made by the men to pay for their meals and drink.

The saloonkeeper, Manfri Pannell, and one of his adult sons, Vano, came running from the kitchen. They stormed into the alley just as the cowboy who'd first grabbed the girl stripped her of her dress, tearing the garment entirely from her body.

Manfri and Vano, both sturdy, muscular men, ran to the girl's aid. The other two cowboys, despite their drunkenness, sensed the duo advancing behind them. Both gunmen spun and fired.

Manfri was struck in the shoulder. A .44 slug spun him around and sent him tumbling to the ground. His son Vano was struck squarely in the belly by a bullet fired from the other cowboy's .45. Like his father, he collapsed.

"You idjits," the first cowboy scolded. "Them shots'll bring the law down on us fer sure."

"What was we supposed to do?" one of the other two cowboys retorted. "Let them two yokels whomp us?"

"We'd best git," the third cowboy said, holstering his gun. "I'll go around front and fetch our horses."

"What about her?" the second cowboy asked, pointing to the terrified, gagged, and naked teenager, still trapped in his companion's thick arms.

"We'll take her along with us," he said with a leer.

Pritchard had been out in the county serving an arrest warrant on a livestock thief when the incident occurred. When he rode back into town after dark, with his passive prisoner in tow, he was greeted at the jail by a crowd of townspeople bearing grim news.

One of Pritchard's only two full-time deputy marshals, Toby "Tater" Jessup, reported what transpired. Tater, a kind-hearted, middle-aged, former liveryman, tearfully relayed what Doctor Mauldin had reported to him; that Manfri Pannell would recover, but his son Vano had succumbed to his belly-wound shortly after being shot.

Manfri Pannell and his entire immigrant, Romanichal, clan, had been personally shepherded into Atherton by Pritchard himself. He considered Manfri and his family more than friends.

The girl, named Vadoma, was one of Manfri's nieces. She was last seen, nude and sobbing, on the back of one of the horses as the trio of intoxicated cowboys rode hell-bent-for-leather out of town. All three riders fired their pistols indiscriminately at shop windows, lampposts, and anything else they believed would dissuade pursuers as they galloped out.

Pritchard wasted no time. He turned over his prisoner to Tater to be locked up, retrieved his Winchester from the jail, loaded his saddlebags with provisions, grain, ammunition, and an extra canteen, and re-mounted. Deputy Strobl, who had been awaiting Pritchard's return, and Mayor Ditch Clemson, a veteran of the late war who'd grown up with Pritchard and fought alongside him too many times to remember, and who'd been deputized on more than one occasion, joined him.

The portly Tater halted Pritchard, Strobl, and Ditch with a raised hand before they departed. He extended three sets of manacles to the mounted marshal.

"Ain't you forgettin' these, Marshal?" Tater asked. "They're for your prisoners."

"Won't have need for 'em," Pritchard told his deputy.

The three lawmen rode wordlessly out of Atherton, heading west. None were strangers to hunting armed men.

Chapter Two

The cowboys had several hours' start on Pritchard, Ditch, and Strobl, but left an easy-enough trail to follow, even at night. Pritchard and Ditch had grown up in the woods along the Missouri River, and knew every inch of ground for twenty miles in all directions. Five miles west of Atherton they found the girl.

Vadoma lay on a patch of grass near a creek, quietly crying, which was how they located her in the darkness. She was still naked, and covered in bruises and welts. After her three captors took turns violating her, they stole her shoes to slow her return to town.

The oldest of Vadoma's assailants, the leader of the trio and the one who'd initially grabbed her at her uncle's inn, had drawn his revolver, cocked the hammer, and placed the barrel against her head.

"You're gonna deliver a message to the posse which'll be a-comin' after us," he said.

Vadoma nodded, her eyes tightly shut.

"You're gonna tell whoever is a-comin' after us to stop comin'," the leader said, as his partners fastened their britches. "You're gonna remind that posse that we didn't kill you, even though we could've. You're also gonna let 'em know if they don't heed this warning, we'll be waitin' up the trail for 'em. If'n they find us, we'll plant 'em all. Can you remember to tell 'em that?"

"I'll relay your message," the girl said in her British accent. Her Romanichal Tribe heralded from England, and had emigrated to America less than two years before. "But it will make no difference. The marshal will disregard your warning. He will hunt you down. He will shoot all of you like the dogs you are or hang you from the nearest tree."

"We ain't afraid of no tinhorn marshal from no backwater, Missouri town," one of the other cowboys scoffed. "Nor of any posse of shopkeepers and stable boys."

"The marshal was once a Texas Ranger," she said. "He's known far and wide as a killer of men."

"She's lyin'," the third cowboy said to his companions. "Tryin' to put a spook into us 'cause we done had our way with her."

"What's this marshal's name?" the leader asked.

"His name is Samuel Pritchard," Vadoma answered. She opened her eyes and looked up at the man holding a gun to her head.

"Never heard of him."

"He used to go by another name," she said. "Perhaps you have heard of that one?"

"What name would that be?"

"Joe Atherton."

"Joe Atherton?" the youngest cowboy said. "You're tellin' me Smokin' Joe Atherton is the marshal of that hogslop of a town back there?"

Vadoma nodded. "It is said he took the name of his hometown during the war."

"Now I know she's lyin'," the other cowboy said. "Ain't no way a famous pistoleer like Smokin' Joe is the sheriff of no backwoods river town."

"What's this marshal look like?" the leader asked.

"Tall as a barn, and as wide in the shoulders," Vadoma answered. "He's young. He's not even thirty years old. He has white-blond hair, blue eyes, and a bullet scar on his forehead."

"Is that so?" The youngest cowboy laughed. "Tall as a barn-hah! A bullet hole in his noggin! Sounds like she's describin' the booger man. Does he sport horns and fangs, too?"

"Shut up," the leader snapped. He prodded Vadoma with the barrel of his revolver. "You ain't fibbin'? You tellin' us the truth?"

"You already beat me, defiled me, and are going to shoot me," the girl said defiantly. "What do I gain by lying?"

The gun was removed from her head. "Get mounted," the leader said to the other two cowboys, as he lowered the hammer.

"Maybe we'd best finish her?" one of the other cowboys said. He drew his own revolver. "It ain't savvy to leave the bitch above ground. She knows our faces."

"Put that lead pusher away," the leader barked. "Nobody's givin' her a pill."

"What're you afraid of?" the cowboy said. "You don't actually believe her made-up fairy tale, do you?"

"I saw Smokin' Joe gun a man in the Oklahoma Territory," the leader said, "a few years after the war. He was with a company of Texas Rangers. He wasn't much more than a kid then. A giant of a kid. But she's described him, dead-on, all right."

"She's probably heard campfire stories," the second cowboy argued. "She's only repeatin' what others have told her about his appearance."

"Maybe not," the leader said. "I heard tell a while ago Smokin' Joe had given up the Rangers and was sheriffin' somewhere's up north under a different name." He holstered his revolver. "Get mounted, like I told you."

All three cowboys climbed aboard their horses. This time their leader pointed his finger, and not his gun, at Vadoma.

"You remember what I told you to tell that posse," he admonished her. "Smokin' Joe or not, anyone who comes after us is gonna wish they didn't."

"I'll tell them," the naked, abused, girl said. "Have fun looking over your shoulder."

Ditch wrapped the exhausted Vadoma in his coat and gently put her up on his horse. It was agreed since he was married, and his wife, Pritchard's sister Idelle, was due to give birth in a few months, he should be the one to escort her back to Atherton.

"Soon as I drop her off in town with Doc Mauldin and her folks," Ditch said, "I'll turn around and catch up to you and Florian."

"Don't bother," Pritchard said. "You'll be needed in Atherton. With me and Strobl gone for who knows how long, it'll be just you and Tater to look after the town.

What if some other hard cases ride in? You're a solid gun hand, and we both know the only thing Tater's ever wrestled with is indigestion."

"But Samuel," Ditch protested, "there's three of 'em, and—"

"No 'buts,'" Pritchard cut him off. "I've faced worse odds a hundred times over, and you know it. As much as I welcome your company, you belong back in Atherton lookin' after your pregnant wife and our town. You're not just a part-time deputy, Ditch, you're the mayor, remember? Now get goin'."

Pritchard's logic was irrefutable. Ditch nodded to Strobl and his friend and began leading his horse, with Vadoma astride, back toward town.

"I told those three animals you'd be coming after them, Marshal," Vadoma suddenly spoke up. "I told them it was Joe Atherton on their trail. I said you would find them and shoot them like dogs or string them up. I hope you aren't angry with me for saying such a thing?"

"Of course not," Pritchard soothed. "Marshal Pritchard, or Smokin' Joe, it don't matter a whit. Those boys'll get what's comin' to them for what they done to you and your family. You have my word on the matter."

"My word, as well," Strobl said.

"You just get on back to your folks and get to healin'," Pritchard said.

"Thank you, Marshal."

Pritchard tipped his hat to Vadoma and climbed into the saddle. Strobl took the cue and followed suit.

"Let's ride," he said to his deputy.

Connect with

Visit us online at
KensingtonBooks.com
to read more from your favorite authors, see books
by series, view reading group guides, and more.

for sneak peeks, chances to win books and prize packs,
and to share your thoughts with other readers.

facebook.com/kensingtonpublishing
twitter.com/kensingtonbooks

Tell us what you think!

To share your thoughts, submit a review,
or sign up for our eNewsletters, please visit:
KensingtonBooks.com/TellUs.